PRAISE FOR BELLA OSBORNE

'A well written and very intriguing tale that I really enjoyed'
Katie Fforde

'A warm and engaging story with relatable characters who will
worm their way into your heart'
Talli Roland

'Loved it! Believable characters, a sweetly told, lovely story…a
great read'
Jane Lovering

'Romance, comedy, and mystery abound in this delightful
British novel'
I Read That Book!

'So beautiful and romantic'
Annie's Book Corner

'A well-written and charming tale'
Paris Baker's Book Nook

'I wasn't expecting a debut novel to be this good'
The Bookish & The Romantic

'Makes me feel like I should be reading it while wearing a tea
dress, drinking posh coffee from a china cup and eating
Victoria sandwich cake with a dainty little fork. It's charming,
adorable, amusing and all those sorts of words'
Escape Into Words

'This book is perfect chick lit'
Gidget Girls Reading

A Family Holiday

BELLA OSBORNE

A division of HarperCollins*Publishers*
www.harpercollins.co.uk

Harper*Impulse* an imprint of
HarperCollins*Publishers*
1 London Bridge Street
London SE1 9GF

www.harpercollins.co.uk

A Paperback Original 2016

First published in Great Britain in ebook format by Harper*Impulse* 2016

A catalogue record for this book
is available from the British Library

ISBN: 978-0-00-820820-2

This novel is entirely a work of fiction.
The names, characters and incidents portrayed in it are
the work of the author's imagination. Any resemblance to
actual persons, living or dead, events or localities is
entirely coincidental.

Set in Minion by Palimpsest Book Production Limited, Falkirk, Stirlingshire

Printed and bound in Great Britain

MIX
Paper from
responsible sources
FSC
www.fsc.org
FSC™ C007454

For my amazingly supportive husband and daughter –
I love you with all of my heart.

Chapter One

Millie had forgotten her knickers again. The grinning toddler swung her legs happily as she sat on the toilet at the solicitor's office. With all the children still off school and having been let down at the last moment, Charlie had been forced to bring them with her to the meeting. This was far from ideal. She was their nanny; not a member of the family, just a paid employee whose job stability was now very unclear.

'Millie, it's important that you keep your skirt down. Keep your bottom covered up, okay?' said Charlie as they washed and dried their hands.

'Bottom,' repeated Millie with a giggle. She gripped Charlie's hand tightly as they left the toilets, something the three-year-old would have resisted a couple of months ago due to her desire to be independent, but things had changed and Millie now needed Charlie close to her.

In the waiting room sat the other three children: Ted, George and Eleanor. Ted, the eldest at fifteen, was studiously ignoring everything around him. George had had a recent growth spurt and looked older than his ten years, making the two-year gap between him and Eleanor appear to be a lot more.

Eleanor's face looked thin and pale and her eyes were full of sadness. Charlie sat down next to her and gently patted her hand as Millie inelegantly climbed onto the seat next to her, clutching her beloved Winnie the Pooh toy and immediately revealing her bare bottom to the rest of the solicitor's waiting clients.

George sniggered and tried to exchange smiles with his older brother but Ted was looking deeply serious as he stared at the floor. George's smile disappeared and he too started to study the carpet.

Eventually a very young-looking man called them into his office. He met them all solemnly at the door, introduced himself as Jonathan Steeple, and shook Charlie's hand. 'I'm sorry for your loss,' he said and all Charlie could do was swallow hard and nod her response. They settled themselves into chairs as the solicitor squeezed behind a giant desk.

'Normally I would read out the wills word for word but…' he looked at the children all staring back at him. 'It's probably more appropriate to just focus on the key elements.'

'Yes, I think that would be best, Mr Steeple,' said Charlie.

'Please call me Jonathan.'

A loud repetitive knock came at the door as it was simultaneously opened.

'I'm so sorry, Mr Steeple, this is Miss Talbot, she's…' but the young receptionist could no longer be heard.

'I'm Ruth Talbot, we had an appointment.' A thin ordinary-looking woman had shut the door and was stood glaring at the solicitor, until she noticed Charlie and her glare immediately changed direction.

'Hello Ruth. I'm Charlie. We met at the funeral.' Charlie stood balancing Millie on her hip and belatedly offered a hand to shake. Charlie always felt awkward in serious situations and this was one of the worst. Ruth nodded and only now seemed to notice her nieces and nephews.

'Edward, George… girls,' she bobbed her head in what Charlie assumed was her best attempt at a greeting, before returning her stare to Charlie. 'You're the au pair.'

'No, I'm the nanny,' replied Charlie, sitting down. If anything was designed to annoy Charlie it was being demoted.

'An unqualified one, I understand, which I think you'll find makes you an au pair.'

It was hard but Charlie held her tongue. Now was not the time to start a fight.

Jonathan introduced himself again and pulled forward a chair for Ruth to sit down.

'I'm sorry but this is a family matter, you shouldn't be here.' Ruth was pointing at Charlie. She was clearly not one for sugar-coating what she thought.

'Your father asked me to come,' Charlie gave a smug smile and turned away from Ruth.

'But he's in a nursing home…'

'Yep, he calls every week. He's seized up with arthritis, Ruth, but he still has all his marbles.'

'Well, really…' Ruth shook her head, but said no more.

Jonathan waited a moment and when nobody else objected he cleared his throat and proceeded to read through the high-lights, if you could call them that, of Helen and Toby Cobley's wills. Written shortly after they'd had Millie, the mirror wills appointed Felix Cobley and Ruth Talbot as joint guardians and trustees. The wills were very clear that the children should be kept together, despite Toby not being Ted's natural father.

Ted was frowning as he took in the information. The sudden loss of his parents meant he had quickly become the adult he so longed to be.

'We're going to be looked after by Felix?' asked Ted.

Eleanor blew her nose and cried quietly into a tissue as Charlie tried to comfort her with one arm and restrain a bored Millie with the other.

3

'Who's Felix?' asked Charlie, having not heard him mentioned before.

'Will you stop interrupting?' said Ruth, followed by a series of tutting noises.

'How rude!' said Charlie, but Ted was already answering her question.

'Felix is Dad's loser of a brother who flipped out and ran off years ago,' explained Ted, throwing himself back into the office chair and making it topple precariously. Jonathan opened his mouth to speak but was cut off by Charlie.

'Where does this leave us right now?' she asked, more than a little confused by the information overload.

'Well,' cut in Ruth, although she was speaking directly to Jonathan. 'As we have no contact details for Felix, that makes me effectively sole guardian.'

Jonathan gave her what looked like a very practised smile. 'Not exactly. We have finally managed to track down Mr Cobley and we're awaiting a response.'

'Good luck with that,' snorted Ted.

'We don't have to move house, do we?' asked Eleanor, her eyes wide.

'For now it's best if everything stays as it is. We will pay all essential bills, including your salary,' Jonathan nodded reassuringly at Charlie. 'As long as you are happy to carry on in your role as primary care giver until a guardian is appointed. It is an unusual situation but Social Services will be able to help you through this.' Charlie felt her stomach clench at the mention of Social Services and bile rose in her throat. Jonathan quickly passed her a pre-poured glass of water.

'Thank you.'

Ruth was checking her watch and frowning. 'Would you put all of this in writing and confirm what powers we have over the estate. 'We' being the family, obviously.' Ruth gave a withering glance in Charlie's direction as she stood up.

'Only the executors, which is us, Sedgley, Steeple and Thomas, have the power to administer the estate until guardians and trustees are formally appointed. And the guardians' appointment will be subject to Social Services' approval.'

'Do Aunt Ruth and Uncle Felix have to fight to the death?' said George, leaning forward as Eleanor automatically recoiled.

'How ridiculous!' said Ruth. She turned to Jonathan, 'I'll be expecting you to send minutes of this meeting,' she said, before addressing the children. 'Take care of each other, and call me if you have any problems.' This successfully made Charlie bristle but she didn't react; instead she gave her sweetest smile as Ruth left.

Ted looked at Charlie, colour rising in his cheeks. 'So basically, we've been left in their wills like an old tea set. Worst still, we've been left to two people, neither of whom has done anything for us in the past.'

'Aunt Ruth sends book tokens at Christmas,' added Eleanor, ever the voice of diplomacy, as George snorted his derision.

Ted was shaking his head. Charlie could feel the frustration emanating from him but before she could attempt to allay his fears he stood up abruptly.

'This is bloody ridiculous!' he bellowed before roughly pushing back his chair and stomping out of the room.

'Bloody ridiculous!' repeated Millie as she lifted her skirt and flashed at the solicitor. Charlie let a heavy sigh escape.

Looking back, Ted had been more than a challenge to care for; underneath his couldn't-care-less exterior was a boy who longed to have more of his mother's time. In Ted's eyes Charlie's arrival had further displaced his mother. At the start there were full-blown shouting matches between them, and Charlie had placed Ted at the top of her 'Kipper List'.

The 'Kipper List' was a long list of people that Charlie would like to beat around the head with a wet kipper. Yes, a wet kipper was her weapon of choice. Over the years she had been offered various suggestions for how to manage her fiery temper and she had found this the most effective. The original suggestion had been a lot less colourful and nowhere near as effective, but Charlie's variation seemed to work a treat. Charlie could happily visualise slapping the offending individual with a wet kipper and she felt it was a fitting approach to those who upset her, whilst unlikely to get her into any serious trouble. Charlie had only ever told one person about her 'Kipper List' method of anger management; a particularly uptight therapist who looked like she needed her own stress-release mechanism. However, when Charlie had explained the process the therapist had unhelpfully pointed out that kippers were not large and wet, as Charlie had described, and had provided a detailed account of the herring-to-kipper process, during which Charlie had visualised the therapist being battered senseless with a giant wet kipper whilst she herself stayed completely calm, which proved beyond doubt that the method truly worked.

Charlie made her apologies to the solicitor over the top of Millie's repetition of 'Bloody ridiculous!' There were much simpler words she struggled to pronounce like 'banana' or 'cereal' but 'bloody' and 'ridiculous' evidently weren't causing her any such issues.

As Charlie tried to herd the children through the waiting area as quickly as possible a tall blonde-haired man strode past them. He glanced at Charlie, but as he saw the miserable-looking children surrounding her he quickly turned his head away. Still, he wasn't to know that she was only the nanny.

Chapter Two

Back at home Ted and Charlie stared into their respective mugs.

'What do you know about Aunt Ruth and Uncle Felix?' asked Charlie, trying to sound relaxed, but it still came out like the start of an inquisition. Ted sighed heavily.

'You've met Aunt Ruthless,' he said, and looked up as if that was explanation enough.

'She seems… okay,' said Charlie, sipping her drink and avoiding eye contact.

'Okay?' questioned Ted. 'Yeah, if you were stuck next to her on a train for an hour, perhaps, but okay to take the place of our parents?' Charlie pulled a face like someone discovering a maggot in an apple. Ted continued, 'She would only look okay when compared to a rabid wolf and then it would be touch and go who to choose. In fact, I think wolves have quite a strong nurturing instinct.' He gave a wry smile.

'I agree she's not the warmest of people, but she seemed, um, efficient.'

'Charlie, I am not having Aunt Ruthless move in here so she can bully all of us and use the trust fund to shore up her failing company.'

'She's not that bad and don't call her Ruthless or Millie will pick it up and...'

Ted grinned over his coffee mug. Charlie shook her head in mock despondency. They sat in silence again, the only sound was of muffled footsteps upstairs as Fleur played with the other children. Fleur was Charlie's oldest friend and should have been baby-sitting that morning so Charlie could have gone to the solicitor's alone, but something had come up and Fleur hadn't made it in time. Better late than never, thought Charlie.

The sound of frantic high-speed paws almost tumbling down the stairs towards them made them both turn to see the arrival of Wriggly. He was a brown-and-white Llasa Apso puppy with an amazing pedigree birth line and an even longer pedigree name that was no good for day-to-day use. After much debate and a secret vote, they had finally settled on the name Mr Wriggly. Charlie still felt that it had some inappropriate overtones, but she'd been outvoted. Thankfully it had soon been shortened to Wriggly. Today Wriggly was wearing a Star Wars Ewok costume and was closely followed by Princess Leia, a storm trooper and a mini version of Darth Vader.

'George, Wriggly will overheat in that outfit. Take it off, please,' asked Charlie as the storm trooper removed his mask.

'But we're being chased by a Cyberman!' said Eleanor, adjusting her Princess Leia Chelsea-bun-style hairband.

'Shhhhh,' said Darth Vader. Not having seen the films, this was Millie's interpretation of the Darth Vader breathing noise. George had given up trying to teach her how to do it properly.

'Cyberman?' queried Ted and he glanced at Charlie with raised eyebrows.

An odd-looking Cyberman walked awkwardly down the stairs like an Egyptian mummy from a black-and-white film. The key differences being the swathes of auburn hair bouncing behind it and the patent high-heeled shoes. George and Eleanor screamed and ran for the garden.

'Shhhhh,' said Darth Vader before giggling and following the others.

'Fleur, you are useless when it comes to sci-fi,' said Charlie.

The Cyberman spun in her direction, removed the mask and studied it. 'Is this not *Star Wars*?'

Charlie shook her head, 'Dr Who.'

'Bugger,' said Fleur as she flopped onto a barstool.

'Thanks for baby-sitting, Fleur. They love playing with you.'

'It's the least I can do after messing up this morning. Sorry. How are things?'

'Not great, but we're managing,' said Charlie, exchanging grimaces with Ted.

'I think you're all amazing. I'd be a mess if it were me. Ma and Pa send their love and Pa says thanks for keeping me busy. He says if I mention the wedding at home once more he's moving into the stables.' She huffed. 'You'd think I'd turned into some sort of Bridezilla.'

Charlie and Ted exchanged looks and sipped their drinks in unison.

'What? I can't help being excited, it's not long now. Eeeek!' squealed Fleur. Ted winced.

The back doors opened and the compact version of the *Star Wars* cast came thundering back in. 'George! Remove the Ewok costume!' said Charlie with authority. 'Go on, all of you back upstairs, I'll call you when dinner is ready,' and Charlie dismissed them with a wave of her hand. George undid the Velcro on Wriggly's costume, the little dog shook himself free and chased up the stairs after Eleanor, closely followed by the storm trooper and unconvincing Cyberman.

'Shhhhh,' said Darth Vader in passing. The kitchen was calm again.

'Uncle Felix, what do we know about him?' Charlie didn't like to admit that she hadn't known that Toby even had a brother.

'There was some family upset and he did a runner some years

ago…' Ted paused. 'It doesn't matter, though, does it really? Mum and Dad are dead and nobody else is going to love us like they did.'

The doorbell rang and both Charlie and Ted jumped. Piccadilly Circus was as calm and serene as a spa compared to their house. Charlie slid off the barstool. 'I'll go,' she said, as she downed the last of her coffee and tried to push her own grief to the back of her mind. The children were coping incredibly well now; they were quite matter-of-fact at times. The funeral had been the worst experience of her life as she had tried to keep things together and let them all deal with it in their own way. The last thing she wanted was for them to bottle this up, as she knew from her own experience that repressing emotions would never end well.

Charlie opened the front door and surveyed the uncomfort-able-looking man fidgeting on the doorstep. His striking features looked familiar. A baseball cap covered his hair but wisps of blonde were sticking out at odd angles. He was wearing a new-looking jacket and ill-fitting jeans and his hands were thrust deep into his pockets, making the jeans sag even more.

'Hi,' he said at last. His accent was British with a hint of something difficult to identify.

'Hi,' said Charlie, feeling her cheeks rise into an involuntary smile.

'Are you the nanny?'

'Yes, I'm Charlie French.' The attractive stranger intrigued her.

'I'm Felix. Felix Cobley.'

Charlie's smile evaporated in a haze of confusion. Was this some sort of hostile takeover?

'What's going on?' she said, folding her arms tight as if holding down the anger within her.

'Oh,' said Felix, looking awkward. 'I thought the solicitor had explained?'

'Err, no!' In her mind Charlie matched Felix to the tall man she'd passed in the solicitor's waiting room.

'Can I come in?' asked Felix with a shudder. What was wrong with him? It was summer, for goodness sake!

'I think there's lots to discuss before we spring a long-lost relative on the children.' Especially one with a record for running off, she thought.

'Look, I can come back later,' suggested Felix with a shrug.

'Fine by me,' said Charlie quickly.

'But I thought it might be best the sooner we all talked. Seriously, can I come inside please?'

'No,' said Charlie, 'not until I know what you're planning to say to them. It's me who'll have to deal with the fallout!' She tightened her folded arms.

'There are no definite plans as yet, that's why I thought a chat might be a good idea.'

Charlie heard a faint noise coming from the stairs and she knew one of the children was listening, which in reality meant that they would all know about Uncle Felix within the next few moments anyway. Charlie took a slow, deep breath and tried to calm herself. She needed to have her wits about her.

'Okay, let's get this over with.' She stood back and ushered an apologetic-looking Felix into the hall and through to the living room.

'Guys, can you come down, please,' she called and immediately George appeared, closely followed by Eleanor, who was carrying Wriggly. So that was who was listening. George was eager to get into the living room and take a look at his uncle and Eleanor followed behind with her pale face buried in Wriggly's coat. He was living up to his name and she was struggling to keep hold of him.

Charlie tried to remove Millie's mask as she marched into the living room but she was not giving it up willingly so Charlie relented. Felix sat down in Toby's spot on the sofa and Charlie and the children all stood and stared at him as he now removed his cap to reveal a mass of unruly blonde hair and the full might of the Cobley blue eyes. He was by no means his brother's double; he was younger and more olive-skinned, but the obvious likeness was uncanny and more than a little creepy as he sat in Toby's place. Millie shuffled a little closer to Charlie and leaned into her leg, even she could sense something.

Felix self-consciously brushed back his hair with his fingers and tried to look anywhere except at the many eyes trained on him.

'You might want to sit over here,' suggested Charlie gently as she gestured for Felix to move to the opposite sofa.

'No, I'm fine. Thanks.'

Charlie gave him a look that communicated that staying seated where he was was not an option. Felix looked around him in bemusement. 'What?'

'Please move,' said Charlie. He sighed but did as he was asked and looked further confused when nobody took the place he had vacated. Millie decided to sit on the rug at Charlie's feet.

Charlie gave a forced smile. 'This is…'

'You're Uncle Felix, aren't you?' blurted out George and Millie responded with a dramatic gasp and covered Darth Vader's mouth with her hand. It was one of her favourite things to do at the moment and for once her timing was spot on.

'Why are you here exactly?' asked Ted, leaning forward, his shoulders hunched and his hands clasped tightly together in front of him.

'Well, the solicitor thought we should meet up and…'

'Not because you wanted to see how we were,' stated Ted coldly, as his knuckles turned white.

'Of course I did.' Felix looked uncomfortable. 'You've changed since I last saw you, Teddy,' said Felix.

'It's Ted. And yeah that tends to happen when you sod off for years. Things change, Felix.' He emphasised the name before slumping back into his seat.

'Look I don't have all the answers and I'm not here to cause trouble.' Felix rested his hands on his knees as if trying to keep them still.

Millie climbed up onto Charlie's lap and turned her back on the room. Charlie removed the Darth Vader mask.

'Why did you run off?' asked George.

Felix ran his hand through his hair, 'It's complicated, mate. You'd not really understand.'

'You could at least try to explain,' said Charlie, locking eyes with Felix and she saw a flash of something – anger, irritation? She wasn't sure.

Felix swallowed hard. 'Our father died and it was difficult…'

'Yes, we know how that feels,' said Eleanor in a soft and genuinely sympathetic voice.

'I'm so sorry, of course you do…' Felix looked suitably chastened.

'Did you kill him?' asked George, his interest piqued.

'Err, no. Of course not.' Felix was frowning and shaking his head but there was something about his expression that worried Charlie. His words said one thing but his face said another.

'Why didn't you come to the funeral?' Ted asked belligerently.

Felix went pale. 'Your dad and I… didn't keep in touch. I suppose it took the solicitors a while to find me and by then I'd missed it. I'm… so sorry.'

There was an uneasy silence before Felix spoke again. 'I'm seeing Ruth later about the guardianship and the trust fund.'

Ted snorted and shook his head. 'You know the money comes with strings attached and we're those strings,' he said, pointing at himself and the other children.

'Perhaps this was a bad idea,' said Felix, looking decidedly awkward.

Charlie raised her eyebrows but said nothing.

'I am truly sorry about your mum and dad. I loved them too.' He stood and left the room and Charlie felt she should see him out, so she shifted Millie off her lap and followed him.

'Here, call first if you want to come again. It's best they're forewarned, okay?' said Charlie, handing him the phone number she'd quickly scribbled on the back of an old envelope.

He nodded, turned up his collar and stepped out into a mild summery London.

Felix raced into the small coffee shop and immediately spotted a vaguely familiar woman, who was staring unblinking at the door.

'Hello Ruth,' said Felix, reaching forward to air-kiss her. 'Really sorry I'm late, I was...'

Ruth recoiled. 'Yes, well, I still need to be in a meeting at three o'clock, which means we only have thirteen minutes.'

Felix looked longingly at the conga-line queue for coffee and Ruth blinked hard. Felix's shoulders sagged as he accepted his disappointment and sat down opposite her.

'I'm truly sorry about your sister. Helen was such a genuinely lovely person, I remember when...'

'Thank you,' cut in Ruth, glancing at her watch, 'I'll keep this brief. The lawyers are going to keep burning money the longer they debate how we split the guardian role. I've spoken to Social Services and they would prefer us to work this out for ourselves and then they'll review the candidate. I am very happy to take on that responsibility.'

Felix slumped back into his chair and clapped his hands. 'That is great news. Thank you. The solicitor I spoke to implied you didn't want to look after the kids but kind of made it clear that one of us had to. So that is a huge relief.'

Ruth scowled, 'The responsibility of guardian enables me to ensure they have a financially secure future and appoint a child-care professional to administer their care. And let's be clear, I do not mean the current incumbent.'

Felix looked like he'd just been beaten at Scrabble. 'What?'

'Their current nanny will be leaving as soon as I can find a replacement. She isn't qualified and the children are out of control. She is some stray that my sister took in. I queried it with Helen at the time. I told her she should do proper checks, but Helen was always too soft and naive.' Ruth's voice caught in her throat. 'Anyway, I've done some investigating of my own and she's not fit to care for those children but I'm sure she's already looking for another job, so we'll soon be rid of her.' Ruth checked her watch again and moved her handbag onto her lap. 'If you could inform the solicitor that you concur, I will notify Social Services of the agreed approach, and we should be able to get things wrapped up quite quickly.' Ruth stood to leave.

'Hang on, hang on,' said Felix, waving her to sit down again. 'Let's get this straight. You will be their guardian, and you'll administer the trust fund. There will be a new nanny...'

'A qualified nanny,' interjected Ruth.

'Yep, to do washing, cleaning and day-to-day stuff. But what's missing is who is actually looking after them?'

Ruth pursed her lips. 'A full-time nanny will be there to care for them, they'll be fine. We could, of course, consider boarding school for the older children,' said Ruth, with almost a smile. 'I need to leave.'

'Yeah, of course. Sorry I was late but I think we need more time to work something else out. I really don't think Helen and Tobes would have wanted their kids to be left to manage by themselves like this, and certainly not just packed off to boarding school.'

Ruth stood up. 'Very well, I'll check my diary so we can discuss this further, but I assure you they'll be fine. Children are very resilient. Good bye.'

Chapter Three

Millie took a big breath for another rendition of the chorus. 'All the birds of the air, fell a-sighing and a-sobbing, when they heard of the death of poor Cock Robin...'

'Stop it!' shouted Eleanor at close range before almost knocking over the high chair as she ran past. Eleanor's temper had turned to tears before she'd reached the top of the stairs.

'I'll go,' said Charlie, giving the others a wan smile.

'Silly Billy,' giggled Millie, thankfully oblivious to the impact of the upsetting faux pas before continuing with what she remembered of the old rhyme.

Eleanor lay face down on her bed, her small body shaking with the force of her sobs, her butterfly duvet muffling the pain. Wriggly sat on the pillow, looking worried and helpless, as he tilted his head from side to side and whimpered. Charlie got on the bed next to Eleanor, wrapped her arms around her and rocked her gently until the sobs turned to sniffles.

'Mum and Dad...' started Eleanor, but the noisy sobs returned and Charlie cradled her again until she could control them. At last they both sat up and Eleanor clung to Charlie, as she had done yesterday and the day before.

'I know,' said Charlie, 'it's total rubbish.' She pushed a strand of damp hair off the eight-year-old's face. Wriggly came to sit on Charlie's lap and tried to lick Eleanor's tears. A tiny smile appeared fleetingly on Eleanor's lips.

'That stupid song,' grumbled Eleanor.

'Granddad Roger taught it to her. She doesn't know what it's about, though.'

'I know. Even Millie is being braver than me,' said Eleanor, wiping her eyes with the tissue that was now permanently in her pocket.

Millie had been deeply affected by the emotions in the house and had cried constantly for the first few days after the accident. She had then moved onto calling out 'My Mummy and My Daddy!' and searching the house for them as if playing some twisted game of hide and seek. Thankfully, after repeated attempts by Charlie to explain that Mummy and Daddy had gone to Heaven, where they could see her but she couldn't see them, she had calmed down a little and mercifully had now stopped looking for them and was very nearly back to her usual cheeky self.

'You don't have to be brave, Elle. It's different for Millie; she's only three. She won't fully understand everything until she's bigger. As long as Millie has food, drink and her Winnie the Pooh her basic needs are met. For the rest of you it's a lot more complicated. You need to get through this however you can.'

'I feel sad all the time and I cry… all the time,' said Eleanor, looking wretched.

'I know, sweetie, and that's completely normal. Someone once told me that grief is like any wound, it needs time to heal. Thing is, it's not a scab on your knee, so you can't see how it's getting on.'

'It won't get better though, will it? Mum and Dad are never coming back. We'll never be a happy family again.' She paused for a moment. 'I know we argue sometimes but we did used to be happy.' Eleanor pulled Wriggly onto her lap and he wagged his tail excitedly.

'We did,' nodded Charlie. 'It will take time, lots of tears and lots of cuddles but I promise you you'll get back to being happy. It'll just be a different kind of happy,' she said but Eleanor didn't look convinced. 'When you're ready, come and get some food. Okay?'

The last couple of months had been a blur and too awful to put into words. They had all been suffering. It was probably Eleanor who worried Charlie the most as she had gone into her shell and spent all her time with Wriggly, barely speaking to anyone and surviving almost entirely on milkshakes.

The accident had hit Charlie hard too. She had learnt so much from the Cobleys. She'd learnt that if there was ever a cement shortage Weetabix was a viable substitute, having tried to remove it from a myriad surfaces, including her own hair. She'd learnt that you never leave a baby to play innocently with a thread in a Berber carpet, as it soon becomes a four-foot-long bald strip. She'd learnt to change a nappy at record speed, to avoid the horror of a poo-covered bottom rolling across a vanilla-coloured wool rug. But, most importantly, she'd learnt that whatever happens, you stick together as a family.

Charlie struggled to believe it herself, that Helen and Toby Cobley were both dead. When she heard a car stop outside she still occasionally had a quick look to check it wasn't them. How quickly their world had been changed. A simple car accident on a wet motorway had become a multiple-car pile up, with the Cobley's car somewhere in the middle.

Charlie's immediate fear had been that the children would be taken into the care of Social Services. That fear still hung over her and it would do until the question of guardianship had been resolved. She knew too well what it was like to be a child in the care system and she was desperate for the Cobley children to avoid this fate.

Charlie joined the others at the table, where Millie was using her carrot sticks to beat out an interesting rhythm.

Ted put his cutlery down when she approached. 'Is she okay?' he asked, but before Charlie could get a reply out George threw his cutlery down hard onto the table, making Millie jump.

'Of course she's not bloody well okay!' George shouted at his brother. 'She's never going to be okay. None of us are. What made you suddenly care?'

'Come on, George, don't be an arse,' said Ted as he went to give George a friendly nudge.

'Don't shove me! You're not in charge,' yelled George, scraping his chair across the floor as he stood up sharply. George stood over Ted with his fists clenched.

'Hey, calm down. I'm not trying to be in charge. Nobody is in charge any more.'

'You think you're the man of the house now. But you're not!'

'Technically, I think I am,' said Ted, standing up and towering over George, 'but I'm not going to fight with you.' However, it seemed George had other ideas and launched himself at Ted, pummelling his torso with his fists. Charlie leapt forward but Ted raised a hand to stop her. Instead of hitting back or even defending himself, Ted pulled George to him, enveloped him in a hug and took the blows until George wore himself out. The happy-go-lucky George was missing and an angry boy was in his place, ready to shout and argue with anyone, about anything. Charlie sorely hoped this was a temporary phase of the grieving process.

Charlie looked at Ted, and right at that moment she was immensely proud of him. He'd been up and down emotionally himself, but it was clear he was trying to hold it together for the younger ones. George clung onto Ted until the worst of the crying had left him and then he pushed him harshly away and stormed off. Charlie listened and was pleased to hear his bedroom door slam; at least it wasn't the front door.

'Naughty step! Naughty step!' chanted Millie happily, waving a carrot stick in time.

As Charlie was clearing away the lunch things in an empty kitchen the doorbell rang. Whilst Charlie loved the house, a stuccoed townhouse in the heart of Pimlico, the fact that it was split over five floors could be a pain sometimes. She sprinted up the steps from the kitchen, taking a towel with her to dry her hands. They had a state-of-the-art dishwasher but recently she'd taken to washing up, as she'd found if she kept herself busy it made things a fraction easier.

She opened the door to the hunched figure of Felix, his jacket collar turned up and his hands thrust into his jeans pockets.

'Oh, it's you.'

Felix rolled his lips in on themselves like a chimp. 'Thought I should call round.'

'A phone call first would have been good.'

'I lost the number.' He shrugged. 'Last time didn't go well. I thought I should try to get to know the kids a bit better.'

Charlie eyed him warily, stepped outside and pulled the door almost closed behind her.

'Look, that's all very well but if you're planning on buggering off again at a moment's notice it's best you don't bother in the first place.' Charlie belatedly added a brief smile. 'I'm really not trying to be unkind but...'

'It's not up to you, though, is it?' said Felix, quickly zipping up his jacket as a light breeze dawdled down the overcast London street. 'Can I come inside?' He stepped towards the front door. He and Charlie were now stood very close to each other, he smelled soapy. Charlie held tight to the door. 'I don't know...'

'Please,' added Felix and Charlie let the door go. Maybe Charlie wasn't the most tactful of people but she wanted him to understand that she was trying to protect the children.

Ted was sitting at the kitchen table spinning a coin repeatedly and staring at it intently. He picked it up and put it in his pocket as Charlie and Felix entered the room. Ted sat up straight, narrowed his eyes and stared at Felix.

'It's very quiet. Have the children run away?' asked Charlie, as she filled the kettle.

'Last time I looked they were trying to put clothes on Wriggly for a fashion show.'

'Not again! Ted, can you stop them, please? Last time he went outside wearing a teddy bear's Arsenal kit he peed all over it. See if you can interest them in playing something outside with Uncle Felix.'

'I can try,' said Ted as he stood up and shrugged at Felix.

'Best thing to happen to an Arsenal kit,' chuckled Felix.

'Arsenal fan,' said Ted, pointing at Charlie, and he idly swatted at a fly as it flew past.

'Argh!' shouted Charlie as the fly flew near her face. She grabbed a tea towel and started wildly thrashing it around her head. 'Did I get it?'

'No, it's gone out of the window. Thank goodness it wasn't a spider!' Felix laughed.

'Spiders I can cope with,' said Charlie, shuddering as she shut the window. 'Tea?'

'Coffee please.'

Felix stood awkwardly by the table, and when the silence got too much he got a yo-yo out of his pocket and started to expertly spin it. Charlie raised her eyebrows but didn't want to show him that she was impressed with his yo-yo skills, as it didn't exactly automatically qualify him as a capable guardian.

'Where do you live now?' asked Charlie as she passed Felix his coffee and he flicked up the yo-yo and returned it to his pocket.

'Oh, I'm staying in a hotel for a bit while I'm here. I can give you the details if you like.'

The fact that he had sidestepped the question did not go unnoticed. 'No, it's okay. Where's home?'

'I'm a bit… nomadic. How's the job-hunting going?'

'What the …' Charlie was wrong-footed by the question and the sound of the tribe hurtling down the stairs thankfully drowned out her other words. Led by Ted the children all ignored Felix and ran shouting and hollering into the garden. Felix stared open-mouthed after them.

'Are they always like that?'

'They're children; it's what children do. Sure they're playing up a bit to their new audience, that's you by the way, but it's to be expected. What do you mean job-hunting?'

'I thought…'

'You thought wrong. Have you met with Ruth yet?'

Felix's attention was now outside as he saw the shady figures darting in different directions. 'Yeah, we're trying to work something out.'

Charlie was getting increasingly frustrated with everyone's lack of communication. 'Who is going to talk to the children about that? Don't you think they should be included in any big decisions?'

Felix briefly looked away from the window. 'No, not really. It's not like we've got a lot of choices.'

'Ruth or you, is that it?' She couldn't help but think, 'The devil and the deep-blue eyed…' But her thoughts abruptly trailed off and he was speaking again.

'Ruth is keen to be the trustee but I'd like her to do a bit more than just look after the finances.'

'Good luck trying to persuade Ruth,' laughed Charlie and Felix turned to stare at her.

'I can be very persuasive,' he said with a beaming smile. It was the first time Charlie had seen him look happy. His previous frowns couldn't exactly make him look ugly, but a smile like that lit up his whole face.

The noise from the garden reached a crescendo.

'Do you not think you should check on them?' asked Felix, straining to look out of the window, but with the garden raised higher than the kitchen it was hard to see.

Charlie could feel the annoyance rising within her. 'They're fine.'

'I think someone should go and take a look.'

'Be my guest,' said Charlie, leaning back against the worktop and mentally rearranging her 'Kipper List'.

He glared at her, roughly put down his coffee mug and walked outside and up the steps to the garden.

Charlie smiled to herself, sipped her coffee and waited. There was a brief pause in the noise before the screaming erupted again. Charlie got the kitchen roll out of the cupboard and picked up a damp cloth. She counted to three and, right on cue, Felix stumbled down the steps and tumbled into the kitchen as mud pellets showered down on him. He quickly shut the door behind him and leant against it like a scene from the Wild West as a banshee-like Millie hurled a large mud pie at the doors, hitting the glass with a tremendous thump, making Felix jump and turn round. Millie stuck out her tongue at Felix and stomped back up to the garden, where the rest of the tribe were whooping in celebration.

Felix took a deep breath and turned to face Charlie. Mud dripped from his once blonde hair and trickled off his chin. 'They're feral!'

Charlie couldn't contain her grin any longer. 'They're great, aren't they?' she said handing him the cloth and kitchen roll.

Felix looked decidedly rattled as he wiped himself down. 'Was that some elaborate initiation ceremony?'

Charlie thought for a moment. 'They hosed me down when I first came. So, yeah, I guess it's their way of welcoming you.'

'Ruth said they were out of control but I hadn't realised it was this bad.'

Charlie felt a flash of anger rampage over her. 'Children are not meant to be CONTROLLED, especially not kids that have had their world turned arse-up!'

Felix shook his head and a lump of mud plopped onto the floor. 'They could kill each other,' he said, snatching some kitchen roll and smearing the mud into his once-white rugby shirt. Charlie's temper hitched up a notch.

'You're such a drama queen! They're only playing. Have a sense of humour, will you? Nobody's going to get killed by mud.'

Felix looked even more irritated as he appeared to realise the uselessness of his rubbing. 'Have you any idea how much bacteria is probably in this?' he said, showing her the muddied kitchen roll.

'Nope, but seeing as they play in it a lot, I'm guessing they must be immune. I do hope you don't catch anything deadly,' she said with a smirk.

Felix glared at her. 'I need a shower.'

'You can't have one here,' Charlie said, without thinking. After all, it was his brother's house, he had every right to use the facilities, but right now this was Charlie's territory and he was the invader.

Colour rose in Felix's cheeks and he screwed up the used kitchen roll and threw it, with force, into the bin, making the muscles under his rugby shirt show up. 'I'll be back,' he said as he headed for the front door, leaving a trail of muddy footprints. Charlie threw an imaginary kipper at the back of his head.

Chapter Four

Charlie was feeling a little sweaty as she walked out of Green Park tube station and into the warm summer sunshine. She walked along Piccadilly, trying to flap air up her t-shirt to cool herself down. It was the first time Charlie had left all of the children since their parents had died and thoughts of how they were getting on filled her head.

She thought about the first time she had been here with Helen Cobley. All the years she'd lived in and around London she'd never seen the Ritz Hotel or encountered the wonders of Fortnum and Mason's food hall or the delights of the small exclusive shops in the Burlington Arcade. She made a last-minute decision to go to Ladurée and treat the children to macarons before she met up with Fleur. The Burlington Arcade was barely out of her way and the bizarre little shop swathed in molten gold never failed to make Charlie smile – and she needed to smile right now.

With her treasure of macarons swinging gently at her side, Charlie walked down Old Bond Street and quickened her pace when she spotted Fleur pacing up and down outside the exclusive bridal shop. Fleur's parents were super-wealthy thanks to her mother's family money and her father's very successful business, so this wedding was going to be the no-expense-spared variety.

Charlie gave a friendly wave and Fleur stamped her foot and beckoned her closer, like a New York policewoman directing traffic.

'You're late, Charlie!'

Charlie glanced at her watch. 'Three minutes!'

'They don't like it when you're late,' said Fleur, turning her back on Charlie and leading the way under the scalloped canopy and inside.

'They don't like me, whatever time I'm here,' mumbled Charlie as the door triggered a disturbingly elongated buzzing noise to announce their arrival.

An overly made-up young woman appeared instantly. 'Good Morning, Miss Van Benton, final fitting for the last of the brides-maids,' she said, her eyes flicking to the clock.

'Yes, I'm sorry we're late,' said Fleur, with an involuntary nod towards Charlie. 'Three minutes!' mouthed Charlie. It seemed a funny little shop to Charlie; three wedding dresses were displayed on one wall, next to a giant arched mirror. Cream high-backed chairs, a matching chaise longue and low glass tables were strewn with designer brochures but still failed to make the place look welcoming.

'I understand,' said the shop assistant briskly. 'Shall we get along?'

Charlie followed them out of the sparse room, through a narrow corridor and into a fitting room decorated like a French palace. Charlie went to place her Ladurée bag on the chaise longue, this time in a shade of deep purple, but the glare of the shop assistant made her think better of it, so at the last second relegated it to a place on the floor. The shop assistant, who Charlie remem-bered was called Amber, proceeded to undo probably the longest zip in the world. Charlie followed it all the way to the top of the specialist dress carrier. Instantly the insipid flesh-coloured dress poured out like something out of a horror film. It was a colour that Fleur had spent the last two months insisting was 'peaches

26

and cream'. Charlie swallowed hard, trying to dispel the terror she knew was written all over her face and quickly checked that Fleur wasn't watching her. It was worse than she'd remembered.

Fleur was clapping her hands together excitedly. 'Isn't it simply divine?' she said, stepping closer to it and slowly reaching out a tentative hand to touch it. Charlie couldn't be less impressed if she tried but this was Fleur's special day and she wanted it to be perfect for her. But this dress was pushing their long friendship to the limits.

'It's...' Charlie frantically searched her tired brain for the right word and settled on the closest she could find, 'special,' she said.

'Oh, you're right. It is. Isn't it?' this time Fleur turned to Amber, who had now unleashed the full awfulness of the dress. Amber nodded earnestly and Charlie rolled her eyes and wondered how much you had to be paid to be that convincing to deluded strangers.

'Do you need help getting dressed?' offered Amber.

'No thanks, I've managed all right for twenty-odd years, I think I'll be okay,' Charlie was aware of the dagger glances Fleur was hurling in her direction, so she quickly added, 'but that was really kind of you to offer. Thank you.'

Amber studied Charlie's trainers. 'I'll bring you some suitable heels to try on with it. That way you get the full effect,' said Amber. 'What size?'

'Eight and half,' said Charlie, but quickly altered it as a result of the look of revulsion on Amber's face, 'Eight is fine. Thanks.' Amber gave a practised neutral smile and left the room.

Charlie was very pleased with herself as she had remembered to wear her best matching underwear in a soft cream. This was a big improvement on her slightly grey sports bra and her red Mickey Mouse pants that she had worn to the first fitting without having properly thought it through.

'Before I forget, here's your hair piece for the wedding,' Fleur said, handing her a cord-strung bag.

27

'Right. Why do I need that again?' asked Charlie, running a hand through her mass of dark hair.

'We're all having seriously big up–dos, so you'll need it. Trust me,' said Fleur with a giggle. Charlie peered into the bag and eyed what looked like something that had been run over many times.

'Great,' said Charlie, using up the last of her fake enthusiasm.

Fleur hopped about excitedly while Charlie turned herself into the sugar puke fairy. Charlie stared forlornly at herself in the giant mirror. It was difficult to tell where the dress ended and where Charlie started. The only bit that obviously wasn't Charlie was the obscene number of layers in the skirt. If it got too much on the day she could always smuggle all four of the children out underneath it, she thought.

'What are you thinking?' asked Fleur.

How fabulous you will look compared to me in this, I look like a negative of Barbie, but what she actually said was, 'How lovely we'll all look.'

'You should have seen Tilly in hers. She looked totally stunning. I'm not standing too close to her!' squealed Fleur.

Tilly was another of Fleur's bridesmaids and her best friend from the very posh private school they had both attended. Tilly had an olive complexion and neat straight caramel hair so stood a fighting chance in the dress, unlike Charlie with her pale skin and mop of unruly black curls – she looked beyond anaemic in the dress.

Amber announced her presence and came back in. She handed Charlie some sling-back pinpoint high heels for her to balance on and proceeded to stalk around her like a wolf surveying its prey. 'Have you lost weight?' she asked with a disbelieving look.

'Might have done. Don't know. I don't weigh myself regularly.' Come to think of it, Charlie had noticed that she'd had to do up the belt on her jeans another notch. Amber fussed around the waist and shoulders and tutted to herself. She grabbed a handful of dress at the back and nearly pulled Charlie off the silly little pin heels.

'Steady on!' said Charlie, resisting the urge to clout Amber.

'Sorry. But look at this, it's all excess,' she indicated the mass of material in her fist.

'You really should have let us know if you were dieting. This will have to be altered.' Charlie started to protest, but Fleur was already wincing with embarrassment so she stopped and shrugged instead. At a guess the stress of everything must have impacted her weight.

'Can you do it in time for the wedding?' asked Fleur in a small voice and Charlie instantly felt for her. This wedding mattered so much to her. Charlie couldn't imagine getting that caught up in something. It wasn't healthy, but she sympathised with Fleur all the same. Amber was sucking in air though her teeth like a car mechanic shortly before they tell you that your car is terminally ill.

'We'll do our best, but it is a very busy time of year.'

'We need to know a definite yes or no,' said Charlie firmly.

'I should think so,' offered Amber, but seeing the glint in Charlie's eye she added, 'Yes. Of course Miss Van Benton, we won't let you down.'

Fleur started to breathe properly again. Amber fussed some more and used the thinly veiled excuse of marking where alterations were needed, to stick pins in Charlie. When she'd finished she gave Charlie a last once-over. 'I take it you'll be getting rid of those t-shirt tan lines with a spray tan? Otherwise it will detract from the dress.'

It was all Charlie could do not to batter her with the Ladurée macarons, but they simply weren't heavy enough to do a proper job.

'I bought macarons,' said Charlie, placing the bag on the table and suddenly commanding the full attention of every child. The children oohed and aahed as they opened the large box and studied the intensely coloured contents. Ted grabbed a pistachio green macaroon, stuffed it in whole and slid off the sofa. He gave Charlie a nudge and she followed him out of the room and downstairs into the kitchen.

Ted slumped against the wall and casually crossed his legs. He glanced at Charlie through his fringe. I must take these children to a hairdresser, she thought.

'Thought you should know that Elle was crying again,' said Ted, his voice flat.

'Right, what did you do?'

He shrugged. 'Just hugged her and fed her ice-cream.'

'Good call,' said Charlie with a smile.

'And Granddad Roger rang and someone called Jonathan too, but he mumbled a lot.'

'Right, thanks,' said Charlie, as a thought struck her. Perhaps Roger could be the guardian? He was family and, unlike Ruth, he liked Charlie. Perhaps Roger was the answer to their problems and she started to think about how she could broach this with him, the solicitors and Social Services.

A bundle of screams came flying down the stairs with Wriggly in the lead. He appeared to be wearing a pink tutu and he was carrying something black and hairy in his mouth. Charlie's first thought was that it was a rat, but she quickly dismissed it as she'd never seen a longhaired rat and Wriggly simply wasn't that brave. That stupid, perhaps, but certainly not that brave. As he came past Charlie's feet she grabbed him and he went into wriggle overdrive.

'Charlie we couldn't stop him, honest,' said Eleanor breathlessly.

'What is it?' said Charlie, trying to part Wriggly from the mass of black. 'It's my hair piece for the wedding!' she said, as realisation dawned and she gave one more tug to free most of it from Wriggly's jaw. He started frantically trying to spit out the stray pieces that had been left behind. Charlie put the dog down and surveyed the hairpiece. It was now a ball of knotted hair.

'Oh God, I'll look like a budget Amy Winehouse impersonator!'

'Oh God! Oh God! Oh God!' chanted Millie happily.

Chapter Five

Fleur was the epitome of the beautiful bride. She glided down the stairs in her designer gown to greet her beamingly proud father. He'd been waiting patiently in the entrance hall of their modernised farmhouse. Fleur's hair had been expertly crafted into an elegantly sculptured up-do or, as George had put it, a pile of ginger horse poos. Charlie wasn't proud of the fact that she'd paid him five pounds not to repeat the phrase in front of Millie, but it seemed the best option.

A kindly, but foolish, cousin of Fleur's had offered to take Ted, George and Millie to the church, so that Charlie was able to be part of the wedding party and fulfil her duties as bridesmaid. There had been some consternation from the children about attending the wedding and Charlie had agonised at first over whether it was the right thing to do, given the recent tragedy. But she knew that the sooner the children started to do normal things, rather than being shut up in the house all day, the sooner they would be able to manage their grief and start to carry on with their lives.

The wedding had given them all something else to focus on and, although for Ted and George that was mainly moaning about having to wear a suit and tie, it was at least something a little jollier. Eleanor was still quiet but a last-minute decision by Fleur to make her a flower girl had given her a definite boost that Charlie was very grateful for. A simple cream-satin dress had been purchased and the posh bridal shop had couriered across a sash in the same pasty colour as the bridesmaids' dresses and it was now tied around Eleanor's waist with a neat bow at the back.

Eleanor's warm hand snaked its way around Charlie's fingers and she squeezed it gently and felt the squeeze returned. Charlie looked down at Eleanor and felt a lump in her throat at the sight of the little girl smiling up at her. But with the sound of heels on polished parquet their attention was drawn back to the bride.

'Fleur, you look like a princess!' blurted out Eleanor excitedly and Fleur flushed with pleasure.

'She's right,' said Mr Van Benton, 'you are truly beautiful. I am a very proud father today,' he said, his tone surprisingly even given the emotion in his eyes. Fleur forgot her composure and hugged her father tightly, letting him go and then embracing her mother, who was already dabbing her eyes with a handkerchief.

'I was hoping I wouldn't have to use that,' said her mother, folding it neatly and returning it to her Chanel clutch bag. 'Now we'd best be off. Come on, bridesmaids,' said Mrs Van Benton, linking arms with Fleur's sister Polly, 'and of course flower girls too, they're very important,' added Mrs Van Benton, catching sight of Eleanor's face. Charlie stood for a moment and looked at Fleur, who was now straightening her dress after its crushing experience in her parents' arms. Fleur instinctively looked up and beamed at Charlie, who gave a little sigh and returned the smile.

'Go on, get going. I was hoping to have a glass of champagne with Pa before we have to leave.'

'Na, uh,' said Charlie, shaking her head, 'you can't go staggering down the aisle,' although *I* probably will in these silly heels, she thought. Fleur came over and hugged Charlie.

'I'll be fine. Now go!'

Charlie had missed the rehearsals for obvious reasons, but she was familiar with the local church as it sat virtually in the town centre. It was, however, the first time Eleanor had seen it and she was suitably impressed. The magnificent oak-timbered spire had her looking like she had a flip-top head as she craned backwards to see it.

'It's lovely, it's like the one at Disney but not as brightly coloured,' said Eleanor.

'The one at Disney is a castle,' pointed out Charlie.

'Oh, yes,' said Eleanor, still staring at the building, 'it's nearly as lovely, though.'

'Yes, it is lovely.'

'I love you, Charlie,' said Eleanor as she got out of the car, leaving Charlie a little stunned. She quickly composed herself and stepped out.

'Straighten up a little, Charlie,' said Mrs Van Benton gently. 'There, you look perfect,' she said with a smile. Charlie suddenly felt emotional and had to give herself a stern talking-to to keep things in check. She knew that Fleur's mother was only being kind. Charlie's hair was behaving itself after a master craftsman from a top salon had wrestled it into submission and pinned it into a neat pleat with the required tumbling tendrils at the front and thankfully without the need for the Wriggly-chewed road-kill wig. However fabulous her hair looked the dress still made her look like she was sickening for something.

There was a little breeze but the sun was out and any clouds were politely darting across the sky without, for a change, causing any fear of rain. Guests appeared to have taken the arrival of the bridesmaids to mean that it was time to go inside. After a few photographs and the usual comments, guests started to be devoured by the church. The vicar was standing outside with the bridegroom, who had scrubbed up very well indeed. His usually shaven head had a couple of weeks of hair growth on it, making him look less like he had undergone nit-prevention measures.

He waved enthusiastically when he saw them and jogged over.

'Mum!' he said, giving Mrs Van Benton a kiss on the cheek. She smiled and her cheeks flushed. Rob would most likely not have been her first choice of husband for her youngest daughter but despite his rough-diamond persona he was quite sweet and when Fleur made up her mind about something it was pointless to argue – it only made her more determined. Charlie felt that the family had hoped that it would fizzle out with Rob as it had with the other odd choices of boyfriend Fleur had made, but unfortunately this had snowballed very quickly into a full blown fairy tale and now here they were at the climax.

'Ladies!' he said, turning to the three bridesmaids with outstretched arms, 'Poppy, Tilly, Charles,' he said to them in turn, 'you look divine.' There was a likeability factor to Rob. He wasn't a naturally charming person but there was something about him that drew you in. Unfortunately, Charlie had already had to have a word with him about his keenness to continue to share that loveable side with his ex-girlfriend but hopefully he was a man of his word and things would change after today.

'You look smart,' said Charlie, stifling the urge to joke about him usually only being in a suit for court appearances but that would only embarrass Mrs Van Benton and Charlie was too fond of her to do that. Instead, she concentrated on showing Eleanor how to hold her flowers so that the stalks didn't show.

'I take it Fleur's on her way?' he said, sounding a little less confident.

'Yes, they'll be setting off in approximately seven minutes,' said Mrs Van Benton checking her Cartier wristwatch.

'Shouldn't you be inside?' asked Tilly.

'What? Imprisoned for being too handsome?' joked Rob. Charlie gave him a look. 'You are absolutely right.' He gave each of them brief air kisses and a flash of his cheeky grin before bounding towards the church. The thing with Rob was that he was rough around the edges, he hadn't had the best upbringing and he was feckless, but he wasn't bad. He just looked a little bit like he was, but Charlie guessed that was exactly why Fleur was attracted to him.

The vintage Rolls Royce swung in front of the church as the bridesmaids and flower girl stood in a line behind the low chain and wood-stake fence. The organ was barely audible as the delicate sound carried through the open doors of the church. A small group of well-wishers and nosey shoppers stood nearby and a smattering of applause went up as Mr Van Benton helped Fleur from the car.

'This is it,' said Fleur, with a grin, and Poppy and Tilly squealed excitedly.

'Are you ready?' asked her father.

'Absolutely. Let's get married!' she said, and linked her arm through his.

Charlie followed them, with Eleanor gripping her hand through excitement and hard concentration. The wedding was doing her the world of good. As the organist broke into the opening bars of 'Here Comes the Bride', Mr Van Benton gave Fleur a kiss on top of her head and they entered the church.

Charlie and Eleanor kept pace a short distance behind them and turned to walk down the aisle. Charlie could see the smiling vicar standing at the front of the church and the back of Rob's stubbled head. Then, over to the left, about halfway down, she saw the children. Millie was standing on the pew, looking angelic in a purple dress with a layered full skirt and a daisy hair band. Ted stood next to her, with a cautious hand hovering nearby ready to catch her if she fell or, more likely, jumped. George was looking bored. Charlie's heart swelled at the sight of them and she gave a little sigh of relief that they were all fine. Millie started to wave as soon as she saw Charlie and to point excitedly towards the vicar.

'Look Charlie, it's God!' she shouted.

Charlie and Mr Van Benton had been enjoying the reception but were now silently sipping wine watching the body language as the bride and groom had their first row as husband and wife.

'How could you do this? Now! Today! What's wrong with you?' screeched Fleur, as she wiped away a tear of temper.

'Ah, Babe, I thought it best to tell you. You know, I wanted to start the marriage with a clean slate, no surprises. It's a good thing.'

'No, it isn't! Why didn't you tell me this morning?'

'In case you overreacted and then you wouldn't have had your dream wedding. I couldn't let anything get in the way of today, now could I?' Rob's attempts at reasoning were not getting him far.

'But this does get in the way! I told you to choose and it looks like you haven't chosen me. So it's over, Rob.'

Charlie realised that the argument must be about Rob's recent activity with his ex-girlfriend and she tottered over in her stupid high heels. She slammed a hand onto Rob's shoulder. 'What did I say to you?'

'Now, Charlie Boy, don't you go sticking your finger in the plug socket. This isn't anything for you to get involved in, okay?' He tried to convey something with his eyes.

'Charlie, please!' pleaded Fleur and, after a pause, where Rob stared pointedly at Charlie's invading hand, she reluctantly stepped back.

'Come on, Babe, you don't want to miss the surprise I have for you tonight and I don't just mean the bedroom jousting,' grinned Rob. Charlie screwed her face up. Didn't jousting involve long poles and horses? Fleur's face softened a little and Charlie became worried. If Fleur backed down now she could be a doormat forever. Fleur was a rich girl at heart and whatever she said about wanting the simple things in life, and her choice in men was testament to this, she could wobble if Rob had booked the wedding night somewhere stunning like the Savoy or, worse still, Browns.

'It doesn't actually make a difference,' said Fleur unconvincingly, 'but where is it? I may as well know.'

'You wanted something special, right?' said Rob, looking exceedingly smug as Fleur nodded. 'And there's always somewhere that you talk about that you loved to go to, right?' Still no breath was drawn and Charlie was now crossing her fingers. Please don't let it be Browns. 'I found this awesome little B and B in Great Yarmouth!' And, with that, Rob took a wet kipper to the head as well as Fleur's right fist to his chin.

Mr Van Benton surprisingly came to Rob's rescue and instructed Fleur to stop. He had a very clear view of the world, and of right and wrong, and whatever Rob had done, in his eyes, didn't warrant any violence on Fleur's part.

'That hurt,' said Rob rubbing his chin. 'I thought you loved that place! You always talk about how you used to have lovely summers there when you were a child.' He smiled at Fleur's mother. Mrs Van Benton had now silently manoeuvred herself to be next to Fleur.

'I liked it when I was four! I liked it when I was into making sandcastles and going on teacup rides!' said Fleur, her voice rising again. 'Not for my bloody, buggery wedding night!'

'Fleur, dear, language please,' implored her mother. Charlie stood the other side of Fleur and gently rubbed her back.

'To be honest, Fleur, that was actually quite a nice thought… for Rob,' said Charlie, who was immensely relieved that it wasn't a posh London hotel he'd chosen. Poppy Van Benton appeared in a flurry of pallid bridesmaid's dress.

'Sis! What's happened?' The assembled support group all looked in Rob's direction. He was now trying to reason with Fleur from a slightly safer distance. As nobody was providing Poppy with an explanation, Charlie stepped in.

'Rob is still seeing that Sophie girl, even after I told him I would have his gentleman's vegetables for earrings and guess what as a matching pendant. That still holds true, by the way,' said

Charlie, glaring at Rob. Rob was now shaking his head vigorously, which didn't surprise Charlie. He was bound to deny that Charlie had bumped into him outside a tube station kissing his meant-to-be ex-girlfriend, Sophie.

'What!' spluttered Fleur, dragging her tear-stained face away from her mother's now-make-up-smeared Chanel ensemble.

'What?' repeated Charlie, feeling that odd sensation in her stomach when something is not quite adding up but you know that it should be. She looked at Rob, who was scratching his head nervously.

'I told Fleur that I'm going on tour, with the Headless Rodents,' said Rob, fishing business cards out of his suit pocket and handing them round, and wisely missing out Fleur for fear of another punch.

'Your pop group?' asked Mrs Van Benton, taking the card.

'It's more indie rock, Mrs VB, but yeah. We've got this opportunity to support that Goth group that came fourth in a TV Talent show, so we jumped at it and we leave in a few weeks. Couple of visa issues need sorting out first and then we're off. This could be our big break,' he said, turning his best appealing eyes onto Fleur.

Charlie's unease was steadily growing. She knew that Rob and his merry band of equally feckless individuals were talking to some agent but she hadn't thought for a moment that it would ever come to anything. She had instantly assumed that Rob's recent return to the expertly tattooed arms of Sophie was the cause for the outburst.

'You're still seeing Sophie?' A little spit flew in his direction as Fleur literally spat out the words as she pointed at Rob. She spun round, almost knocking over her mother 'And you knew,' she said, jabbing a close-range finger at Charlie. Mrs Van Benton gasped in time to the finger-pointing and Charlie felt her stomach do a triple salchow.

Fleur looked around for the heaviest thing to throw at Rob.

She grabbed the top tier of the wedding cake in both hands and, propelled by her anger, launched it into Rob's face. The reception, which had been in full swing, abruptly halted as everyone turned to stare at the bride and groom, apart from little Millie and Fleur's Uncle Steve, who carried on doing their version of the Macarena, even though the band had stopped.

'Ow! One of the figures went in my eye!' complained Rob, as chunks of elaborately decorated chocolate cake fell to the floor.

'That would be the bride!' shouted Fleur.

'You're overreacting!'

'You think!' snapped Fleur as she hastily gathered up the acres of her dress and exited the room with as much flounce as she could muster.

Chapter Six

Sunday was a very strange day for Fleur. She awoke in her own bed, in her own bedroom, to the usual sound of birdsong, but this was the last place she had expected to be the morning after her wedding. She pulled the duvet tight around her and had a little weep to herself. She had cried a lot yesterday and now told herself that after this little cry, that was it. Rob simply was not worth it. Despite everything he'd promised, he was never going to stay faithful to her, he was a charmer and charming women was what he did. On top of that, who would decide to leave their new bride only a couple of weeks after the wedding and go off around the world with a band? Especially a band that changed their lead singer virtually monthly, due to what they loosely termed 'artistic differences'. All the things that she had thought were exciting and made Rob stand out from the others seemed silly today, and she hated the fact that he was dominating her thoughts.

Fleur felt bad for her parents too. She had been waiting for the 'I told you so' lecture but it hadn't been presented yet – and something told her that it wouldn't be either. She also felt their relief – they were never keen on her boyfriends and Rob was no exception, but this time there was a divorce to sort out. Fleur rubbed her eyes and slid out of bed. At least she could make herself useful, seeing as she wasn't getting on a plane to Borneo any more.

After her shower she checked her phone. No messages, no missed calls. She'd asked Rob not to get in touch and it looked like he was doing as he'd been told. Fleur pulled on some leggings and a big jumper and made her way out of the house. It was a little chilly as the sky was all clouds today – a mass of painted stripes, aspirin-white on more aspirin-white and a drizzle in the air.

Fleur could hear the noise long before she reached the stables. Of all the ponies and horses Fleur's family had owned, Ralph was the most demanding. Fleur was a fraction late with his breakfast this morning so he was making his presence known. As she opened the main door the bucket came flying out at head height, narrowly missing her.

'Ralph!' she shouted. The small fat Shetland pony stared her down. His big brown eyes full of the devil. He hated having to wait for his breakfast. He snorted and turned around to present Fleur with his particularly large backside.

'Delightful,' said Fleur, 'Morning Clyde,' she said. Clyde was her oldest love. The heavy head of her horse lolled over his stable door in welcome. 'Ralph's in a bad mood,' she said and Clyde vigorously nodded his agreement. He didn't, actually, but he always liked to shake his head in a variety of directions first thing in a morning once his stable was open, so it always entertained Fleur to ask him a question.

'Sorry Clyde,' she said sneaking him a polo mint. 'You looked lonely. That was the only reason we got you a stable mate. Shame it turned out to be one with satanic tendencies.' Fleur wondered if it was because Ralph was so small and Clyde was so big, but eventually she'd come to the conclusion that Ralph's bad attitude was simply because he was a little bastard.

As it turned out, Clyde would have been far better off being lonely as, from the second he stepped out of the horsebox, Ralph decided he was in charge and proceeded to nip at Clyde's fetlocks. At any given opportunity Ralph would chase Clyde away and generally make his life a misery, but none of the Van Bentons had the heart to send him back to the rescue centre.

Ralph stamped his hoof in frustration as Fleur hung up his hay bag.

'Darling, you don't need to be doing this today,' said her mother, marching across the yard. 'I was all set to sort out the boys this morning. You could have had a lie-in.' She kissed Fleur lightly on the cheek.

'I'm okay, thanks. I might take Clyde out for a ride.'

'Good idea, but come and have breakfast first. Poppy will be leaving shortly and she'll want to see you before she goes.'

'All right,' conceded Fleur.

'Any contact at all from you know who?'

'He's not Voldemort, mother! You can use his name, but no I've heard nothing from him,' she said as she felt a buzzing sensation from the mobile in her pocket.

Charlie opened the door and then wished she could instantly slam it shut again.

'Hi,' said Felix, 'look we got off on the wrong foot.'

'Twice,' stated Charlie with a bored, slow blink.

'Yeah, sorry. Everything feels like such a mess, I wondered if we could have a chat. Just you and me.'

'Is this so you can give me my notice?'

Felix chuckled, 'No, suspicious Londoner. I want to talk to you about the kids. I think you're a moody cow but I also think you know them the best.'

At least he was honest, thought Charlie. 'Wait there.' She left Ted in charge, grabbed her umbrella and met Felix on the doorstep. 'Posh coffee?'

'Yeah, sounds good,' he said.

'You're paying,' smiled Charlie as she led the way.

The coffee shop was busy and they stood awkwardly in silence in the queue next to each other and gave their orders separately. They found a small table shoved into a corner and settled down. Felix looked around.

'So many miserable people,' he said. 'Do you think it's the weather that makes them like that?'

'It's summer.'

'Not so as you'd notice. It's raining most of the time.'

Charlie looked at him. 'Are you not a fan of London?'

'Hate it. It's cold, wet, there's too much traffic, it's noisy, nothing feels clean, nothing *is* clean and nobody cares about anyone else.'

'Definitely not a fan, then,' she sipped her coffee. 'Thanks for this,' she said, raising her mug.

'And everything is ludicrously expensive,' he said, with a broad smile.

They sipped drinks and glanced at each other for a minute or so and Charlie felt her cheeks colour up. What was that all about?

'We need to talk about the kids,' said Felix at last. 'I don't think there is anyone who can be the kind of guardian that Tobes and Helen would have wanted. You know, someone in the family who could love the children like their own.'

Charlie swallowed hard. It wasn't meant to be but it felt like a blow to her relationship with them.

'What about Roger?' she suggested. 'He's their grandfather and he wouldn't actually have to do anything.'

'He's a bit of a long shot, being elderly, and wasn't he a bit unsteady on his feet?'

'He's got arthritis. He's in a nursing home.'

Felix shrugged and fiddled with the handle of his mug. 'He wouldn't be very involved, so I don't know what Social Services would say about that. Or the solicitors, as it was me and Ruth who were named in the will.'

Charlie knew the odds were stacking up against Roger. 'I'm not saying he's a great option but he could be *an* option.'

'So is Ruth. She's keen to make sure the children have a financially secure future, but she's not the mothering type.'

'That's an understatement,' said Charlie and they both smiled at each other and held eye contact. 'So that leaves you,' said Charlie, and she knew she looked like a puppy as she eyed him hopefully.

Felix blinked and broke the intensity. 'I am the last thing those kids need.'

'But you don't have to actually do anything. I would look after them...'

'That's not what their parents would have wanted.'

'Then stump up!' said Charlie, sounding crosser than she intended. Felix looked taken aback. Charlie tried to relax the situation with a smile. 'What I mean is...' she thought for a moment, this was tricky because stump up was exactly what she meant. 'Nobody is ever going to replace their parents. They just need someone to love them. You could do that.'

Felix stood up abruptly, bumping into the table and knocking over what was left of Charlie's coffee. 'I'm sorry,' he said waving at the coffee. 'I'll be in touch.' He squeezed his way out of the coffee shop repeatedly saying 'excuse me' as he went and repeatedly he was ignored.

On Monday morning, Charlie sat on the floor of the living room, her ear getting quite soggy from the prolonged closeness of the telephone. She had been listening to Fleur for the last fifty-two minutes and if she didn't manage to get her off the phone soon she wouldn't have time to put the vacuum cleaner round before the lady from Social Services arrived. She probably didn't need to do it as the cleaning company did the house every Wednesday but, what with Wriggly, who did so love to get on the sofas and roll around on the carpet, Charlie was keen to make sure that everything looked in place. And Charlie thought that fifty-two minutes of being conciliatory was enough for her blunder. Thankfully, Fleur had quickly forgiven Charlie for not telling her about Rob's infidelity as she was far too busy directing all her venom at Rob.

Charlie tuned back to what Fleur was saying.

'I think Ma is secretly pleased. She won't admit it, but she hadn't really taken to him.' Fleur had now followed her mother's lead and taken to avoiding using Rob's name and instead he was either referred to as 'him', 'Rob the Knob' or Charlie's personal favourite and all her own work, the 'bridegloom'.

'Like all of us you want someone who will make you happy, Fleur, and Knob simply wasn't the man for the job.'

'But I loved him, Charlie.' Fleur's voice faltered. Charlie couldn't endure another round of tears. There simply wasn't time.

'He didn't deserve you. Look, Fleur, what you need is a duvet day with a bunch of rubbish films. Shall I come round later?'

'No, thank you. I'm okay. But lunch somewhere special on Wednesday or Thursday might be nice.'

'Okay, let's do that. Text me.'

'Will do. And when we meet I'll give you the details of Pa's friend, whose nanny is about to go on maternity leave. Pa's already put a good word in for you so I think the job's yours. Bye.'

With relief, Charlie put the phone down. Her head was swimming. Should she be thinking about looking for a new job? Perhaps it was foolish to think that whoever became the children's guardian would want to keep her on. It was a huge assumption. In which case there would no longer be a role for her to play. The trouble was that although Fleur's suggestion made absolute sense Charlie couldn't deal with the amount of emotion her thoughts were stirring up. Right now she didn't want anything else to change, so she would stick her head in the sand – or in this case, the cupboard – and carry on.

She was tugging the vacuum cleaner out of the cupboard when

she heard the doorbell go. Surely that couldn't be the social worker? If it was they were twenty minutes early. Charlie pushed the cleaner back in and ran up to the front door. Sure enough, there, on the doorstep, was a petite woman with an insipid smile and very floral clothes. She was most definitely a social worker and, unfortunately, one of those who could have been made with a cookie cutter. Sometimes you had one who was bright, cheerful, knew a bit about the world and then there were the rest; this woman was most definitely one of the rest, decided Charlie.

'Hi,' said Charlie, stepping back to let her in.

'Hello, I'm Camille,' she simpered and Charlie inwardly sighed. 'Would you like to see some identification?' she asked.

'No, it's okay. You're from Social Services. We're expecting you.'

'I am,' said Camille, looking totally surprised.

'Although you're a little early.'

'So I am,' said Camille, without looking at her watch. Charlie was already suspicious. Was this an attempt to catch Charlie off guard? Charlie showed her through to the living room and shut the door.

Charlie went down the stairs at speed, through the kitchen and into the playroom. George and Millie were play wrestling and Millie's hair looked as if a troupe of monkeys had rampaged through it.

'George, Millie! Stop it now,' said Charlie, trying not to shout. Millie jumped up and promptly stomped on George's groin.

George let out a yelp. 'My testicles!' said George, nursing the front of his trousers.

'George!' Charlie pointed at Millie and tried very hard not to laugh.

Chapter Seven

For the first fifteen minutes the meeting with Camille went fine. Camille had introduced herself and gone through what usually happened in this situation and the process they would need to go through. Charlie had given her the children's birth certificates so that she could copy down their details correctly.

'I see that Edward is Mrs Cobley's child from a previous relationship.' It didn't bode well for them that, despite her appearance, this social worker was on the ball.

'Yes, Ted was the result of a relationship at university, as I understand it,' said Charlie. 'His father doesn't keep in touch and Toby always brought him up as his own.'

'However, this does mean that technically he isn't orphaned, so if his father was able to look after him that would be an option for Edward.'

'Ted is sixteen in September, he doesn't know his father at all and Mr and Mrs Cobley wanted the children to stay together. It specifically stated it in their wills.'

'Yes, of course, but Edward's father should be made aware of the situation.'

'Okay. I'll tell him,' said Charlie, who had absolutely no intention of doing so. 'I know that it's not straightforward having joint guardians so we wondered if Helen's father, Roger Talbot, could be the children's guardian instead?'

'Oh, I wasn't aware there were any other family members?' Camille seemed to brighten up, as she poised her pen over her notebook. 'How old is Mr Talbot and where does he live?'

'He was seventy last year, they had a big party for him at the nursing home,' said Charlie and she saw Camille's brightness fade. 'He has all his marbles, he's only there because he's got really bad arthritis.'

'I see,' said Camille as she made some notes.

'Will I be able to stay on after the guardian is appointed?'

'I don't know, that would be up to the guardian, but what if you get a better job offer? What then?'

'I stay here,' said Charlie bluntly. 'It's not just a job to me.'

'Yes, of course, but people's priorities change and I need to check that everyone understands the implications of any arrangements. And, as I explained, the final decision will rest with a judge.' She gave a weak smile and Charlie started to feel sweat form on her top lip.

'Have the children returned to school?' asked Camille.

'No, not yet but both the schools have been really supportive. The tutors are in regular contact and have sent work across so that they don't fall behind on their studies. I guess that's the benefit of private schools.'

'You'll need to talk to the tutors about a plan for them to return.' said Camille as she jotted down more notes but didn't look up.

'Yep, and talk to the children about it too,' said Charlie as she wondered how she would broach that subject.

The door opened and in came Millie carrying a struggling Wriggly.

'Wriggly needs a nappy,' stated Millie, plonking the dog momentarily onto Charlie's lap before he made his escape.

'Come here, sweetheart,' said Charlie, lifting Millie onto her knee. Millie snuggled into Charlie's shoulder and stared at Camille.

'So who do we have here?' asked Camille, her business-like approach lost at the sight of the beautiful child with pouting lips.

'This is Millie,' said Charlie.

'Ah, Amelia Alexandra Cobley,' said Camille, checking her notes.

'Th-b-th-sssssss,' said Millie, blowing a magnificent raspberry at Camille.

'Be nice,' whispered Charlie in Millie's ear and she instantly put on a beaming and slightly scary smile. Camille sat back a little. 'How do you think the children are coping?'

'I think the phrase is as well as can be expected.'

Camille nodded, 'Any drastic changes in behaviour? Anything you need help with?'

'Testicles,' said Millie and Camille's eyebrows shot up. Charlie inwardly cried.

'Testicles! Testicles!' chanted Millie happily.

Thankfully, Camille hadn't seemed too shocked by Millie's inappropriate chanting. She arranged to visit the following week and also to talk to each of the older children, to understand their wishes. Charlie saw Camille out and returned to the living room. She flopped down on to the sofa next to Millie.

'How did you think that went?' asked Charlie.

'Testicles!' said Millie.

'Precisely,' said Charlie.

Charlie was sound asleep when the phone went. She hated it when the phone rang in the middle of the night; it was usually a wrong number. Charlie didn't have a landline in her room so it meant she would have to get out of bed and go downstairs. She tried to move an arm but realised that it was dead and trapped underneath a sleeping Eleanor. It seemed Eleanor had rolled that way, having been squeezed out by Millie, who was taking up an inordinate amount of room by sleeping in a star formation. This was not going to be an easy habit to break. Charlie pulled her arm from underneath the sleeping child and removed the weight from her feet that was in the form of a snoring Wriggly. That was another habit that needed to stop too, she thought, as she went downstairs on autopilot. The caller was persistent, so Charlie decided it was worth making the effort to answer it.

'Hello?' she said wearily.

'Thank the Lord. I only had one call and I thought your mobile might be off so I called the house phone and you did pick up. Thank you, thank you,' said a high-speed Fleur.

'Uh, Fleur, it's…' Charlie looked at the clock 'ten past two. What do you want?'

'Um, I need you to come and get me, or I can get a taxi to yours, if that's easier,' said Fleur hurriedly.

'Fleur, talk sense. What's going on? Are you okay?'

'Kind of yes and kind of no.'

'Fleur!' barked Charlie, her patience worn through already.

'I went to Rob's digs and I slashed his tyres, but their neighbourhood watch is really very good so they called the police, who arrested me. I'm in Harold Hill police station and I can't ring Ma and Pa – they'll kill me and I don't think a taxi would risk taking me home as it's quite far and I don't have any cash. So I called you and the nice policeman says I need to wind up the call.' Her voice was getting faster and faster, like someone declaring all the terms and conditions on a lending advert.

'You prize idiot. Get a taxi here. I'll pay for it, but you're paying me back,' and Charlie put the phone down because, if she didn't put it down now, in about ten seconds she was going hurl it across the room.

Charlie's cold feet were pacing the living-room floor, the boiling-mad sensation she could feel elsewhere hadn't yet travelled that far. When she heard a car pull up outside she sprang towards the front door, grabbing her purse on the way. She opened the door briskly and a startled-looking Fleur stood outside with a knuckle aloft, ready to tap on the door. Charlie held out twenty-pound notes; Fleur took them and delivered them to the waiting cab driver. She slunk back up the steps, past Charlie and into the house. Even in an oversized jumper and her hair roughly tied back she still looked like she could be on the front of a magazine. Her hooded eyes were the only thing that gave her away.

Charlie held the door tightly and, with a lot of effort, shut it silently. She would far rather have let some of her temper out and slam it shut but that would wake the whole house and the children needed their sleep. She was so cross with Fleur she didn't know where to start.

'I actually got arrested,' said Fleur, trying to hide a smile by biting her bottom lip.

'You idiot! What the hell did you think you were doing?'

Fleur crept onto one of the big chairs, pulled her feet underneath her and covered her knees with her jumper. 'Come on, Charlie, it's not really serious. Even the policeman laughed when I told him the story. I think he thought Knob deserved it too.'

Charlie knew that Fleur could charm anyone and a gullible policeman would not be a challenge. A quick flutter of the eyelashes and the 'I got dumped at my own wedding' story and he didn't stand a chance. But Charlie was full of temper and she had to channel it somewhere.

'They charged you, so you have a criminal record now. What happens when you want to get a job? These things hang around forever,' said Charlie, speaking from bitter experience. 'And what will your parents say when they find out?'

'Knob will drop the charges when he's calmed down and, well, Ma and Pa don't need to know. I told them I was most likely going to be staying at a friend's.'

'Did you plan to get arrested?' Charlie couldn't control the higher-octave voice that escaped.

'No! I was going to sit outside his flat. I know that's sad but I wanted to know who he was with, what he was doing. If he was sad or sorry or… I don't know.'

'And was he any of those things?' said Charlie, trying to maintain her temper because annoyingly it was starting to ebb away.

'No. He pulled up in his car and it was like a party spilled out. He was with Jed and Sophie and two other girls and they were laughing and messing about… and I watched them go inside and I flipped out. You know when you say the red mist descends and you can't control it?' Charlie knew exactly what that was like. She nodded and sat on the arm of the chair next to Fleur. 'I flipped out and I stabbed his tyres with my penknife. I got a bit carried away and then there was this man with a torch shouting at me and then Knob came out and went crazy and then the police arrived.' Fleur's bottom lip sagged and Charlie leaned in to give her a hug before she started to cry.

'You are a prize idiot.' She hugged her for a bit until Fleur released her grip.

'I'm tired.'

'Hot chocolate?' suggested Charlie.

'No, thank you. Where am I sleeping?'

'Sofa or one of the children's beds – half of them are free as far as I can make out,' said Charlie, thinking about the warm bodies squirrelled under her duvet.

Charlie could hear the phone ringing again and dragged herself to consciousness. It was light outside but still early. She looked around and realised she was asleep on the sofa. When she had gone back to bed it had still been full of children and dog, so she had settled Fleur in Eleanor's bed and had taken a blanket and opted for the sofa. It had been adequate and at least she hadn't spent the night disentangling herself from paws, legs and countless pointy elbows.

She dragged herself upright, picked up the phone and mumbled into it.

'Who is this?' asked Ruth.

'It's Charlie, the nanny,' said Charlie, waking up as a shot of something lunged uncomfortably around her system.

'I want an update on the Social Services meeting,' she stated firmly.

'I'd be happy to do that for you,' said Charlie, relaxing into the sofa. She could feel Ruth's reaction on the other end and it was quite entertaining.

'I still don't see why they wanted to see you at all,' said Ruth, her voice fading out a little.

Charlie really did dislike this woman. 'I'm going to be the children's primary carer so it concerns me very much.' There, that felt better.

'What gives you that idea? We can, and will, employ who we like to care for the children. As you've brought up the subject, I'll see if I can get along to you this afternoon...' said Ruth.

Charlie wanted to reach down the phone and pull her out, like they did in cartoons, and give her a good slap. Count to ten, she thought, count to ten. One, two, three... bugger it!

'You can employ anyone you like, Ruth, and you can change them weekly, especially if you'd like to totally fuck up your sister's children. If that's what you want, you go ahead!' and she switched off the phone. Charlie instantly wished she hadn't done it. That may have been tantamount to handing in her resignation. It was stupid and rash. She flung herself back against the sofa. What had she done?

Chapter Eight

Fleur came into the room wrapped in Charlie's dressing gown and wearing Ted's old slippers. She was closely followed by Millie.

'Good morning, Gorgeous,' said Charlie, as Millie plonked herself onto her lap and started to suck her thumb.

'Good morning,' said Fleur, curling herself into the chair opposite.

'Do you have plans for today?' asked Charlie, as she ran her fingers through Millie's hair in an effort to remove the worst of the knots before she had to drag a reluctant comb through it.

'I need a lift to Harold Hill to get my car.'

'Or what's left of it,' snorted Charlie.

'Don't. That's not funny.'

'Nor is Harold Hill,' said Charlie. 'Yes, I'll take you there. What time?'

'No rush,' said Fleur, with a yawn. 'Maybe I could help you?'

'That would be nice. I think I may have blown it with Ruth. She's coming to see me later.'

'Don't worry, she's all hot air.'

'I'm not so sure that she is,' said Charlie, feeling the ominous cloud of Ruth's words hanging above her, raining down pellets of dread.

Fleur clapped her hands together. 'What you need is a bit of fun!'

They decided that they would all have a walk to the park and take a picnic lunch. Charlie felt she needed to broach the subject of the children returning to school – and a bit of moral support from Fleur would be nice. After breakfast Fleur was playing mummies and babies with Millie and hadn't appeared to see the irony of the game, but both she and Millie seemed content enough. George was playing something unsuitable on the games console with Ted so they were both happy and Eleanor was giving Wriggly a bath.

Charlie was counting out drinks into the cool box as the phone rang and it was answered somewhere else in the house. Ted strolled into the kitchen and mouthed that it was Ruth on the phone, followed by a roll of his eyes. This way she could at least listen to one side of the conversation and decide if she needed to pack now or later.

The conversation that followed was rather one-sided as Ted listened and Charlie could hear Ruth getting crosser in the background. After a couple of minutes, he handed the phone to Charlie. 'She wants to talk to you,' he said, taking the plate of toast and sitting down at the table. Charlie took the phone and regarded it as if it were a hand grenade with its pin missing.

'Hello Ruth,' said Charlie, trying to brazen it out.

'We got cut off this morning,' said Ruth, and Charlie thought for a bizarre moment that perhaps Ruth was being kind. 'I think there's a problem with my phone, it keeps doing it,' but it turned out that, for once, luck was on Charlie's side.

'And there was me thinking you'd put the phone down on me, but who would be so rude?'

'Quite,' said Ruth. 'Is Edward all right? He doesn't speak.'

It was Charlie's turn to roll her eyes. 'He's a teenager, Ruth. You're lucky if you can get a grunt out of him.'

Charlie felt the toast hit the back of her head and turned

around to see Ted holding a second slice aloft. She gave him a death stare and he grinned before biting into the toast.

'Can you explain why my father seems to think he's going to be the children's guardian?'

'I suggested it to Roger and he seemed quite keen. I spoke to Social Services about it too. Is there a problem?'

'Yes, there's a problem. My father was never one of the options. He is in a nursing home for a reason. He is not in a fit state to be the children's guardian.'

'But Social Services explained everything. They need to do an assessment of whoever puts themselves forward as guardian, they fill in some forms and it goes to court to grant the formal guardianship. I think they want someone who really wants to be the guardian to do it. Either way, I can go on looking after the children here in their own home,' said Charlie. It was worth a try, she thought.

There was a slight pause and Charlie bit her lip. 'I have power of attorney for my father. Do you know what that means?'

Charlie let out a defeated sigh. 'That you're going to say no.'

'It means I have the legal right to make decisions for him. My decision is that he will not be the children's guardian. I'll be along later to discuss…'

'Ruth, hold on. I only want what's best for the children. And I know that sounds really big-headed of me, and before you say it, I know I'm not a qualified nanny, but it works. The children and I get on really well. This isn't just a job to me, I love these kids.' There was no response from the other end of the line so Charlie continued. 'Ruth, I don't want to upset you or anyone else in the family, I want to do what I think Helen and Toby would have wanted and I honestly believe that they would have wanted the children to stay in their own home.' She felt an unwelcome tear poke the back of her eyes. There was still no response. 'Ruth, are you still there?' There was silence. 'Bloody phone!' said Charlie as she switched it off.

The mood was decidedly un-picnic-y as they threw down the rugs, including a plastic-coated Winnie the Pooh one for Millie. The grass was damp but the rain was currently holding off. Millie was the only one who was disappointed about this as she had brought her umbrella in the hope of a downpour. George flopped down onto a rug, looking intensely bored already. Millie spotted the play area and started running.

'Here you go!' said Charlie as she threw the Frisbee towards Ted, who sidestepped it and wandered off after Millie. He walked with a slouch these days. Charlie wasn't sure if he always had but it seemed more noticeable recently. And his ear buds were permanently attached to his ears. 'Football?' said Charlie, offering the ball up to George and Eleanor.

'I'm going to take Wriggly for a walk,' said Eleanor glumly.

'Keep where I can see you, okay?'

'I'll go with her,' said George, dragging himself up from the rug.

'And then there were two,' said Fleur.

'At least they're getting some fresh air,' said Charlie, trying to ignore the distant rumble of London traffic.

Fleur's phone beeped for the umpteenth time that morning. 'It's Knob,' she said, 'he's dropping the charges.'

'You were right,' said Charlie, feeling relieved. 'Anything else?' she added, suspecting that the lovely Fleur wasn't telling all. She settled herself down so she had a good view of the play area and of George and Eleanor, who were already quite a distance away.

'He still loves me.'

'Uh, huh, that explains kissing Sophie and dumping you at your own wedding reception.'

'He says he didn't know what to do for the best, what with all the money my parents had spent.'

'Yes, I can see that that would concern Knob. You're not thinking of taking him back are you?' asked Charlie, dragging her eyes away from Millie, who was squealing happily as a nonchalant Ted tried to push her swing one-handed and without looking.

'No… No! Honestly, it's over. It's just… don't laugh,' said Fleur, lying back on the rug, her auburn hair splaying out around her head like a giant halo.

'Go on,' said Charlie, scanning the park and spotting Wriggly trying to pull Eleanor's arm off with his lead so that he could chase a pigeon.

'There was so much to do before the wedding. There was this massive list of things that had to be perfect and I was busy every day sorting it all out. The caterers, the marquee, the church, the place names, the champagne, the honeymoon, it was a very long list. But now, I have nothing to do. There was this big full stop and I don't know what to do now.'

'But after the honeymoon, what had you planned to do?' asked Charlie, feeling this was possibly the most ridiculous dilemma ever.

'Be with Rob… the Knob,' said Fleur, with a clear hesitation before she added the insult. Charlie feared that she was wavering and Fleur was as robust as a wet paper bag when it came to men.

'Really? That was the rest of your life. You following him around while he pratted about with the Headless Hamsters.'

'Rodents,' corrected Fleur.

'I know. Come on, Fleur, maybe this is the wake-up call you need. Do something with your life. You can do anything. You simply need to make it happen.' And with Mummy and Daddy's money and unwavering support behind you, you really could do anything you wanted, thought Charlie.

'Do you ever think about when we were in foster care?' asked Fleur.

Charlie turned away from her surveillance operation to look at Fleur. 'Blimey, that was a long time ago, Fleur.'

'I can't remember any of it,' said Fleur, her eyes filled with sadness.

Charlie turned back to watch George poking something in the grass with a stick. 'Nobody can remember stuff from when they were that young. I was four and I only have vague memories and you were what? Eighteen months old?'

Fleur nodded. 'It's like a book with the first chapter missing.'

Charlie glanced over her shoulder and smiled indulgently. 'Oh, Fleur, that's very poetic but it's a right load of crap!'

Fleur looked tense. 'Don't you want to know about your early life?'

'Nope,' said Charlie, with a shrug. 'Why would you want to know about a time when people didn't care enough to look after you properly?'

Fleur bit her lip. 'It feels like I've got something missing.'

Charlie resisted the opportunity to make a joke. 'Fleur, I think you're looking for excuses. You have the most amazing family, who love you to bits. Knowing about the past might fill in a few blanks but that's all it will do. It won't suddenly unlock the key to your future.' Fleur sighed and Charlie decided to leave things there.

Fleur and Charlie's childhood experiences had been very different. Charlie had been like a pinball in the care system, bouncing from one place to another and from one misadventure to the next. It wasn't an excuse, it was simply fact and, coupled with the usual teenaged angst, it had made for an explosive cocktail. Thanks to the kindness and unrelenting persistence of her last foster parents, Charlie had finally straightened herself out. The Van Bentons had also been a constant presence, letting Charlie and Fleur keep in touch after they adopted Fleur, as the girls had shared an early bond in their foster placement together. It was thanks to the Van Bentons that she had got this job. They were good friends with Helen and Toby and knowing the Cobley's situation they had engineered a meeting and waxed lyrical about how well Charlie was doing, having achieved her level one in childcare. The Van Bentons had been incredibly good to her.

'Maybe I should have gone to Borneo for the honeymoon on my own,' mused Fleur, staring up at the branches of the tree above her.

'Great, so that would have kept you occupied for two weeks. Still leaves the question of the next seventy or so years,' said Charlie, losing sight of Millie and half getting to her feet before spotting Ted supporting Millie on the climbing equipment.

'Pa is driving me potty as well, so a break from the parents would be a good thing.'

'What's your dad done?'

'Nothing he hasn't done before. He just takes over everything. He cancelled the honeymoon, sorted out the return of all the presents. He's sorting out the divorce. He does everything and it drives me mad,' said Fleur, waving her arms and from her prone position looking a little like a dying fly.

'Eleanor washes her own hair now,' said Charlie after a pause.

'Random.'

'I don't remind her, because I know she can do it herself. Before, I used to have to remind her and before that I had to do it for her.'

'Riveting,' said Fleur. 'Should I book a holiday?'

'What I mean is, you need to show your parents that you can do things for yourself. Start by sorting out the divorce. Show them you're not a little girl any more,' said Charlie, taking a quick glance at Fleur, who was pouting.

'Pa knows solicitors and it's all a bit upsetting.'

'Don't be so lazy! Google solicitors and pick one. Ring them up and ask them if they'll take you on as their client. It's not hard!' said Charlie, shaking her head in dismay. Sometimes she wanted to give Fleur a good shake and this was one of them. 'Right, I'll round up the troops, you unpack the hamper,' and Charlie strode off towards where she'd last seen Wriggly trying to wee up a litterbin.

The children all ate their sandwiches in silence apart from

Eleanor, who lay on the rug copying Fleur. Some teenagers walked close by them and Millie waved at them. When this elicited no response, she happily called after them, 'Riff Raff!' George started to chuckle and a smile broke out on Eleanor's face and then, like the best disease ever, they all started to laugh. Fleur lifted her sunglasses to survey them all. It was like a release valve and the laughter went on a fraction longer than was sane.

The laughter trickled away and Charlie saw her opportunity. 'I'm glad we're together. I need to talk to you about going back to school,' she said, checking each face in turn and waiting for the deluge of complaints. 'I've been speaking to your schools regularly and they're keen to have you back.'

Ted looked at his siblings and shrugged at Charlie. 'Fine, it's boring at home,' he said.

'Even more boring than school,' said George. They all turned to look at Eleanor.

'I've missed school. Can I go tomorrow?'

'If you want to,' said Charlie, totally stunned by the reaction. Maybe getting back into their normal routine was what they were missing, but she couldn't help but worry how they would manage all the questions and curiosity that would surely come their way from their classmates. She knew she couldn't protect them from that. All she could do was be there when they came home.

'Are there any crisps?' asked Eleanor, and Charlie handed them over and resisted the urge to hug her.

After the food, the children disappeared with the football and whatever the game was they were playing Wriggly appeared to be at the centre of it. Charlie packed away all the leftover food before any flies got interested and Fleur grabbed the last couple of chunks of celery before they were hastily wrapped in cling film. Charlie leant back against the tree and felt herself relax a little.

'Here you go,' said Fleur, handing Charlie a thick cream embossed business card. 'Sorry, I forget to give it to you earlier.'

'Melvyn Halsey, Chiropractor. What do I need that for?'

'Job, Duh? Their nanny is having a baby. They've got two girls… no two boys… or is it one of each? Anyway they've got two children and they'll soon need a new nanny and they only live ten minutes away from me, so it would be perfect.'

Charlie gazed at the business card. This was her get-out clause; the easy answer. 'Um, thanks,' she said, stuffing it into her jeans pocket and trying to halt all the questions it was triggering in her mind. Was this the point where she made a decision? She could wish the children well and walk into a new job. That would be the sensible thing to do. She'd worked hard to get her life on track and this would be another step in the right direction, with another professional family on her CV. Or she could risk everything and fight for the children she loved.

'Pa will give you a reference because, well, the Cobleys can't.'

Charlie felt a wave of grief come over her. Why did the Cobleys have to die? Why did everything that was so perfect have to change? She lay back on the grass and fought hard to stop the tears she knew were brimming in her eyes.

They had to visit the Joy of Life Fountain before they left the park, as Millie always loved to hurl coins in. Charlie already had a few pennies in her pocket in anticipation. The others usually wandered off when they got to the fountain, but today they all took a penny from Charlie, tossed them in and stood silently. Charlie wondered what wishes they were making and if any of them could possibly come true. Millie asked for another coin and this time did an impressive over-arm lob and narrowly missed Fleur.

'I bet your wish was that you weren't standing in Millie's firing line,' joked George.

Charlie flipped in a coin and watched it disappear under the water. Her wish was a simple one – she wished she knew what to do.

The walk back was definitely more upbeat, the children seemed to have perked up at the thought of returning to school and it was good to feel that they were taking steps in the right direction, even though they were baby ones. Ted was still looking slouchy but even he had a fleeting smile on his face. Charlie started to mentally go through all the school things she would need to get ready for tomorrow. She would also get Millie back into her toddler groups, which she knew she had been missing. That would also mean that Charlie was back in her old routine and she felt a great wave of comfort at the thought of it and realised that this must have been the same for the children.

'Is that people at the house?' asked Fleur, pointing up the road to where two figures were standing on the steps.

Charlie squinted. 'Oh great, it's Ruth and she's got some woman with her.'

Chapter Nine

'Hello,' said Charlie, turning to the smiley woman wearing a funny little brown hat with a gold letter N on it, a white-edged beige dress and white gloves. Charlie couldn't help grinning, but it was more in response to the outfit than the woman's smile. 'Children, say hi,' added Charlie, as they streamed up the steps.

There was a mumbled chorus of 'Hi'.

Charlie opened the front door and the children trooped in followed by Fleur. Charlie turned to address Ruth and the oddly dressed woman.

'I'm Charlie,' she said, offering the woman her hand to shake, which she did enthusiastically.

'Hello! I'm Sally.'

Charlie nodded and looked to Ruth for an explanation. Ruth was looking rather smug. 'Sally is a Norland Nanny, and actually... shall we go inside?' said Ruth, stepping past a stunned Charlie and into the house. Charlie took a moment to get the sudden rush of emotions in check before following them inside.

'What's going on?' whispered Ted, as his eyes followed the Norland Nanny.

'I think this is a hostile takeover,' said Charlie, handing all the picnic stuff to him, which he took and put on the floor at his feet.

'Edward could you show Sally round the house while I speak to Charlie?' asked Ruth. Ted looked to Charlie and she nodded that he should do as he'd been asked.

'I know this will come as a shock,' said Ruth, handing Charlie an envelope, 'but I think you'll find I've been more than generous.'

Charlie said nothing but she felt sick. She tore open the envelope and as she opened the letter that was inside a cheque floated to the floor. Fleur picked up the cheque as Charlie scanned the typed letter. There was lots of jargon and long words but the two things that hit her were 'one week's notice' and 'terminating your employment'.

'Ooh, this is good, Charlie, look,' said Fleur, trying to distract Charlie with the cheque. Charlie closed her eyes for a moment, reviewed her 'Kipper List', and proceeded, in her mind's eye, to whack Ruth with a kipper. When she felt she was in control she opened her eyes again as Ted and Sally returned to the hall.

'It's a lovely house. It's a shame I'm only here as a stopgap for a permanent placement. I would like the en-suite room, if that's possible?' said Sally.

Charlie turned to her and spoke slowly and deliberately. 'That's the Cobley's bedroom. I don't think that's appropriate.'

'Right, well. I only wanted to serve you your notice and introduce Sally to the children, so we'll be off,' said Ruth, her tone jolly. 'Bye, children.'

'Hang on,' said Charlie. 'If you're sacking me you need a reason.'

'You can't do that!' said Ted, before turning to Charlie. 'She can't do that, can she?'

'Your friend, Charlie, is not all she pretends to be,' said Ruth to Ted, before leaning towards Charlie. 'I know about your past and because of that I can dismiss you without notice. But, like I said, I think you'll find I've been more than generous in the circumstances.'

Charlie slowly sucked in a steadying breath. 'Ruth I am going to call the solicitor and take advice from him about this situation. Would you both like a cup of tea?' asked Charlie, looking from Ruth to Sally and back again. Ruth was eyeing Charlie suspiciously, perhaps this wasn't the reaction she was expecting or hoping for.

On Charlie's suggestion Ted took Ruth and Sally into the living room whilst Charlie and Fleur went to the kitchen. Fleur put the kettle on.

'This has worked out quite well,' said Fleur, distracting Charlie from dialling the solicitor's number.

'What?'

'You can leave here with a big fat cheque, have a few weeks' holiday away somewhere, then start the new job. I'd say that's great timing!'

Charlie blinked hard. She was tired and she did need a holiday, but what she wanted above everything was a family holiday like the ones she used to go on when the Cobleys were alive, not a week on her own. 'Fleur, the children need me.'

Fleur gave a reticent smile. 'Perhaps it's time to give in gracefully?' she said, taking Charlie's hand and giving it a supportive squeeze. 'Ruth's got a Norland Nanny for the children. They don't come any better than that, Charlie. The Royal Family have Norland Nannies. Ooh, I wonder if Sally has met the Queen…'

Charlie shook her head and left Fleur to make the tea and prattle on while she phoned Jonathan Steeple. Thankfully he was available and was quick to respond once Charlie had read him the letter.

'The guardianship has not been formally agreed and Miss Talbot does not have the authority to terminate your employment,' said Jonathan, and Charlie felt relief wash over her, although she still felt quite sick.

'Thank you. That's brilliant news. Now what do we do about Miss Talbot and her Nanny, who are sitting in the living room?'

'Let me speak to her, would you?' asked Jonathan.

'With pleasure,' said Charlie, as she hurried Fleur and two clinking cups and saucers up the stairs. They entered the living room and Fleur put the drinks on the low table and sat on the sofa to watch the proceedings. Sally was perched on the edge of a chair, looking uncomfortable, and her cup and saucer rattled when she picked them up.

'Ruth, I have Jonathan Steeple on the phone and he would like to speak to you,' said Charlie, as she tried to hand her the phone.

'I do not wish to speak to him.'

Charlie thrust the phone towards her. 'I think you should.'

Ruth picked up her cup and saucer and Charlie now had nowhere to hand the phone to. She spoke into the receiver, 'She won't speak to you. What should I do?'

Jonathan suggested that she put the phone on loudspeaker, which she did, and she placed it on the coffee table near Ruth.

'Miss French is employed legally by the Cobley Executors. They and only they can terminate her employment and...' started Jonathan.

'Unless that employment was based on lies,' said Ruth, before taking a sip of her tea.

'Hold on, Jonathan,' said Charlie. 'What lies, Ruth?'

'You have been in trouble with the police. If my sister had known that she would not have employed you. Therefore you got this job on false pretences; therefore you have breached the terms of your employ. I spoke to a solicitor too.' Charlie's head started to spin and she sat down on the sofa with an inelegant thump. All the old memories and emotions so well buried surged up and momentarily took her breath away.

Ted was sitting forward, looking worried. 'Is that true?'

Charlie swallowed hard and tried to compose herself. 'It is true about me being in trouble a very long time ago, yes. But your parents were aware of my background and they employed me knowing that.'

'I can vouch for that,' said Fleur. 'My parents introduced Charlie to the Cobleys and they are the most honest people on the planet. I can call them if you like?'

There was a moment where everyone's eyes were darting around the room but nobody spoke. Eventually there was a noise from the telephone and they all tuned back in to Jonathan.

'There is no reason to believe that Mr and Mrs Cobley were not aware of Miss French's record and I repeat that legally only the executors can dismiss her. We should have been consulted before you did this, Miss Talbot, and...'

Charlie cut in and addressed Ruth, 'And you should leave before I call the police and have you removed,' said Charlie, her face starting to colour. She picked up the phone and took it off loudspeaker. 'Thank you, Mr Steeple, you've been ace, good-bye.' Charlie ended the call.

Sally looked shocked and placed her rattling cup and saucer back on the table. 'I should leave,' said Sally, standing up and facing Ruth. 'Good-bye, Miss Talbot, perhaps we should speak once these issues have been resolved,' she added, before heading for the door double-quick.

'Good decision, Sally. Lovely to meet you. Nice hat,' said Charlie.

'This isn't over,' said Ruth, rising to her feet. 'I will not rest while these children are in the care of a convict.'

Fleur was pleased to be back in her own little car, albeit crawling along the M25. She was even more pleased to find that her car was still in one piece and had all its wheels, but she had known that the neighbourhood watch were a vigilant lot. There had been a surprise; there was a note left on her car. At first she had held it in her hands, a little afraid to open it, assuming that the message inside would be something abusive. But the only way to find out was to unfold and read it. As soon as she opened out the scrap of white paper she recognised Rob's slopey handwriting. She read the note and looked around, expecting to see him appear nearby or to be watching her from a window. But he wasn't there. His car wasn't there either.

As she drove home, Fleur was still trying to work out if the note was a nice surprise or not. She turned up her latest favourite song and sang along. She glanced across at the passenger seat and the small, simple white business card with its blue edging. Maybe she shouldn't have taken it without checking with Charlie, but it was Charlie who had told her to take control, to show her parents that she could sort out her own problems. She had even told her to get a solicitor, and there on a shelf in the Cobley's hall had been their solicitor's business card and from the loud-speaker Mr Steeple had sounded like he knew what he was doing and he had a nice voice, which made him ideal, in Fleur's view.

As soon as she got home she had to have a much-needed talk with her parents. Charlie was right, she needed to be in charge of her own life and a good start would be to come clean about last night's escapade. Fleur knew she was drifting in life, the sudden void after the wedding had told her that and it had to stop. The question was, if she wasn't drifting, what was she doing? And right now Fleur had absolutely no idea.

Charlie hated the feeling that she was fast running out of options and after some thought she decided that it might be worth a call to Ted's birth father. The last thing she wanted to do was split the family up, but if there was anything that held the merest possibility it was worth checking out.

'Anthony Penton,' said the brusque male voice.

'Hello. You don't know me, but I'm Charlie, Helen and Toby Cobley's nanny. Have you got a minute?'

'Not really.'

'But it's important…' started Charlie, but Anthony Penton talked over her.

'Fine. I'll call you back,' he said and the line went dead. Charlie stared at the phone, thinking what an unpleasant man and wondering exactly when, or even if, he would bother to call her back when the phone rang.

'Hello,' said Charlie, noting the 'number withheld' message on the small screen. She was half expecting it to be a telesales call, which she now particularly hated as they didn't always seem to understand when Charlie told them that 'Mr and Mrs Cobley had both died.'

'Anthony Penton. You've got five minutes.'

Oh, you are a complete delight, thought Charlie, I'm so glad something pricked my conscience and I called you. 'Okay. I'm very sorry to have to tell you that Helen and Toby died in a car accident a couple of months ago.' Charlie paused to give him time to digest the sad information. He may have been bolshie to start with but she knew this would come as a shock. But apparently Anthony Penton didn't need time to digest what she'd said as he came straight back in the same business-like tone.

'I see. I don't know what I thought you were going to say but it definitely wasn't that.'

'I'm sorry,' said Charlie and she meant it. This man must have loved Helen once, so it couldn't have been easy for him to hear.

'So how does this affect me?'

'Social Services said I should inform you. There's a lot of confusion over who will be guardian for the children, but it was Helen's wish that they should all be kept together. There's four of them,' she said, trying to mimic his unemotional tone and failing badly. 'That includes your child, Ted,' she added in haste, just in case that wasn't blindingly obvious.

'Thank you for letting me know,' he said and this was followed by a long pause, which Charlie filled by silently waving her right arm in circles like a prompter on a film set.

'Is that it?' she said at last.

'As far as I can tell, there is nothing for me to do. Do tell me if I'm wrong.'

71

'Maybe there isn't anything for you to *do*. But your child has been orphaned…' as she said the word she knew it wasn't technically correct, but to hell with it, she was on a roll now, 'so I guess I thought that you might want to know how he was feeling.' A chilly silence ensued. There was a brief sigh from Anthony's end and Charlie pulled the phone away from her ear to give it a stern look.

'How is he?' asked Anthony, at last starting to sound a little uncomfortable.

'Not great, he's recently lost his parents, who loved him very much.' Charlie couldn't help herself. She was trying very hard not to turn completely unreasonable but she knew it wouldn't take much. After the events of the last few days the emotions had been building up inside her.

'Quite. Look, Charlie was it? I don't do kids. I don't know the person you're talking about. I'm not about to give you my life story, but Helen and I went our separate ways after university. It was her decision to have the baby and she wanted to do it alone.'

'Because it's every woman's dream to be a single parent?' she said. Or because you were, and apparently still are, a useless, unfeeling tosser, she added silently?

'Thank you for calling. You've done what Social Services asked you to do, but let's leave things as they are. I don't know if you thought this would be a long-lost family reunion opportunity but I can assure you that it isn't and it never will be. Am I making myself clear?' he said with a firmness that sent Charlie's irritation level up another notch.

'Perfectly,' she said, with as much venom as she could inject into the all-too-short word. She put the phone back on its holder with force and it gave a friendly chirrup of acknowledgement. The 'Kipper List' had a new starring member.

Charlie was about to tidy up when she was aware of a figure in the doorway. She turned around to see Ted standing there.

'Are you going to bed?' Charlie asked him. He was fresh out

of the shower and wearing his dad's dressing gown, which she noted looked only a little too big for him.

'In a bit. Who was that?' he asked, trying and failing badly to look uninterested. Charlie was good at many things and in her time she had been an Oscar-winning liar, but not any more, and certainly not with the children.

'It was Anthony Penton, your birth father. Social Services asked me to call him so he knew what had happened.'

Ted gave a half-pout and nodded.

'You okay?' asked Charlie.

'Yeah. So he doesn't want to meet up or anything?'

'No, I'm afraid not.'

'No, that's good, because I don't want to either. He's like… not bothered with me before… so he's no one, right?'

'He's still your birth father, Ted, but that doesn't make him an instant replacement dad, especially if he doesn't want to be.' Charlie was trying to be as honest as she could without sounding heartless. This sort of thing was very cut-and-dried for Charlie; parents were the people who looked after you and earned the right to have the title 'mum' or 'dad', not some donor who never got in touch. What they had supplied you could pick up off the internet at a reasonable price.

'Charlie, it's all right. Look I'm fine,' and Ted gave a cheesy grin. 'I'm not interested in him. I lost my dad in a car accident and I get that he's the only one I'm likely to have. But, hey, if you're going to only have one, then I was lucky to have the best…' and that was where Ted's voice broke and he disappeared upstairs two at a time. Charlie hesitated for a second but decided to let him go. She knew he was hurting exactly same as the younger children, but she had only seen him cry at the funeral and even then he had stifled it. She could go upstairs now, but she and Ted had never had a relationship where a cuddle was acceptable, and now wasn't the time to start.

Charlie checked on the other children, as she did every night before she went to bed herself. She stood outside Ted's door and listened to the muffled sniffs of a boy trying very hard to control his tears. She placed her hand on the door handle and stood there fighting with her choices and the implications of opening the door. When at last it went silent inside, her hand fell away from the doorknob and she went to bed.

Fleur's parents had been out when she had got home, but there was a long note from her mother on the breakfast bar about Clyde throwing a shoe and Ralph causing all sorts of upset when the blacksmith came, plus details of a potential meal that was in the freezer, with instructions for reheating and directions as to where to find the salad to accompany it and a dessert. She had also left contact details, as they were at some National Trust dinner. Fleur suspected that the hosts were after her father's company to provide some sort of sponsorship; that was what a free meal or trip usually meant. She re-read the note and ran her fingers over the last line – All our love M & P xxxx. Her mother always put four kisses on the bottom of notes and cards to Fleur or her sister Poppy.

Poppy had an altogether different relationship with their parents. Fleur wondered when they had stopped treating Poppy like a child and tried not to get grumpy about it. She helped herself to a glass of water and leant on the cool granite surface. Poppy had always been more independent that she had. She was always an 'I can do it myself' sort of child and that had developed further as they had grown up, but the point was that Charlie was right, Fleur had never completely grown up. She hated it when Charlie was right. She didn't want to admit it and she certainly wasn't going to let Charlie know, but it was foolish not to accept it herself.

She missed Poppy. They were closer than most sisters she knew of. Over the years they had had their moments, as all siblings did. Sometimes they seemed perfectly suited but at other times it would feel as if Poppy had left her behind and that she was playing catch-up. She loved Poppy immensely, but as they had grown up it had become clear that they were two very different people. Poppy was academic and wanted to make her own way in the world, ideally without any input from her father's name or money. Whereas Fleur had taken the scenic route, had drifted through school and had completely lost her way after her exams. Her forays into various college courses had amounted to nothing. And here she was again with absolutely nothing to do.

Fleur put her hand in her pocket and pulled out the folded note and the business card and placed them side by side on the granite top. There was the temptation to do 'eeny, meeny' over them, but she resisted. If she was going to grow up, now was a good time to start. She pulled her phone from her pocket and dialled the number.

When her parents arrived home they were laughing and it cheered Fleur to hear it. They were her parents and she rarely thought of them as a couple, but the recent events had made her see how perfect they were for each other. She could just make out her father whispering something inaudible, to which her mother was giggling. Fleur decided that she had better make her presence known or she could become privy to something that might scar her for life.

'Dirty stop-outs! What time do you call this?'

'Fleur, sweetheart.' Her mother homed in on the disembodied voice and found Fleur curled up on a sofa hugging a large mug of tea. 'Have you eaten?'

'Yes. Thanks for leaving me a meal and the note and everything. But, honestly, you don't need to. I know you're being kind, but I'm an adult and you wouldn't do it for Poppy.'

'Oh,' said her mother, a little crestfallen. Fleur's father joined them in the room and wrapped a protective arm around his wife. He looked a little flushed as he kissed his wife's neck and Fleur felt an unpleasant shiver go down her spine. Don't think about it, she told herself.

'The child is right. I'll work out what you owe us in rent,' he said with a wink. Fleur dismissively stuck her tongue out at him.

Her mother gave her a hug and perched on the arm of the sofa. 'Did you have a nice time last night?' she asked.

'Um, I really need to talk to you about that. It's all right, nothing to worry about but you might want to get a large glass of something alcoholic and sit down first.'

Chapter Ten

Breakfast was utter mayhem. Despite Charlie having laid out their uniforms and instructing them to check their school bags yesterday, somehow today everyone had lost something. For Millie it was her temper as she was lashing out at anyone who came within swiping distance. Eleanor was organising a production line and filled lunch boxes as quickly as Charlie could make the sandwiches.

'Millie, we've got Music and Rhythm today.'

'Yay!' shouted Millie. 'Zinging!' she launched into a very off-key version of Humpty Dumpty.

Ted sat at the table, slowly stirring his cereal. He retrieved Millie's toast when it went flying across the table and dangerously close to the edge. His blazer was definitely shorter in the arms and Charlie realised how much he had grown in the last few months, and not only physically.

Charlie herded the children to the front door and equipped them with bags as they filed out onto the pavement.

'Eleanor, put the dog down and stop letting him lick your face. He was washing his bum earlier!' said Charlie.

'Eugh,' said Eleanor, before she gave Wriggly one last kiss and deposited him back inside the house.

'Bum, bum, b-bum,' sang Millie, which for once sounded quite melodious and could very easily be mistaken for a nursery rhyme rather than her latest word obsession. But for Charlie anything was better than the 'testicles' incident.

George was chattering away to Ted and seemed completely unaware that Ted was not responding. Charlie buckled everyone into their seats in the back whilst Ted loaded the school bags into the boot. Charlie and Ted reached their respective doors at the same time and she looked at him across the roof of the car. She wanted to say something to him, after what had happened with his birth father last night, but nothing suitable came to her lips, so she shrugged instead. Ted nodded and they both got in the car.

Charlie was surprised how pleased she was to be going back to her old routine – she hadn't realised how much she had missed it.

Millie's playgroup was the best of her toddler activity groups as most people were friendly there; Music and Rhythm was different. Everyone had been friendly to start with but as the mothers realised that Charlie was the nanny and not Millie's mother they were noticeably less chatty to her. As this was London, there were quite a few nannies in attendance so she had soon found the breakaway gang she was meant to belong to. There were two distinct groups: one for mums and one for carers. Even within the carers group there was a hierarchy as there were a couple of au pairs who were barely allowed to break into the conversation.

'Hello, Millie, we haven't seen you for a while. Have you brought Pooh Bear?' asked Jane, the lady who ran the group. Millie nodded and went to grab a fish-shaped mat and dragged it to her favourite spot.

'Hi, Jane, sorry we've not been for a while,' said Charlie, realising instantly that none of the people here would be aware of why they had been missing for so many weeks. They had been in their dark bubble while the world carried on as usual.

'No problem, you're all paid up,' said Jane.

The session went well and it made Charlie feel so much better to see Millie bashing the life out of a tambourine and belting out the words to 'Buns in a Baker's Shop'.

Charlie's phone was on silent but she felt it vibrate in her pocket. A quick look told her that it was Fleur. She would have to wait.

Tea and biscuits at the end gave the opportunity for some much-needed natter in each of the two groups, whilst the children wore most of their biscuits and spilled their drinks happily.

'Have you been away? You're not very brown. I texted you, did you get it?' said Ali, who was one of the friendliest of the group and someone who Charlie got on okay with. Ali was a talker and Charlie was more tolerant than others as she wasn't so desperate to fight for airtime.

'In that order: No, not been away which is why I'm not very brown. I did get your text and I'm very sorry that I didn't reply,' said Charlie, frantically wondering what she should say about Helen and Toby. These people didn't know them, so should she tell them? Would they treat her differently? More importantly, they were sure to treat Millie differently. Charlie decided to avoid the conversation if she possibly could.

'I thought you'd been sacked,' said the blonde girl whose name was either Ada or Ida, but she had an accent and Charlie still wasn't sure so she simply never used the woman's name in conversation.

'Not yet, still working. How is Zander eating now?' asked Charlie, deciding to turn the conversation onto the child the woman looked after. This was a stroke of genius as that and the eating habits of the other charges then dominated the conversation.

In the car park Charlie was once again strapping Millie back into her car seat before attempting to strap Pooh Bear into the seat next to her, when Ali appeared.

'Are you okay?' she asked.

'Yeah, I'm fine,' said Charlie.

'You look… you look under the weather. I'm not being unkind, I just thought I'd check. I know what it can be like sometimes, if it all gets a bit much and the parents take the pee,' elaborated Ali, not stopping for breath.

'No, really. I'm fine. My friend's had a bad time with her fiancé, that's all.'

'Oh, okay,' said Ali, looking decidedly disappointed.

'Because you can always call me, you know. The last parents I worked for were awful.'

'No, it's not the parents. Really, I'm fine.'

Millie had been quiet as she studied the exchange between the adults closely.

'Mummy and Daddy have gone d'evon,' said Millie, speaking very deliberately and looking very serious. Charlie felt as if her heart was breaking. She and Ali both looked at the pretty face that was looking so stern. Charlie reached out a hand and stroked Millie's plump cheek.

'I know, sweetheart, I know.'

'You see what I mean, they sod off to Devon and leave you with four kids. Taking the pee. Call me!' Ali hollered, as she headed off towards her car.

Fleur had changed twice because she wasn't sure what was most appropriate to wear when meeting a solicitor. She had a meeting arranged at the offices of Sedgley, Steeple and Thomas and was really quite nervous about it. She was going alone and it did feel like a huge milestone for her. She straightened her shift dress and walked into the plush waiting area with as much confidence as she could muster. The receptionist was about her age but very polite and efficient and she found herself upstairs in another waiting area reading *Country Life* within a moment. Fleur wasn't reading the magazine, though she was turning the pages in a timely manner. She was thinking through what she was going to say. She wanted to sound business-like but not cold. She wished Charlie would pick up her phone, she was sick of calling. Charlie didn't even use the answer service, so it rang out interminably.

Fleur was being distracted by an article claiming the debutante season was back when a young awkward-looking man, with neat hair not dissimilar to a Lego mini-figure, walked out of a nearby office and hovered in front of her.

'Mrs Van Benton?' he asked tentatively.

'No, that's my mother. I'm Miss Van Benton… well, at least I was. Can we go in your office?' said Fleur, keen to stop rambling within earshot of others.

'Yes, of course,' and he pointed the way, staring after her as she picked up her Gucci clutch bag and cat-walked past him.

A very large old-style desk dominated the office and the solicitor had to squeeze between it and a bookcase to get past. Fleur was watching him with a tiny smirk.

'Gift from my grandfather,' he said, reading her mind. 'I'm Jonathan Steeple. Can I get you anything to drink?'

'No, thank you.'

'Then let's get down to business,' he said, leaning forward and smiling warmly. 'You mentioned a divorce on the telephone. Could you elaborate?' he asked, having a quick look around for that box of large tissues and wondering, at the same time, who could be so deranged that they would do anything to lose this beautiful woman.

After a shaky start, Fleur found her flow and, encouraged by Jonathan, she was able to explain the situation and the desired outcome she was looking for without getting emotional and without sounding heartless.

Jonathan could have happily listened to her for hours, her voice was soft and caressing with a hint of public school. She kept good eye contact, or was that simply him staring at her? He couldn't be sure. The problem he had was that, as he had suspected from the phone call, this young woman most probably didn't need his services at all. Jonathan carefully played back the situation to her.

'So you and Mr Crane,' he said, glancing down at his very brief notes, 'are in agreement that the marriage has no future and that you wish for it to be dissolved?'

'Yes,' said Fleur, with confidence, and then added, 'That's what I want. He says he still loves me and wants to make it work, but he also said he would do whatever I want. And I want a divorce.'

'I'm very sorry for the personal nature of the next question, but can you confirm that you haven't had sexual relations with Mr Crane since the wedding service.' Jonathan felt his face flush and he ran his finger around his tightening collar. Fleur looked equally embarrassed.

'No. Not since the wedding but we did… before.'

'Good… I mean good that you haven't… well, you know… it makes things simpler.'

'Good,' agreed Fleur, her cheeks flushing with embarrassment.

'The good news is that this is very straightforward. You don't actually need a solicitor. The marriage is voidable as it hasn't been consummated. Therefore, you can apply for annulment by completing a nullity petition and that can be done over the internet. There is a fee. Would you like me to write down the details?'

'Please,' said Fleur. 'It seems all a bit too easy to get divorced or annulled, or whatever it is. Are you sure you don't need to check with someone?'

Jonathan laughed a squeaky little-girl laugh and Fleur giggled along. 'No, I do know what I'm doing, honestly. There you go.' He handed her a piece of cream embossed paper with a website link and a few key words. 'Go to that link and follow the instructions. Pay the fee and the documents will come through the post to be signed. You and Mr Crane return them to the court, there's a cooling-off period and the marriage will be over. Was there anything else I could help you with, Miss Van Benton?' and Jonathan sent a silent prayer that maybe there was a death in the family he could deal with.

'Um,' Fleur pondered and bit her lip as she folded the paper in half, 'no, I guess not. Thank you, Jonathan, you've been most helpful.' They shook hands and both felt the flush of blood to their cheeks and the sensation of sweat on their palms. Jonathan watched her leave and tried very hard not to stare at her arse. He was loosening his tie when her doll-like face and cascades of auburn hair bobbed back into view.

'Actually, Jonathan, would you be a sweetie and do it for me?' she said, handing him back the piece of paper. He went to take it, but Fleur snatched the paper back, causing him to almost launch himself onto his desk. 'Sorry, I know I should really do this myself, but it feels like a bit too big a step. Do you under-stand?' she asked.

'Of course,' said Jonathan, nodding vigorously, '...actually, sorry, no I don't know what you're talking about. I've got twenty minutes before my next meeting. Do you want to get a coffee?' He had never been so brave in all his life and, whatever happened next, he would always be mightily proud of himself for seizing this moment and not dithering, as he frequently did.

'Yes, that would be lovely. Let's do that,' said Fleur, perking up and putting the piece of paper back into her bag.

School pick-up was the usual noisy and chaotic affair but it was full of life, and Charlie found it oddly reassuring as the children were all cosseted back into the womb of her car and she could return them to the safety of the house. As she started the engine the radio kicked into life and out blared 'We Are Family' by Sister Sledge. Charlie had a moment's hesitation. This was a special song for them. It was the one they all sang along to – well if you could call the out-of-tune warbling from Millie and the shouting from George and Ted 'singing'.

Charlie needn't have worried because, as if on autopilot, all the children did exactly what they always did when they heard that song – they all joined in with gusto. Ted and George, particularly, liked to emphasise the line 'I've got all my sisters with me' whilst pointing at each other. And even now, after what had happened in their lives, this song still meant what it always had – a fun sing-along. Charlie laughed and joined in. The song finished and the volume in the car reduced a fraction as the singing was replaced with voices.

George was slightly hyper and he and Eleanor were clamouring to be the first to re-tell what had happened at school. Charlie knew none of it would have anything to do with what they had actually learnt in class and a question of that nature was a sure-fire way to shut them up. But that wasn't what she wanted today. She wanted them to be excitable, she wanted them to come back to the world of the living and start being children again instead of the little mourners they had become.

'Okay, okay, you guys. Let Ted go first. Ted, how was your day?' she flicked the car's indicator and pulled it out into the traffic. There was no response, so she gave a quick look to her left to see Ted repeat his shrugged reply. 'Right, so is that a bad day or an okay day?'

'Okay, I s'pose,' said Ted, without moving his eyes from his mobile phone, which his thumbs were traversing at high speed.

'We went to Music and Rhythm, didn't we, Millie?' said Charlie, checking her rear-view mirror for a response.

'Did zinging. Bum, bum, b-bum,' she sang happily.

'Can I go next? Pleeeeeeeeeeeeeeeeeeeeeeeeeeeeeeeeeease!' pleaded George. And a diatribe ensued, covering everything he had missed including who had fallen out with whom, who had been dropped from the cricket team and who was on regular detention. Eleanor sat quietly the whole time, until it was her turn, and then brandished a printed sheet of A4 in the air.

'It's parents' evening next week,' she said in a hushed voice.

Chapter Eleven

Fleur moaned gently as she felt his fingers tease the inside of her thigh. She was hot and she wanted him badly. She reached out to cup his face and pull him to her. His hair was different, she noticed; it wasn't as neat as it had been, it was all roughed up and she liked it much better. His body was surprisingly muscular and she could feel the weight of it on top of her. She heard a voice whisper in her ear… but it was a female voice. Fleur screwed her face up and tried to listen.

'What are you dreaming about?' asked Poppy, who was sitting on the bed, though technically she was half on the bed and half on Fleur.

'Urgh, you could knock, you know,' grumbled Fleur, feeling slightly violated.

'I did, but as you didn't reply I thought I had better check that the Rozzers hadn't been here in the night and carted you off to the nick.'

'You sound so authentic, you could be in *EastEnders*,' said Fleur, briefly checking that the other side of her bed was empty, though she knew it was.

'Is this still your winter quilt? You look a bit red in the cheeks. Anyway, I got the late train last night but by the time I'd arrived, you'd all gone to bed, you wild lot,' said Poppy, giving Fleur an affectionate nudge.

'Poppy, there's something on my mind that I can't talk to Ma and Pa about.'

'You're not pregnant, are you?'

'No! Thank goodness. Don't get cross when I tell you but it's about me being adopted.'

'I won't get cross, Fleur, come on, what is it?'

'Ma and Pa have been the best and everything but I feel like there's a piece of me missing.' She paused and watched Poppy closely, waiting for the dismissive eye roll that didn't come. Fleur continued. 'They've told me all they know, or at least everything they are comfortable to share, but I get the feeling there is some-thing else. Something they're not telling me.'

'Like?' prompted Poppy her tone gentle.

Fleur shrugged her delicate shoulders. 'I don't know – that's kind of my point.' She pulled a resigned face. 'Maybe the family that didn't want me were criminals or something.'

Poppy smiled. 'If you're looking for something exciting you're looking in the wrong place. The point is whoever those people were, they don't make you who you are. You have to do that.'

'It's all those missing months of my life with just a couple of random photos of places I can no longer remember. Maybe if I knew more about that I'd be able to work out who I am now and who I want to be?'

Poppy puffed out her cheeks and let the air escape slowly, as if taking her time before responding. 'Ma and Pa took hundreds of photos from the moment they brought you home. But if there were any more photos from before that I'm sure they would have been kept on file. You could ask Social Services.'

Fleur shook her head. 'I couldn't bear to upset Ma and Pa and I'm not looking for another family, just the bit of my past that's missing.'

'You were a beautiful toddler,' said Poppy, her voice soft as she studied Fleur's face.

'Really?'

Poppy nodded, a hint of a tear in her eye. 'You used to chatter to yourself and giggle as if you'd told a joke.' Poppy chuckled at the memory. 'You were happy. You've always been happy, Fleur, as far back as I can remember. No child can recall those early months that you're searching for. You're looking for answers because you're trying to figure out who you are and you're looking here because you were adopted, but I think that could be the wrong place to look.'

'But that's the missing piece of the puzzle.'

'I can see why you think that, and if you want to try to find out more you know I'll help you. But I'm not sure that's the answer '

'So what is?' said Fleur, tilting her head to one side.

'I think it's getting on and living your life and discovering the person you want to be, and there's no magic way of discovering it. I have bad news for you, Fleur – you're normal!'

'Normal?' Fleur was frowning hard.

'I'm afraid so. Come on, let's get breakfast before I steal your horse and go for a ride.'

'Charming,' said Fleur, rolling her eyes, and Poppy sprang from the bed and headed for the door. 'Sis?'

'Yep,' said Poppy, almost jogging on the spot she was so full of energy.

'It's nice to have you home.'

Charlie re-read the text message and was quick to craft a reply. She couldn't help feeling a little excited that Felix was back in touch. It was purely for the children, of course, a small spark of hope. Charlie opted for neutral territory so they were meeting at the park. If they were now back to two options for guardian she much preferred the prospect of it being Felix rather than Ruth.

At least with Felix she stood a chance of keeping her job and he was much easier on the eye.

The children seemed to be coping well with being back at school. The teachers were keeping a watchful eye on them and their friends appeared to be sympathetic. Eleanor was excited that Charlie had agreed she could order a birthday present for her best friend, Victoria, and Charlie was pleased to see Eleanor getting excited about going to birthday parties again.

Charlie managed to get the children out of school clothes and to the park earlier than planned, which was a miracle in itself, but now they had hoovered up the snacks she'd brought along they were getting bored.

'Play football or Frisbee?' she suggested to Ted and George, who were arm-wrestling. George was the colour of an overripe tomato and looked as if he was about to rupture something. Please show Felix what great kids you are, she pleaded in her head.

'Bored! Bored! Bored!' yelled Millie as she started spinning in circles.

'Charlie! Wriggly's done a poo! Have you got a poo bag?' called Eleanor from nearby.

'Hi,' said a voice from behind them as Felix appeared. Perfect timing, thought Charlie.

As Charlie had forgotten the poo bag she had to use an empty crisp packet. When she returned from the bin Eleanor and Millie were playing patter-cake and Felix was watching them.

'Where are the boys?' she asked, spinning around, not unlike Millie had been doing earlier.

'Gone to play Frisbee,' said Felix.

'Where exactly?' Charlie was scanning the park and could feel a twinge of fear making itself known in the pit of her stomach.

'Umm…' Felix stayed where he was relaxing on the grass.

'You must have seen which way they went.'

'No, not really. I wasn't really paying attention.'

'For Christ sake, Felix! This is London. You don't take your eyes off them for a second!' Charlie spun around frantically. 'You irresponsible id…'

'Hey, it's only a joke.' Felix looked alarmed by Charlie's outburst. 'They're hiding behind that tree.' Felix pointed to a large horse chestnut, where behind the huge trunk a slice of George's blue t-shirt was barely visible. 'Boys! She sussed you, out you come!'

George high-fived Felix when he reached him and Felix looked pleased. Even Ted looked less hostile. Felix snatched the Frisbee from Ted and ran off as the others gave chase. Charlie's heart was starting to return to its normal rhythm. She sat on the picnic rug and tried to relax. She watched Felix and the boys as they played with the Frisbee, thinking that this was a huge improvement. She started to let herself wonder if this could actually work.

A happy half hour passed until Millie demanded the toilet urgently. Why did they always leave it until the last moment? Charlie called and waved to Felix and the boys and Felix jogged over. He was still wearing a jacket even on a warm day like this one.

'Could you move your Frisbee game nearer to Eleanor so you can keep an eye on her too please?'

'Why? Where are you going?'

'I need a hoooooge wee wee,' explained Millie, elaborating with her arms.

'Yep, no problem,' he said, beckoning the boys nearer to the horse-chestnut tree.

A few minutes later Charlie and Millie were skipping back towards the others, when the sound of raised voices put Charlie on high alert.

'Get the hell down here right now!' shouted Felix, pulling roughly at his own hair.

George was barely visible as he was engulfed in the foliage of the horse chestnut, edging closer to the marooned Frisbee, stuck on an outer bough.

'I'm all right,' called back George.

Ted was standing underneath the tree, looking as if he was ready to attempt to catch George if he fell.

'Bloody hell, do you kids ever do as you're told?' Felix's voice was growing louder and more frantic. 'Get down before you fall and break your sodding neck!'

George inched forward and the branch took a dip, making him wobble precariously.

'You idiot, you'll kill yourself!' screamed Felix as he made a grab for George's ankle and missed.

Felix got a foothold on the ageing trunk and made another lunge for George – this time he managed to catch hold of his jeans. Why was he tugging at George like that? Was he trying to pull him out of the tree, thought Charlie as she quickened her pace, but kept hold of Millie's hand? Whatever Felix thought he was doing he was definitely making the situation worse.

George was at full stretch, his fingers almost touching the Frisbee until the sudden attack unbalanced him and made him cling to the branch. 'Get off me, you nutter!' shouted George.

'No, you let go, you little bugger!' Felix pulled at the jeans and George's leg dislodged from the branch.

'Bugger! Bug...' started Millie.

'No!' said Charlie forcefully to Millie as she popped her on the picnic rug next to a terrified-looking Eleanor. Felix yanked on the now-hanging leg and George lost his grip. 'No!' she repeated as she approached Felix.

'Argh!' yelled George as he tumbled from the tree. Ted stepped forward to break his fall. George landed clumsily on the ground with a thump and a yell.

Felix clutched at George's shirt and hauled him to his feet. 'What were you thinking?' he snapped, clutching the boy's arms.

'Let me go, you psycho!' said George, trying to pull himself free.

Charlie grabbed Felix's shoulder and pulled him off. 'What the f… heck are you doing?' she said, pushing him away, before turning to George. 'Are you okay? What hurts?' she asked, almost frisking him down for injuries.

'Everything,' said George glumly, his lip starting to wobble. He sniffed back a tear.

'Anything broken?' Charlie inspected the graze on his arm. She did not want to have to explain a broken bone to Ruth. George shook his head.

Felix stood back, took out his yo-yo and started rhythmically spinning it up and down. Satisfied that George's injuries were all superficial, she turned her angst on Felix. 'What is wrong with you?' she said, striding up to him.

He let the yo-yo hang and shook his head. 'I'm sorry. I panicked. I was trying to…'

'What? Kill him?'

Felix's eyes widened. 'God no.' His voice was diminished.

Ted marched over and stood at Charlie's shoulder. 'You need to go now,' he said calmly.

Felix rubbed his chin and Charlie noticed a small scar. He looked as if he was about to say something but instead he nodded and turned to leave.

'Yeah, that's it, run away again!' yelled George. 'Nutter,' he added quietly.

'Can we go home now?' asked Eleanor from the relative safety of the picnic blanket, her skin looking a shade paler than before.

On the school run, Charlie sent Eleanor off with a letter asking if they could be excused from parents' evening this time as, given the situation at home, it was another can of worms that didn't need unleashing right now. Millie was having her morning at nursery and had barely given Charlie a wave as she skipped inside.

George already had his sleeve rolled up, ready to show off his impressive scab from the tree fall even before he was dropped off. Ted was last. He got out of the car and paused.

'Are you seeing that social worker today?' asked Ted, flicking his hair out of his eyes. I still haven't sorted out the hairdresser, thought Charlie.

'Yeah, and Auntie Ruth. Lucky me.'

'So who do you think will be our guardian?'

'I don't know, Ted,' said Charlie honestly.

'But you'd still be our nanny, right?'

'I don't know, but I promise to let you know whatever I find out when you get in from school, okay?'

'Thanks, Charlie,' he said and he walked away.

Charlie's mobile rang. 'Hi Charlie, it's Felix. Can we meet up so I can apologise properly?'

There wasn't a lot she could say apart from. 'Okay, same coffee place and you're definitely paying again.'

Felix was already sitting at a table and he raised a lidded cup to indicate that he'd already got the drinks.

'Peace offering in a non-spill cup. Americano with hot milk. Right?'

'Thanks,' said Charlie, sitting down. 'Why did you pull George out of the tree?'

Felix held up his hands in surrender. 'I am truly sorry. I don't know what happened. I just panicked. Is he okay?'

'Yes, but no thanks to you.'

'Charlie, you'll never know how sorry I am. So no major injuries?' He looked sincere and Charlie felt the bubble of irritation dissipate.

'Scratches and bruises only. He'll live. I don't think it's something we should mention to Social Services, though, if you're still aiming to be guardian,' she said. He looked uncomfortable as he took a mouthful of coffee. Charlie noticed the delicate pink of his lips.

'I'm glad he's all right.' He held her gaze over his cup and she found herself staring into his eyes. They were so incredibly blue, beyond pretty. In fact, she had to admit that he was a pleasure to behold. He blinked first and she felt a flush of colour to her cheeks.

'Thanks for the ludicrously expensive coffee,' she said, with a twinkle of mischief in her eyes.

'That's one of a million things on my ever-growing list of stuff I hate about London.'

'I'm getting a subtle feeling that London's not your favourite place, but please tell me if I'm wrong.' She sipped her coffee.

'I can't stay here.' Felix shook his head and sighed heavily. Charlie felt another straw being wrenched from her clutches.

'But you're doing so much better with the children. Well, you were getting on fine with them before… well, you know what I mean.'

'I agree. I think there's a possibility that I might be able to be a part of their lives, but not here. Not in London.'

'What does that mean?'

'If I was to feature in their lives I would need to move them away from London.'

'But you'd be uprooting them from everything familiar. Taking them away from the only place they've ever lived. Dragging them off to a far-flung corner of the country is not the answer. You must see that?' Charlie paused, realising she was gasping for breath.

Felix was studying the tabletop in a similar way to how George did before he owned up to something.

'I do understand, but I've got a life in another country,' he said finally.

Charlie frowned. 'What?'

'I can't stay in the UK. There's too many memories haunting me here.'

'This is getting worse. Now you want to change the language

they speak. Seriously, have you thought this through at all?'

'And you don't listen. I'm not planning on taking them away, but if they have to stay in London that means I can't be part of their lives.'

Charlie paused while she processed the information. 'It's Ruth or the care system. Is that what you're saying?'

Felix ran his hands through his hair and blinked hard. 'Nobody is going to let them go into care.'

'Okay, but if Ruth is the only option left...' Charlie felt a lump rise in her throat. 'I'll be sacked.'

'I'm truly sorry,' said Felix and he looked it. 'There's something that's come up at home so I need to leave sooner than planned.'

'Something more important than the children?'

Felix sighed. 'There's someone who kind of relies on me. They don't have anyone else. At least the children have you.'

But for how much longer, she thought? Was this the moment that Charlie lost the battle? How on earth was she expected to walk away? She tried to calm the rising panic in her head.

'When do you leave?' she asked.

'As soon as I can get a flight.'

Charlie felt something churn inside her. She wasn't going to see him again, but she was sure the churning sensation was more to do with her losing the best option as guardian for the children as well as the prospect of losing her job and the children altogether. Because what else could it be? Whatever it was, it suddenly mixed with her feeling of abject frustration.

'How predictable Felix! You're running away yet again.' Although she felt like throwing the coffee, she pushed it across the table instead. 'Here, we don't want anything from you.' She stood up and shoved her chair so hard it slammed into the table and knocked over both coffees. She heard Felix swearing as she walked away.

The nursery pick-up had taken Charlie's mind off things briefly but her heart sank a little further as she saw both Camille and

Ruth on the doorstep, talking. She was pleased to find a parking space nearby for once, got Millie out of the car, locked it and walked over.

Ruth was wearing a skirt suit with sturdy shoes; her usual efficient outfit. Camille was wearing a long denim skirt and matching waistcoat and she smiled as Charlie and Millie came up the steps.

Charlie unlocked the door and followed Ruth and Camille inside. As Ruth was trying very hard to hold a conversation with Millie, Charlie took Camille to one side. 'I've just come from seeing Felix. He's dropping out of the guardian race.'

'That explains why he's not returning my calls.'

'As you've probably heard, Ruth has said no to Roger being guardian.'

'I had,' said Camille kindly. 'It probably wasn't the best option for the children.'

'The thing is, that leaves Ruth as the only other relative,' said Charlie, trying desperately to convey all of her concerns without actually having to voice them. Camille turned to listen to Ruth trying to explain the horrors of the internet to Millie in the other room.

'I see,' said Camille, 'but you would still be primary carer?'

'That would depend on the guardian, wouldn't it?'

'Yes, I'm afraid it would,' said Camille.

'Then we definitely have a problem.'

Charlie went to get something to entertain Millie. Charlie heard the noise before she saw it and she spun around quickly as a dozy-looking fly took an uneasy trajectory towards her cup of tea. She picked up a nearby magazine and swatted the fly like a world-class cricketer and it fell dead onto the cabinet. Scooping up the remains with barely a flinch, she binned the filthy creature.

Charlie returned to the living room and handed Millie the touch-screen tablet with her favourite game ready to play. Ruth and Camille were on opposing sofas, so Charlie opted for the big comfy chair. She realised that the conversation that had been in full flow had stopped abruptly so she looked at the two women for clues as to what was going on. Camille gave her usual weak smile.

'Millie will be okay for a bit. What did I miss?' asked Charlie, clasping her hands together and letting them fall into her lap.

'We were discussing options for the...' said Camille, before Ruth talked over the top of her.

'Nothing that concerns you at this stage. I will decide what's best for the children and when I have, I will inform you,' said Ruth, almost snorting the words through her nose.

'We need to keep things consistent for the children, so if you could carry on day to day...' said Camille.

'Unless I tell you otherwise,' interjected Ruth, 'that will be all,' she said, looking from Charlie to the door. Charlie couldn't help herself and she started to laugh.

'Have we stepped back in time, like a hundred years? Don't you think, as the primary care giver, I should be included in this discussion?'

'No,' said Ruth.

'Yes,' said Camille at almost the same time. Charlie was surprised but she was warming to Camille as she was clearly made of stronger stuff than Charlie had first thought.

'Could you leave now, please? I don't have much time.'

'Yes, Ma'am. Beggin' your pardon Ma'am. I'll be blackening the coal scuttle Ma'am,' said Charlie, tugging at her forelock as she collected Millie, who was glued to the game on the tablet and reversed out of the room. 'Bloody woman,' she said, as she shut the living-room door.

'I heard that,' said Ruth.

'You were meant to,' said Charlie, hastily reviewing her 'Kipper List' and mentally underlining Ruth's name, as she was already joint top with Felix.

Charlie had just opened the dishwasher when there was a buzz on the doorbell and she grumbled as she headed back upstairs. At the door was a far-too-jolly postman.

'Hiya, Farishta,' said Charlie trying not to yawn in the man's face.

'Somebody is not getting their beauty sleep,' he said, followed with an unwarranted amount of laughter at his own joke. 'Things to sign for,' he said, handing Charlie the strange little black box and pretend pen. She made a mark, which resembled something that Millie would have drawn rather than a signature. Charlie was searching her brain for what she had ordered that might need signing for and remembered the birthday present for Eleanor's friend.

'Thanks,' she said as she took the two small packets and closed the door. Farishta was still chuckling as he left. Charlie popped the padded envelopes on the side and returned to the kitchen.

After about forty minutes the women emerged from the living room. Charlie smiled, but Ruth ignored her and she and Camille left together, with Camille mouthing 'thanks' over her shoulder. Charlie shut the door and headed upstairs.

She was tidying up when the doorbell rang and, to Charlie's surprise, it was Camille again.

'Ruth's gone. Can we talk? Off the record?'

'Absolutely,' said Charlie, 'but I've got Millie, so you should be careful because she's young but she's not stupid.'

'I know exactly what you mean,' said Camille, following her downstairs. Charlie popped Millie on a kitchen chair and set her up with some colouring. Within moments she had her tongue stuck out of the side of her mouth in total concentration as she feverishly coloured in a picture of a fish with an orange crayon.

'I can't disclose what I've discussed with Ruth,' she said and Charlie's shoulders tensed, 'but I can tell you this. If there wasn't a satisfactory guardian the children could be fostered.' Charlie's eyes widened in shock and she held up her hands to indicate Millie. Camille nodded, 'and that fos… carer could be a new

carer. Someone who applied specifically to care for these children.'
Camille nodded again slowly. Camille and Charlie looked at each other.

The penny rattled around and finally dropped. 'Me?' asked Charlie, narrowing her eyes in disbelief.

'Why not?'

'I didn't think I could.' Charlie's mind was sifting through her past exploits, which she was sure Ruth would have shared with Camille already. She had done some stupid stuff as a teenager but that was a long time ago and clearly it no longer mattered.

'It's different if there is an approved guardian but if there's no one suitable the children would go into care. This would be the same, but with a carer they know. A permanent placement with you as their foster mother.'

'Are you saying Ruth isn't suitable?'

'No. I'm saying we need to undertake a full and fair assessment and that will include looking at the relationship the guardian has with the children, their experience, their level of commitment and other things like that,' said Camille.

'I get you. So what would happen about the trust fund?'

'I'm not certain, but I think it would be administered by appointed trustees instead of the guardian.'

'I like that idea,' said Charlie, feeling the smile spread across her face. 'Does Ruth know about this option?'

'No, and I will undertake a fair assessment with her, but I felt it was wise to look at back-up options. Like you, I want what's best for the children. Anyway, here's the form. Fill it in and post it back and I can start to progress things in the background in case a backup plan is needed, which of course it may not be if Ruth is approved...'

'...as guardian,' finished Charlie. 'I get it.'

'Mum's the word.'

'Apparently so,' said Charlie with a grin. Things were definitely starting to look up.

Chapter Twelve

Charlie had just come back downstairs after putting the younger three children to bed and had flopped into the armchair when Ted appeared with a mug of tea. He didn't say anything, he just put it down in front of her.

She tried to hide her surprise. 'Thanks. You okay?'

Ted slumped onto the sofa. He'd been quiet all evening. 'Yeah. How'd it go with Felix?

'Don't ask,' said Charlie, as she realised she would have to tell them sooner or later.

'Run off again?'

'Yep, exactly that. I'm sorry, Ted.'

Ted shrugged. 'And the social worker?' Charlie could see he was trying very hard to look uninterested.

'Good. They will assess Ruth. It'll take about six visits.' Charlie pondered for a moment. 'She's also thinking about a back-up plan. You know, in case Ruth... changes her mind,' Charlie thought it best not to badmouth one of their remaining family members.

'What sort of back-up plan?' Ted looked troubled.

'Me,' said Charlie, taking a sip of her tea and smiling across at Ted over the rim of her mug. 'Apparently, I could be your foster parent. It would be a permanent placement, so you'd be stuck with me.'

Ted smiled automatically and then remembered himself and flicked his too-long fringe out of his eyes and shrugged, 'Millie would like that,' he said.

'I hope so,' said Charlie, feeling a mild pang of panic.

Charlie lay in her bed, wide awake. Her brain was as wired as if she'd had a double espresso and a litre of cola. The implications of being a full-time foster carer for the children were looming large and there was no getting away from them. Charlie knew this would mean sacrificing a lot. This would be her life for, well, the rest of her life. It was huge and it scared her hair straight.

Fleur found herself in an unhappy place. She was no longer planning an exciting wedding or setting off on the adventure of married life, she was at home and she was alone. Poppy was back at work, climbing the corporate ladder, and was dating a highly suitable accountant from Richmond. Her father was in the City doing whatever it was that a managing director of a security systems company did; he had a flat in London so frequently stayed away. Even her mother was out finalising the nitty-gritty details of the local summer fete, which was grandly titled the 'extravaganza' – the ladies of the WI were not the best when it came to expectation management.

So, here she was mulling everything over and she was finding it hard to come up with anything other than asking Ma and Pa what she should do. But she had promised herself that this time she was going to sort things out on her own. Fleur was really proud of the fact that, with a little help from Jonathan Steeple and the internet café, she had completed the first stage of the annulment process. There wasn't much else to do on that front apart from wait. It was a shame, really, as she had quite liked

Jonathan in a 'he's a nice person' sort of way, but now she didn't really have any reason to see him again.

Fleur stared at her phone. She wondered what Rob was doing now. Tomorrow he was flying out to the Netherlands. She knew that from the note he'd left on her car. I bet he's not packed the right things, she thought. He was hopeless with anything practical; these creative types often were. She picked her phone up and ran her thumb over the screen. She remembered Rob's note promising her lots of sex and shopping if she went to the Netherlands with him. She scrolled down to his name; well, actually, he was still saved under 'husband to be'.

Fleur hastily switched the phone to standby and got up. She had to keep busy, but the problem was that she needed something to be busy with. Something came to mind; the horses were a bit low on hay, so she decided she would use up some time by walking over to the farm nearby and also take the chance to have a think on the way.

'You walked over?' asked the farmer, raising one out-of-control eyebrow, as he saw there was no car in the yard.

'It's a lovely day so I thought I'd get some fresh air,' said Fleur, knowing that she sounded like a complete loser and not like herself at all.

'Shall I drop them bales over tomorrow or do you want 'em now?' asked the farmer.

'I can't take them with me,' said Fleur, suppressing the temptation to add 'duh' at the end of the sentence.

'I know that. But I've got a lad working here that can bring them over on the trailer. He could give you a lift n'all if you'd like.'

'On a trailer?'

'Up t'you,' he shrugged, lifting up a bale to hurry her decision.

'Fine, I'll take them now… thanks.'

'Duggan!' shouted the farmer, his bellow making Fleur step backwards and her ears hurt.

The farmer started pulling bales off the pile and stacking them up in front of Fleur, who smiled awkwardly as she waited. The sound of thudding footsteps caught her attention long before Duggan appeared. Duggan strode around the corner and for a moment Fleur thought he came with his own theme tune as she heard some cheesy Wild West music, which was oddly appropriate, accompanying his impressive entrance.

'Aw, sos. That'll be me girlfriend,' he said, pulling a battered-looking phone from his pocket as the theme tune to *The Good, The Bad and The Ugly* continued. Duggan hit the answer call button and listened. The girlfriend talked in an alarmingly high-pitched voice that made it sound as if there was an irate budgie on the other end. Fleur appraised the new arrival. He was tall and muscular and certainly rugged. His hair was cropped and he had matching dark stubble. His face had a sheen to it from working in the heat.

'Look, I gotta go,' he said into the phone and shook his head a few times. It was a shame that the voice didn't match the body, but you rarely got the whole package.

'Can you load these onto the trailer and drive them and 'er over to the Van Benton's house. That big place over there,' said the farmer, pointing in a vague direction behind Duggan, who swivelled around to look. Duggan stayed facing in that general direction, apparently straining to see if he could see a house.

'It's all right, I can show you where it is,' said Fleur in her sweetest voice. The force with which Duggan spun around nearly made him fall over. He regained his balance and stared at Fleur, who had now stepped from behind the wall of hay. Duggan grinned at her.

'All right,' he said with a nod as he started wildly grabbing up the bales and marching off with them. Perhaps this is the sort of busy I need, thought Fleur.

'That is precisely not the sort of busy you need!' said Charlie, growing more and more frustrated by the phone call. She'd only called to see if Fleur was in as she was at a bit of a loose end and the kids were driving her round the hat rack.

'If you come over you can meet him. He's fit!' said Fleur. Charlie shook her head but realised it was pointless when you were on the phone.

'Yes, we're coming over but no, I don't want to meet him. Please tell me you're not getting involved,' said Charlie, removing a screwdriver from George's hand as he went past her. What followed was very like a mime fight, where no words were uttered but George gave exaggerated gestures towards the screwdriver and made a twisting motion with his right hand. Charlie simply shook her head and put it in her pocket. George threw up his hands and went upstairs. The sooner they left, the better, before George started taking things apart to relieve the boredom.

'No, of course not. Sadly Duggan's got a girlfriend. But if they were to split up I might be interested,' said Fleur, and Charlie imagined her doing a pirouette at the other end of the line. She shook her head again.

'Right, see you in about an hour,' said Charlie, as she ended the call and started her sweep of the house in an effort to round up the children as quickly as possible.

In reality, it took them a good twenty minutes to even leave the house. Ted was engrossed in the latest barbaric army game on the games console, George was busy trying to take his alarm clock apart with the nail clippers and Eleanor and Millie were drawing pictures of a new fashion range for Wriggly, who was chasing his tail like the tiny-brained creature that he was.

The journey was on a par with most – Ted had his headphones on, George and Eleanor bickered over who was sitting in which seat and Millie sang out of tune with Wriggly joining in at various points. It was a wonder that Charlie had never crashed the car. However, as they turned into the tree-lined drive of Fleur's parents' house, the noise abated and the occupants of the car started taking an interest in the world outside.

'There's Clyde!' said Eleanor loudly as she spotted the horse at the other side of the paddock.

'Where Ralph?' asked Millie, trying to look out of both sides of the car at the same time and making herself look like a demented tennis fan.

'He's too naughty to be out in the same paddock as Clyde,' said Eleanor with authority.

Charlie stopped, opened the car doors and the children swarmed out and disappeared into the house. Fleur met Charlie at the car and gave her a big hug. 'I've missed you,' she said, giving her another tighter, but slightly briefer, hug.

'We only spoke on the phone an hour ago,' said Charlie.

'I know, but it's not the same.'

A walk down to the stables provided them with much-needed talking time, where Fleur was able to proudly tell Charlie about the progression of the annulment and the very helpful Duggan. Charlie, in return, updated her on Felix and Ruth and also on the foster parent application, the latter literally stopping Fleur in her tracks.

Fleur spun around to face Charlie, her mouth already open. 'Charlie? Four children? Seriously?'

'It makes sense,' said Charlie, trying to appear nonchalant.

'Uh, no, it doesn't. You're what? Twenty-five?'

'Twenty-four, but birthday coming up, thanks for the reminder.'

'Whatever, it's far too early to be a single parent of four. Come on, this is taking the Sister Teresa thing a bit too far!'

'Mother Teresa,' laughed Charlie. 'They don't have anyone else, Fleur,' she added, her voice suddenly grave.

'That is *so* not your problem. They were your employers. Lovely people, but still your employers. You have no obligation to do this. I can't believe this is what you had planned for your life!' said Fleur, getting more animated than Charlie had seen her since the wedding-cake-hurling incident.

'No, it's not what I planned because I have no plan. Surely this is better than a lot of things I could be doing?'

'Like what?'

'I don't know, like sitting around waiting for the next loser with a shaved head and a rebellious side to pitch up and offer me a sob story,' she said, staying calm.

'This is about me now, is it?' said Fleur, her hands on her hips like the petulant child she was trying so hard to leave behind.

'Fleur, you can do whatever you want to with your life. You could go anywhere in the world and you could be pretty much anything you wanted to be and it baffles me to the point of doing you bodily harm that you choose to do bugger-all.' Charlie was quite surprised at how calm she was.

'I've been places, done things …'

'You've been on lots of amazing holidays organised by, and mostly with, your parents and you've started lots of courses but what have you actually achieved by yourself?' Charlie was quite enjoying this, not in a sadistic way but in an 'I've been wanting to tell you this for a long time' sort of way. She knew Fleur wouldn't like it but it might actually do her some good.

'Sometimes, Charlie, you are really… obtuse!' and she went off after the children, who were now all milling about waiting for the gate to be opened, having been instructed to wait there on pain of death.

Charlie followed Fleur down and, like the children, became aware of the horrible noise coming from the stables. Like a rumbling bang of a noise 'Dun, dun, d'd'd'd'd'dun,' being repeated over and over again. Millie had her hands over her ears and was shouting. 'No like it!'

'Sorry Millie, it's naughty Ralph,' said Fleur, opening the gate and trying hard to hide her annoyance with Charlie, who was sauntering up behind them. 'He doesn't like being shut inside, especially when Clyde is out, so he drags his bucket along the metal bar gate to get attention.'

'Like a prisoner in a film,' said George.

'Yes, exactly like that. Who's got the Polos?' asked Fleur, and Eleanor responded by nearly shoving them up her left nostril in her enthusiasm.

'Steady on. Let's cheer up Ralphy with the Polos, then who wants a ride?'

'Me!' shouted the girls together.

When the children were happily having a hay fight in the stable, Fleur gave Charlie a hug. 'I'm sorry, you don't need a lecture from me.'

'I can live without it,' smiled Charlie.

'You're amazing.' She caught sight of the face Charlie pulled. 'No, you are. Who else would do something like this? I wouldn't, and you're right – I do need to do more for myself. I'm guessing that's what you meant before.'

'Yeah, I'm sorry too. But sometimes with all the useless men, I get a bit frustrated with you. Sorry,' said Charlie, swatting a fly that came too close.

'Not all the men were useless,' said Fleur. Evidently she couldn't let that comment go. Charlie gave a non-committal shrug and leant against the stable wall. 'Charlie, I'm not going to argue with you about this, it's silly, but you know I've had some nice boyfriends. They just didn't work out, that's all.'

'Nice?'

'You're going to criticise again, aren't you?'

'No, quite the opposite, I admire your perseverance on a theme that clearly isn't working well for you.'

'What theme?' said Fleur, as she too leaned against the stables.

'Well, let's see. There was Veggie Victor, ran a stall on Romford market and had a laugh like a sonic boom – failed because?'

'He got too possessive,' answered Fleur on cue.

'Swampy, part of the TA at the weekend and painter and decorator during the week – failed because?'

'I don't like the word 'failed'. It's very critical.'

'Okay, it didn't work out because?'

'Quite a lot of pent-up aggression, so not really my type after all.'

'Steve the window cleaner, who clearly didn't apply the same level of cleaning to himself as he did the windows?'

'A bit clingy.'

'Do you see a theme here?'

'No, not at all. All very different and not suitable for a long-term relationship for different reasons.'

'Or – all manual workers, a bit of rough, call it what you like and whatever you say you got bored with them.'

Charlie's phone started to ring and seeing that it was Camille's number she walked away from the stables before answering it.

Felix was back home, where the air was clean and warm. The food was being passed around the table like some elaborate game as everyone dived into the meal. The chatter was boisterous and happy. Felix watched the way they interacted with each other with such ease. A mixture of friends was gathered together for no apparent reason other than to share a meal. There was lots of teasing and an abundance of laughter. He was usually part of this but today he felt like an outsider. As if he was separated from them and only observing. His mind was filled with thoughts of his own family, those that had gone and those few left behind, and he hated himself for dwelling on decisions that could not be undone. The children were better off without him and he knew he should keep it that way, so why was it all he could think about?

As the meal ended and people moved outside, Felix found himself sitting on the decking tuning in and out of the lively debate about fishing that was going on behind him. He was back where he belonged, where he was happiest, but things had changed. The trip to London had made his brother's death very real and perhaps the feelings he had now were simply part of the grieving process. He wanted to feel happy and carefree again but it felt just out of reach, like George and his Frisbee, he thought, with a smile.

Felix sighed to himself and took out the yo-yo. It felt sticky in his hand. He hadn't noticed until now that he was sweating. The rhythm of the yo-yo was usually soothing but tonight it wasn't working its magic. He really wasn't good company this evening so he made his apologies and left.

It was dark as he walked down to the water's edge. He breathed deeply, letting the scent of the sea engulf his lungs and calm his muddled thoughts. The sea reminded him of his place in the world and that place was right here – and he repeated it over and over in his head like a mantra.

'Hi Camille, is everything okay?' Charlie knew social workers were often dedicated but to call on a Saturday seemed unusual.

'Hi Charlie, I'm sorry to call but I wanted to tell you as soon as I found out.'

'What's wrong?' Charlie could sense Camille's unease and immediately she felt apprehensive herself.

'It's about the fostering application. You've ticked the box for criminal convictions and your record shows that it was for actual bodily harm.'

'But I thought Ruth had already told you,' said Charlie, as her body went hot and cold in quick succession.

'No, she had a lot to say but she didn't mention any convictions.' Charlie was surprised that Ruth hadn't seized that opportunity and now wished she hadn't been quite so honest on her application form. But either way, she knew they would have found out eventually.

'But it was years ago, Camille, surely that's not going to affect things now…'

'I'm sorry, Charlie, serious convictions don't disappear. I'm sure you have changed as a person but ABH is a violent crime. Your fostering application would have to go through additional processes and it's unlikely to be approved. I would recommend that we don't progress this.'

Charlie clutched the phone as she paced up and down. She didn't know what to say, she was utterly devastated.

Chapter Thirteen

When the call ended, Charlie stared at the screen for a few moments before shoving it into her jeans pocket. How could the answer to all their problems have been whipped away in such a short call? Charlie wished she had realised all those years ago the long-term repercussions of her actions, but now it was too late.

'Problem?' asked Fleur.

'You won't think so,' sighed Charlie.

'Whatever it is, I'm sure we can fix it,' said Fleur, very unconvincingly.

Charlie snorted. 'They've declined my fostering application… because of the conviction. We're back to square one. But it's worse than square one because at some point I'll have to tell Ted that our last straw has been decimated by my crappy past.'

Fleur gave Charlie a hug, which she reluctantly accepted. 'It'll be all right. I know you don't believe me,' said Fleur hastily as she saw Charlie's reaction, 'but maybe it's for the best. There's plenty of time to be a mum and have children of your own when you're ready.' Charlie didn't have the energy to remonstrate with Fleur and her inimitable optimism, it was simply too tiring. Charlie felt as if her final spark had been extinguished.

'I can't be a mum,' she said flatly.

'I don't know anyone better qualified!'

'I mean, I physically can't be a mum.' Fleur showed a complete lack of comprehension, so Charlie continued. 'You remember when I had a ruptured appendix when I was seventeen?'

'Yes, you nearly died. We came to visit you in hospital.'

'It wasn't my appendix. It was a ruptured ectopic pregnancy. They had to remove my fallopian tube and it turns out that was the only one I had.'

Fleur looked dazed. 'That's why your scar was in a different place than Poppy's.' She paused. 'And that means you can't have children.' Fleur looked like she had lots of questions she wanted to ask, but she knew Charlie well and instead pulled her into a tight hug and rocked her gently until the children came running out of the stables laughing loudly.

'Ralphy done a hooooge poo!' announced Millie before collapsing into hysterics.

The afternoon was a happy one for the children, with the girls taking turns to ride Ralph, who was surprisingly good-natured with people considering his bullying behaviour towards poor Clyde. The boys had a lesson each on Clyde and Ted even took him over a small jump, which he was obviously thrilled about but didn't show a flicker of emotion for fear of looking uncool – or whatever it was fifteen-year-old boys called it this week.

Charlie found herself lost in her own thoughts. The past she had tried so hard to bury was at last coming back to haunt her. All the years she had spent in foster care, all the rows, the strangers and the anger washed over her and made her scalp prickle. The pregnancy had been a shock at the time, but she remembered being puzzled by the elation she had felt when she'd seen the pregnancy test turn positive. For a few short weeks she'd imagined being a little family of two, just her and the baby. She'd loved that little ball of cells more than anything else in her life, but in an instant it was all over and everyone was telling her what a lucky escape she'd had.

All she had ever dreamed of was a proper family and time after time her hopes had been dashed either by others or by her own self-destruct button. The Cobleys had offered her a job, but what they had actually given her was a place in their family. Any doubts she may have had about fostering the children long-term had gone, but sadly so too had that option.

'Here,' said Fleur, handing Charlie her mobile phone, which Charlie took cautiously and looked at the photo on the screen.

'Who's this?' she asked, already guessing the answer as she studied the picture of a gormless youth wearing dirty outdoor clothing and looking like the evidence for the cautionary tale of what happens when cousins marry. He had cropped hair and the matching stubble on his chin made Charlie think that his head could go on either way up. She even tilted the phone a little to prove the point to herself. It was quite fascinating.

'What do you think?' said Fleur, doing a little jig.

'I'm guessing it's Duggan.'

'You're right!' Fleur looked genuinely surprised.

'Oh Fleur, here we go again.'

'Excuse me?' said Fleur in mock shock as she reclaimed her phone from Charlie, who was tilting it upside down again.

'Okay, who am I?' said Charlie, 'I'm in love, I'm in love, I'm in love… I'm bored. He's dumped… Ooh, I'm in love, I'm in love… you get the idea,' said Charlie, stopping the accompanying Disney Princess facial expressions and hand gestures that had come with the short game of charades.

'Actually, you have a cruel streak, you do,' said Fleur, giving Charlie a nudge in the back with a bony elbow.

'Frighteningly accurate, though, wasn't it?'

Mrs Van Benton arrived home mid-afternoon and set about making dinner for everyone. Charlie saw how she kept a watchful eye on Fleur, who was doing a great job of playing a multitude of games with the children so that Charlie could have a cup of tea in peace.

'Those poor little mites,' said Mrs Van Benton half to herself. Charlie nodded. 'What a to-do. Fleur says this aunt is a monstrous woman. I knew Helen had a sister but she rarely talked about her.' Charlie sipped her tea. She didn't know what to say. She was fast running out of options, so it would seem that the monstrous woman was all she had left.

'She might not be so bad. I need to give her a proper chance really,' said Charlie, being far more charitable than she felt.

'Well, as long as she does the same.'

'I think she's made her mind up about me already. People do,' said Charlie with a practised shrug.

'Look, Charlie,' said Mrs Van Benton, turning to face her, 'I don't care if I embarrass you. I've watched you grow up. Heaven knows, you haven't had it easy, but you've turned out to be a lovely young woman,' and she kissed Charlie on the top of her head as she was en route to the fridge.

'Doesn't change the past, though, does it?' said Charlie.

Mr Van Benton arrived home in time for dinner and the oversized table was burdened with a variety of home-cooked favourites rustled up expertly at a moment's notice by Mrs Van Benton. Bowls of spaghetti, a variety of sauces, garlic focaccia and salad in a variety of coloured dishes littered the giant white tablecloth. Eleanor was keen to serve herself but Charlie kept a watchful eye whilst she sorted out Millie, who was shaking her head at everything.

'Millie, you have to choose something to eat. How about some salad?'

'Don't eat leaves,' said Millie with a firm shake of her head. After more persuasion she eventually settled on bolognaise sauce on the focaccia. It wasn't ideal but, if it kept her happy, it was the least of Charlie's worries.

'There's a message on the answerphone for you,' said Mr Van Benton to Fleur.

Fleur looked a little puzzled until recognition struck. 'We were down at the stables. Anyone exciting?'

'Yes, actually I think it is,' said her father, taking a large forkful of his pasta and exchanging glances with his wife. Mrs Van Benton paused with a neatly spun fork of spaghetti carbonara inches from her lips.

'Go on,' urged Fleur, who was probably worrying in case it was a message from Duggan.

'It was a solicitor... from Sedgely, something and someone. Jonathan...'

'Steeple?' said Charlie, putting down her fork with a clatter, which instantly stopped the giggling from the other end of the table. Fleur went a little pink.

'You all said I needed to sort things out for myself and I have. I went to see Jonathan... Mr Steeple and he advised an annulment, which is going through.'

Charlie was looking less accusatory.

'Sorry, Charlie, I saw the business card and took it. I should have asked,' said Fleur.

'It's okay, I'm glad he could help,' said Charlie.

Fleur's father's face was full of pride and he conveyed it to his daughter with a simple look and she smiled in response. Mrs Van Benton appeared to be tearing up as she finally delivered the carbonara to its destination now a little cooler than it had been a couple of minutes ago.

The distraction had provided the perfect opportunity for Millie to undertake a little artwork involving the once-white tablecloth and a handful of bolognaise. But Mrs Van Benton seemed too pleased with her youngest daughter's developments to worry about the state of her table linen.

With the younger children suitably exhausted and settled in bed Charlie picked up the packages that had been minding their own business in the hall for too long. She went through to the lounge, flopped into a chair and started to open them. The first one was the computer game for Eleanor's friend, the second was more than a bit of a shock. Charlie had ripped it open and inside was a glossy cardboard wallet and a letter. On the front of the letter was a sticky note. It read – 'Dear Mr & Mrs Cobley, Enclosed are your travel documents for your forthcoming family holiday to Antigua. Thanks again for booking with us. We hope you have an amazing time. Jayne.'

Charlie had thumbed through the contents of the wallet and, sure enough, there were details of flight tickets for all of them, including herself, and a leaflet about a place called Wild Cane Villa that had been booked for the first four weeks of the school summer holidays. There was also a credit card receipt for the balance of the holiday dated a couple of weeks before the Cobleys had had their accident. Charlie's heart was racing as she bundled it all back into the envelope and rammed it at the back of a drawer in the cabinet. Right now she couldn't think about the tickets because she knew anything involving them could never end well.

Late that evening, Charlie found herself having another difficult conversation with Ted, who, as usual, wasn't keen to engage in anything that didn't involve music or shooting people through a television screen.

'Look, Ted, I'm so sorry, but there's a problem with my application to foster,' Ted looked bored and continued to concentrate on aiming at the car trying to escape from him on the screen. She carried on. 'When I was younger I did some stuff I'm not proud of and because of that they won't progress the application.'

Ted sat up and looked decidedly more interested, but not enough to actually stop playing. 'Is this what Ruthless was on about?' Charlie nodded. 'What did you do?'

'Just stuff,' she shrugged, feeling awkward and ashamed.

'No. There's no way you get away with saying 'just stuff'. Come on, spill,' he said, for once looking wide-eyed and eager to hear all the gory details. He pressed pause and dropped the controller onto the bed.

'The short version is that I had a temper. Years ago I used to get into these rages and… I couldn't control it, so it got out of hand. There's nothing to worry about, I'm fine now, and I can control it rather than it controlling me.'

'So what did you do? Did you kill someone?' Ted was learning forward and looked extremely excited at the prospect.

'Yeah,' said Charlie, her shoulders slumping down together as she spoke. 'I murdered this kid that played computer games all day. I battered his head in with his controller.'

'Really?' said Ted, his eyes wider than a bush baby.

'No! Of course not. Christ, you're gullible.' Ted was visibly disappointed. 'I hit a few people and I got into fights and was arrested a few times. Eventually I got charged, so now I have a criminal record.' Charlie was feeling the need to hang her head so she forced it back into an unnaturally rigid pose. 'It turned out to be the best thing that could have happened because it was the shock I needed to get some help and sort myself out.'

'What does it mean for the foster thing exactly?' said Ted and Charlie thought she had sadly probably gone up in his estimation for not being the total goody-goody he had assumed she was.

'It means I can't be your foster parent. So we have no plan B. I'm really sorry but I don't know what else I can do,' said Charlie, raking her hands through her hair and making it look slightly wilder.

'I don't get what you're stressing about, Charlie,' said Ted, slumping back on his bed, 'like you said that was plan B. We'll just do plan A; Ruth is guardian, you are the nanny. What's the problem?'

Charlie was determined that she wasn't going to flip out with Ted, even though the tiredness and panic were goading her.

'Ted, it's serious. I don't want to worry you, but… look, trust me that we need to think of another plan.'

'I think you need to chill.'

'I think you need to wake up! You have no idea what could

117

happen. You've had a charmed life being spoiled by people that love you and you expect someone to work everything out for you because that's what always happens. But not this time!'

'I don't call losing your parents 'a charmed life'!' shouted Ted as he was about to make a dramatic exit, but Charlie stood in front of the door and blocked his way.

'Ted, I can't sort this out,' said Charlie as calmly as she could.

'Well, go on then, leave. We'll get another au pair.' He knew the phrase would irritate her a little more. Perhaps he was intrigued to see if he could spark this temper that had marred her past.

'And where do you think you'll all end up? Hey? Ruth is only interested in the money. She doesn't give a stuff about you. Heck she barely knows all your names! When it all starts getting in the way of her life she'll hand you all over to Social Services.'

Ted looked suitably shocked but carried on the argument all the same, 'Maybe she won't. Maybe she'll get someone to do a better job than you.' He reached for the door handle, but Charlie stepped in front of it.

'*Maybe* she will get someone better, like that Norland Nanny, because she has no intention of caring for you herself. And when you get too much for too many nannies you'll become Social Services' problem. And *maybe* you will be too difficult to place together so you'll go to separate foster homes. And *maybe* you, Ted, will end up in a home for teens, where you live on your wits waiting for someone with more problems than you to beat the crap out of you. But that'll only be until you get booted out onto your arse at eighteen to fend for yourself.' Charlie's voice was a low snarl and her hands were shaking uncontrollably. 'Yeah, you hold onto 'maybe' Ted, because maybe it won't happen, but let me tell you that sometimes... sometimes it does.' She stepped aside and waited for Ted to charge out, but Ted was looking as though someone had hit him full in the face with a large wet kipper.

Chapter Fourteen

Sunday dawned and Charlie was very much hoping for a day off. Whilst it had been good to have some help from Fleur the day before, Charlie was fast realising that it wasn't the same as a day off. The constant responsibility and the dark cloud drizzling overhead – the guardianship issue – was all dragging her down. She checked her clock, strained her ear and when she heard no sign of life, turned over. Perhaps she could squeeze in another half an hour before Millie woke the house up. She closed her eyes and a very slight click jolted her to consciousness. There was someone out of bed and they were heading downstairs.

Charlie tried to convince herself that it would be one of the boys, in which case she could leave them to fend for themselves for half an hour, but something kept poking at her and she realised that she simply had to get up. She let out a low groan as she swung her legs out of bed, put on her penguin slipper socks and went to investigate.

Whoever it was, was being very considerate, she decided, as she tiptoed down the stairs that led down from the ground floor to the kitchen as they were opening cupboards and taking extra care not to disturb anyone. As she reached the last step she saw it was Ted and she was about to ask him if he wanted a cuppa when the reality of the situation permeated her consciousness. Ted spun around with the look of a burglar caught in the act, as he held an open rucksack with one hand and a pack of twelve small Kit Kats in the other. Charlie stared from the bag to Ted. He was wearing his walking boots, activity trousers and a light-weight designer jacket.

'I'm... I'm...' faltered Ted, still stuck in the same pose.

'Running away?' offered Charlie.

'Yes,' said Ted, plunging the packet of Kit Kats into the rucksack and doing it up, defiance and determination etched across his face. Charlie knew now was the time to stay calm. She walked nonchalantly across the kitchen, checked there was water in the kettle and flicked the switch, aware that Ted was waiting for a reaction.

'So where are you planning to stay?'

'Don't know yet. On the streets if I have to.' The defiance flared in his eyes.

'You got everything you need?' she said, giving a cursory nod at the rucksack and Ted followed her eyes.

'Er, yeah. I think so.' This was obviously not the response he'd been expecting and he was still on high alert, having been rumbled.

'There's no rush. The others won't be up for ages. Do you want a cuppa before you go? It may be a while before you get another one.'

'No, thanks.'

'Have you got some cash?'

'Thirty pounds and my bank card.'

'Where is it?'

'In my wallet, in my pocket,' said Ted, as if it was a trick ques-tion. Charlie pulled a face and gave a little shake of her head as the kettle boiled behind her. 'What?' he asked.

'First place they'll look. Neat boy like you turns up with all the latest in outdoor gear, they'll have you stripped and beaten up within seconds. My advice is to stick it into your socks. I would have said boots but they'll have nicked those too. You sure you don't want a cuppa?'

'No, I need to get going.'

'Have you got phone numbers written down?'

'No, I've got my phone,' said Ted pulling the latest model from Apple out of his pocket. Charlie pulled a page off the nearby shopping list pad and scribbled down numbers.

'You won't have that by this time tomorrow. Here, telephone numbers: the house and my mobile. If it gets too much, call me. Anytime, okay?' said Charlie firmly, as she pushed the piece of paper across the counter towards him. Ted took it and folded it in half. She could see that he was thinking. He stood there for a moment staring at the folded paper in his hand.

He looked up, his expression unreadable. 'Bye, Charlie. Thanks for… everything,' he said, losing eye contact. He swung his rucksack onto his shoulder and turned to leave.

Charlie felt a pang of panic in her gut. She had to hit him with something substantial to make him stay. 'Pee in the street,' she said hastily.

'What?' said Ted with a half-laugh as he turned to look at her, his foot already on the bottom stair, so close to carrying him out of the house. 'I'm not going to be weeing in the street.'

'I mean don't use public toilets. Use pubs or McDonalds. They're usually all right, but if there's not one open find a side street and pee there.'

'Right… okay,' said Ted slowly, his face showing that he was still trying to work out exactly what the point of this weird bit of advice was.

'Ted, you do know what happens to good-looking boys like you when they live on the streets, don't you?' asked Charlie, looking directly at him, the fear dancing across her face. Ted pulled his rucksack further onto his shoulder.

'You're just trying to scare me now,' he said, some of his lost cockiness starting to return as he turned around to climb the stairs.

'No, I'm not Ted. There are plenty of messed-up people out there that'll scare the crap out of you far better than I ever could. Take pleasure in it, even,' she said, picking up her mug and praying that she'd said enough. She sipped her tea and stared at the back of Ted's head, as he stood motionless, with one boot lightly placed on the bottom step. Charlie took another sip of tea and listened to the seconds thud by in her ears.

At last Ted let the rucksack slide off his shoulder and he slowly turned around.

'I am going to leave. I'm not going into care,' he said, his jaw tight. Charlie checked the water in the kettle and got another mug out of the cupboard in silence. Ted trudged over to the counter and put down his rucksack.

'I know you meant to go, Ted,' said Charlie, handing him his tea.

'And I still will, but I need to think through the details a bit more.' He pointed to his logo-emblazoned t-shirt and Charlie nodded her agreement.

'Mind if I have a look?' asked Charlie, pointing at the fat rucksack. Ted shrugged and climbed onto the shiny black barstool. She opened the rucksack, still stiff from being new. She pulled out the contents and laid them on the counter between herself and Ted. For the first time that morning he looked sheepish.

'Sorry for taking all this.'

'It's fine, you'll need to learn to do a lot worse than that to survive on the streets.'

'There are hostels and places you can stay,' said Ted, with authority. 'I Googled them.'

'Yep, not a lot better than the streets, but they are warm and dry and you can get a shower. However, you only get to stay for the odd night. Also you usually have to queue for hours and you can't go back for a while – to give others their turn.'

'Huh,' said Ted, taking a slug of hot tea, 'I didn't realise.'

Charlie surveyed the collected treasures from the rucksack. She pulled a few items to one side, 'Bottle of water, torch, spare clothes, toothbrush and paste… and a razor,' she said with a flick of amusement making her eyebrow jump. Ted responded by rubbing a hand over his sparsely populated chin. 'These are all good choices,' she continued. 'You need more socks, though. Dry socks are vital.'

'Okay,' said Ted, without questioning why.

'The rest of it is only good for today,' she said, pointing at the remaining items that looked like a selection of primary-school raffle prizes.

'I wouldn't eat that lot in a day,' he said, looking incredulous, and he put down his tea.

'No, but they won't last any longer in a sweaty rucksack. Chocolate bars and chocolate biscuits will melt,' she pointed to each item in turn, 'cheese sweats and goes mouldy. Bread sweats, gets squashed into a lump and also goes mouldy. Fruit juice will go off, which makes it expand and you don't want that exploding in your bag. Yoghurt? Seriously?'

'I'm a bit rubbish at this, aren't I?' said Ted, keeping his eyes on his tea, his shoulders sloping forward.

'You need to think it through, that's all.'

Ted blew gently on the surface of his tea, making it ripple. 'What would you take?'

'As well as your good pile here and your waterproofs, I'd take ginger nuts – they're good. They're tougher than most biscuits so don't turn to crumbs too easily and they last quite well. Layers: you need short sleeves, long sleeves, jumper and fleece because sometimes you'll need to wear it all. And you always, *always* take honey.'

'Honey? I don't really like the stuff.'

'It's the only food that never goes bad, so you keep it for emergencies. It's a good energy hit when there's nothing else left.'

'You know a lot about this.' He nodded at the lame survival kit he'd packed. 'Have you lived on the streets?'

'No!' said Charlie with a shake of her head, 'I couldn't hack it. I've done the odd couple of nights here and there but that was enough for me. It really would be my last resort.'

The sound of claws on polished wood alerted them to Wriggly, who was in the hallway. He appeared at the top of the stairs and gave a giant yawn. Then spotting them on the barstools he started to wag his tail in greeting. He had a stretch and started his descent. He always looked alarmed when he came downstairs, as if he thought his back end was chasing him and might overtake his front. He came over and started some half-hearted jumps up at Ted's leg as he knew he couldn't make it up onto the high stool with his little legs but usually someone took pity on him and picked him up. When nobody did, he went and sat at Charlie's feet and looked up hopefully in search of someone to get his breakfast.

Ted was quiet for the rest of the morning and Charlie felt it was best to leave him to his thoughts. Let him work it out in his own way. She would be forever thankful that she had come down that morning and caught him before he had done something rash. She hoped he would have had the sense to come home when he realised his mistake, but teenage boys could be very stubborn so there was no guarantee that he would have done and she dreaded to think what fate could have befallen him in the meantime. She would never have forgiven herself if he'd come to any harm. Never. She knew she'd lost her temper the night before and said things she shouldn't have said to him. At the end of the day, no matter how grown up he seemed, he was still only a fifteen-year-old boy. Her intention had been to make him understand the seriousness of the situation, she hadn't bargained on him running away from it. She had to make sure that she kept an even tighter rein on her temper from now on.

Charlie let the children have a lazy day and she cooked a roast dinner with all the trimmings. There was always something comforting to Charlie about a roast dinner – it felt like the food of families. She and Eleanor, with a small amount of hindrance from Millie, had made a chocolate swirl cheesecake for dessert and there had almost been a bout of all-in wrestling when it came to licking out the bowl. The children were very keen to have dessert, so all had made a good effort with their main course.

After dinner it had stopped raining so they played in the garden. They built a den out of twigs and some plastic sheeting and played a game of boules; even Ted joined in. The game kept Millie occupied for all of twenty seconds. Wriggly ran after each boule that was rolled and barked at it excitedly until it stopped, then he strutted back to the bowlers looking very proud of himself. This was highly funny until he ran over the white jack ball and sent it skidding across the lawn, causing a huge debate about whose boule had been the closest at the time. Unsurprisingly, all the children were adamant that their coloured boule had been the winner until the incident had occurred, even Millie, whose boule had somehow ended up on the patio.

George stood in front of Charlie with his hands clasped in prayer, 'Please can we have the water pistols out,' he pleaded. Charlie knew it was a bad idea. It always ended badly, with someone getting hurt or cross, but it was so much harder to say no to them these days. She gave a nod and George was off like an Olympic sprinter.

As Charlie had rightly predicted, Eleanor was in tears within ten minutes and ended up sitting on Charlie's lap after she'd been accidently shot in the eye. George was out of action soon after when he fell over backwards trying to get away from Ted, who was conducting a pretty conclusive annihilation. Apparently the console games had been good training for something after all.

When they were all wet and cold, she pointed them in the direction of the various baths and showers in the house and they all got into their pyjamas early. They sat on the living-room floor together and played some board games, with Charlie taking Millie's turn when she got distracted, which was most of the time.

Charlie got the calendar down and she went through what the week ahead had in store for them, dishing out instructions for school bags. They had sandwiches and cake on a picnic rug in the living room and they all curled up wherever there was space on a sofa or a chair and watched a Disney film chosen by democratic vote.

'Ickle Mermaid, Ickle Mermaid!' chanted Millie, waving her favourite DVD. Thankfully the children were kind enough to all vote for *The Little Mermaid*. When it was time for bed, Charlie felt something she hadn't noticed was missing until then – the sense of being unsettled had waned. There was a calmness about them all, a sense of things being back in their rightful place. Not exactly as they should be, obviously, but it felt better all the same.

She tucked the girls into their respective beds and set the nightlight how they liked it, kissed them each in turn, followed by Eleanor's sausage-dog toy that had lost its tail long ago and finally kissed Millie's Pooh Bear as many times as she presented it, which was a lot. She watched them snuggle down and heard them giggling as she shut the door.

Charlie went to give George a high-five hand slap and she found herself in a hug that nearly toppled her over. 'Night,' he said, suddenly looking embarrassed at his show of emotion.

'Night, George,' she said, giving his shoulder a squeeze and he grinned back at her as he switched off his light.

Charlie tidied up downstairs, returned the calendar to its rightful place and as she went to put the lights out in the living room she saw that Ted was sitting on the sofa.

'I'm turning in. Night, Ted.'

'Thanks for today... it was a bit like Christmas,' said Ted, looking thoughtful.

'Yeah, I guess it was, but not as cold,' she smiled.

'Did you do it to show me what I would be losing if I ran

away?' he asked, leaning over the sofa to assess her reaction.

'No, I didn't plan to.' She thought for a moment. 'Perhaps on some other level I might have. I don't know.'

'Whatever, thanks. It was a good day,' he said, unfolding his long legs and giving her a friendly nudge as he walked past.

If I'd realised it was showing you what you'd be losing I never would have done it, she thought, because I fear you will be losing it all too soon anyway.

Chapter Fifteen

Fleur loved the Criterion restaurant and was suitably impressed when Jonathan had suggested that they meet up there so that he could support her with progressing her annulment, even though she wasn't officially his client. Fleur suspected that Jonathan liked her but she was very grateful for his support, as she felt completely out of her depth. The wedding had seemed so easy to arrange, whereas this felt serious. She had arrived early and was comfortably settled in the neo-Byzantine extravagance of the long thin restaurant, covered in marble and gold. The utter decadence of the room had always enchanted her, ever since her parents had brought here as a child and she'd imagined that the coloured mosaic shapes were sweets.

She sipped her mineral water and checked her phone. Sure enough, a text had arrived silently from Duggan. He wanted to know if she fancied a drink in the local pub later. She smiled to herself and hoped that this meant he was now single. She was tapping out her reply when a waiter escorted Jonathan to the table.

'I'm sorry you've been waiting,' he said, giving her an appropriately distanced air kiss before taking his seat.

'I'm always early. I love this place and could sit here for hours simply looking at the décor. Sorry, you must think me very dull.'

'No, not at all. It's a beautiful room – it's a place of history. Churchill and Lloyd George regularly dined here.'

'Sherlock Holmes and Dr Watson,' suggested Fleur, with a coy smile. She knew the history of the Criterion well, including its references in film and literature.

'Martine McCutcheon is a regular,' he said, nodding over Fleur's left shoulder.

'She is; must be a favourite of hers.'

'It's one of my favourites too,' he said, reaching for the menu. 'Have you ordered?'

'Not yet,' she said, hastily sending her acceptance to Duggan and putting her mobile away.

They discussed the menu at great length and both decided on the lemon sole. Jonathan didn't have time for three courses as he had appointments booked in. He looked more relaxed today and his hair was a little less regimented than before.

'Have you spoken to Charlie?'

'I'm sorry, Fleur, I can't discuss another case,' he said softly.

'No, I wasn't asking you to.'

'I see. Are you and Charlie close?'

'Yes, very.'

There was a short silence whilst they both sipped their glasses of water until Fleur broke it by asking about other favourite restaurants and the conversation moved on from there to jobs, which was a very short conversation. Next was music and a quick-fire question-and-answer round provided some laughter.

'Most embarrassing song you love,' asked Jonathan, leaning closer to the table.

'Oh, easy. But I can't say, or you'll think that's the real reason for my divorce!'

'Okay, if I tell you mine, you have to divulge yours and I bet mine's far worse. Deal?'

'Deal,' said Fleur, fidgeting in her seat and staring expectantly at Jonathan.

'Barry Manilow…'

'Copacabana!' they said in unison and Fleur's hands shot to her face in surprise as the laughter tumbled out.

'I can't believe we have the same taste in bad songs,' she laughed.

'What do you mean bad song? I love that song!' Jonathan protested.

Jonathan ordered coffee for them both as well as the bill. He was a traditional man at heart; he expected to pay and Fleur was happy to let him. The chatter and laughter had continued throughout lunch until Jonathan turned the conversation around to the legal discussion he'd used as the pretence for the meeting.

'Do you have any questions about the annulment or are you happy with the process?'

'I think I'm all right, actually. Rob isn't going to contest it. I think all I do now is wait to hear from the court.'

'That's about it. You don't even have to attend court as they'll send you the decree nisi, which is the same document you'd receive for a divorce, and the decree absolute will follow two months later.'

'And that's when I'm officially unmarried?'

'Yes, precisely,' he said, his eyes lingering on her face. 'Look, I'm really sorry but I have to go. It's been a delight to see you again.'

Fleur giggled at his choice of words, 'I've enjoyed it too. Can we keep in touch… in case I have any more legal questions?'

'Absolutely, you have my number, call any time.'

On the train home, Fleur thought about Jonathan and she felt pleased to have found such an approachable solicitor. She'd expected him to be stuffy and intimidating, but she felt they were becoming friends and this was quite a new thing for her. The men in her life had always been quite similar and relationships had never been platonic, because that was never what they wanted. Jonathan appeared happy to settle for platonic and that appealed to her.

Fleur also had a good think about the one awkward moment they had encountered in their conversation when he had asked her what she did for a living and she had no answer at all. There had been a brief silence before Jonathan had expertly steered the subject to a more palatable topic. She had taken charge of the Rob situation and that was all progressing well and now she realised that she needed to take charge of the rest of her life as chasing Ralph around the stable with a grooming brush was not a long-term career choice.

She tipped her head back, closed her eyes and let the rumble of the train take over. She tried to empty her head of all other thoughts. Now all she needed was for a genius idea to pop into her mind. She needed a job. Actually, more than that she needed a career or, even better, a business idea. However, the journey to Godalming apparently wasn't sufficient time for a genius of an idea to materialise.

Camille arrived before Ruth and looked suitably embarrassed as Charlie let her in. Charlie was by now resigned to the fact that there was no point arguing about the fostering situation and even less point blaming Camille. There was only one person to blame for the situation she was now in, and that was herself. Over the years she had looked back on things she had done in her youth. She had been able to square them for the situations they had been at the time and the fact that she had monumentally turned her life around in recent years, but now all that counted for diddly squat.

Charlie was hovering in the doorway expecting Ruth at the door at any second. Millie was a bit clingy after they'd done the school run, Charlie wasn't sure if she was coming down with something, but she was insisting on being carried around the house and was looking forlorn.

'Are you okay?' asked Camille, as she perched uncomfortably on the edge of the sofa.

'I'll be honest. No, I'm not okay. But we need to think of another plan. If Ruth takes on the guardianship and takes on the trust fund they'll end up in 'care', she mouthed the word for Millie's benefit, 'by Christmas – I'd put money on it,' said Charlie, who was struggling to stand still as she spoke.

'We need to give her a chance. That's the idea of conducting the visits here. That way I can see how she interacts with the children,' said Camille. Charlie wanted to argue but she knew it was a pointless waste of energy. Millie gave a little whinge as Charlie swapped her dead weight to the other hip.

'I want the best for the children, Camille. That's all.'

The doorbell rang and it was like winter arriving as Charlie opened the door to the frostiness that was Ruth. The rain lashing down behind her added to the scene. Ruth barely acknowledged Charlie and completely ignored Millie as she walked past them and into the living room.

'Good morning, Ruth,' said Charlie to the swirling draught she had left behind. 'How are you?' she added as she joined them in the living room.

'Fine.'

'Coffee?' asked Charlie, rocking Millie, who was now trying to plait Charlie's hair, which basically involved twisting it into elaborate knots. Ruth ignored her.

'Shall we start?' said Ruth to Camille with a brief smile and Charlie rolled her eyes.

'Would you like me to leave Millie with you,' said Charlie, who went to pass her to Ruth, who visibly recoiled from the already fretting toddler.

'Yes, please,' said Camille. Charlie carefully deposited Millie on the rug between Camille and Ruth. She handed Millie her precious Pooh Bear and went in search of something else to keep her amused. She returned with some bricks to a grizzling Millie, who was pointing forcibly at Ruth and repeating, 'Go way! Go way!' That's my girl, thought Charlie. Camille started to comfort

Millie, so Charlie put down the bricks and reluctantly left them to it.

She knew the right thing to do was to keep herself busy, especially as she had plenty that needed doing around the house, but she couldn't. She had to listen at the door. She felt like the naughtiest of schoolgirls but it had to be done. Ruth was the opposition and she now had a significant head start; Charlie needed to discover something miraculous if she was to stand half a chance of beating her. Not that it was a competition, but it most definitely was a race she felt she had to win.

Eventually, Millie calmed down but was reluctant to leave Camille and wouldn't show Ruth what she was making with the bricks, preferring to turn her back on her and glare pointedly over her shoulder at selected intervals. When Ruth smiled at her Millie responded to the gesture by sticking her tongue out.

'That sort of behaviour simply shouldn't be tolerated. Do you see what I'm up against?' said Ruth.

'She is still very young, Ruth. How do you think you will go about improving your relationship with each of the children?'

'By hiring a proper nanny,' stated Ruth simply. 'I am not the best person for the job, I never claimed to be, but I can employ someone who will teach them good manners and care for them. Up until now it's been very much an amateur job, as you can see.'

'You might surprise yourself if you spent more time with the children. I'm not going to force you into something, but I would like you to consider being a bit more hands-on with them.'

Ruth took a deep breath and held it for a moment. 'Perhaps I could try, but if that didn't work then I could get a nanny.'

Camille looked pleased. 'Splendid approach.'

Millie started to throw the bricks at Ruth.

'How quickly can we move things along?' asked Ruth, failing to dodge a brick that Millie lobbed over as it bounced off her temple. 'Stop it!' she said in a harsh tone. Millie started to wail.

'Quite quickly, assuming there aren't any issues. If we fail to find a suitable guardian I think they said the trust will be administered independently,' said Camille, struggling to be heard over Millie's noise. Camille looked from Ruth to Millie in the vain hope that the woman would register the child's distress, but there wasn't a flicker from Ruth.

'Are you saying I'm unfit?'

'No, I'm saying that we have to complete a full assessment and report our findings.' Camille was close to pointing at the now bright-red and distressed child, as there was still no response from Ruth.

'For goodness sake,' said Charlie, barely separating her teeth to speak as she barged into the room and scooped Millie up into her arms. Millie's wail reduced quickly to a whimper as she buried her tear-stained face into Charlie's t-shirt. Charlie went and held the front door open so that the two women could leave; she couldn't bear to speak to either of them. How could they use Millie like that? Even a minute of distress was too much in Charlie's book. Camille muttered something about being in touch as she left. Ruth hovered slightly in the doorway and looked as if she was trying to think of something to say to Millie. Millie decided to fill the silence instead and started waving manically in Ruth's face.

'Bye, bye stupid man! Bye, bye stupid man!' Ruth shook her head in exasperation and left and, as the door shut with a satisfying slam, Millie and Charlie both cheered.

After school, Eleanor wanted to put on a show and Millie had a leading role, which kept them nicely entertained whilst Charlie had a serious word with Ted in the kitchen. She updated him on everything and posed the question of what their next move should be. Ted thought for a while, which Charlie found highly annoying; she hated wasting time, even just a few minutes.

'We need to persuade Felix to do it. Perhaps we could pay him?'

'We'd need to find him first,' said Charlie with a snort, trying very hard not to wonder where he had gone. Despite his many shortcomings he had made an impression on her, he was someone she would find hard to forget.

'Private detective?'

'I think we have to accept that Felix has gone,' said Charlie and she swallowed hard. 'If he doesn't want to be found it's a waste of time and effort.'

Ted scratched his chin thoughtfully. 'What we need is Ruth to get through the assessment but to agree to you being our permanent carer,' he said eventually.

'Yes, that would be ideal, but she hates me and even if we did convince her to keep me on we can't trust her not to change her mind later.'

'No, but we could get her to sign something legal. Couldn't we?'

'Mmm, some sort of contract. I like that idea. But what is her incentive? Why would she do that?' asked Charlie as Ted nodded sagely and another long, annoying pause followed.

'We need something on her,' said Ted flatly, brushing away imaginary crumbs from the granite counter.

'Blackmail?'

'Ooh, dirty word, Charlie. I'm thinking something to persuade her.'

'Yep, that's blackmail,' said Charlie, almost leaning back, before realising that the barstools had no backs to them. How did Ted manage to be almost horizontal on his and not fall off? 'Okay, so what dirt do we have on Aunt Ruthless?'

Meeting up at the pub with Duggan had made for a fun evening. Sadly the wet weather had meant they couldn't sit outside, but that was the continued unpredictability of the British summer. The conversation had been a little stilted to start with, but once Fleur had asked Duggan if he had any plans for his future and where he thought the farm job might lead him, he was away. Fleur half-listened to his plans, which centred around learning all he could at the farm and setting up his own small holding. He even had an idea for managed allotments.

'People these days are very busy but what they'd really like to be doing is planting, growing and eating their own organic veg, but it ain't that easy. I think if someone was to come along and say here's an allotment, you do as much as you have time for and I'll do the rest, they'll pay for that. In case you weren't sure, the person that comes along would be me,' said Duggan as Fleur continued to display a glazed expression. 'My dad says they'd be paying for the dream,' said Duggan with a snort, and he downed the rest of his pint and looked hopefully at Fleur. By rights it was her turn to get a round in.

As she stood at the bar she had a horrible thought, that perhaps she was the only person who really did have absolutely no idea what to do with their life. The shock that even Duggan had a life plan was quite mortifying and made her pledge then and there that she would make some changes, set some direction, and it was all going to start from… tomorrow.

Chapter Sixteen

Fleur rarely ventured into her father's study, unless it was to distract him, but he was in his London offices today. She was a woman on a mission and she came out of the small room with her arms laden with stationery supplies. She staggered to the kitchen table and put down her procured treasures. There was a large pad of flipchart paper, marker pens in a variety of colours and equally brightly coloured sticky notes. She laid everything out, picked up a marker pen and stared at the large expanse of white paper. After twenty minutes of inactivity she realised that this brainstorming technique was harder than it looked. She'd looked it up on the internet and now knew all the possibilities it could deliver, but the key thing was having some ideas to brainstorm in the first place. Something she was clearly lacking in.

Fleur's mind was starting to wander to the summer dress she'd seen in Selfridges when her mother arrived home. She looked the epitome of domestication, wearing smart navy trousers, a crisp white blouse with an expertly knotted patterned scarf and carrying a wicker basket in the crook of her arm.

'Ooh, now this looks exciting. What are we doing?' asked her mother, placing the basket on the floor and pulling up a chair to sit down next to Fleur.

'I'm brainstorming ideas for my new business venture. I'm going to run my own business,' said Fleur in a matter-of-fact tone that would have sounded a lot more convincing if she hadn't just spent an idea-free twenty minutes staring at the blank paper.

'Excellent, what have we got so far?' asked her mother, scanning the pristine flipchart for clues.

'Nothing as yet. I'm still thinking them through.'

'I think you're meant to do it quick fire. Like biscuits.'

'Excuse me?'

'Biscuits. Write it down, it's an idea, you have to say the first thing you think of.'

'No, that's word association, Ma,' said Fleur, trying hard not to be too unkind.

'No, I meant biscuits could be a business. You used to make lovely biscuits. You could make biscuits, decorate them and sell them,' said Mrs Van Benton, who looked very pleased with herself.

'I was what? Twelve at the time?'

'It's an idea, write it down,' she said, tapping the paper impatiently.

Fleur stared at the shoal of sticky notes swimming across the flip chart. This was hopeless, she thought. She was about to give up and go to bed when she heard her father's car swing onto the gravel drive.

'Hello love,' he said, coming inside, 'I wasn't expecting to find anyone up at this time.'

'I thought you were staying in London?' she said, as a giant yawn escaped.

'No, I'd rather be home, if I can. So what's all this?' he said, placing his hands on her shoulders and leaning over for a better look. Fleur groaned.

'I tried brainstorming to get some ideas of what sort of business I could set up, but Ma joined in,' said Fleur, tilting back her head to look at her father and widening her eyes.

'There are some good ideas here. Which are you going to develop?'

'Er, that would be none of them!'

'Come on,' he said, giving her an affectionate pat on the arm as he slid into the seat next to her. 'What about pretty saddles?' he pointed to a blue sticky note in the middle.

'Don't, that's one of Ma's, along with dog-walking, biscuits, horse whisperer...'

'Right, let's see what we can do with it,' he pulled across another sheet of flip paper and picked up a marker pen. 'Tell me about pretty saddles,' he said, his pen poised.

'They're pretty and only exist in Ma's fluffy world,' said Fleur, slumping back into the chair and realising that hours spent on a hard kitchen chair weren't kind to your back whatever age you were.

'So, they're pretty,' he said, as he wrote down 'pretty' and drew a circle around it. 'What makes them pretty?' he asked. Fleur shrugged. 'Come on!' he said, looking like he'd just got up after a long peaceful sleep rather than a gruelling day in London. Fleur felt a pang of guilt for her father's enthusiasm and her lack of it.

'I don't know. I guess... their colour,' said Fleur with another shrug.

'Great, what colours?'

'Could be pastels, fashion colours...'

'Like luminous. That comes and goes with the trend,' he said, writing it all down.

'We could personalise them,' said Fleur, sitting up, 'we could emboss the leather with patterns or initials or names,' she said, her enthusiasm building gradually.

'And who would be your customers?' he said, drawing another circle.

'Kids?'

'Middle-class children with wealthy family like parents, grand-parents, aunts, uncles. Anyone really,' he corrected and carried on scribbling at speed. 'Where would you sell them?'

'Stables, riding schools, specialist equine shops?'

'Definitely and online. This could easily go global. The Americans love eccentric British goods, especially if they're good quality.' He put the cap back on the pen and put it down on the table with a sense of accomplishment. 'I think you really have something here, Fleur. Well done, love. I'm really proud of you.'

Fleur stared at the words 'pretty saddles' on the flip chart. She was proud of herself too and slightly stunned.

Chapter Seventeen

Fleur almost bounced out of bed the next morning, she was that excited. It was like the pretty saddles idea had fermented in her brain overnight and now she could picture it all. She could see the designs, the colours, the whole thing. She was soon joined in the kitchen by her parents, who were all smoochy, and she turned away quickly.

'Eugh, someone trying to eat here, people. Let's keep it clean,' she chided.

'Morning, Fleur.'

'Pa, I'm glad you're up. What do I need to do first? How do I get this business started?' she asked.

'First of all, you need a business plan.'

'All right.' She wasn't exactly sure what that was but it didn't sound too scary. 'What else?'

'You'll need to do some market research, check that there are enough people out there willing to buy your product. You'll need to do some costing so that you can work out your profit margin. Before that you'll need to have prototyped your product. You'll need to think about manufacturing and BS kite standards.'

Fleur started to feel as if she was drowning in his words and her expression reflected her thoughts.

'But you can help her with all that, can't you?' said her mother, nodding faster than a wobbly-headed dog in a grand prix car.

'Of course,' he said, checking his watch. 'Not right now, though.'

Once her father had left, Fleur was determined that she wasn't going to sit still and do nothing until he got home; she wasn't completely helpless, she could Google the things he'd said and a few sites were bound to pop up with some advice.

While Charlie was sorting breakfast, Ted appeared and did a secret-agent check that there was nobody else about.

'I've had an idea about blackmailing Ruthless,' he said with a gleeful look, as he stuck his head in the fridge and surveyed the contents.

'Ted, some respect please. It's Aunt Ruthless.' Ted dragged his head out of the large American-style fridge long enough to smile at Charlie. 'Granted that the rest of her kind are living under bridges terrorising little billy goats as we speak, but she still deserves some respect.' Ted broadened his grin. 'Come on, what's this amazing idea?' said Charlie, getting out the cereals.

'We get Granddad Roger to threaten to cut her out of his will,' he said, waving a box of grapes at her as he popped them down his throat, showing the same speed and flare that Charlie could when consuming a box of chocolates.

'Slight problem with that one. Ruth already has Power of Attorney.' Ted gave her his 'I don't comprehend' look. 'He's signed over all his legal and financial rights to Ruth anyway, so no dice.'

'Huh. I'll have another think,' he said, popping in three more grapes.

'Okay, well, do it with the fridge door shut, could you?'

As Ted shut the door it revealed a 'caught in the act' George, who was doing an over-exaggerated creeping-away manoeuvre.

'Hello George,' said Charlie, without turning her head, 'how much did you hear?'

'All of it. Sorry,' said George.

'Don't suppose you know any dirt on Aunt Ruth, do you Squirt?' asked Ted.

'Mmm, no, sorry…' He disappeared up the stairs at high speed.

Charlie had been making pasta pictures all afternoon with Millie and now that she had finally got the glue and paint off Millie and herself she was running a little late for school pick-up. She had Millie on her hip when the phone rang and her first instinct was to leave it, but she couldn't. She let out a growl of frustration as she picked it up – it was probably going to be one of those very annoying callers who always started the conversation by saying they weren't trying to sell you anything, which was the golden clue that that was exactly what they were about to do.

'Hello Charlie, it's Jonathan Steeple,' said the familiar voice.

'I'm about to leave the house. Can I call you back?'

'No, I won't be more than a few seconds,' Jonathan said quickly.

'Okay, fire away,' she said, hopping around in a futile attempt to hurry him along. It really was bad timing. Thirty minutes ago she would have loved a break from gluing down pasta.

'Look we haven't had this conversation, Charlie. But, as the primary carer of the Cobley children, I think you should be aware that someone has formally approached us as the Cobley executors and requested that we relieve you of your duties.' Charlie stood motionless, apart from her left hip, which was moving involuntarily as Millie happily jigged up and down on it.

'Charlie, are you still there?'

'Ruth can't sack me, though, we've been through this.'

'We have, but now she's asking us to do it and technically we could do that, assuming we also had Mr Felix Cobley's agreement.'

'It's just a matter of time, then?'

'I'm sorry, Charlie, that's why I thought you should know.'

Charlie didn't see the very large red four by four as she pulled out into its path. Thankfully the driver saw her and leant heavily on his horn. Charlie waved an apology out of the window and returned to gripping the steering wheel tightly. Thoughts of the Antigua holiday the Cobleys had booked before the accident bounced around her mind, she had clearly run out of straws to clutch at. It was difficult to hide her turmoil as she picked up the children. George was oblivious and had another scintillating cricket tale to tell everyone, but Eleanor and Ted noticed immediately. Charlie waved away their concerns by saying she had a migraine. When she finally found a parking space in their street and moored the car within walking distance of the kerb she tapped Ted's arm. He pulled one ear bud out.

'We have a problem,' she said, her voice matching the despondency she felt. Ted nodded; he was quickly becoming a good sounding board, for which Charlie was grateful. She let the other children out of the car and they walked up to the house, apart from Millie, who skipped.

'Tell me while they're getting changed,' said Ted, pointing at the party of three in front. Charlie nodded.

As it turned out, the problem was about to get even bigger as she listened to the answerphone message from Camille. Camille sounded like she was dispensing the best news in the world, so Charlie guessed it was probably her idea. Camille was suggesting that Ruth do some baby-sitting as a chance to spend some quality time with the children and enable both Ruth and Social Services to see how she coped. Charlie wasn't sure if Camille was still on her side and, if she was, perhaps this was an opportunity to showcase Ruth's epic failure. Well, that was how she was going to play it, anyway.

As the children thundered upstairs to get changed, Charlie shoved Ted into the living room and shut the door.

'I think Ruthless is pretending to Social Services that she's going to look after you all. I bet that's what the conniving cow is up to,' said Charlie in hushed tones, even though the other children were out of earshot.

'Then she'll say she doesn't need you and kick you out,' said Ted.

'And later she'll claim she can't cope, what with her busy high-flying business and four troubled children... sorry, no offence.'

Ted didn't appear to have taken any. He slumped into the nearest sofa. 'We're going to end up in care, aren't we?'

'Don't think about that. What we need to do is come up with a plan – and fast,' said Charlie, trying to push the pictures of white sand beaches and swaying palm trees to the back of her mind.

Charlie had called Camille back and enthusiastically accepted the offer of Ruth's baby-sitting and suggested that if Ruth could come round that evening they could start tonight. Camille had rung back to say Ruth was equally keen and that she would be round at six o'clock sharp and she was true to that word, at least.

Charlie was completely professional as she took Ruth through the house and explained what needed to happen. Ruth didn't speak, in fact she just followed Charlie around, checking her watch at two-minute intervals. Charlie was hoping her request of same-day baby-sitting had been inconvenient for her. The woman only had to cope for two hours and all she had to do was keep the children amused for an hour or so and then start putting them each to bed. It wasn't the most taxing thing.

Ruth stood next to Charlie as she put on her jacket. It had been trying to rain all day and, knowing Charlie's luck, it would start to pour down as soon as she stepped outside. Charlie had written her mobile number on a post-it note, which she handed to Ruth. The children all filed into the hall like the Walton family, but with glum faces every one. Charlie kissed them each good-bye and Ruth tutted.

'Good God, woman, you're not leaving the country,' she scoffed. Charlie gave Ruth her best death stare and left. It was all down to the children now.

For the first ten minutes peace reigned until Eleanor screamed loudly.

'What is it?' shouted Ruth, but she got no reply other than more screaming, so reluctantly she went to investigate. Eleanor was in the main bathroom standing on the toilet seat pointing into the bath at a huge spider. Ruth took a slightly closer look.

'It's a toy,' she stated and looked Eleanor up and down. 'What's wrong with you?'

'I thought it was real, one of those deadly Australian ones that kill you with one tiny bite,' said Eleanor, as if she was at an amateur dramatics audition.

'Silly girl. You might as well get washed and go to bed whilst you're here.'

'It's not time yet,' and she scurried quickly past Ruth and out of the room.

Ruth trudged back downstairs to the living room, where she'd left Ted, George and Millie quietly watching the television, but there was no sign of them and the television was blathering on to no one at all. She turned it off and looked around the now-quiet room. She checked behind a sofa in case someone was about to jump out and surprise her but nobody did.

Ruth followed the faint sound that was coming from the kitchen. She found Millie sitting happily on the kitchen floor.

'I make cake. Want some?' she asked, waving a clump of something in Ruth's direction. Ruth stared, her expression one of disbelief. In the two minutes she had been upstairs it would appear that Millie had found a large bag of flour and a container of milk.

'How did you open the fridge?' asked Ruth with suspicion in her voice, but Millie merrily carried on mixing her ingredients on the floor with her hands as Ruth stood and stared at the vastness of the mess. Not only was the floor a mass of white goo but the kitchen stools were covered in white lumps too and so were a good selection of the kitchen cupboards.

'Edward!' bellowed Ruth, but there was no reply. Millie looked up briefly and carried on stirring her hands in circles and giggling.

Ruth bent down to tackle the mess when Wriggly came hurtling down the stairs at high speed. Ruth tried to intercept him but it was like a very one-sided rugby match of schoolboy versus England professional as Wriggly gave her a false dodge, charged past her and ran through the milky puddle and out into the garden, where he started to frantically roll around on the grass. Ruth stepped around Millie and followed after the dog. He soon came to say hello once he'd had a good roll and was now nicely coated in grass cuttings and looked like a neatly clipped bonsai bush version of himself.

'Edward!' screeched Ruth, louder this time. She looked at the now-green Wriggly and touched a small patch of grass-free fur – it was slimy and coated in something. Wriggly started to scratch and clumps of grass flew in Ruth's general direction. 'Edwaaaard!'

'Hiya,' said Ted, casually appearing in the kitchen, 'Oh dear, you didn't leave Millie unattended did you? Tut, tut, tut,' he said, shaking his head wisely.

'Don't be cocky with me. Clear this up,' said Ruth, pointing at Millie, who responded by throwing a handful of goo, which landed expertly on Ruth's shoe. Ted resisted the urge to laugh but gave Millie a thumbs-up when Ruth looked down at her shoe and Millie giggled. 'Where are the other two?' demanded Ruth, trying to shake off the sticky white mass.

'Playing with someone's phone I think?' said Ted casually. Ruth nodded, then as if realising the implications went back up the stairs quickly. In the living room she found George and Eleanor laughing hysterically as they quickly hid something behind a cushion.

'Give me back my mobile.'

'Here you go,' said George with a smile and he handed Ruth the phone before trying to make good his escape. Ruth grabbed him and Eleanor by an arm each.

'What have you been doing?'

'Nothing,' said Eleanor, but a quick scroll through her recent call list and her emails would later reveal that that wasn't strictly true.

'You can go and wash the baby and the dog right away, and no funny business otherwise there will be trouble. Do you understand me?' her voice was quivering and sounded as if she was bordering on losing control. George and Eleanor stopped smirking so that Ruth would let go of them, then quickly left the room before bursting into fits of giggles.

After a lot of shouting Millie and Wriggly were sharing a bath and being supervised by George and Eleanor whilst Ted finished cleaning the kitchen under the watchful eye of Ruth.

Ruth checked her watch.

'Are you counting down the minutes until you can hand us back?' asked Ted.

'Not at all. I know what you're trying to do and it's not working.'

'And we know what you're doing too,' said Ted pausing mid-scrub.

'I'm doing what's best for your future.'

'Yeah, right.'

'I know you don't want to hear this but I suspect Charlie conned her way into your mother's affections. Helen was always a pushover for waifs and strays. But I can see through Charlie's thin façade and identify her as the scheming gold-digger she is.'

'That's unfair. She loves us!'

Ruth's eyebrows arched. 'I doubt it and anyway that's not a nanny's job. I am determined to find someone better to care for you. I need to do it for your mother.'

'You weren't exactly close,' scoffed Ted.

'That's as maybe, but Helen knew that if she ever needed me I would always have been there. It is unfortunate that the time she needs me is after her demise, but it is therefore even more important that I ensure that you all have the best possible care.'

Ted shook his head and got back to clearing up. Ruth went to check on the others. She met them at the top of the stairs and apart from Millie running around naked and the dog shaking himself dry and, in so doing, spraying everyone else, it all seemed in order. George looked at her before glancing at the bathroom door. Ruth followed his gaze and for a moment they all listened to the sound of running water coming from behind the door.

She rushed to open the door and splashed into the room. She hastily turned off the taps and surveyed the flooded room.

'You children are totally out of control. I won't tolerate behaviour like this!'

'But we've lost our parents,' said Eleanor her arms straight down by her sides and her fists tightly clenched.

'That's irrelevant. You will not behave like this! I am in charge!' As Ruth shouted there was a scary quivering tone in her voice that matched the almost imperceptible shaking that had taken over her whole body. Millie clutched Eleanor's leg, her eyes widening like a cartoon version of herself and she stared up at Ruth.

'Hi Honey, I'm home!' called Charlie gaily from downstairs. The next noise was a thundering of feet on the stairs, both human and animal, as they all rushed to her. Eleanor started to cry and Millie joined in. Ruth came stomping down the stairs and past the hugging bundle of people.

'I suppose you put them up to all this?'

'Ruth, they're distressed. What's happened?' said Charlie, trying hard not to shout as her brain wiped the 'Kipper List' clear, leaving Ruth with a starring role.

'You won't put me off, you know,' she said, reaching for the door. 'Oh, and you might want to get a plumber in. They've flooded the bathroom,' she said, with a brief head-tilt and she left.

'Sorry,' said the children in unison, followed by a belated effort from a sniffing Millie, 'bye bye stupid man.'

The tiled floor in the bathroom turned out to be a blessing and after Charlie and Ted had done a team effort with towels and put the extractor fan on full blast it was drying out nicely. George, Eleanor and Millie were settled and it was time for a debrief with Ted.

'I went to see Granddad Roger. He seems okay – a bit quiet, but he's grieving just like you guys. He said it was okay if I wanted to take you all away on holiday for a bit.'

'That's good. So, do you want to know what we did to Ruth?'

'I said, don't give her an easy time,' said Charlie. 'What exactly did you do?'

Ted thought for a moment and started to reel off a list, counting on his fingers as he went, 'Milk and flour pies on the kitchen floor, moisturised the dog, rang China on her phone and sent a silly text to everyone on her contacts list and flooded the bathroom. Oh and George has put slime in her handbag, but she most probably won't find that until she looks for her keys,' he smiled.

'Ted, mate, that was a bit over the top.' Charlie almost felt guilty.

'Be thankful that she didn't need the loo whilst she was here. George had set up the web cam again.'

'Ted, that would have been a step too far,' said Charlie, giving a little shiver at the memory of her own five minutes of YouTube fame thanks to the same prank.

'But it's all for a good cause. Didn't you say Camille would ask you how it went?'

'She probably will, I guess. I don't know. It depends on whether Ruth gets to her first.'

'Well, if Camille does ask you, we have some great video footage to show her…' Ted handed Charlie his phone. She pressed play and heard Ruth shouting at the children. Millie stood naked clutching Eleanor's leg and they all looked suitably terrified. 'I think that should do it, don't you?'

Chapter Eighteen

Charlie couldn't tell anyone about the Antigua tickets because they were bound to tell her what every molecule of her being was screaming, which was that to take the children that far away was tantamount to kidnap. She knew it wasn't a viable option, but options were something she was fast running out of.

Ruth and Camille were conducting their now-regular assessment sessions at the Cobley house. After Millie had been so upset last time it was agreed that Charlie was allowed to stay in the room if she promised not to interact. Ruth brought some virtually luminous sweets and a long-haired toy cat that looked highly flammable and displayed an expression you'd expect to see if someone had dropped a fully laden skip on its tail. It was a blatant act of bribery that worked perfectly on Millie. Millie climbed up to sit next to Ruth and showed Ruth her Pooh Bear. When Ruth went to tentatively take the much-loved, manky toy Millie snatched it away, but for her to even present it for inspection was a positive signal on Millie's part and the gesture sent a physical stab of pain through Charlie.

The only mention of the baby-sitting came from Camille. 'Did everything go all right the other night?' she asked. Charlie stared at Ruth and Ruth stared back.

'Yes, fine. It was a breeze,' said Ruth, as Camille made notes.

'Millie, did you have fun with Auntie Ruth?' asked Charlie.

'I am in charge!' shouted Millie at Ruth. Ruth laughed awkwardly and handed Millie another sweet, which she snatched. Camille continued to write as Charlie and Ruth exchanged a series of increasingly menacing nods and twitches until Millie stole their attention with a little role-play between the cat and Pooh Bear.

'I am in charge!' she shouted, before Ruth distracted her with another sweet. Charlie slumped back into the chair in resignation.

The following thirty minutes were a slow form of torture for Charlie as Camille asked mundane question after mundane question and Ruth tried to answer them at lightning speed whilst maintaining minimal interaction with Millie. She'd be good at commentating on the horse racing, thought Charlie.

When they eventually came to leave, Charlie said her goodbyes to Camille and asked Ruth for a couple of minutes of her time.

'I hope this won't take long,' said Ruth, her eyes darting after a hyperactive Millie, who was running about like an errant firework, most likely thanks to the E-number overdose from the sweets Ruth had fed her.

'No, it won't. I just wanted to say sorry.' Charlie took a deep breath and tried very hard to look conciliatory, but it was extremely difficult. 'I'm sorry if we got off to a bad start. I'd like us to get on for the sake of the children. I want this to be a long-term arrangement – me looking after the children with you as guardian,' Charlie offered her hand to shake, she wasn't sure what else to do and Ruth definitely wasn't a high-five kind of gal.

'I bet you do. For someone with a criminal record and precious little experience you have a cosy little set-up here, don't you? Free lodging in a much-sought-after London postcode, a car and free rein on what you spend as long as you claim it's for the benefit of the children. I don't doubt that you'd like it to be a long-term arrangement, however, I suggest you swiftly find alternative employment. In fact, I'm surprised you haven't already done so.'

Charlie decided to give Ruth one last chance, 'It's not about what I want, it's about what the children need.'

'So we are clear – I don't trust you. I don't think you are qualified for this job, heaven only knows why Helen employed you. She always did favour the penurious.' Ruth, for once, looked awkward at her own word choice and hastily continued, 'I am making it my mission to get you out of this house and away from these children. It's the last thing I can do for my sister.' The stony, emotionless look had returned to her face and she reached to open the door, but something made her freeze in mid-motion.

Charlie leaned over Ruth's shoulder and hissed in her ear, 'Okay, let's play it your way. In which case I have video footage of you shouting at the children and terrifying them when you baby-sat. That's just the beginning, Ruth.' Ruth looked suitably shocked, so Charlie opened the door for her and she walked out in silence. As Charlie slammed the door behind her she knew the battle lines were drawn and now she needed to get ready to fight.

Felix was sat at his computer, the ceiling fan whirring overhead as he reread the email from Ruth. She wanted him to confirm he was handing over all decisions to her and formally relinquishing his role as joint guardian. This was his get-out clause, the opportunity he thought he had been hoping for. He could walk away, learn to forget and carry on with his own life. But life was never quite that simple. He shook his head at the screen. He knew very well that Ruth's first decision would be giving Charlie her notice. At least it did sound as if Ruth was going to attempt to care for the children herself, that was a definite breakthrough, even though she had worded it as 'keeping a closer eye on day-to-day function'. He believed Ruth's intentions were good, but it was sometimes difficult to feel that when you were facing her matter-of-fact tone and brusque manner.

His mind drifted back to Charlie and the children. It surprised him that the thought of them made him smile. Ted had changed so much from the young boy he'd made Lego creations with when he'd last seen him. Eleanor was like the nicest slice of Helen: gentle, calm and caring, but she appeared to lack the drive that Helen had shown, perhaps this would come later? It was scary how much George reminded him of himself, but George had a more confident air to him than Felix had at that age. Millie baffled him a little and he chuckled to himself as he thought how like Charlie she was: striking, stubborn and ever-so-slightly bonkers.

His thoughts changed to the backdrop of their lives and its stark contrast to his own. He loved where he was living now, the climate was perfect for him, the people welcoming, it was relaxed and happy and the pressures of life were nothing that couldn't be solved over a cold beer. He thought of London – cold, miserable and grey with its unsmiling busy people. No, he definitely couldn't go back there, but the question was, could he write the email that Ruth wanted him to and effectively sever all ties with what was left of his family?

Fleur searched her father's office for the key to his London bolt-hole. It was only a studio apartment, which was London-speak for one room barely bigger than a cupboard with a sink and sofa-bed, but it meant he didn't have to commute every day and, having bought it a few years ago he was very proud of calling out the price of similar properties when he saw them in the *Sunday Times*. And as he didn't use it at weekends it was just the place to escape to with Duggan.

Fleur sat back in the oversized office chair. He usually kept the spare key in his office drawer, but it wasn't there now. She saw his suit jacket hanging up; it wasn't like her father not to have put it away, but it was worth a quick rummage, she thought. She checked his pockets and pulled out some small change, along with the key she was looking for and a couple of receipts. She put the key in her pocket and had a quick glance at the receipts. One was for a meatball sandwich, yuk, and another for something altogether more worrying; a receipt for a night in a London hotel. Fleur's buoyant mood was deflated quicker than a skewered lilo.

Fleur was like a cartoon rabbit as she bounced into the Cobley house jabbering something about all men being untrustworthy bastards. After what seemed like a yard and a half of listening to her wittering but actually saying very little, Charlie finally saw an opportunity to speak as Fleur paused to recall something specific.

'The Cobleys paid for a holiday before they died. The tickets arrived a couple of days ago. It's four weeks in Antigua during the school holidays. I'm thinking of taking the children because I think I'm about to be cut out of their lives forever and I don't know what else to do.' Charlie was shocked by the sound of her own voice cracking. She didn't cry, she never cried. Fleur flung her arms around Charlie and hugged her tightly. Charlie knew what was coming next and braced herself for the lecture on not being such an idiot and let's look for a practical solution. But it didn't come.

'Just don't get caught or they'll lock you up and, let me tell you, it is no walk in the park living in a tiny grey cell,' said Fleur, with an expression of someone who was speaking from bitter experience. The effect was somewhat lessened by the fact that Fleur's experience was limited to the couple of hours she'd spent following the debacle of stabbing Rob's tyres.

'It's a bad idea, though, isn't it?' asked Charlie, biting a thumbnail.

'Let's break it down. Four weeks in sunny Antigua, definitely a good idea. Time with the children would be fabulous especially if… you know, the worst happens. A chance to forget about reality and have fun together, lovely. But, and it's quite a big but,' she emphasised, with a wise nod of her head, and Charlie resisted a smirk, 'if you're about to be sacked then it's a bit like kidnap and that could get you on every news channel across the globe.'

'Oh God! Don't say that.'

'And don't you need permission to take them abroad without their parents?'

Charlie nodded and handed her a scruffy piece of folded paper. Fleur opened it and read it. 'This is in Toby's writing and signed by both of them. How?'

'It's the one they did for skiing last year. They booked late and we couldn't all get on the same flight, so the children and I flew out earlier the same day. It had the holiday destination at the very top of the page so I've trimmed that off and added Antigua and the flight number. The dates were in numbers so I've gone over them with the new dates in words,' said Charlie, leaning over her shoulder and pointing out the alterations.

'Oh, that is very good recycling. You wouldn't notice unless you studied it very closely. Okay, that's one hurdle sorted. Let's think who would shout 'kidnap'? Who would go to the police? Obviously Ruth would…'

'Or possibly Camille?'

'You need to work out what will keep both of them silent for four weeks.'

'I think I may have enough on Ruth to keep her quiet. If it wasn't for the guardian assessments being held here Camille wouldn't need to visit more than once every six weeks.'

'There you go! Tell Camille to meet somewhere else and we have a plan.' Fleur hugged Charlie again and she looked at Charlie's sad face. 'You do know when you come back you probably won't see the children again?' Charlie nodded and dug her fingernails into her palms in an attempt to keep the tears at bay.

Ruth finished watching the video on the laptop, her expression pure distaste as she looked from Ted to Charlie.

'Is this some crude blackmail attempt?'

'Blackmail is a criminal offence,' said Charlie. 'So, no, it's definitely not that.'

Ruth's eyebrows twitched. 'Out with it.'

'I want to look after these children and you want to be their guardian. If Camille sees this, it's game-over for you. It's that simple.'

'In exchange for deleting this, you want what? A job for life?' said Ruth with a half-snort. 'Because you can do what you like, but I'm not agreeing to that. In fact I'm interviewing another Norland Nanny next week.' Charlie mentally lined up her wet kippers.

Ted leaned forward. 'Charlie stays in exchange for us not putting this video all over YouTube and making you Britain's most wanted…' He sounded very adult, his voice somehow deeper than usual. Ruth's scowl looked a little less derogatory and she seemed to be thinking things through.

'I understand this is hard for you as children but I have to make, what I feel is, the right decision for your future and that is a professionally qualified nanny. So do your worst.' Ruth inched forward, as if to stand, and Charlie raised a hand to stop her. This was it – her very last chance.

'Fine, but I'm guessing it'll take a few weeks to line up another new nanny.' Charlie paused and took a deep breath. 'I want to take the children away for a holiday and have a proper handover with the new nanny, no sudden replacements. That's all I'm asking. I want to get them away from all of this. Give them a chance to unwind and relax. In exchange, I will support you in becoming their guardian. It's not blackmail, just an arrangement – okay?'

'You can dress it up however you like, but it's still blackmail.'

'Yeah, I guess it is and YouTube is one click away,' said Ted, now starting to sound quite menacing.

'I don't want any trouble. I want to have some time with the children, well, four weeks, to be precise,' said Charlie, the real truth unexpectedly seeping out.

There was a long pause as Ruth studied them both. 'I'll think about it,' she said, and that was the best Charlie was going to get from her for the time being.

Charlie decided to tackle Camille next. It was a short phone call as Camille sounded harassed, but she seemed to like the idea of the children having a holiday and was immediately more receptive having been told that Ruth and Roger had already agreed.

'Where are you going?' asked Camille.

Charlie was slightly wrong-footed before a suitably vague response popped into her head. 'I was thinking of somewhere with a nice beach.' It wasn't a complete lie. There definitely would be a nice beach in Antigua. Three hundred and sixty-five of them, to be precise.

From a practical perspective Camille agreed to find somewhere else to continue the meetings with Ruth. Charlie had to end the call abruptly as Millie started to use the saucepan lids as musical instruments and it was impossible to continue. She was not going to miss these wet-play days at all.

When Jonathan's phone went to voicemail Charlie had all of three seconds whilst his message played to think about what she was going to say. 'Hi Jonathan, it's Charlie. I'm sorry we keep missing each other. I'm going to take the children away for a holiday. I honestly hope that doesn't cause you any problems ... and thanks for, you know...' and the computerised voice told her that her time was up.

There had been no response from Ruth and the flights were tomorrow, so Charlie left a casual message on Ruth's voicemail to say that she was off with the children for four weeks and she doubted that there would be much in the way of telephone reception. She hoped that Ruth would make the same assumption that Camille had done, that it was a UK-based trip. She also subtly slipped in the fact that she still had the recording, just in case there were any problems. As she put the phone down she wasn't sure if it would have been better to have spoken to Ruth. This way she would be leaving without having a strong sense of whether or not Ruth was going to make trouble.

School pick-up on the last day of term was utter chaos as each child had a mountain of work and projects and rank PE kits to bring home. Eleanor was thrilled to have received a certificate for English, for her poem about someone killing a fly. George was complaining that he didn't have a mobile phone and had been forced to write down lots of phone numbers so that he could meet up with people in the holidays. Ted was quiet.

Charlie's idea of having a barbecue was scuppered by the persistent rain. So an indoor grill-up was the best she could do. She had mulled over in her mind how best to tell the children about the holiday and had worried about how they might react. They were now all sitting at the table eating in relative quiet, so she seized her opportunity.

'Guys, I've got something to tell you,' she said, her brow furrowed. All faces turned her way, apart from Millie, who was having a serious talk to her hot-dog sausage.

Ted gave her an encouraging nod, as he knew what was coming next.

'We're going on holiday tomorrow. All of us.'

'How long for? I've got cricket on Wednesday,' said George, looking concerned.

'Where are we going?' asked Eleanor, looking more positive than the others, before she added, 'Can Wriggly come?'

'It's four weeks in Antigua,' said Charlie. For the first time she was grateful for the sound of the rain lashing against the windows to break the silence. 'Your mum and dad booked it before...' She didn't need to finish the sentence, so they all listened to the rain for a moment.

'Do you think they would have wanted us to go without them?' asked Eleanor, her small perfect face so serious.

'I think so, sweetie.'

'Antigua?' asked Ted, looking bewildered. 'You hadn't said it was long-haul.'

Charlie shook her head. 'Does it make a difference?'

Ted pondered for a moment. 'Guess not. I'll get the cases down,' and he left the table. It wasn't the response she had hoped for, but it was probably best that they didn't see it as the hugely significant event that Charlie did.

Fleur came to collect Wriggly and, much to Eleanor's disappointment, he merrily trotted off with her for his own holiday. Fleur had been over-dramatic in her farewell embraces and her parting shot had been to check that Charlie had Jonathan's phone number with her as it was likely she would be needing a good solicitor on her return. This all helped to pique Charlie's paranoia. All she had to do now was finish packing and check the passports and tickets again. She took a deep breath; she really was going to do this.

Chapter Nineteen

Charlie kept giving the taxi driver her best apologetic look when he glanced at her. Millie was singing at the top of her voice 'Juicy pineapple, juicy pineapple!' to the tune of 'Bermuda Triangle' and Eleanor was struggling to contain her bladder contents as she was laughing so hard. The children had wanted to know a song about Antigua and that was the closest thing Charlie could come up with under pressure and Millie had made it her own. It was all starting to feel a bit real and Charlie felt the panic try to take hold. She took deep breaths and tried to slow her heart rate.

'You all right? You a bad traveller?' asked the taxi driver, looking a bit worried.

'No, I'm fine, I'm not going to be sick.'

'I'm scared of flying too. You won't get me up in one of those things. On average there are over one hundred and fifty plane crashes every year!' he said, looking very pleased with his random fact. Charlie couldn't help but look alarmed and she prayed that Millie hadn't heard what he'd said, but the sudden silence from the back seats meant that all the children were now very quiet and listening intently.

'How about we play a travel game?' she suggested.

'Guess the road kill?' offered George, leaning forward in his seat.

'No!' said Charlie and Ted together.

They spent the rest of the journey in virtual silence, for which Charlie was thankful. The windscreen wipers beat a soothing rhythm as they neared the airport; there was always an element of schadenfreude about going somewhere warm when it was raining at home.

There wasn't a long queue at check-in, there never was for Premium Economy, but it still seemed to take too long and Charlie was getting twitchy. She was resisting the urge to keep checking over her shoulder. It wasn't going to be the stress-free break she'd hoped for if this was the level of paranoia she could conjure up. Millie had been causing a bit of an upset in the queue, thanks to George's sick sense of humour. It appeared that the phrase 'One hundred and fifty plane crashes every year!' was a little alarming to quite a few people. Millie had thankfully now been distracted by the challenge of undoing the combination lock on her Disney case. Eleanor was very fidgety, so Charlie gave her the children's passports to hold; she felt that a little responsibility under supervision was good for her.

'Can I have your passport too please, Charlie?' asked Eleanor.

'Er, no, it's okay. I'll keep hold of it. Thanks.'

'Ooh, someone has a dodgy passport photo,' said Ted, making a grab for the passport and missing. 'Come on, it can't be that bad. You aren't meant to look good in your passport photo and they fine you, or something, if you do. Even Millie looks rough on hers and she's super-cute,' he said, ruffling Millie's hair. As Charlie was trying to think up a good excuse not to hand it over and wishing the queue would hurry up, she felt the passport leave her hand. She was too slow to retrieve it from George, who was prancing around the luggage and waving his trophy aloft.

'Got it! Ha, Ha,' he laughed, 'Bad photo. Miss... Chardonnay Paige French!' he blurted.

'Chardonnay?' said Ted, looking from George to Charlie to see who was going to explain, 'I thought Charlie was short for Charlotte?'

'It can be, but not in my case,' she said, swiping back the passport from George, who was grinning so hard he looked unhinged.

'Chardonnay?' repeated Eleanor, 'Didn't we go skiing there last year?' she asked.

'No, that was Chamonix,' said George, 'Chardonnay is like a proper chav name,' he said, still grinning until he caught sight of the look Charlie was giving him and his grin disappeared.

'Well, I like it,' said Eleanor emphatically as she gave Charlie's hand a squeeze.

'Shar-don-yay,' said Millie slowly, trying out the sounds, but as it was getting no reaction she went back to trying to undo her combination lock.

When the pretty cloned young woman with the red uniform, red lipstick and high ponytail hair beckoned her forward, Charlie's feet were difficult to move. Millie ran forward, dragging her Disney princess trolley bag and ran over Charlie's toes as she did so. Charlie realised her hands were shaking as she went to hand over the documents, so she quickly placed the passports, tickets and Toby's letter on the high counter and shoved her hands into the safety of her hoody pockets.

'Two of our party are unable to travel,' said Charlie, almost in a whisper.

'Not a problem, they'll be 'no shows'.' The smartly dressed woman opened the scruffy letter. It had been at the bottom of Charlie's rucksack for months. Charlie held her breath. The woman checked the details on the letter to Charlie's passport and tapped away on the keyboard as she asked the usual questions about items in hand luggage. Charlie waited for a question about her travelling alone with the children but it didn't come, the recycled letter had done its job.

Ted hauled the largest case onto the scales, which surprised Charlie because he didn't seem to struggle with its weight like she had. The woman confirmed their seat numbers and handed back the documents, along with the boarding cards. 'Enjoy your flight,' she said, without looking up. Charlie waited for something else to happen.

'Sorry, was there anything else?' asked the woman, with a forced smile.

Charlie shook her head and shooed the children away from the desk. The next hurdle was getting through security. If anyone was going to stop her, she felt that someone who worked in security would likely fit the bill. The queue was moving quickly and by the time she had helped Eleanor get the glittery belt off her jeans without losing too many sparkles and convinced Millie to put Pooh Bear in a tray, they were being ushered through the scanner. The children all went through and Ted started supervising the return of their items as the beeping went off around Charlie. The sense of panic that shot up her spine almost took her breath away. A uniformed lady with a stern face beckoned Charlie over.

'Arms out, please,' she asked, but if she'd asked her to put her hands together so that she could cuff them it wouldn't have been a surprise. The lady waved a handheld device over her and smiled.

'It's probably an underwired bra,' she said conspiratorially.

Charlie was stunned for a moment, 'Yes, sorry, I am wearing one.'

'That'll do it every time. Have a good flight,' she said as she moved on to the next beeper, who was coming through wearing the more usual resigned expression.

As Charlie re-joined the others, Ted greeted her with a warm smile.

'Home and dry. You can relax now,' he said. Charlie thought she would most likely never be able to relax again.

The children were regular flyers so the aeroplane experience was a normal one for them. There was always the excitement of take-off and for Eleanor and George the delights of what the films would be. Millie loved having her own headphones but always forgot about the cable and would regularly start wandering about and be bungeed back to her seat by the headphone cord.

Ted made an impassioned speech about why he should be able to have a beer on the flight, especially if Charlie was turning the alcohol away, which she was. Hostess after hostess kept trying to offer her something. With the choice of five seats, they were struggling to make a final decision on where they should each sit and moves in seating were akin to musical chairs without the tuneful accompaniment. The frequent shifting around of seats was starting to annoy the poor random person that had been allocated the last seat in the third pair they were occupying, so Charlie took the seat next to the 'Rando' as Ted had christened her. Ted sat with Millie whilst George and Eleanor implemented a complicated system they had invented that revolved around how much time each of them could spend in the window seat.

Eventually, one by one, they began to fall asleep and Charlie started to feel the ache of tiredness and stress take over her own body. The cabin lights were dimmed and she reluctantly drifted off to sleep too.

Fleur had had a difficult day, what with saying good-bye to Charlie and not knowing if the next time she saw her would be on a news flash. Wriggly had been well behaved until she'd let him off the lead and he'd gone careering down to the stables. It had taken her a good half hour to recapture him as he was too engrossed in yapping at Ralph's heels. It made a change to see Ralph on the receiving end of being harassed and he was not impressed. He had kicked out a couple of times and narrowly missed the little dog. Fleur couldn't bear the thought of what Eleanor would do if anything happened to Wriggly. She had gone through the instructions of his routine with Fleur about a dozen times. So she persevered and eventually tempted Wriggly away from the stables with a sausage roll – the WI wouldn't miss one. Fleur was pretty sure that she saw a smile on Clyde's face as she carried Wriggly back up to the house.

That evening she was sitting at the kitchen table sipping a glass of white wine and jotting down key points she wanted to cover in her business plan. She'd found some helpful sites on the internet and now had a day-by-day list of what she needed to do. The familiar sound of car on gravel and key in door made her put down her pen and clutch her glass.

'Hello love, you still up. Oh, are you working?' he said, scanning the paper in front of his daughter.

'Only to fill the time until you came home,' she said, her voice formal.

'Let me get a drink and I'm all yours,' he said with a smile.

'Is that what you say to her?' said Fleur, her eyes narrowing.

'What?' he laughed, not getting the joke.

'I wasn't sure if you would be home or if you'd be staying at the Marriott,' said Fleur, banging the receipts onto the table. Her father stared at her, ran his fingers through his grey speckled hair and sighed deeply.

'It's not what you think, Fleur.'

'That's a bit of a cliché. Can't you think of something more original, like… like…' she was so cross she couldn't actually think of something more original and that annoyed her all the more. She didn't want to shout as she didn't want to wake her mother and this was not the way for her to find out that her husband was a lying, cheating scumbag. Fleur felt the warm tears trickle down her face. 'How could you? How could you do this to Ma? To me and Poppy?

'Fleur, love…'

'Was the flat not good enough for her? The sofa-bed not glamorous enough?'

'Fleur. Please let me explain.'

'Don't go fobbing me off with a long list of excuses. I'm not a child. I know how it works. You get bored, find some young floozy and dump us.' She was starting to sob in between words, which wasn't what she'd planned when she'd rehearsed her speech.

'Sweetheart. There isn't anyone else.' Fleur went to interrupt and he stopped her by putting both his hands firmly on her shoulders and gently pushing her back into her seat. He kept his eyes firmly fixed on hers. She could see that it hurt him to see her cry like this. 'Fleur, please listen to what I'm going to tell you. But you must promise not to say anything to your mother.'

Charlie was woken by distant screaming and the sensation of being rocked, which was more than a little confusing.

'She's okay, she has bad dreams. She's had a lot to deal with lately,' Ted explained as Charlie came to. She found she was staring at something very floral and was working it out when she realised that she was lying with her head on the Rando's lap. She jerked upright, which instantly gave her a headache.

'I'm sorry,' offered Charlie, as she hastily wiped her mouth in case she was dribbling and gave a quick check that the woman's dress didn't have a wet patch. It was difficult to tell due to the wild pattern, which was handy.

'You had me worried there, I thought you were having some sort of fit,' said the Rando with a strangled laugh that said she wasn't joking. Ted returned to his seat and redid Millie's seat belt for the umpteenth time.

'Sorry about the whole falling-asleep-on-you thing,' said Charlie, tucking her hair behind her ear and realising that the embarrassed flush had reached that far.

'Don't worry, dear. You've got your hands full there. I had two and that was bad enough...' and the woman went on to recall in detail the highlights of her child-rearing years. Charlie reluctantly listened for the rest of the flight. She felt it was the least she could do.

Nobody boarded the plane to arrest her when they landed and there was nobody waiting at security either. They collected their luggage and drifted out of the 'Nothing to Declare' doors. George started jumping up and down until he remembered how uncool that was and pointed instead. 'Look,' he said. There was a hand-written sign being held up that said 'Wild Cane Villa'. The man holding it was grinning at them, having seen George's reaction. He was quite short and had his Afro-Caribbean hair braided into many strands with a variety of coloured beads dotted about them.

'Hi, I'm Tigi. Welcome to Antigua!' he said it with too much energy for anyone not high on something quite strong, thought Charlie. 'I thought there were seven of you?' he asked, giving a cursory glance behind them.

'Er, no, sorry only five now,' said Charlie, hoping that the children didn't react. The tiredness must have been taking over as they all remained silent and Tigi carried on smiling.

Their ride was a slightly battered mini bus but it had air conditioning and plenty of seats. Tigi was very attentive and insisted on taking virtually every bag, even managing to prise Millie away from her Disney trolley case with a smile.

'You wanna go up front, my man?' Tigi asked Ted as he was about to try to fold himself into a seat at the very back.

'Thanks,' said Ted, jumping in the passenger seat and grinning at George, who stuck his tongue out. Eleanor and Millie both snuggled close to Charlie as if they were going to try to catch a few minutes' sleep on the journey to the villa. However, there was no possibility of sleep. As soon as Tigi swung the van out of the airport they were onto Antiguan roads, which had obvi-ously not seen any maintenance for some time. Tigi swerved the van violently and everyone gasped and sat up straight. George was gripping his seat. Tigi looked at Charlie through the rear-view mirror.

'No problem, I'll get you there safe and sound, safe and sound,' he said in his smooth accent, which was a vast contrast to the bumps and jerks of the van.

'Pot holes!' said Ted, realising why Tigi was swerving with such little notice. As the light from the headlights danced randomly about, they could see a glimpse of what was around them. The odd tree and clumps of long grass here and there, and occasionally small wooden buildings like large colourful beach huts. Charlie pulled Millie to her and realised that despite the four-wheeled roller-coaster experience she had gone to sleep. Eleanor was looking about and taking in all the snippets she could see as the headlights alighted on them. She must have sensed Charlie watching her as she turned briefly and smiled. George was in the back looking decidedly green.

'Is it much further, Tigi?' she asked.

'I'll soon have you home,' he smiled into the mirror. He was true to his word and within a couple of minutes the van slowed and stopped in front of some white gates. Tigi leaned out of the cab, pressed a button on an ageing entry device and waved at the surveillance camera.

'Wah gwan,' he said into the crackling device and received an inaudible reply, but the gates began to open and they started to descend a narrow, steep road. He turned off and parked in front of a large hedge. Tigi sprang out and disappeared behind the hedge so, assuming this was it, Charlie lifted Millie into her arms and rounded up the others.

'Come on!' called Tigi from behind the hedge. They all followed the sound of his voice like tired sheep. He was standing on some steps that led up to the villa. It was a vast imposing structure in lemon and white that looked pretty in the half-light. They dutifully followed Tigi up the steps and past the shaped infinity pool, where there was lots of pointing and open-mouthed expressions.

Through the open door, they found themselves in a large entrance hall complete with black-and-white-tiled floor and sweeping staircase.

'Welcome home,' said Tigi, 'you can relax now.' He patted Charlie gently on the shoulder as she cradled a sleepy Millie. And, more than anything, Charlie wanted that to be true.

Chapter Twenty

Fleur was tapping her fingers impatiently on the pub table. She'd drunk two large glasses of white wine and was ready for another one. She could buy it herself but she was meant to be meeting Duggan and she didn't want to be legless before he even arrived. She checked her phone again; still nothing. She flicked her hair off her face impatiently and rang him.

'Duggan, have you stood me up?' she demanded.

'No, Fleur, like I said I'm having a bad day, baby,' said Duggan, his frustration evident in the huffing that followed. Fleur wondered what a bad day at work looked like for a farm hand. 'I've been working on my allotment and there's something making the salad vegetables wilt, the rocket has got it bad and…'

'Duggan!' said Fleur snapping, 'I don't care about the sodding rocket. I care whether or not you are going to bother turning up this evening.'

'Look Fleur, I did want to talk to you. I think you still have feelings for Rob…'

'Don't you dare mention that name! The only feelings I have for him are purely murderous…'

'Anyway,' said Duggan, sounding keen to end the call, 'I think maybe we should take a break…'

'Argh! You arse!' she said, slamming the phone down on the table. When she could still hear a muffled Duggan she realised she hadn't ended the call, so reluctantly picked it up and stabbed the end-call button. The other faces in the pub were either blatantly looking her way or having a sneaky glance.

The ageing barman looked over, 'You all right, love?'

'Another white wine, please. Make it a large one,' said Fleur, picking up her phone and scrolling through to find Jonathan's number.

The pub was getting busy when Jonathan arrived. The summer evenings were good for business, despite the poor weather, and Fleur was easily lost in the hum. Jonathan excused his way through the crowded bar out into the garden. He looked around at the damp bench seats and the chattering smokers huddled under a gazebo, as he turned to come back inside he spotted Fleur. She was seated at a table tucked the other side of an unemployed fireplace. She was scrolling through her phone directory and she'd been crying. Three empty wine glasses were on the small table in front of her.

Jonathan pulled up a backless stool, placed it opposite her and sat down, his smile greeting her sad eyes.

'Oh Jonathan, you came…' she said, fresh tears starting to flow. 'It's all such a mess.'

'Shh, it's going to be all right,' he said, quickly moving to sit next to her, only just able to squeeze himself onto the tiny bench seat.

'Oh, Jonathan,' Fleur sobbed onto his shoulder, 'Poppy is on Pa's side and Charlie has gone on holiday. I miss Charlie.' She looked up at him and took the handkerchief he offered her. She pulled her hair off her face and scooped it round to lie on one shoulder, exposing her neck, distracting Jonathan for a moment.

'You and Charlie are very close, aren't you?'

'She always knows what to do.'

'Give her a call. Even if she's on holiday she'll want to help you.'

'No, I think this time I have to sort it out for myself.'

Charlie was disorientated when she woke up; the cool cotton covers were unfamiliar and there was the hum of a ceiling fan. She was in Antigua. She'd really done it and now they were here, hopefully they had four weeks of perfect relaxation time together ahead of them. Whatever faced them when they got home she would worry about when they touched down at Gatwick, but for the next four weeks she was going to make sure that they had some amazing memories and that the bond between them all was strong. That would only serve to help them face whatever came next.

The room was vast and painted pale yellow with simple white furniture and a large bed. There was also a huge pair of curtains. Charlie threw them back and was met by the most amazing view. The curtains had been hiding patio doors and a balcony beyond. Charlie stepped out and clutched the wooden railings for support. In front of her was something she'd only ever seen in films. They were on a hillside, overlooking a perfect crescent bay. Boats of different shapes and sizes were painted onto the water. The sea was perfectly calm, as if spread with a hot knife. Palm trees lined the white sandy beach and everything that was not sea or sand was lush and green. Charlie wanted to shout for the children, but it was still early so she settled for sitting on the conveniently placed sun-lounger and staring at the view. She couldn't help grinning to herself, it was so beautiful. 'Paradise' summed it up brilliantly.

Charlie had a shower in the cavernous en-suite bathroom and was running a brush through her wet hair when she heard movement in the villa. Eleanor and Millie were padding about the glossy tiled floor in bare feet and came running in as soon as Charlie opened the door.

'I slept in a castle!' announced Millie, proudly pointing back to the bedroom she'd shared with Eleanor.

'It's a four-poster bed, Millie,' said Eleanor with a very grown-up roll of her eyes.

'Castle!' said Millie emphatically. 'Charlie got one too!' she exclaimed delightedly.

'Can we go to the beach?' asked Eleanor. 'Please!' she added hastily.

'Yes, but let's wait till everyone's up and we've had something to eat.'

'Ahhh,' groaned Eleanor, lying back on Charlie's bed. Millie wandered out onto the balcony and climbed onto the sun-lounger. Charlie was right behind her.

'Millie, you need to be careful. No climbing and no coming onto the balcony without me. Okay?' Millie nodded, but had already lost interest and was opening the door to the walk-in wardrobe.

'Wow, ickle room!' she exclaimed, going in and pulling the door closed behind her.

'It's a wardrobe and don't go shutting yourself in there. That's not very smart,' said Charlie, but Millie was now heading off to explore the rest of the house.

From downstairs came the sound of someone singing, which was odd but somehow quite pleasant too. It was a stranger, but Tigi had warned Charlie that a local woman would be in to cook for them. Charlie guessed this was the source of the melody. Millie covered her mouth dramatically as she laughed, and she and Eleanor giggled their way to the kitchen.

'Morning, morning, welcome to Wild Cane Villa. My name is Berta and I'm here to cook for you,' said a large smiley-faced black woman. 'I'm doing hedgehogs for breakfast,' she said to the girls with a wink.

'Hedgehog?' queried Eleanor, 'yuk!' Millie gripped Pooh Bear tighter and stared at Berta, her eyes wide with awe.

'You are going to love my mango hedgehogs,' said Berta, showing them a mango half, the surface of which had been cut into cubes and turned inside out so it did vaguely resemble a hedgehog.

'Mine, please,' said Millie, holding out her hand for the mango.

'Of course, baby girl,' said Berta, leading Millie to the table with the mango as bait. She's good, thought Charlie.

'Hi, I'm Charlie. This looks lovely,' she said, pointing to the dishes of fruit and pastries already on the big table.

'Whatever you want, I can make it… with a bit of notice, anyway.' She gave a robust chuckle and Charlie felt obliged to join in.

'That sounds wonderful. Thank you,' said Charlie. There was a big temptation to give herself a pinch to check it wasn't a dream, but she knew it wasn't – she'd never had dreams as good as this.

'Who do we have here?' asked Berta. Charlie realised it might have been a good idea to work out a story about Toby and Helen before now. Charlie did the introductions and explained that the older boys would most likely surface later. As Berta didn't ask about the two missing people, Charlie didn't volunteer anything. Perhaps Tigi had already tipped her off.

Eleanor started firing all sorts of suggestions at Berta to try to find something that Berta was unable to cook. She only succeeded when it started to get silly and they were on stewed donkey and barbecued pencil case. Berta was lovely with the girls and was one of those people who you knew genuinely loved children and saw them for the wonderful little people they were.

As the girls were finishing breakfast, George and Ted stumbled into the kitchen. Whilst Charlie got the girls showered and covered in sun cream, Berta made fluffy pancakes for the boys. Charlie admitted defeat and let Millie do her own sun cream and wiped off the excess and used it on Eleanor, which was easier said than done in all the excitement, when you were getting repeatedly whacked by Millie's cream-clad flailing hands.

175

Berta gave them the easiest directions in the world to get to the beach, 'Turn right onto the road, walk down the hill and there it is.' Even Charlie couldn't get that wrong. She had also given them all strict instructions to avoid the east end of the beach, which was popular with sea urchins – apparently very prickly and not good for either you or the sea urchin if you stood on them. There were buckets and spades that belonged to the villa along with an assortment of inflatable toys so, after a discussion that went on way longer than it needed to, they democratically decided on what to take to the beach. Millie clutched hold of a bright-yellow bucket protectively and Ted gathered up the other items.

Berta was right, it was a short walk to the beach and all down-hill. En route they met a couple of locals who stopped to chat and Charlie automatically went into suspicious city-dweller mode, wondering what they were about to sell them, or worse still, about to steal from them, but she quickly realised that they genuinely did just want to chat. They wished them a happy holiday and waved them on their way. Charlie couldn't help thinking that if it had been London and you'd told them where you were staying their next stop may have been to burgle the place, but this was Antigua and Berta was still at the villa, so it was bound to be okay.

As they got closer and the road straightened, the full glory of the beach and the sea appeared. Had Charlie been on her own she would have stopped to take in the beautiful sight, but as she had Millie she had to start running to catch up with the high-speed child, who was now careering towards the water at a rate of knots. As she reached the water's edge, she applied emergency braking and stopped dead. Millie clutched her Winnie the Pooh swim ring as if she was about to be shipwrecked and tentatively dipped a single toe in the water as it washed close to her. The others now joined her and awaited her response.

'Yay!' she shouted and waded in up to her knees and bobbed

down to wet her bottom. Her face was one huge grin and she was giggling. Eleanor took a bucket and went in search of the perfect place to make sandcastles and George set about digging a trench. Ted lay out a towel, switched his phone to music and lay down. Charlie looked around; this was why she'd come to Antigua – they could all be themselves, have fun, try to relax and make some new memories to sit alongside the old ones.

Millie was enlisted by George to fill up the trench he was still digging, so Eleanor magnanimously gave up her bucket and went for a swim. Charlie paddled on the shore to keep an eye on her. She was a competent swimmer for an eight-year-old and it was calm, but this was still the ocean and she didn't want her going too far out.

Charlie adjusted the straps on her swimming costume. She didn't know why she'd bought the size twelve – it was too big all over. Ever since the accident she'd been steadily losing weight and nothing seemed to fit any more. She'd grabbed the costume when she was shopping and didn't bother to try it on. It was a plain black one-piece, which was functional rather than glamorous, but as she never wore a bikini it would have to do. George grinned as he went past Charlie and stood in the sea scooping up water in the bucket and hurling it in Eleanor's direction.

'Stop it George! Look at these creatures,' said Eleanor, and George waded out to join her.

Charlie's mind returned to her clothing crisis. Most likely all the summer things she'd thrown in the case were going to be too big for her now. Oh well, she thought, I'll only need swimming costumes, shorts and t-shirts while I'm here and if Berta is cooking for us I'll soon put the weight back on. Charlie's thoughts were interrupted by Eleanor screaming. This wasn't play-screaming this was the noise of someone in pain and Charlie was bounding through the water in an instant.

'It's a sea urchin!' yelled George, as Charlie hoiked Eleanor into her arms and carried her back to the beach.

'Where does it hurt, Elle?' asked Charlie and Eleanor held up her hands.

'I'm sorry!' said George and Charlie dragged her eyes off the now very pale Eleanor to glare at George. 'I scooped it up in the bucket because I thought it was seaweed going past and… I threw it and Eleanor…' George stopped talking and stared at his sister. Ted was now kneeling next to her.

'George!' shouted Ted, bringing George back to the now.

'Eleanor caught it but… it was a sea urchin,' tears started to pour down George's already wet face.

Ted turned to Charlie. 'They're poisonous, aren't they?'

Before Charlie could think of an answer there was a shadow over them all. She looked up and through the blinding sun she could just about make out a fair-haired, golden tanned Adonis in sunglasses.

'Was it small, black and spiky?' the Adonis asked George. George sniffed and nodded. 'Nasty sting but it's not dangerous.' He crouched down next to Eleanor and uncurled her fingers to reveal very red palms dotted with black spots. Eleanor winced. 'Let's get these sorted,' and he lifted her into his arms and marched off across the sand. There was something very familiar about that voice. Charlie stared after the muscular figure in swim shorts who was now striding away from them, with George in hot pursuit. Ted took Millie's hand and stood up nudging Charlie as he did so, urging, 'Come on,' and they had to jog to catch them up.

'But isn't that…?' asked Charlie, but everyone was too far away. She felt like a very large wet kipper had hit her, that or the jet leg was doing very crazy things to her hearing.

The Adonis took Eleanor to a small beach bar attached to the nearby hotel and as Charlie and Ted joined them the barman was already filling a bowl with hot water. Eleanor was deposited gently onto a bar stool and the Adonis tested the water.

'It's going to be hot, but that will help the pain,' he said. 'Okay Eleanor?'

The children suddenly stopped staring at Eleanor's hands and looked at the Adonis.

'Felix?' said Charlie as everyone did a double-take.

'Have you turned into our stalker?' asked George.

Felix ignored them and focused on Eleanor. 'I'm going to get these little black dots out of your palms because that's what's making them sting. Okay?' Eleanor gave a teary nod. The barman produced some tweezers, dipped them in some boiling water and handed them to him. Everyone stayed quiet and watched intently as he carefully teased the little black dots from Eleanor's palms. After a lot of wincing from all assembled, the worst of the stings were out and Eleanor was jiggling her fingers in a fresh bowl of hot water.

Charlie picked Millie up and she eyed Felix suspiciously from the safety of Charlie's arms. He smiled at her but soon turned his attention to Charlie.

'It's nasty – a bit like running your hands down a cheese grater, but nothing serious. The stings will dissolve themselves in a few days if I've missed any.'

'Thanks, I wouldn't have known what to do.'

'Good job it wasn't a local that came to help; they still favour urine for healing urchin stings!'

'Ewww!' said Eleanor with feeling.

'Cool,' said George, 'I could pee on her if you like?' he said keenly, and was met by a chorus of 'No!'

'I knew it was you as soon as I heard Millie,' said Felix as he leaned against the bar, making his abs appear to ripple and Charlie had to try very hard not to stare. 'I thought I was dreaming for a bit watching you all together on the beach and...' he seemed to run out of words.

Felix waved to get the barman's attention. 'Four fruit punches and two beers please.'

'No problem, Blue,' replied the barman.

'Why did he call you Blue?' came Eleanor's feeble voice from the bar stool.

'It's what everyone calls me here. Because of these,' he said, as he nonchalantly slid his sunglasses up to rest in his unruly sun-streaked hair. Even though she knew what was coming it was all Charlie could do not to gasp at those amazing eyes – they put the ocean to shame.

'Yes, I remember those,' said Charlie, who was feeling as if she had woken up in a parallel universe.

The first of the drinks appeared on the bar and Felix handed over a staff card and some dollars.

'You work here?' asked Ted taking a beer, which Charlie swiftly took from him and pointed at the fruit punch instead.

'No, not exactly. Look Ted, could you keep an eye on the others while I find out from Charlie what exactly is going on.'

Ted was busy tasting the fruit punch, so had no chance to reply as Felix put his hand on Charlie's shoulder and guided her quickly away.

'So?' he prompted when they were out of earshot.

Charlie resisted the very childish urge to go 'found you!' 'We're on holiday, how about you?' she asked, feeling an odd sense of calm. Her emotions were all over the place.

'Did Ruth agree that?'

Charlie took a swig of her beer. 'She knows we're on holiday but she didn't exactly agree to it and she doesn't know where we are.' The beer was cold and refreshing as she savoured another mouthful.

He stared at her. 'How did you find me?' The way he was frowning made him look a little cross.

'You found us,' said Charlie, enjoying being annoying. It was nice to see him again, especially topless, but she still hadn't forgiven him for running out on the children. He looked so very different in a pair of shorts. To think he'd been hiding that amazing body under all those layers the whole time he'd been in London. 'You came along the beach and found us, Felix.'

'Please can you not call me that? Just stick with Blue.' Charlie

180

pulled a noncommittal facial expression. 'Why have you brought the children here? Oh God, you're not planning on leaving them with me, are you?'

Charlie laughed and started to choke at the same time as her beer went down the wrong way. 'Fe… Blue, calm down I had no idea that you lived here. The holiday details came in the post, Toby had booked it ages ago.'

'Right,' said Blue slowly. He finally took a long drink of beer. 'Why here?'

'I don't know. Maybe Toby knew where you were and wanted to see you. Perhaps he thought it might be nice for you to get to know them.' She pointed at the children, who were now playing stacking games with their empty cups.

'I'm sorry, but nothing has changed. I can't be their guardian.' There was the frown again.

'I know that. But you're still their uncle.' Charlie didn't want to have this fight again, not here. 'I'd better get these back to the villa. Thanks again for your help. We're here to have a quiet holiday but I expect we'll see you around,' she said, downing the last of her beer.

'So it's really just a holiday?' asked Blue.

'Yep. Just a holiday.' Although Charlie was already thinking what a stroke of luck it was to have found their runaway uncle. This was a definite opportunity for the children to get to know him better and there was always a chance he might change his mind, however minuscule that chance was.

Blue followed her back to the bar, where she started to round up the children. Charlie tucked Eleanor's damp hair behind her ear. She was still looking very sorry for herself, slumped on the bar stool with her hands in the bowl.

'Try soaking them in vinegar for a bit, pat them dry and put some cream on, Eleanor,' said Blue and she gave him a brief nod.

'Good to see you guys,' he said awkwardly to Ted and George. 'I'm sure I'll see you about if you're here for a couple of weeks.'

'Four,' said Charlie, hardly believing it herself. Blue's forehead scrunched up in response but he didn't say anything. He watched them gather up their belongings and walk across the beach. He flicked down his sunglasses and turned his head slightly so it looked as if he was looking out to sea, but what he was actually doing was following every step of their slow progress until they disappeared from view.

Tigi was sat on the porch of a small wooden building decorated in faded pink. He was making the rocking chair sway gently as Blue pulled up outside.

'You feeling any better?' Blue asked as he bounded up the steps.

'Ah, don't fuss, man. I'm fine.'

'Tigi, you have multiple sclerosis and your flare-ups are getting more frequent.'

Tigi waved his words away. 'I'm fine. You need to feel the breeze,' said Tigi, rocking a little slower.

'I worry, that's all.'

'I don't and you shouldn't either. It's one of the wonders of life that we don't know what is coming around the corner to challenge us next. It keeps us on our toes,' said Tigi, with a throaty laugh.

Blue let out a heavy sigh. 'I don't know, it feels like everything is changing. The easy life is… well, not as easy as it once was, that's all.'

'You need to lighten up, Blue, I'll be back to normal soon enough. But in the meantime a cold beer would be good.'

Blue shook his head and disappeared into the small dwelling. He returned with two beers and handed one to Tigi, together with a lipstick. 'Found this in the truck. Is it yours?'

'Not my colour, but I'll return it to its owner,' said Tigi, taking it from him.

'This week's golf widow?' Blue sat down on the top wooden step.

'Never you mind,' said Tigi, tapping his nose. 'I heard you were a hero today,' he said, changing the subject.

'News travels quicker than a barrel over a waterfall here.'

'You should know by now that it's a small island.' Tigi closed his eyes as he sipped his beer.

'Yeah, I know. It was some kid with an urchin sting, that's all.'

Tigi watched Blue closely and rocked steadily in his chair. 'I heard it was your niece?' he said, raising one eyebrow.

Blue laughed and shook his head. 'God damn it, it *is* a small island!'

Chapter Twenty-One

Fleur was enjoying the feel of the cotton against her bare skin and snuggled her face into the pillow, aware that her torso was uncovered and felt cool but comfortable. She stirred and turned onto her back as she heard a door shut, which made her sit up quickly. She pulled the duvet up to cover her bare chest even quicker. Fleur's mind was foggy but she recalled the previous evening in the pub, a discussion about her refusing to go home and Jonathan suggesting that she go to his. She vaguely remembered being helped into a car but the rest was a mystery.

'Jonathan, is that you?' asked Fleur to the empty room. The door opened just a crack.

'There's a fresh cup of coffee on the bedside cabinet for you,' he said, before the door was closed again.

'Thanks, Jonathan,' she said, but the words fell away as she realised he must have seen her half-naked. She shrugged. Oh well, he was most likely more embarrassed by that than she was.

Fleur looked around the small bedroom and her eyes found the plain-white coffee mug. The room was painted a pale grey and had a huge bookcase on the far wall, which was so full of books they were double stacked on every shelf and also piled on top.

Fleur put on the dark-grey dressing gown from the back of the bedroom door and took her coffee cup with her. Jonathan's flat was compact, a couple of steps along the short hallway brought her into a living room cum kitchen and dining area. There was a large black leather corner sofa scattered with red and cream cushions, where Jonathan sat with his feet up on a low glass coffee table. When Fleur walked in he almost spilled his coffee with the speed that he stood up.

'Oh, you're up. Look I'm sorry about before. I hadn't realised you were… that you hadn't… I was concentrating on not spilling the coffee… I hadn't realised that you didn't… you know…'

'Well, someone undressed me last night. Was that not you?'

'No! Goodness, no. I took off your jacket and shoes, but that was all. I swear!'

'Don't worry, I believe you. Thousands wouldn't,' she said with a sly smile and sat down on the edge of the sofa. Jonathan remained standing and rubbed his unshaven chin. Fleur indicated for him to join her. 'Oh, relax.' She patted the seat.

Jonathan sat down, picked up his mug and they sipped coffee in a silent synchronised motion. 'How are you feeling? You had quite a bit of wine last night.'

'I'm fine… a little fuzzy round the edges, but fine. Was I frightful?'

'No. Not at all,' said Jonathan, vehemently shaking his head. Fleur gave him a sideways look. 'Well, perhaps a bit. Yes,' he conceded. 'What's the plan for today?'

Fleur let out a big slow breath, put her mug on the coffee table and wrapped the now slightly gaping dressing gown tightly around her petite frame. 'I don't know. I can't go home. There's nobody at Charlie's. I don't know what to do.'

'I have to work, but you're very welcome to stay here.'

'That's kind, but I think I'll book into a hotel and let you have your bed back.'

'Up to you. No rush,' he said, getting to his feet and taking the mugs to the sink. 'There are cereals in the cupboard. Fruit in the fridge and more coffee in the pot. I'm going to shave and get going.'

After Jonathan had said good-bye for the fourth time she found herself alone. She decided to formulate a plan whilst she was in the shower. She raided Jonathan's shelves and quite liked the citrus smell of his Penhaligon's shower gel; she thought she detected a hint of basil in there too somewhere. She realised the smell reminded her of Jonathan, she'd smelt it when he'd greeted her yesterday and before at the Criterion. She breathed in the fresh scent and started to form a plan of action.

Whatever her father said about there being a bed-bug infestation at his London flat, she didn't believe him. It was a good cover story because she could see why he wouldn't tell her mother as she most likely wouldn't have let him back into bed with her for years and he clearly thought it was enough to put Fleur off the scent too. But he was underestimating his daughter. There was something going on and she was going to find out exactly what it was.

Fleur had decided to take the tube and, although it hadn't been too busy with most of the commuter traffic now dispersed to their office cubicles and designated squares of utility carpet, she had rather wished that she'd taken a cab. At least she was now outside in the open air and a slight whiff of Thames was assaulting her nostrils as she clip-clopped her way across the South Quay footbridge. Each metal-heeled footstep rang out across the modern metal structure and echoed around her. She confidently followed its slightly snaking path until she was on the paved edge of the water and her heels sounded altogether less impressive. It wasn't far to her father's apartment from here but already she was wishing that she had worn flats, but all she had available was what she'd worn last night for her date with Duggan the Dumper.

Thankfully, she turned the last corner, promising herself that it was a taxi all the way back. The block of flats was like a series of boxes stuck together, some wood-clad, some with cream rectangular tiles and some in a menacing dark grey, but it was modern, low-maintenance and it fitted into its surroundings on the Isle of Dogs. She pulled out the key and used the magic key fob to open the communal entrance door. She took the stairs to the first floor and stood outside the door for a few moments collecting her thoughts, few that there were. She hadn't really thought this bit through. If there were a bug infestation she really didn't want to go inside, and she wasn't sure how she would know. How big were bed bugs? Could you see them with the naked eye or were they microscopic little beasts? She had no idea. She wasn't expecting to find any evidence of the other woman because clearly the flat wasn't good enough for her. So what was she expecting to find on the other side of that door?

Charlie was lying on a sun lounger by the villa's pool, sipping fresh pineapple juice and listening hard as she tried to hear the sea, which was a little too far away to be heard. She was starting to think that if she lay there any longer she was going to fall asleep and be eaten alive by tiny winged biting things, when she heard footsteps bounding up the steps behind her. She lurched forward, ready to fight, and was greeted by Blue, who nonchalantly sat down on the sun lounger next to her.

'Evening Charlie,' he said, as casual as you like.

'Er, hello,' she said, giving him the once-over. He was still wearing the shorts he'd had on at the beach, but now his rippling stomach muscles were hidden from view by a pale-green t-shirt advertising Wadadli Beer, which according to the logo under the picture purported to be 'the beer of Antigua'.

'How's Eleanor?' he asked, leaning forward, his forearms resting on his tanned legs. Charlie noticed the hairs on his legs had been bleached blonde by the sun and she tried to drag her eyes back up to his face.

'Yeah, she's fine. Tonight I bathed them a second time in vinegar and put some cream on. They look loads better, thanks. She's asleep now, anyway.'

'That's good to hear.'

'How did you know where we were staying?'

'Small island,' he said, with a grin. 'Interesting suntan,' he added, failing to hide a smirk.

'Oh, I put sun cream on the kids and forgot about myself,' said Charlie, who had noticed the heat of her burnt shoulders kick in a while ago but had yet to thoroughly inspect the damage.

'Right. So the white hand print, just above your...' he tailed off and pointed abstractly in the direction of her left breast. 'That wasn't intentional, then?'

Charlie followed his gaze and gave a little gasp as she saw Millie's perfect handprint immortalised on her chest and her mind rewound itself to the moment that a factor-fifty-clad Millie had landed a slap on that exact spot.

'Terrific!' she said, as she pulled her chin down to her chest to get a better look. The redness offset the milk-white patch of skin brilliantly. 'You know, that's better than the expensive baby hand print she has in a frame at home,' she laughed.

'Hang on a sec,' said Blue and he jogged off across the garden. He produced a penknife from his pocket and sliced the top off a spikey plant. He walked back and presented it to Charlie, who looked doubtfully at the oozing goo that was seeping out of the end.

'It's aloe vera and if you spread it on your skin it will relieve the burn.' Charlie looked suspicious. 'Trust me,' he said, with a grin. She took it from him and tentatively spread it on her shoulders.

Blue watched her before making himself comfy on a sun lounger. 'How are you settling in?'

It was so very strange to see him. Here in Antigua he was somehow different and now he was so much more relaxed than he had been at the beach. 'Yeah, it's fine thanks… no that's unfair, it's amazing. The villa is totally beautiful and the beach is paradise so, yeah, everything is great, thanks.'

'You've only seen the villa and the beach?'

'Apart from what we can see from the balcony. I expect we'll venture a bit further when we've found our bearings.'

'I was going to ask if you'd like me to show you round the island tomorrow?'

'I see. You're selling me a tour?'

'No, suspicious Londoner, I'm not going to charge you. I'm not working tomorrow and I thought it would be a nice thing to do. Okay?'

'Okay,' smiled Charlie.

'Anyway I figured while you're here we should make the most of the time together.'

'What you and the kids?' said Charlie, pausing with the now very squished aloe vera plant held aloft.

Blue moved very slowly as he turned to face her, his expression unreadable. 'Yeah, and you and me.'

Charlie felt the colour rise in her cheeks so at least now they matched her shoulders. She nodded and asked the question that had been buzzing around her head since the incident on the beach. 'Are you going to tell anyone at home that we're here?'

Charlie was still trying to dress the wriggling octopus that was Millie when she heard the friendly beep of a car horn outside.

'He's here!' shouted George, all thoughts of being pulled out of a tree a few weeks ago long forgotten as he ran downstairs, bumping into Eleanor as he went.

'Ow!' she protested, and started to cry.

Millie escaped from Charlie's grip wearing her pants and t-shirt and Charlie decided that would probably be all right for today, seeing as she had been covered from head to the very tip of her toes in factor-fifty sun cream and her swimming costume was in

189

one of the bags. Charlie put her arm around Eleanor and guided her downstairs.

'Is it a sad day?' Charlie asked her.

Eleanor nodded and wiped her nose on the back of her hand. Charlie produced a tissue and handed it to her. 'But it's not why you think. I miss Wriggly,' his name was almost lost in the sob.

'Oh, sweetie, come here.' Charlie pulled her into a hug. 'He will be having the best holiday ever. He will be driving Ralph crazy, he'll be having walks in the fields and he'll be sleeping on Fleur's bed, I bet.'

'But I love him,' said Eleanor with a sniff.

'And he loves you too, but it won't stop him having a good time. And it shouldn't stop you. Okay?'

Eleanor nodded. 'I'm missing Mum and Dad too,' she added. 'It feels like we've left them behind.'

'I know,' said Charlie, kissing the top of her fair hair, 'But we've not left them behind, they're always with us.'

'In our hearts?'

'I was going to say in our memories, but yeah if you like, in our hearts too.' Eleanor wiped away a tear with her arm and it left a streak. Charlie thought she might have overdone the sun cream on her too.

'Are we ready for the Amazing Antiguan Island Tour?' Blue announced through the open doors.

The children answered him in varying levels of shrill reply, making Charlie smile as she joined the others in the entrance hall. She handed Blue a selection of rucksacks, buckets and more hats than there were heads and he pulled a puzzled face but took them anyway. She couldn't help noticing the muscle definition under his t-shirt and, for a moment, her mind wandered off. Whatever the Antiguan air was doing to her, it needed to stop.

'Is Winnie excited about his adventure?' Blue asked Millie and in reply she took hold of the only free finger he had and went with him.

Outside there was a large white truck-like vehicle that, according to its bonnet, had been made by Range Rover. It had a canvas roof and open sides and, with ten seats in the back and two up front, there was plenty of space for them all and their detritus.

'Front or back?' asked Blue, with a very cheeky grin.

'I don't think I can leave the children in the back on their own, do you?' said Charlie.

'Good point. Okay, Teddy you can come up front with me if you like.'

'It's Ted. I'll be fine in the back.' Ted was not going to be so quick to forgive and forget, it seemed.

'Sure thing,' said Blue, jumping into the driver's seat and starting the engine, making Millie squeal with delight. Eleanor looked alarmed as Charlie was still making her way round to the back of the truck.

Berta came to wave them off, which added to the excitement in the jeep. Charlie checked she had the sick bags, returned Millie's hat to her head once again and they set off. With Blue up front it was a magical mystery tour, as only he knew where they were heading. The Range Rover could cope much better with the Antiguan roads than Tigi's mini bus and in daylight there was so much to take in that the small bumps were quickly forgotten. The breeze that the open-sided truck created was welcome. Charlie closed her eyes and breathed in deeply; it did smell so very different here, she couldn't really describe it – it was simply clean, fresh and somehow sweeter and lighter than the air at home. Someone once told Charlie that 'Fresh air blows in a contented spirit' and that felt true today. She could feel her lungs rejoice as the unsullied breeze was gulped down.

It wasn't far to their first stop. 'Windmill!' shouted Eleanor as they trundled along a dirt track.

'Welcome to Betty's Hope,' said Blue as he helped them out of the jeep. Millie was the last one and she kept hold of Blue's hand as they walked over the uneven ground. He acknowledged two men sitting in chairs a few yards away and ushered everyone towards the large sugar mill. Inside was a large piece of faded red machinery, which, Blue explained, was what had once crushed the sugar cane. He took them through the whole process of sugar production. Ted read the information boards behind him, suddenly becoming interested when Blue got to the part about making rum.

There was a small museum with a model of what the area would have looked like when it was at the height of sugar production, which Millie was desperate to play with but thankfully was safely encased in glass. They read the information boards whilst Blue chatted to the men outside. Charlie listened for a bit but wasn't always able to follow what they were saying. When they had taken in as much as they could, they climbed back on board the jeep.

'What language do they speak?' asked Charlie, as Blue checked the jeep door was secure.

'It's called Dialect. Kind of a mix of English, Creole and something the slaves developed. I can't really speak it. I only know a few bits, which is enough to get by. But everyone speaks English as well, they just take pride in using Dialect.'

'Cool, can you teach us the swear words?' asked George, blunt as ever.

Blue laughed, 'No. But you do need to know how to greet someone. You can say 'Hello' in English or 'Wah Gwan' in Dialect.'

Everyone started practising 'Wah gwan', all trying to mimic Blue's proficient local accent. He left them to it and they set off on the next leg of their tour.

Next stop was a short one, but Charlie was impressed with the thought that Blue had put into it. It was a donkey sanctuary. Lots of friendly donkeys that liked to be petted, a couple of foals – and toilets. Charlie stayed in the shade and watched the donkeys from afar, because wherever there were donkeys there were flies, although there were a lot less than she was expecting. Once everyone had washed their hands and was back in the jeep, the engine roared into life again. They took a short cut up Red Hill, a steep and rocky track that made the vehicle bounce about, even at a snail's pace. The children loved it, and shouted and squealed with each bump. Once back on slightly more level roads they were off again.

'Nelson's Dockyard!' announced Blue, as he swung the jeep past a giant anchor and brought it to a halt. Ted and George were already piling out of the jeep and eagerly looking around. Blue bounded round to the rear of the jeep and helped the others down. He picked Millie up and lifted her expertly onto his shoulders before leading the way. He was greeted warmly by a local woman who pretended to tickle Blue for Millie's benefit. Charlie saw Blue slip her some dollar bills, but she couldn't make out the denominations and then their private tour began.

'Can you see the giant doors up ahead?' he asked, 'on the other side is the naval base and dockyard. What do you think they were trying to keep out?' He was met with a barrage of responses: 'Wild animals,' said George. 'The enemy?' said Ted, trying to appear uninterested and failing badly. 'Disease?' said Eleanor, all of which he dismissed.

'Nope. Women. The gates were to keep out the women!' he gave Charlie a cheeky wink as he said it and went on to explain that the navy was very keen that the sailors should concentrate on working and not falling in love with the beautiful local ladies.

Blue was clearly very knowledgeable about the area and was able to make it engaging for each of them, which was a trick in itself. Charlie noticed that he talked to Eleanor about the slaves but to Ted and George he pointed out the restored military buildings and gave an insight into the life of a soldier in the early eighteen hundreds.

'Admiral Horatio Nelson lived here for three years, but he wasn't popular and never really liked Antigua so he spent most of the time on his ship.'

'That's weird,' said George. 'Was he a nutter?'

'Nope, just very set in his ways.'

He told Millie tales of pirates sheltering in the harbour from treacherous seas and the might of the British Army. Charlie couldn't fail to be a little impressed.

They walked round to the small museum housed in a beautifully restored pale-blue colonial building which had once been the Naval Officers' House. Millie oohed and ahhed as Blue pointed out historical artefacts and the boys were mesmerised by the cannons. Before there was a chance for anyone to get bored Blue was herding them back to the jeep. He produced a large flask and poured out fruit punch for everyone.

'Would you like some island rum in that?' he asked Charlie.

'Yes, please,' said George, holding out his plastic cup.

'No, thanks,' said Charlie, shaking her head at George.

Once everyone was bundled back on the jeep they were off again. The rainbow colours of the houses flashed past; many pastel shades and some a bit on the bright side. Some perfect, with that recently painted look and others in need of repair. A few had small verandas at the front, sometimes occupied by people who waved as they passed and one that had a washing machine by the front door. The backdrop of lush green framed it all beautifully.

'Who likes pineapple?' shouted Blue from the front and everybody shouted back 'Me!'

'Great. You're going to love our next stop!'

He wasn't wrong. He stopped at the roadside and greeted an elderly man with a handshake and a hug. Soon pineapples were being sliced up with a small but deadly looking machete of some description and being handed out to the children. Charlie liked pineapple but she'd never tasted anything so sweet or as delicious as this. She knew she was gobbling it down but she couldn't help herself, it was divine. Blue took a close-up photo of their juice-covered faces and handed out more slices. This time Charlie tried really hard to eat it slowly and savour the exquisite taste. She closed her eyes as she nibbled at the last piece.

'You're enjoying that, aren't you?' whispered Blue, and Charlie opened her eyes quickly and grinned. She really hoped she didn't have strings of pineapple flesh hanging between her teeth.

'It's amazing.'

'Black pineapple,' explained Blue, 'it's the best in the world.'

'Why black?' asked Eleanor, studying the pineapples on the wooden cart that looked just like any other pineapple.

'They are darker in colour, sort of dark grey until they ripen and then they go this golden colour,' explained Blue.

'Juicy pineapple, juicy pineapple!' sang Millie and the others groaned.

They meandered through the countryside with Blue calling out the odd point of interest until they were bumping their way through residential areas scattered with more small homes. After three attempts at shouting to the back they finally worked out that Blue was telling them he was going to avoid the capital of St John's as there were two particularly large cruise ships in dock and it would be crowded. They suddenly left the houses and people balanced on mopeds behind and were bumping along a path that was getting narrower and narrower.

'Hold on,' yelled Blue as the jeep lurched and he slowed its speed so that it could navigate the crater-sized hole in the track. The bushes turned a darker shade of green and a few palm trees appeared before Blue brought the jeep to rest on an almost deserted piece of headland.

'Welcome to Blue's Bay,' he said, as he leapt from the cab.

'It's yours?' asked George, looking mightily impressed as he jumped off the back of the truck.

'No, but as it doesn't have a name on any maps and only the locals know about it, what's the harm? I'm letting you in on a big secret by bringing you here. Shh.'

'Ooooh,' said Millie, her eyes wide with intrigue.

Charlie sat on the lonely picnic bench, as Blue had instructed, as he ferried various containers from the jeep and assembled them on the picnic table behind her. The unspoiled little white sand beach spread out in front of her and gently sloped down to the clear water caressing the sand in a languid way that seemed to embody what the Caribbean way of life was all about.

A bit further along, and thankfully a safe distance away, Ted and George were playing extreme Frisbee, where they threw it out of reach and points were scored for the most dramatic dive that resulted in a successful catch. Millie had been awarding a million points each time but had quickly got bored and was burying her own legs in wet sand.

Eleanor was paddling and studying the shells that she came across, and beyond her Charlie saw a series of small boats bobbing gently on the rippling surface of the water. The boats were all slightly different but they were motorboats of some description.

Charlie could hear Blue setting up the lunch things behind her. She adjusted her sunglasses and breathed out a relaxed sigh. Her relaxation was short-lived as two huge flies suddenly came out of nowhere and started to frantically loop the loop around her head. She spun round to see that the picnic table behind her displayed a buffet of uncovered food and more flies were fast approaching.

'Blue!' she shouted.

Blue bounded over to her, looking from her to the children and back again, 'What's up?' he said, having another look at Eleanor who was still paddling in the shallows.

'There are flies everywhere!' she said, scrambling to her feet and skidding out of her flip-flops in an attempt to get away from the food.

Blue laughed and waved an arm over the table as a couple of the flies threatened to settle. 'Is that all? You're such a city dweller.'

'I just don't like flies. They're dirty, filthy creatures that spread germs and land on all sorts of vile stuff. Cover the food up,' she said, taking a tentative step towards the table, but stopping as a fly made a last-minute change of trajectory and headed straight for her. Charlie stumbled backwards and Blue grabbed her arm with a steadying hand and kept her upright.

'You're not joking are you?'

'It's no big thing. Nobody likes flies,' said Charlie, shrugging off his strong hand. She felt foolish but her heart was thundering in her chest and the flies were still circling.

Blue gave her a sympathetic smile. 'Why don't you finish burying Millie and I'll cover this lot up? They'll soon clear off, I promise.'

Charlie backed away. She covered her eyes with her sunglasses and walked away as calmly as she could muster with her heart racing. She swatted away an imaginary fly and pasted a smile on her face as she approached Millie.

'You okay, Millie?'

'Poo,' said Millie without looking up as she continued to busy herself with slapping wet sand onto her thighs.

'Pooh is safe in the car. We don't want him to get all sandy, do we?'

'Silly Charlie! I need a poo. Now,' said Millie, suddenly looking very serious.

'Oh, right,' said Charlie, scanning the small beach and up towards the small lane they had come down but she knew she hadn't seen any buildings nearby. 'This could be tricky. Hang on.'

'No,' said Millie shaking her head vigorously. 'Hooooooge Poo now!' she added, her facial expression changing as the rumble that was ripping through her swimming costume was audible, despite the muffling qualities of the sand.

'Oh no!' said Charlie, lifting Millie up under her arms and wading out into the sea as far as she could before dunking Millie's bottom half. The water around her changed colour as the sand was returned to its rightful place with a little something extra.

Charlie bobbed Millie up and down in the water, which made Millie chuckle.

'Ploppy puddles!' she giggled as Charlie stifled her laughter.

When the rumbling stopped Charlie got Millie out of her costume and spun her around in the warm water. She gave a quick check to Millie's behind before carrying her to the shore and setting her down to collect shells with Eleanor. Charlie swam out to deep water and tried to make herself feel clean, but it was going to take more than a dip in the same corner of the ocean into which Millie had emptied her bowel contents. She was starting to turn back to shore when she heard splashing and to her horror saw Ted and George chasing each other straight into the ploppy puddle.

'Nooooo!'

Chapter Twenty-Two

Lunch turned out to be less stressful than Charlie had envisaged after Blue filled two plastic bags with water, tied them at the top and put one on each end of the table to fend off the flies. Despite Charlie's reservations it did seem to work. It also kept Millie entertained as she could see her distorted reflection in them and apparently when you're three that's hilarious. Lunch was all local fare, made up of conch salad, a tasty rice pilaf, ducana and chop up with homemade ginger beer.

Blue explained each dish to the children and got them all to try a little bit. The ducana was a big hit, although it didn't look the most appetising of the selection. Blue explained that it was made from sweet potato, sugar, flour, vanilla, water and raisins. Chop up caused a lot of laughter at the table as George performed pretend Karate chops over the dish of spinach, eggplant and okra. Thankfully they all found something they liked and it was demolished in record time.

After lunch Charlie lay on the sand, feeling the sun on her skin, interrupted only by the gently wafting breeze. Blue cleared up, had a game of ultimate Frisbee with the boys and put Millie's sun hat back on at least half a dozen times. Eleanor was sitting at the now-empty picnic table in a small spot of shade, reading a book. At one point, Charlie almost fell asleep and she smiled to herself; it was a good feeling and she could get used to it. Blue left the boys to it and came over and sat down on the edge of Charlie's towel.

'Are you ready for the second half of the tour?'

'Do we have to?' asked Charlie, without opening her eyes.

'It'll be worth it. Better than this morning, I promise.'

Charlie slid her sunglasses up off her face to rest in her hair like a hairband and leaned up on one elbow. 'That's quite a claim. Okay, count me in,' and she stood up and shook her towel half over Blue.

'Oy!' he shouted as the sand landed on him. He was quick to his feet and started to chase Charlie and, although she didn't know why, she started to run. She narrowly missed being decked by the Frisbee as she dived between the boys and splashed through the shallows before she remembered her closeness to the ploppy puddle but her quick turn up the beach was a mistake. Blue grabbed her and started to tickle her. He was immediately joined by Millie, who was trying to join in but was basically pinching Charlie, which made her laugh all the more.

It was only day two and even if it all ended now she knew this island, this family holiday had done them all some good.

Fleur stamped her foot, her tiny heel making an impressive sound in the echoey stairwell. It was an attempt to steel herself, to get a grip on the nerves that were threatening to make her call a cab and hot-foot it out of there. She paused with the key hovering over the lock and just before she inserted it she heard a noise coming from inside. Either the bed bugs had worked out how to operate the radio or there was someone inside. With a renewed sense of courage she opened the door and marched in with authority. Whatever she had expected to see, whoever she had thought she might find there, Rob the Knob was not even an addendum to that list of remote possibilities.

'Shit!' said Rob, clutching the duvet to him.

'And it's an utter delight to see you too,' said Fleur, shutting the door and striding forcefully across the laminate floor.

'Christ, Fleur, you gave me a fright, I thought it was... Well, I thought it was someone else. How are you?'

'Drop dead, Rob. What the hell are you doing in my father's apartment?'

'That's what I love about you, Fleur, you get straight to the heart of the matter. How've you been? I've thought of you every single day. How's your Mum?'

'Rob, I want an answer or I'm going to start screaming and people will start running and very shortly you'll probably be hanging head first over that balcony, with any luck.'

Rob laughed and Fleur felt her left eye twitch. 'You think there's anyone left in this building after eight-thirty? It's like the Marie Celeste on a Bank Holiday.'

Fleur had so many questions that needed answering and she needed to boil them down to one simple one quickly, while she still felt in control.

'Why are you living here, Rob?'

'So, Papa was good to his word and didn't tell you,' said Rob, appearing to suddenly gain confidence as he threw back the covers and got out of bed, wearing only his tight designer pants, his taut abs giving Fleur a reminder of what she was missing. 'Can I get you a coffee?'

'If you get me a coffee I would like it red hot because I will be pouring it over your head.'

'Chill out, Fleur, we've come to a business arrangement, that's all. It's what men like me and your Dad do,' he said, with an exaggerated wink. 'I need to go to the loo and I'll tell you everything,' he added, as he started to jog for the toilet. 'I'll have three sugars in mine,' he said as he disappeared into the small bathroom. What was going on, wondered Fleur?

When Rob returned, still adjusting his underwear, Fleur was standing by the window, trying to think straight.

'Sit down, babe,' said Rob, straightening out the duvet. 'Don't worry, that's a coffee stain, honest.'

'I'm fine, thanks.' Fleur moved over to the small table and chairs and hovered there. She still wasn't sure if the whole bed-bug infestation was a reality or not, but she wasn't going to take any risks with the bed. She looked around the small space while Rob fixed himself an instant coffee with a mound of sugar. He sat down on the bed opposite her, parted his legs slightly and leaned forward, making Fleur avert her eyes.

'How've you been, babe?'

'Cut the crap. Either tell me or don't tell me, but don't try to make small talk.'

Rob's eyebrows jerked up his forehead and he sipped his coffee, which was clearly too hot for him, but he had to keep on drinking or admit his mistake. Fleur smiled to herself.

'Look, I don't want to cause any trouble between you and your dad, you know?'

Fleur stood up and put her bag on her shoulder and jangled the keys in her hand.

'Sit down, Fleur. I'll tell you. It's simple, your Dad didn't want me messing up your life so he offered me some money and the flat,' catching sight of Fleur's disbelief he quickly added, 'just the use of the flat for a bit. I had to let my place go but then the tour got delayed and I needed somewhere. Short-term, you understand. The tour is still going ahead, and we've secured some top venues. There's this Olympic stadium in…'

'Rob!' Fleur raised her voice to gain his attention, before returning to her usual volume, 'why would Pa offer you anything after what you did to me?'

'Technically I didn't do anything, you overreacted to…'

'Rob!'

'Okay, okay. He wanted to make sure that I agreed to whatever you wanted. Which I was going to do anyway. I've always wanted the best for you, you know that, yeah?'

'He paid you to agree to the annulment?'

'Pretty much, yeah. I mean I wouldn't usually be manipulated like that but I had a bit of a cash-flow problem and what with the tour dates being…' But Fleur was no longing listening, she was already closing the door behind her.

As Fleur left the apartment building she knew what Charlie meant when she said that the red mist descended. She wanted to lash out at someone, to scream, to release the burning from her lungs. She needed to get home as quickly as she could; she hoped that her father wasn't there because she really couldn't face him right now. Fleur wasn't up to facing anyone. There was only one person she wanted to see and she was a few thousand miles away, sunning herself in the Caribbean.

'Ted, can you give me a hand?' called Blue as he locked up the jeep.

Ted gave George a friendly shove and jogged over to Blue and Charlie. Charlie stood with one bag containing the essentials, the rest now safely locked in the cab of the jeep and she was feeling a bit wrong-footed. Blue had a brief word with Ted.

'This way,' said Blue, handing Charlie his sunglasses and grinning broadly. He patted Ted on the back and headed off down the beach to the water and Ted dutifully followed.

'What's happening?' asked Eleanor, who had been torn away from her book, now safely stored in the cab with most of everything else they'd brought with them.

'I don't know,' said Charlie slowly, 'but I bet it's going to be good.' She had never said a truer word. She watched Blue and Ted wade out into the sea and start to swim, they looked as if they were heading out to sea and Charlie started to walk towards the shore, all the time not taking her eyes off the two almost synchronised swimmers getting further away. Three more strokes and they both stopped swimming and while Ted trod water, Blue hauled himself out of the sea and onto a large white, partially covered, speedboat.

'I sincerely hope they are not stealing that,' she said under her breath.

'I hope they are. This is ace,' breathed George, who had silently joined her at the water's edge and was standing open-mouthed next to her. 'Blue is so much cooler than Uncle Felix.' She had to admit he was right.

The boat was soon in the shallows and Blue was helping everyone up a ladder and on board. Once on the boat, Millie instantly started to jump up and down and was thrilled by the effect it had as the boat rocked gently. George wasn't.

'No, no, no! Stop bouncing, Mills, or you'll fall in and be eaten by the sharks!'

Millie started screaming and Charlie was tempted to return to the beach and wave them off but, however much a quiet afternoon would have been bliss, she had a feeling that the boat trip, even with an excited Millie and a queasy George, would be so much better. And she wasn't wrong.

With life vests on the girls and George under strict instruction to stay seated whilst the boat was in motion, Blue stood at the wheel and started the engines, which roared into life. Charlie clutched Millie to her and as the boat pulled away Charlie felt her grin broaden. Once the boat was into deep water, Blue cranked up the power and the boat tore the sea apart as it sped away. The ride was surprisingly smooth and the cool wind and occasional spray on her face was pleasant. It was noisy, but you could just about hear each other over the engines. As they went round the west side of the island, Blue called out the names of various beaches and bays as they passed them; all equally beautiful as each other. Blue was looking away from the shore and he slowed the engine and pointed to his left.

'Here,' he said, quickly handing out binoculars. He pointed to a small dark blob in the water. 'Turtle,' he said. He added something else but it was drowned out by the shrieks from the children. When the turtle disappeared, Blue fired up the engines and they took off again at speed. Millie was delighted with the 'nockulars' and used them for the entire next leg of the journey. From the sea the island looked so lush and green, small hills became bigger ones and all gloriously swathed in a deep-green carpet of trees and vegetation. Many of the beaches were dotted with palm trees. It was like watching someone flick through a holiday brochure.

As they started making their way across the northern side of the island, Blue started to spout facts and Charlie could see the tour guide in him come to life.

'There are twenty-two small islands off this coast; all sorts of wildlife are reliant on them for food and shelter and we're going to take a bit of a closer look at a couple of them.' Blue introduced them to the weave of mangrove swamp and the mangrove nurseries. His keen eye spotted a mangrove cuckoo that was well camouflaged despite its yellow chest. Blue kept calling out directions and instructions until all the children were able to see it through the binoculars. Millie insisted she saw it, even though her binoculars were aimed at the sky, but she did see the large white heron-like bird that Blue informed them was a cattle egret. But the sighting of a large brownish sea bird diving for fish was too much for any of them to stand and hysterical giggles were all that could be heard once Blue had identified it as a booby.

They took off again and after a while Charlie realised they were getting further away from the main island and another island was coming into view quickly. Blue slowed the engines and introduced them to Jumby Bay, a private island of exclusive villas and an even more exclusive hotel. They weren't close enough to see much but they were still impressed, especially at the long list of celebrities that Blue reeled off who regularly holidayed there.

'One more stop and then home, okay?' asked Blue and he received a series of groans in response. The last stop was to be the best by far. He took them out into the Atlantic Ocean, where a pontoon was floating lazily in shallow water, created by a nearby reef. A man in an orange top helped Blue moor up and introduced himself as Sam the Wrangler.

'Welcome to Stingray City,' said Sam, handing out snorkels and masks before giving them a briefing on what to do and what not to do and reassuring Charlie several times that, despite the name, the stingrays were safe. The highlight was when he explained that the females grew up to four feet long with males being much smaller. However, to compensate for their size they had two penises. George looked at Ted in glee and Ted snorted his suppressed laughter. They waited for a large tourist party to leave before taking their turn in the water.

'Remember to do the stingray shuffle with both your feet on the sand and keep your thumb tucked away when you feed them and we'll be fine,' said Sam, as he eased himself into the water. Charlie waited her turn at the steps and watched the dark shadows circle around the pontoon as Millie clutched at her legs.

'No like sharks,' said Millie, her bottom lip wobbling. Blue, who was already in the water, reached up to her and, despite her fears, she instinctively went to him.

'They're not sharks, Millie. Come and see,' said Blue, holding her tight to him.

Charlie, Blue and Ted could stand up in the water. George and Eleanor swam off in search of the biggest of the rays. Blue put a mask on Millie and showed her how to put her face in the water so she could see the stingrays better and she popped up quickly with a big smile on her face.

'Whale!' she shouted before smacking her face back into the sea. The stingrays were greedy. Blue held Millie in one hand and squid in the other so she could watch the stingray eating from his hand. Eleanor and George were swimming around, surrounded by fish and frantically pointing at every one that came close to them, intermittently calling out Charlie's name to gain her attention to see their latest encounter.

An hour seemed to whiz by. Charlie felt herself relax as she floated and watched the stingrays fly through the water beneath her. Even at a few metres' deep she could see the bottom clearly and when she swam on the surface she felt like she was miles from anywhere. A wonderful sense of calm had engulfed her. The nearby reef had created a shallow pool that teemed with fish and Charlie marvelled how the clear water turned to turquoise nearby and then deep indigo as it became deeper and returned to the ocean.

Blue looked up, his eyes met Charlie's and she grinned back at him, 'This is amazing. Thank you,'

'It's perfect, isn't it?'

Chapter Twenty-Three

It occurred to Fleur that she was probably the only person who didn't know about the pay-off arrangement. They may all have agreed that it was the best thing to buy Rob off, to get helpless Fleur out of another situation she couldn't handle herself. Fleur stopped and looked around her. She'd walked as far as the footbridge and had seen no sign of a taxi. She walked to the middle of the bridge and stood at the edge looking up the river. She took in deep breaths but wished she hadn't, this was London after all. She needed a plan but that was very easy to think about and very hard to actually instigate. People bustled past, even jogged in some cases. All getting on with their lives, good and bad, straightforward and complicated, walk in the park and heartbreakingly difficult, but all getting on with them.

She was staring at nothing when her phone rang.

'How did it go?' asked Jonathan, concern etched into his voice.

'Basically, it is one giant bed bug.'

'I take it that's some sort of metaphor?'

'The bed bug is Rob.'

'Ah, I see. I'll be free at twelve. Do you want to meet for lunch?'

'No thanks, there's things I need to do. Your offer of a bed for a bit, does it still stand?'

'Absolutely, and if you like I could help you with that business plan.'

'Thanks Jonathan, you've been really kind. I don't want to take advantage, but when you keep making offers I can't refuse...'

'Then you should know that I also make a mean Thai red curry.'

Fleur re-joined the trickle of people crossing the footbridge, her step feeling a little lighter despite her unsuitable footwear. She headed into the Canary Wharf shops on a mission to purchase a couple of complete sets of clothes and, most importantly, some sensible shoes. Well, the last bit was a lie to herself, but she would at least attempt to find something slightly more comfortable than the stilts she was currently enduring.

Back at Jonathan's flat, Fleur found herself eagerly anticipating his arrival. She checked herself in the mirror one last time. She was pleased with the casual outfit she'd bought; you could never go wrong with skinny jeans and a Thomas Pink white shirt. She'd also managed to stock up on Jo Malone essentials so she smelt like herself again and not as if Jonathan was shadowing her. Sadly, she had failed to obtain the one thing she went for – sensible shoes. LK Bennett had failed her. The shop was her idea of shoe heaven and every pair was a beauty, so she had made a purchase but she wouldn't be running any marathons in these.

Jonathan arrived home and he was talking on his mobile as well as struggling with a full Waitrose bag and his briefcase. Fleur was almost bouncing on her new heels at the sight of him, she had so much to tell him. When she could see that his call wasn't going to end quickly she decided to look a little less desperate for attention, so relieved him of the shopping and went to put the coffee machine on. She earwigged Jonathan's conversation and was impressed by how official and commanding he sounded. The person he was speaking to was quite irate as she could hear the raised voice but couldn't make out the words and Jonathan was giving as good as he got in an utterly professional manner, of course. Fleur frothed the milk and lost the thread of the conversation for a short time. As she ladled froth onto the coffees she tuned back into the phone discussion.

'…as I have explained repeatedly; Miss French informed us of her intentions and gained verbal agreement from Social Services, yourself and your father, who are currently the closest individuals we have to trustees or guardians, and she confirmed all this in writing to us… No, I do not feel that there is any cause to seek her immediate dismissal on the grounds of… hello?' Jonathan switched off his phone. 'Thank God she's gone.' He smiled at Fleur and, taking in the domestic picture of her making coffee for him, his smile broadened.

Fleur was gripping the steel milk jug. 'That was Ruth, wasn't it?'

He nodded. 'I think Charlie might have a problem, but don't worry I'll do whatever I can. I promise.' He gave a short smile. 'Tell me about your day,' he said, taking one of the coffees and looking at her intently, making the little bean of excitement inside her start to jig about again.

They spent a relaxed and companionable evening that was interrupted only by two calls from Fleur's mother and one from her father. Fleur managed to convince her mother that she was staying in London to focus on her business idea and she ignored her father's call, just seeing his number flash up on her phone had made her cross. Jonathan had listened intently to all the details of Fleur's day and she could tell he was genuinely interested. She didn't get this very often; she knew people found her a bit superficial but Jonathan made her feel valued and that was a lovely trait in a friend.

He had also been true to his word and had made a delicious curry from scratch that she was very impressed by; she wouldn't have known where to start. Her mother had long ago given up on ever passing on her culinary prowess to her youngest child.

When the conversation moved onto Charlie she could sense his unease and he repeatedly mentioned client confidentiality although he told her everything anyway.

'Tomorrow I need to produce a letter from Charlie. It will sit on file as proof, you see, because now I've told Ruth that there is one I need to create one...'

'I see,' said Fleur, nodding earnestly. There was something in Jonathan's eyes that he was trying to get across and she wasn't picking up on it, 'and you're worried because it's not ethical?' she ventured.

'Yes, that too, but I'm also worried because there is no letter and I don't write like a girl ...'

'Oh, you want me to forge a letter from Charlie.' The penny finally dropped. 'Of course, I'd love to. It's no problem. In fact it's quite exciting. Get me a pen and paper!' she said, pulling her chair closer to the table.

They wrote it out in rough first with Jonathan dictating and Fleur changing his words to sound like Charlie and not a lawyer trying to talk street. When they were happy with it, Fleur copied it out onto some thick writing paper in her best Charlie-style scrawl and signed it with a flourish.

'The signature will be damn-near perfect,' she said proudly. 'We used to copy each other's signatures all the time when we were younger. Charlie is particularly good at it. She forged Ma's signature on a sick note for me once and you really couldn't tell the difference. Unfortunately, I'd written the letter and I'd spelled influenza wrong, so that gave it away, but otherwise it was the perfect crime.'

'Let's hope this is enough to buy her a bit more time,' said Jonathan, folding the letter neatly and slipping it into his briefcase.

During their second week in Antigua, Charlie found herself once again lying on a sun lounger watching the lights of the boats in the bay twinkle like Christmas. The children were sleeping well here. Charlie wasn't sure if it was the fact that they were on the go all day – either swimming, digging in the sand or playing cricket, or whether they were taking the Antiguan advice of 'Feel the breeze' to heart, but they were definitely relaxing.

Someone once told her that sea air was charged with healthy negative ions that meant you absorbed more oxygen and that made you sleepy. She didn't know if it was true but she liked the fact that something was working and it was giving her time to relax in the evenings. Time to think through all the things they had done that day and carefully store the memories. Somehow she felt even closer to the children here. Maybe it was because it was just her and them, she wasn't sure. She let out a jaw-aching yawn and heard someone laugh behind her.

'You still awake, party animal?' asked Blue, as he nudged her legs out of the way and joined her on her sun lounger for what was becoming a regular evening visit.

'Only just. How do you manage to get any work done? I have done nothing but walk to the beach, lie there half the day and walk back, and I'm shattered.'

'You get used to it after a while. I was wondering if you fancied a lime tomorrow?'

'I think Berta has got all the fruit we need, thanks.'

'Oh, I think you'll need this type of lime. It's the outdoor party kind. Lime is the local word for get-together and they don't get better than Sunday nights at Shirley Heights. Berta will child-mind and Ted can come if he fancies it. It's a big tradition here. I promise you'll love it.'

'I'm not sure.'

'You could walk from here, mind, but I know what a busy life you lead.' Charlie took a swipe at him and the back of her hand hit the solid muscle of his bicep, making her eyebrows raise in interest.

'Is there drinking?' she asked.

'Most definitely.'

'Then I'm not sure about Ted going…'

'Come on, let the boy live a little. How often does he get to let off a bit of steam? He's got no parents… I mean…' Blue sighed and the air whistled through his teeth.

'That's why we have to be the grown ups,' said Charlie, struggling with her desire to let Ted off the leash and experience things in the adult world and her need to keep him out of harm's way.

'It's your call. I'll not pressure you but if you let him come I promise to keep a close eye on him.'

'I'll think about it. Now clear off, I'm going to bed.'

'Great. I'll pick you both up before sunset,' and he started to jog away.

'When the hell is that exactly?' laughed Charlie, but he'd gone.

Berta had taken Sunday off, apart from the planned baby-sitting in the evening. So the children had toast for breakfast, which was a huge disappointment after the varied selection of omelettes, fruit hedgehogs and pancakes that Berta had been providing. They decided to take breakfast outside, sit out on the deck and take in the early-morning sun. The forlorn sight of the toast was instantly cheered up by the arrival of a hummingbird having its own breakfast from the bright-pink flowering plant that was sprawling out of a large urn.

Charlie felt bad for flinching when she had first caught sight of it, as with a quick glance it looked like a giant fly – the stuff of her nightmares. It appeared black at first but there was a hint of green and in the same split second it jolted to a new position and the true brilliance of its vivid colour was revealed. There was a blur of wings around the small body as it jerked from flower to flower, moving in any and every direction without warning. It was quite mesmerising to watch and all complaints about breakfast were quickly forgotten.

At Blue's suggestion, Charlie had decided to walk the children round to English Harbour; he promised it wasn't far and if they went early-ish they would be out of the worst of the sun. There was also the promise of an Italian restaurant for lunch that interested Ted.

Blue had promised it was a twenty-minute walk, but with four children and an unscheduled toilet stop at Berta's house, which was on the way, it took them nearer forty and Charlie had lost count of how many times she had replaced Millie's hat. Charlie was not surprised to find that English Harbour was pretty much the boat-mooring facility she had envisaged, but still it was a change of scenery and wherever you looked in Antigua it was stunning.

They had a good look at the boats and found somewhere to sit that was a little shady whilst they waited for the restaurant to open. They could see Nelson's Dockyard across the bay, making them feel like old hands as they reminisced about their island tour with Blue.

At twelve sharp the restaurant opened and they flooded in as if they hadn't been fed for days. The menu was familiar and the children debated long and hard over what to have. Soon they were tucking into meatballs, pasta and a selection of pizzas and silence reigned briefly. Charlie spotted the public telephone and felt a pang of guilt. She had no intention of switching on her mobile while she was here in case anyone was tracking it's location so she hadn't even told Fleur that they had arrived safely. She spent the meal tussling with her conscience and whether or not to make the phone call. If she called and things were kicking off – by 'things' she pictured Ruth having a meltdown – what would she do? Would she pack them up and get on the next flight? She wanted to believe that all was well, that nobody had even noticed they were missing and if she didn't call she could go on believing this for the rest of the holiday. Or, if she called, perhaps she could get that confirmed and stop worrying?

Ted was shovelling in chicken and jalapeno when he noticed Charlie's gaze was once again drawn to the phone. 'You can call home if you like?'

'There won't be anyone in, though!' laughed George.

'I hope not because if there is someone there, they're burglars,' pointed out Eleanor, looking a little alarmed.

Millie continued to eat and hum. Charlie stroked her hair and smiled at the others. 'We're okay as we are, and I'm sure everything is fine at home.' Right now everything was good and she didn't want to unsettle anyone, so she focused on her margarita pizza and tried to ignore the temptation of the phone.

An afternoon on the beach followed, with the usual sand-castle and trench building. Charlie was starting to relax a little and didn't watch them constantly, although they didn't stray far and always remained within shouting distance. They weren't the quietest of children so she could usually work out where they were without looking up. Today, Millie had decided she was in charge and this was causing great discussion but Charlie was a firm believer in letting them sort it out themselves wherever possible.

Ted was restless and couldn't seem to settle. He had plugged and unplugged his earphones a dozen times at least, been for a stroll up the beach and back and had a half-hearted attempt at a sandcastle with Millie. He jumped up as he spotted Blue's speedboat appear from behind the ruins of a fort and head for the jetty.

'I'm going to see if Blue needs a hand,' he said, as he jogged off along the sand. Charlie looked at Ted as he jogged away; he was definitely having a growth spurt, in fact he was growing like a weed. George abandoned his trench and ran off after Ted, they were getting on well. They were all getting on well. Antigua suited everyone and Charlie was glad that she hadn't made the phone call home.

'No, Eleanor, I'm in charge!' shouted Millie, instantly dispelling Charlie's happy contemplations.

'Charlie!' called Eleanor, 'Millie meltdown alert!'

'Millie, you're not in charge,' said Charlie.

'I am in charge!'

'Millie,' warned Charlie.

'I. Am. In. Charge!' yelled Millie.

Charlie heard Blue before she saw him, now she was accustomed to his dulcet tones. It was British with a hint of the Caribbean, which was stronger here than in London.

'How was English Harbour?' he said, sitting down cross-legged on the edge of her towel.

'Lovely, thanks. You had a good day?'

'Yep, lots of Americans. They're great, they find everything 'awesome'!' he grinned. 'Have you decided about tonight and me-laddo here?'

'What's this?' asked Ted, flopping down on the sand next to them.

'It's a local party…' started Blue.

'Yeah, count me in,' said Ted.

'Cheers,' said Charlie, giving Blue a mock death stare, 'now I'm the bad guy if I say no.'

'There's no need to say no. You'll behave, won't you Tedward?'

'Oh, yeah, course. Good as gold, me. Is there beer?' he grinned. Charlie shook her head and lay back on her towel as she heard Ted and Blue high-five each other above her.

'I. Am. In. Charge!' repeated a frustrated Millie, turning an unusual colour. Charlie could see the benefits of maybe having a few hours out.

Chapter Twenty-Four

Shirley Heights was ridiculously close to the villa. It was on the peak of the hillside behind it. Blue was greeted warmly by everyone he met, with lots of handshakes, hugs and backslapping. He led Ted and Charlie through the restaurant and bought drinks, before they went and stood with others to watch the sun go down. Charlie was amazed at the speed it travelled. At home it took ages for the sun to set, but here you could actually see it moving, falling, melting into the hills behind Nelson's Dockyard and lighting up the sea.

As it sank lower, Blue leaned in close to Charlie and whispered to her. 'Keep watching, don't even blink. If I'm right, you won't believe what you're about to see.' Charlie dared not move and stayed glued to the falling orange mass. It was a clear night, with barely a cloud. The chatter of those around lessened as others joined them – it wasn't silent, there were too many people, but there was an excited hush. Charlie was beginning to think that Blue was winding her up as the last piece of the sun disappeared but he wasn't. At the last moment, as the sun disappeared, there was a glimpse of green light and it was gone. The crowd gasped and burst into spontaneous applause and a steel band broke into life.

'That was incredible. Does it happen every night?'

'No. Not every night, it's pretty rare but the conditions were good tonight. We caught lucky.' His eyes kept her gaze for a moment.

'You know what? I'm starting to think that too.'

It was still surprisingly light, despite the sun having set, and they meandered about the stalls that sold all sorts of food. There were easily a couple of hundred people in the tiny space and Charlie tried to keep sight of Ted without him seeing her.

'This isn't London, he's fine. Come and dance,' Blue said, taking her arm. Charlie made a pathetic effort to protest but found herself pulled by the hand and then she was dancing. The music felt like it came from within. The steel band mixing up the play list from the traditional 'One Love' by Bob Marley to Daft Punk's 'Get Lucky'. The dancing was an eclectic mix, there were a lot of tourists but there were lots of locals too and the difference in rhythm was strikingly obvious. Blue seemed to have picked up the local ways and was guiding Charlie with his hips. The dancing and the music were seductive and so was the company and with each rum punch Blue grew more and more tempting.

Charlie caught sight of Ted on and off during the evening and each time he was chatting to a girl, the same girl, and the way she was looking at Ted set off alarm bells. It was dark now, the darkness suddenly appearing and cloaking them all. The music had changed – the steel band had handed over to a local calypso group and the pace of the dancers had slowed.

'Sorry, Blue, I'm done in and I think Ted and I should be heading back now.'

'Give him another five minutes – he's only just plucked up the courage to dance.' Blue nodded to the darker side of the dancing couples, where Charlie spotted Ted dancing with the girl – her head was resting on Ted's shoulder and her eyes were closed. 'Come on, let's have one more dance ourselves, then I'll drive you both back.' Charlie was rooted to the spot and was taking in the details of the girl Ted was dancing with. She looked a bit older than Ted, most likely local, with her dark skin and neat cornrows. She was very slim and was wearing a short dress and flat shoes. There was a 'Kipper List' nominee if ever she'd seen one.

Blue tugged on Charlie's hand and she dragged her eyes away from Ted. As they danced and slowly turned to the music Charlie found herself searching the crowd on each turn for a glimpse of Ted until Blue pulled her tighter to him and she could only concentrate on him.

'You don't have to worry about him, you know. He's a sensible lad.'

Charlie pulled her head back so that she could see his face clearly, 'It's my job, it's what I do.' She started to scan again and Blue pulled her closer. 'Charlie, I think I might ask if I can kiss you later, but it depends,' he whispered.

Charlie's heart rate suddenly increased and a million reasons why that would be a bad idea streamed through her head.

'It depends on what?'

'On whether or not you want to be kissed,' he said, his voice growing huskier.

Charlie had to admit that the thought of being kissed by Blue had already crossed her mind more than once over the last few days. 'I think there are a million reasons why that would be a very bad idea.'

'But would you like it?'

'I might,' she said breathily into his ear and she felt him shudder in response.

'That's good to know,' he said, then added, 'we'd best get you home.'

They left the other people dancing and Blue nudged Ted in the back as they past, 'Home time, lover boy.'

Ted said an awkward good-bye to the girl he'd been dancing with and wandered away from the crowds.

Fleur turned over in Jonathan's big bed and looked at the clock again in disbelief, it was three o'clock. She was wide awake and now her mind was racing there was no chance of going back to sleep. She kept going over the day's events and trying to work out what to do next. She felt she needed to talk it over with Jonathan, but he would be asleep. He was such a good listener and as she now had a couple of suggestions for how she could tackle the situation with her father she wanted to know what he thought.

Fleur tried a couple more times to go back to sleep, but eventually gave in to her restlessness and got up. She pulled on Jonathan's dressing gown and traipsed through to the living room. There was no light except the dim glow from the digital clock on the oven that only served to remind her it was still the middle of the night.

She tussled with her choices; switch on the kettle for a cuppa and risk waking the sleeping Jonathan or wander back to bed and fight the boredom for a few more hours. She watched Jonathan sleeping. He had kicked off his duvet and was lying curled up in a foetal position; she leaned over him a little to see if she could see his facial expression. He stretched and started to stir, which pleased Fleur – if he woke up of his own accord she would have nothing to feel guilty about and not only could she then have a cup of coffee, she would also have someone to talk to. Unfortunately for Fleur he quickly snuggled down again and was still sound asleep. She couldn't deliberately wake him, she wasn't that cruel. She huffed involuntarily, turned to leave and walked straight into the coffee table. 'Shit! Ow!' She hopped about as she rubbed her injured shin.

'Fleur?' said Jonathan, frantically feeling for the light switch.

'Argh!' Fleur blinked hard as the light blinded her, and she continued to rub her leg.

'You look like a Premiership footballer trying to get a penalty,' he chuckled before checking his watch.

'I'm really sorry, I didn't mean to wake you… actually I did want you to wake up but not like this. Sorry.' She shrugged and sank down next to him on the sofa, still preoccupied by the bump coming up on her shin. At least she had someone to chat to now, she thought, even if it had resulted in a minor injury.

'Right, I see.' Jonathan looked pleased and he dragged a hand through his hair as his eyes ran up and down Fleur's body. She was wearing a pale-pink lace-edged vest top and matching hot-pants-style bottoms. Fleur lay back on the sofa and sighed loudly as she thought through the potential next steps she had conjured up. Jonathan watched her closely and moved over so that Fleur could lie stretched out next to him. She shuffled over.

'Thanks,' she said, turning to face him and realising just how close they now were. She felt she was invading his space. 'Oh,' she said, assessing the situation, 'would you like…' but she failed to finish the sentence before Jonathan's lips were on hers, full of pent-up passion and desire. Fleur lingered a fraction too long and felt his arms pull her to him and she was up against something intrusive and rigid between them which made her spring away. 'Coffee! I was asking you if you wanted a coffee!'

'What?' said Jonathan, his expression one of total confusion.

Fleur scrambled off the sofa and stood over him, her heart racing. She had held Jonathan up on a pedestal as someone who liked her for who she was, not someone who wanted to get her into bed, and right now he had ceremoniously tumbled off that pedestal. 'Why did you do that?' she said, trying, but failing, to hide her hurt feelings.

'You said … no sorry, I thought you said you came to wake me and you lay here,' he indicated the sofa, his expression was contrite, 'I'm so sorry, I misread the situation, but it was a genuine mistake.'

'It was a mistake to stay here, you're the same as all the rest,' she said sadly. She'd never had a male friend like Jonathan before and now she felt she had lost him. He had unwittingly crossed a line and there was no going back to the easy platonic relationship they'd enjoyed because she'd always know what he really wanted from her. As she shook her head a tear slid down her cheek, and she turned and left the room, her body weighed down by disappointment. Jonathan sighed as he rubbed his face with his palms, blinking hard before slumping back against the sofa – he was the picture of regret.

Back at the villa, Blue was chatting to Berta by the front door whilst Charlie got two beers from the fridge.

'Tigi is a stubborn old chap,' said Blue with a chuckle.

'Less of the old,' said Berta, giving Blue a look worthy of a Hollywood diva. 'He's the same age as me!'

'So obviously he's not old,' said Blue, raking his fingers through his already unkempt hair. 'But he's struggling with the MS more than he'll let on.'

Berta nodded wisely. 'I know he would never admit it but he was frightened when you were in London and so grateful when you came home. When that wicked disease strikes he can't cope on his own,' said Berta, adjusting the bag strap on her shoulder.

'I guessed as much, but don't go saying that to Tig or he'll go off like a fire cracker.'

'Hee-Hee,' screeched Berta as she slapped Blue on the back. 'You're right there.' She left her hand on his back as her smile waned and she patted him gently. 'You're doing a good job looking after him,' she said, her smile sincere but melancholy.

'And don't say that either!' said Blue, his tone light-hearted as he opened the door for Berta to leave.

'I won't, I value my eardrums too much!' she said, her humour quickly returning as she left, chuckling to herself.

Charlie didn't like to admit that she was earwigging their conversation and she jumped slightly as Ted loomed up behind her. 'I thought you'd turned in,' she said, feeling a little guilty.

'Yeah, I'm heading up now. I just wanted to say I had a good time tonight, so if you were going again next week I'd be up for it.'

'I bet you would! Who was she, then?'

Ted looked like he was about to say 'who' but Charlie's expression pre-empted his denial. 'Esther, her name is Esther. She's at school but she helps her mother with hair braiding on the beach. She said she'd do the girls' at a discount,' he said, his voice full of awe.

'She sounds like a good person to know,' said Charlie, giving him a friendly slap on the back as they left the kitchen together. 'Take it easy, okay?'

'Char-lie,' complained Ted and he disappeared upstairs. Charlie joined Blue by the pool and handed him a beer.

'So, what's your story, Charlie?' asked Blue, swigging from the bottle.

'Nothing exciting. I'd rather hear about how you made Antigua your home.'

'That's not very exciting either. I came for a holiday and I stayed. That was six years ago nearly.' He swigged his beer and glanced at Charlie, who was waiting for more of an explanation.

'You stayed? Just like that?'

Blue laughed. 'Not exactly. I did a few odd jobs, bar work in hotels, that sort of thing. I met Tigi and he wanted to expand his business into the boat trips. I spent a lot of time in my youth with boats and I knew I wanted to stay here, so we decided to go into business together.'

'Big decision, though. Will you ever go back to the UK, do you think?'

She saw the muscles tense in his neck. He shook his head. 'This is my home now and there's the business and Tigi. We share a place together. And before you ask, no we're not gay.'

She smiled at the thought. She opened her mouth to speak but decided not to raise the question of the children right now. 'What did you do before you came here?'

223

'University. I was lining up for a job in entomology when I decided to take a look at the world. I shoved a pin in a map and ended up in the Caribbean.'

'That's lucky. If I stuck a pin in a map, knowing my luck, I'd end up in the Arctic or, worse still, Clacton-on-Sea!'

'I like Clacton – good beach, nice pier and big amusement arcades.' Charlie pulled a face at him. 'I was about ten when I visited, so it ticked all my boxes back then.'

'You really stuck a pin in a map and ended up here?'

'Not exactly. I signed up to do a moth study in Barbados but the funding got cut.' He smiled and paused. 'I decided to come anyway. Bummed around Barbados for a bit and got a job moving a boat around the islands, so I ended up here.' He paused for a moment. 'I felt at peace here, something I hadn't felt for a long time. It felt like home.'

They sat in silence for a while listening to the rhythmic calls of the tree frogs. 'I like it here,' said Charlie. 'I can see why you stayed.' She turned and gave him a brief smile.

'Where are you at home, Charlie?'

'London,' she said without thinking.

'No, I don't mean where do you live. I mean where are you at peace?' He turned to study her as she thought.

Charlie sipped her beer and tried to ignore Blue's gaze. When the silence had gone on too long she spoke. 'I was happiest with the Cobleys, but I don't think I've ever had that feeling of being at peace.'

'I hope you find it one day,' said Blue as he finished his beer and put the bottle on the ground. 'I should be making tracks,' he said, but didn't move from his seat.

'Someone waiting for you at home?'

'Only Tigi and he'll be asleep on the porch by now.'

'Right,' said Charlie, and Blue smiled before getting to his feet.

'You don't have to leave,' she said, feeling the colour rush to her cheeks. She thought she'd been promised a kiss and now she really wanted it.

'I think I probably should go,' he said lingering, 'but…'

'You're not great at making decisions, are you?' said Charlie lightly as she stood up. Blue shrugged and gave her a cheeky smile. He stepped forward and Charlie held her breath. As Blue leaned slowly forward she closed her eyes. She waited. Charlie's cheeks were still burning and she was starting to feel awkward. At last Blue's lips met hers with the lightest of kisses, sending shivers all over her body like city lights coming back on after a power cut.

She opened her eyes to see Blue looking coy. She could no longer hear the tree frogs, only the thump of her own pulse in her ears. He stood and stared at her but said nothing. 'So, anyway, I'm going to bed,' she said, finishing her beer and picking up Blue's empty bottle.

'Okay, 'night,' said Blue and he jogged down the steps and disappeared. That wasn't the effect she had hoped the mention of bed would have on him. She sighed. It was probably for the best. It was the drink and the effect of Shirley Heights getting to her, and she knew sex was a complication they didn't need. Charlie wandered inside and set about tidying up in the faint hope that it would return her heart rate to normal.

Upstairs Charlie checked on the girls, who were both fast asleep. She retrieved Pooh from the floor and pushed him gently into Millie's arms. She shut their bedroom door and went across the landing to her own room. It was dark and she padded straight through to the en suite. As she flicked on the light, she saw movement in the bedroom and she grabbed the nearest thing to a weapon she could find.

'Please don't make me look like Edna Turnblad!' said Blue, in mock horror at the sight of Charlie wielding a can of hairspray.

'You complete idiot, I could have sprayed this in your eyes! What are you doing?' She lowered her weapon and took in the sight of Blue in just his snugly fitted briefs, lying on her bed that was now strewn with bright-orange flowers.

'I'm being romantic and spontaneous and you said you were going to bed.' He patted the bed next to him and the flowers bounced about.

'They better not stain that white cover or Berta will be after us,' Charlie grinned at him. He was fun and she was already imagining what sex with him was going to be like and she knew that was going to be fun too.

'They're from the Flamboyant tree,' he said with a grin. 'I think I might have brought in a couple of bugs as well, actually,' said Blue, sweeping them to the floor before leaping back on, 'no pressure,' he grinned as he stroked the space next to him.

Charlie thought for a nanosecond then ran and jumped on the bed next to him and through stifled laughter they kissed each other. It wasn't a particularly coordinated affair but it felt right and it was urgent and exciting. Charlie yanked her dress off over her head and got a bit stuck. 'Er, help me, could you?' she asked, her voice muffled by the dress.

'I could,' purred Blue, 'or I could slowly torture you,' he said, pushing her back onto the bed and feathering kisses across the tiny sliver of exposed skin above her knicker-line. Charlie wriggled a little in an attempt to free herself from the dress and Blue relented and started to pull the dress off for her. The dress revealed Charlie's stomach and as it did so she heard a gasp from Blue, but couldn't see what was happening because the dress was still covering her head.

'Holy crap! What the hell is that?' said Blue staring at Charlie's midriff. Realisation dawned and she no longer wanted her face visible. Total embarrassment was seeping through her. He pulled the dress off her to reveal she had her eyes tight shut. He returned his attention to what was probably the worst tattoo ever inked. It had the face of some sort of black creature in the centre and then something that looked like feathers on its head. Thankfully it was only small, although that didn't diminish its ghastliness.

'Could you just not look at it?' mumbled Charlie, her stomach

226

muscles clenched, partly from the touch of Blue's fingers and partly from the gut-twisting embarrassment.

'Is it a cross between Darth Vader and the Indian from the Village People?' he said, twisting his head to try and work it out.

'Don't,' groaned Charlie.

'There must be a story here,' said Blue as he traced his fingers over the faded blue and black lines on her abs.

Charlie sighed heavily, 'I was seventeen, a mate said they knew someone who was training to be a tattooist and would do it for free,' she said, with her eyes still closed and her concentration waning as Blue's fingers continued to trace the pattern on her flesh.

Blue studied it a little closer, 'I still have absolutely no idea what it is. Could it be the devil wearing a chicken for a hat?' he shuffled down the bed to have a closer look from a different angle and Charlie groaned.

Charlie took a deep breath and sat up. 'It's meant to be a panther's head. It means strength and courage.'

'Right, and is that a scar or part of the feather pattern on its head?'

'It has wings, to symbolise peace and freedom,' said Charlie, ignoring the comment about her scar. The scar was the whole reason she had got it done. Every time she had caught sight of her scar it had reminded her of her operation and the fact that she could never be a mother. The tattoo was meant to hide it. They both stared at the discoloured artwork.

'Do you, um, like how it turned out?' said Blue, failing to stifle his laughter.

Charlie gave him a playful slap, 'I hate it. I hated it the minute I saw it, but it was too late.'

'Oh, it's not that bad,' he said, having another look. A grin spread across his face, 'Actually, it's frigging hideous,' said Blue eventually, and Charlie started to laugh. 'Seriously, it's awful,' said Blue, his face now edging towards Charlie's.

'Someone once told me that if this was the biggest mistake I made in my life I would be doing okay. So, I kind of judge things against the tattoo.'

'Right, so am I a mistake and if so how do I measure up to the tattoo?' he breathed.

'I fear you are going to come close,' said Charlie, feeling her pulse quicken. The frenzied kissing started again and they found they were no more co-ordinated than the last time. Charlie tugged off her underwear and was quickly pulling a naked Blue on top of her. Blue groaned and Charlie quickly put her hand to his mouth. 'Shh, no noise, we mustn't wake the children.'

The sex was hot and sweaty and very physical and they found themselves lying on the bed trying to catch their breath. When her breathing had returned to almost normal Charlie went to get her pants but was pulled back on the bed by Blue.

'Er, excuse me, don't love me and leave me. I haven't finished with you yet,' and he drew her into his arms and kissed her. This time it was slow and measured and Charlie felt her muscles relax as she melted into it. She was so tight against him she could barely breathe. She ran her hands over the arms that held her and squeezed the solid muscles of his biceps. There was no getting away from it, Blue had the most amazing body and Charlie was happy to explore it some more. She didn't like the sense of being trapped beneath Blue, though she wasn't afraid, but she pushed him off her and he released her immediately.

'Are you okay?' There was concern in his voice.

'My turn on top,' she said straddling him. She felt totally uninhibited with him and that was a turn-on in itself. She leant forward and looked into his eyes, those ridiculously blue eyes, and kissed him slowly at first but her own desire soon increased the speed.

'You are so my kind of woman,' he said and she stifled another moan from him as she slid herself onto her target. He took hold of her backside and moved to the rhythm that Charlie was dictating. The sensations pulsed through her body until she finally arched her back and shuddered.

'Slowly!' she pleaded and he released his grip and drew her into his arms. He kissed her lightly on the lips.

'You are something else, Charlie,' he said and he kissed her again.

Chapter Twenty-Five

Charlie smiled as she retrieved her clothes, which were scattered around the room. She felt like such a hussy but it had been fun and the odd thing was that although it was the last thing she'd thought she needed, it turned out it was exactly the right thing. She picked up Blue's t-shirt, folded it carefully and put it on the bed. He would be out of the shower in a minute or two. She reached for his trousers and as she lifted them from their prone position the pocket contents scattered across the floor, making a noise. Charlie winced at the sound, quickly threw the trousers onto the bed and started to collect the scattered items: a bunch of keys, some coins, a printed email and a yo-yo.

As she stuffed the things back into the trouser pocket she caught sight of her name on the email. She didn't mean to pry but she thought her eyes were playing tricks so she had to have a closer look to prove to herself she hadn't imagined it.

The email was confirmation of Felix's agreement for Ruth to be the children's guardian and to relinquish Charlie of her duties – and it was dated two days ago. She was effectively sacked, so was she now here with the children illegally? She heard the water stop in the shower and shoved the email back into his pocket and folded the trousers. Charlie jumped back into bed and pulled up the covers. She didn't feel as uninhibited all of a sudden.

Blue emerged from the bathroom with a towel slung low around his hips and he was rubbing his hair dry with a small towel. He caught sight of Charlie sitting up in bed and checked his watch.

'I don't have time for a repeat performance, I'm afraid, but there's always tomorrow,' he said as he leaned over to kiss her. Charlie froze. It suddenly all felt wrong and she could feel the fire of temper start to burn inside her.

'You okay?' he asked, taking in her rigid form.

'I thought I heard one of the children. They'll be in here in a minute and I don't want them to see you here.' It was only a half-lie.

'I understand. I promise they'll never know I was here,' he said, pulling his t-shirt on and running his fingers through his wet hair, which amazingly seemed to be all it needed to style it. Charlie studied him as he tugged on his clothes. When she looked at him now she could see a glimpse of perhaps what George would look like as he matured; the fair hair, the full lips and the distinct jawline.

He noticed her studying him and his smile radiated something akin to desire in her direction. Blue finished getting dressed and leaned across the bed to kiss Charlie, who was still staring intently at him. Blue grazed her lips. Briefly it lightened her heart and she felt her shoulders relax. She closed her eyes and let him kiss her. What was happening?

There was the faint sound of small bare feet padding across the landing and Charlie took a sharp intake of breath. Blue studied her face for a moment.

'You're beautiful, Charlie. I'll see you later,' and before she could start to panic and work out where to hide him he was climbing over the white-painted balcony railings. She watched him until her bedroom door opened and she had to drag her eyes away. Millie toddled in, yawning, and stood at the side of the bed with her arms in the air, waiting for Charlie to pick her up. She pulled Millie into bed, relishing the little person clinging to her and let her tears silently seep into the pillow.

A couple of days later, Charlie was spending another morning on autopilot, realising that they already had a fairly set routine; they stayed around the villa and pool in the morning then went down to the beach in the afternoon. It was oddly comforting to her. Lunch was a quiet affair with sandwiches and salad on the veranda. Charlie re-basted the children in factor fifty and gathered up the usual collection of towels and buckets and they headed down the now-familiar path to the beach. With the afternoon sun warming them, they walked along to the background noise of George jabbering on about sharks.

'Charlie, can I talk to you about Blue?' asked Ted tentatively and Charlie felt her eyes widen involuntarily. She slowed her pace to let the others get slightly ahead and for once was pleased that George was increasing his volume. She sucked in air and waited for the accusations to fly, but nothing came.

'Out with it, Ted!' Her impatience underlining the words.

'He's actually okay. Right?'

'I'm the wrong person to ask, Ted. I thought I was good at judging people but I don't think I'm as good at it as I thought I was.'

'Riiiight,' said Ted slowly. He appeared to sense Charlie's mood but could not understand why. 'Anyway, yesterday Blue said that he could do with a hand with the boats, because Tigi doesn't work as much as he used to, and I thought I might offer to help him while we're here. What do you think?'

Charlie let out the breath she hadn't realised she'd been holding in. 'I don't see why not. I'd ask him what he's paying first,' she said, looking across at Ted for the first time.

'I'm not doing it for free, I'm no goon,' he said, giving her a playful punch on the arm and she swung a bucket at him.

The beach was quiet and they went to their usual patch, halfway between the beach bar and the sea urchins, and set up their things. Millie and the yellow bucket were almost a blur as she ran up and down in the shallow water squealing happily at her simple game. Charlie sat on the towel, hugging her knees; her mind was full of so many thoughts but her dominant thought was what the hell was Blue up to? She wanted to challenge him on his motivations for spending the night with her. Was it guilt at giving the go-ahead for her to be sacked or perhaps it was a leaving gift? She suddenly felt that she was running out of time and she needed to have a conversation with him about the children. But as Blue was working it would have to wait.

Ted was on child-watch and was supervising the build of an intricate multiple castle-and-moat system while Charlie was engrossed in her latest holiday read. After a few minutes she heard Ted whistle. She nudged her sunglasses onto the top of her head, turned down the corner of her paperback and sat up. Blue was helping tourists out of a boat and onto the small wooden jetty and Ted was now jogging along the beach towards him. Clearly he'd felt that a whistle was enough of a handover in the child-minding department. Charlie watched them exchange greetings and Ted helped the last few passengers off the boat. Blue scanned the beach and, catching sight of Charlie looking in his direction, he waved enthusiastically. Charlie faltered before discreetly putting her hand up in acknowledgement; she could see him grinning even from this distance.

Ted and Blue were laughing as they meandered back along the beach and Charlie could feel her impatience growing. Ted and Blue shook hands and Blue jogged over to Charlie. With George, Eleanor and Millie all manning the moat and fully occupied by trying to bail it out, Charlie saw this as her chance to speak to Blue. She had given herself a good talking to and was happy she knew what she was going to say.

'I've done a deal with Ted. He's going to do a spot of child-minding while we get a drink, assuming you fancy one,' said Blue, his warm disarming smile not working quite as well as it once had.

'Yeah, that would be good,' she said, getting to her feet and pulling on her beach dress. Ted gave her the thumbs-up in between digging furiously to save the sandcastles.

They bought drinks and found a table on the edge of the bar area, away from anyone else. After a few swigs of rum punch, Charlie felt the pleasant warmth in her gut and hoped that would be enough to get her through the conversation.

'So, Felix, when were you going to tell me I'd lost my job?' said Charlie, her voice even and measured in total contrast to her emotions. 'I read the email this morning.'

Blue hesitated for a second as he was about to take a sip of his beer but he recovered quickly. 'Please don't call me that. That was someone I left behind nearly six years ago.'

'Okay, Blue, so if I'm sacked, does this now count as child-kidnap or do I hand them over to you before Ruth gets me arrested?'

'Ruth doesn't know you're here. I stalled as long as I could before answering her email.'

'Not long enough though, eh?'

Sweat glistened on his top lip. 'I can't help the children. Ruth can. I'm really sorry you and her don't get on but…'

'They need you, Blue. They need someone who loves them.'

Blue picked up his beer and took a few gulps before placing the condensation-covered bottle on the table and scowling at it.

'So that was why you came here,' he said, turning his eyes back onto Charlie. A glint of something cold was visible in them now.

'No, I came here because Toby booked a holiday and, if you remember, you had buggered off without telling anyone where you were going. And hang on a minute – if you knew I was sacked and now possibly about to be arrested, why did you sleep with me?' she could feel her annoyance building.

Blue started to laugh and shake his head. 'Because, Charlie, despite my best efforts you have walked into my life and turned everything onto its arse.' His sad eyes were fixed on hers.

Charlie's temper was building at a rate of knots, 'Stop it, Blue, you're making this worse. Let's leave you and me out of it.' Charlie felt the unwelcome emotion catch in her throat and she took one more sip of rum punch before getting to her feet. 'You know where I am when you're ready to talk... about the children.'

Chapter Twenty-Six

Fleur was crying again as she packed a case, grabbing whatever she could see through the tears. The incident with Jonathan had really upset her, and there was only one person left she felt she could trust. She locked the Louis Vuitton and hauled it with difficulty downstairs. Fleur burst into her father's study, almost panting with the effort of the emotion.

'Hang on, Royd, something has come up. I'll call you back,' and her father abruptly ended his call. 'Sweetheart, what's wrong?'

'You. Men. Everything. Where do I start?' She snorted very inelegantly. 'You let me think you were cheating on Ma and now I find out that you've been cheating on me with Rob!' Fleur looked puzzled by her own sentence.

'Fleur, have you been drinking?'

'So what if I had a gin on the train? I'm a grown up. I mean an adult,' she blinked hard as she tried to maintain focus.

'Whatever Rob has said to you has clearly upset you but you know you can't trust that boy,' he said, coming around to Fleur's side of the desk.

'Don't go blaming Rob! You gave him your flat and you gave him money to keep quiet. You treat me like a child and it needs to stop.' She swayed slightly and grabbed the desk for support.

'Fleur, you need to calm down.' Her father's voice was calm and gentle.

'No, I need my passport.' She stared boldly at her father until the pause had gone on too long and she added reluctantly, 'please.'

'Why don't you take some time to think things through, sleep off the alcohol perhaps?'

'Passport, please.'

'Fleur,' he said again, but her face remained adamant. Mr Van Benton opened a cupboard, tapped in a digital code to the small safe and it sprung open. He handed Fleur her passport but kept hold of it as she tried to take it.

'Where shall I tell your mother that you've gone?'

'To see Charlie,' was all she could manage before snatching the passport and, failing badly to stifle more tears, she left the room, slamming the door behind her. Outside the study she came to an abrupt stop as Wriggly sat staring at her. He tilted his head from side to side and Fleur couldn't work out if he was puzzled or if he was shaking his head at her. She crouched down to him.

'Wriggly, you be a good boy for Ma and Pa and I'll be back soon.' She turned around and marched back into the office.

'Uh, hang on a second, Royd, no it's all right, you don't need to call back,' he put his hand over the receiver. 'Yes, sweetheart? No, not you, Royd.'

'You need to take care of Wriggly… and the horses…'

'Of course. Anything else?'

Fleur tried to think but after three large G and Ts it was getting tricky, 'Um. No.'

'Take care, Fleur. Remember that we love you.'

Charlie heard the sound of familiar footsteps coming to join her by the pool and she prepared herself for a confrontation as she sipped her pineapple juice. She kept her gaze on the bay and the innocent twinkling lights of the boats moored there. She eventually looked up to see why her visitor hadn't sat down and was surprised to see Tigi – and it showed on her face.

'Sorry to interrupt your leisure time, Charlie, but…' he paused and held out a scrawled note in his hand. Charlie took it from him and read it. 'Sorry Tig, I need to get away for a few days and clear my head. Ask Ted to help cover. He's a good lad. Will be in touch. Blue.'

'Did he explain what happened?' asked Charlie.

'Nope.'

Charlie didn't know Tigi well enough to tell him everything. 'Do you know where he's gone?'

'Nope, but he's taken one of the small boats. This is all I know,' he said, taking back the note and folding it with care. 'I can ask someone to cover the jeep tours but I will need someone to come on the boat tours with me. Would you be happy to let Ted do that?'

'It's up to Ted, but I'm happy for you to ask him.' She checked her watch, 'He'll still be awake so I'll ask him now if you like?'

Charlie got up from the sun lounger but paused before she headed inside. She turned to Tigi, 'I bet Blue gets through lots of girls, doesn't he?'

'Oh, yeah, he's a mightily popular young man.'

'I thought so,' she said sadly.

Next morning Ted was first up and was chattering to Berta. He was much more like his younger self and less the self-conscious teen and it brought a smile to Charlie's face as she deposited a tired-looking Millie at the breakfast table. Millie instantly got down and went off to the TV room.

'Morning Berta.'

'Good morning, Charlie. I hear your man Blue has taken a sabbatical?'

'It would seem that way,' said Charlie, avoiding making any

238

fuss about the reference to him being her man; she assumed this was just a local phrase.

'I'm off to work, don't know what time I'll be back,' said Ted with a grin and he picked up his phone and almost ran from the room in his enthusiasm.

'You're keen,' said Charlie, but he was already out of the villa. Charlie and Berta were left in the kitchen and the two women smiled at each other. Berta busied herself with checking cupboards and adding items to an already very long shopping list.

'Is Tigi going to be all right with Blue away?' asked Charlie tentatively. She guessed she wasn't meant to know about Tigi's condition.

Berta paused and sighed. 'He'll tell you he's fine on his own, but he's not.'

'Is he safe on the boat with Ted?'

'He wouldn't take any risks with passengers, so don't worry about Ted. It's only himself he doesn't take proper care of.'

'Does he have any family?'

Berta nodded and they were both momentarily distracted as George sidled into the kitchen and slumped onto a chair without speaking. 'He has a brother but he doesn't live here. Tigi's from Saint Martin,' said Berta, getting a plate out of the cupboard.

George leaned forward. 'Does that make Tigi a Martian? Or a Martini?' he giggled as Berta passed him a croissant. They waited for George to leave the room and as the giggling faded Charlie turned back to Berta.

'Ted seems to have made friends with a local girl,' Charlie said, her voice tentative.

'Esther,' said Berta, as she inspected the levels in her flour jar.

'Yep, that's her,' said Charlie, her head snapping around in interest, 'Did he mention her?'

'Nope, but she mentioned him. Esther is my niece,' Berta

straightened up and locked eyes with Charlie before smiling. 'Esther is a good girl, she works hard and she cares for her Momma. I would hate to see that change.'

Charlie felt her hackles rise at the same time as her left eyebrow. 'I'm guessing we feel quite similar about this. I don't want Ted to have his head turned either.'

It was Berta's turn to raise an eyebrow and the warm breeze that had been flowing through the villa suddenly bore a chill.

The next couple of days went by relatively smoothly with the now rigid routine of swimming pool, lunch, beach and sandcastles. Charlie was relaxed at the beach and was speeding through another paperback, which was a particularly gripping thriller. When other people were packing up, Charlie realised it must be getting late. Ted and Tigi had come back from the boat about an hour before but, apart from a wave, he had stayed down at the jetty with Tigi.

Charlie gathered up a yawning Millie and a bucketful of shells that Eleanor had collected.

'How many shells today?'

'I'm going to make something with them,' said Eleanor, looking proudly into the bucket.

'I don't think we can take them all home, but we can pick out the best ones.'

Eleanor took the bucket from Charlie and clutched it protectively. An impatient Millie wriggled in Charlie's arms.

'Are you still grumpy?' Charlie asked her. Millie's face was turning the colour of a beetroot in its prime.

'No! I. Am. Not. Grumpy. Any. More!' she shouted, her body aquiver with rage.

'That's good to know,' smiled Charlie and she gave the beetroot a kiss.

She called to Ted as they headed off the beach and Ted shouted back that he would be another few minutes finishing off.

'He's a good worker!' shouted Tigi before fist-bumping Ted's clenched hand and pulling him into a brief man hug.

It was hard work getting the other children up the hill and she could feel her patience starting to wane. She was very pleased to see the hedge loom into sight and challenged the children to a sprint. 'Race you to the sun loungers,' and she set off, unaware that she was onto a certain win as even George waved away her challenge with a weary flap of his arm.

As she lumbered up the steps to the pool she was surprised to see a slender bikini-clad body stretched out on a sun lounger. And even more surprised to see a familiar mop of red hair cascading out of a bandana.

'Fleur?' She stopped dead and blinked. Perhaps she was hallucinating?

'Charlie, I'm so pleased to see you!' Fleur launched herself off the sun lounger and into Charlie's arms. Fleur took off her sunglasses and stood back to study Charlie, 'You look well. You look thinner. This place suits you!' And she gave her another hug, followed by a huge sigh. 'I have so much to tell you.'

'What's wrong? Actually, tell me later,' said Charlie, conscious of the footsteps coming up behind her.

'Fleur!' shouted Eleanor as soon as she spotted her and, pulling energy from somewhere, she ran up the steps to hug her. 'Did you bring Wriggly?' she said, searching the patio area for any sign of the fluffy pup.

'Sorry, I didn't have enough air miles for him and anyway he's busy playing chase with Ralph. Ma is looking after him, so he's fine.'

Eleanor's face fell. 'I bet he's missing Eleanor, though,' prompted Charlie.

'No, he's fine,' replied Fleur unhelpfully, making Eleanor's face a little glummer. Realising her faux pas she quickly pulled her bag from the shade of the sun lounger. 'I brought you this,' she declared, handing Eleanor a deformed Mars bar.

'Thanks!' said Eleanor and she skipped off to put it in the fridge.

A couple of hours later Berta put out the salads whilst Ted manned the barbecue and they all milled around outside on the veranda. The heat from the barbecue seemed to keep the flies away so Charlie stayed close to that. It was lovely to hear the children all take their turn at recounting holiday stories for Fleur and each joining in and adding to the tales with their own take on things. The sea-urchin incident was a huge dramatic performance starring Eleanor, and cricket on the beach, described by George, was as exciting as the Ashes. Despite Charlie's niggling fears about why Fleur was there, she was reassured that the children were loving Antigua and making the family memories she wanted them to hold onto forever.

The added excitement of Fleur's arrival sent George, Eleanor and Millie off to sleep with ease but Charlie's plan to pump Fleur for details about the home situation was thwarted by Berta.

Berta stopped quite late, much to Charlie's irritation. She liked the woman but the revelation that she was Esther's aunt and wasn't keen on Ted hanging around with her niece hadn't gone in her favour, and delaying Charlie finding out news from home was chipping away at the simple friendship they had built. It seemed that a couple of large tumblers of rum punch was the key to unlocking countless stories from her childhood on the island which, although entertaining, did not carry the same interest as why the hell Fleur had suddenly turned up unannounced. When Berta eventually declared that she had better be going home, Charlie nearly carried the poor woman off the veranda and out of the driveway.

As the sun had long since slid south and the biting insects that the locals called 'no see ums' were on the wing, they went to settle in the lounge area. Ted sat down nearby and plugged in his earphones.

'This is a lovely villa. It reminds me of a place we had in St Kitts when I was about twelve...' recalled Fleur.

'Fleur! Why the bloody hell are you here?' snapped Charlie, unable to hold in her frustration any longer.

'Charlie, don't get on my case. I've come here to escape all that, you know, people getting on my case.'

'So, you're not here to warn me that there's a man hunt for my arrest or that Ruth has put the house up as reward for information as to my whereabouts?' she said, only half in jest.

'No, oh, goodness did you really think I was here because there was a problem?'

'Er, yeah!' she said sarcastically.

'Sorry. I didn't think...' Fleur looked remorseful.

'No, that's just it, you never...' but Charlie looked at Fleur's expression and stopped herself. 'Apology accepted. Has anyone been in touch with you?'

'Ruth was getting herself all aerated but I forged a letter from you so it's all sorted now,' said Fleur, dismissing the conversation as Charlie stared at her wide-eyed. 'But you won't believe what Pa has done!'

Charlie sipped her third rum punch and listened to Fleur's tales of home, a world that had seemed so far away and that now came back to her like a film playing out. Ted came back in a few minutes before midnight and patted Charlie's arm as he headed up to bed and she returned the gesture.

'You know, when it comes down to it, men are all the same. All. The. Same,' Fleur flopped her head back on the sofa and let out a groan.

'Come on, tell me what's happened in your love life and then I really will have to turn in.' Charlie contemplated another drink, but thought better of it.

'Just when you think you're actually building something special. You know, a friendship with someone, um well, special.

He then goes and makes a full on pass at me when I was at my most vulnerable. This proves he didn't want to be my friend – he just wanted sex, like all the others. Have you got a headache? I'm getting a headache. I may have drunk too much.'

'I think you're being a bit hard on Duggan. And, to be fair, given the way you were dribbling over his photo I hadn't assumed it was only friendship that was on your mind...'

Fleur pulled her head upright quickly, 'You know, I'd forgotten about Duggan and his wilting rocket.'

'Is that a euphemism?' asked Charlie, her face spreading into a childish grin.

Fleur ignored her and continued. 'He dumped me. He's Duggan the Dumb-per,' she said, as she wrote it in the air with her finger.

'Okay, I'm officially lost and confused and it's time for bed.' Charlie unfurled her feet from underneath her and wriggled her toes.

'Jonathan was the one that made a lunge at me. I was staying at his place when I was trying to solve the mystery of the bed bugs.'

'Jonathan?' But, as soon as she'd said the name, Charlie knew exactly who it was.

'Jonathan Steeple, he's that solicitor guy. He was really helpful and nice and we became friends. I thought he liked me as a person, but after he did that I knew it was all just a ploy.'

'He's all right, is Jonathan, and I don't think he has a dishonourable bone in his body.'

Fleur huffed. 'As I left he spouted a load of stuff about me, saying that when someone comes into your life and changes the world as you know it, it makes you re-evaluate everything, but that's just typical male bullshit, isn't it?'

'You know, this time I don't think it is,' said Charlie, with a brief smile. 'You might want to think about giving him a second chance.'

Chapter Twenty-Seven

Berta was a bit later starting than usual and Charlie was thankful for the fraction of a lie-in she managed to get. She was slowly climbing the ladder back to consciousness when someone's foot rubbed gently up and down her leg. Charlie blinked and stretched as Fleur turned over.

'Dear God, you need to wax your legs. I thought I was in bed with a builder,' mumbled Fleur, with her eyes still closed.

'Good morning to you too, you cheeky mare. For your information I shaved everywhere a few days ago.'

'Interesting, do tell.'

'Nothing worth telling,' said Charlie, shuffling herself into a sitting position.

'That tells me there is something to tell but you're not telling. So spill, but do it quietly. I have the most frightful head. Bloody rum!'

'There is someone, well, there was someone and they switched on feelings I didn't even know I was capable of.'

Fleur opened one eye, 'Are we talking sex?'

'No! Well, yes, there was sex, but not a one-night stand... although it turns out that it was.'

Fleur closed her eye. 'Either I'm still drunk or you're talking total rubbish, because I am very confused and it's making my head hurt more.'

'I'm very confused too,' said Charlie, her forehead creasing with the effort of analysing her situation. Sleeping with Blue had only made things more complicated. For a second she thought she regretted it but she realised swiftly that she didn't. She had a connection with Blue and it wasn't about the children. The truth was, she felt something when she was with him. She wasn't entirely sure what it was that she felt but with a hangover pounding away behind her eyes, now was not the time to scrutinise her feelings any further.

She was saved from any further consternation as the bedroom door opened and Eleanor came in with Millie in tow. Eleanor jumped onto the bed on Fleur's side and Fleur groaned. Millie toddled round to Charlie to be picked up.

'Not much room today,' she said, slotting Millie between herself and Fleur. Millie stuck her bottom into Fleur's chest to create a bit more space for herself, Fleur grumbled and shoved her head under the pillow.

'I forgot how much you fidget,' said Charlie.

'And you snore,' said Fleur from under the pillow, 'that rum cocktail thingy was a bit strong.'

'Did it take you three of them to work that out?'

'Three! Ahh,' came the muffled grumble.

'Are you stopping long?'

Fleur lifted the pillow. 'Oh, come on, Charlie, don't do that. I only arrived yesterday and already you're booking my flight home.'

'Does that mean you haven't booked a return flight!' said Charlie, her concern evident. 'Look, it is really brilliant to see you, of course, but...' she couldn't see a good way to finish the sentence.

'So I've forgotten the return-flight bit. I've never booked one before, sorry,' said Fleur, coming out from under the pillow and wrinkling up her nose. 'My head feels like a stuffed aubergine,'

246

she groaned. 'I won't overstay my welcome and I won't intrude. I promise. Now please, can I get some more sleep?'

The children had finished breakfast. Millie was repeatedly doing a twelve-piece jigsaw on the table outside and Charlie was staring at the flowers, trying to conjure up another hummingbird whilst George and Eleanor had gone to use the bathroom. Ted had been a fleeting shadow that had planted a brief greeting on each of the people at the table, including a kiss for Millie and a high-five for George, before he had stolen two bananas and jogged off towards the beach. Charlie was pleased that he was enjoying himself and the responsibility would do him good.

Charlie finished her pineapple juice, put the glass on the table and stretched. A small blue-tit sized bird called a yellow breast joined Charlie and proceeded to nose dive into her glass to retrieve the dregs of her juice. It was such a gymnastic feat, she didn't have the heart to stop it. It suddenly took off as a figure loomed in the doorway.

The sorry-looking sight of Fleur in sunglasses, pyjama bottoms and flip-flops shuffled out onto the patio area, wincing at the morning sunshine.

'That needs a dimmer switch,' she said, pointing idly into the sky at the bright sunshine and pulling out a chair. They sat in silence for a bit before Berta came out and joined them. She looked almost as hung-over.

'Coffee?' Berta asked.

'Grande Americano, please,' replied Fleur.

Berta gave her an old-fashioned look as a reply. 'Did the rum hijack you?'

'I think it blatantly mugged me and tied my brain in a knot. Any local remedies that work?' Fleur sounded hopeful.

Berta thought for a while, 'There's souse.'

'What's that exactly?'

'Like a soup,' explained Berta, and Fleur's interest showed as she raised an eyebrow, 'made from pig's head and trotters.'

'Actually, I'll give that a miss, thanks,' said Fleur pulling a face. 'A large black coffee would be wonderful, please.'

A white splat splashed onto the table near Fleur and she recoiled. All three women stared at it and then up to the sky. A second splat landed on the patio and a third landed on the table near to Charlie.

'Eew!' said Fleur, pushing her chair back, 'that's a huge turd.'

'Charlie leaned forward and dipped her finger into the white substance.

'Charlie! That's disgusting!' said Fleur.

Charlie ignored Fleur and sniffed the dipped finger before tasting it. Fleur started to wretch and Berta looked taken aback.

'Toothpaste,' declared Charlie, as she looked up to the bathroom window above. 'Thanks, you two. Now finish washing faces and brushing teeth so someone else can use the bathroom.'

A peal of giggles broke out above them, followed by the slam of the bathroom window.

Fleur decided she would spend the day at the villa again, her monster hangover dictated that she needed to drink lots of water and a day in the sun wasn't going to speed the recovery of her pounding head. She found some peace on the patio and was thrilled by the arrival of the hummingbird that Charlie had enthusiastically told her about earlier. Unfortunately, when she had called to the others, it had disappeared.

Fleur managed to doze off whilst the children were playing in the swimming pool but the shrill squeals from Millie frequently woke her. Berta appeared before lunch and handed Fleur a tumbler of cloudy liquid with a few green bits floating in it.

'Thanks Berta, but I'm not a hair-of-the-dog sort of person,' she said, handing it back.

Berta gave a broad smile. 'It's coconut water and lime, no

rum and no pig. You wanted a local cure,' she said, clinking her glass gently on Fleur's before downing it. Fleur peered into her own tumbler, but decided that studying the contents wasn't going to improve the look of it. She took a sip and, despite the tang of lime catching in her throat, it was surprisingly good. She knocked it back and settled down for another interrupted nap, which was pretty much how she spent the rest of the day.

At the end of the next day Charlie was surprised to learn from a very casual comment from Ted that Blue was back; she totally failed to control her interest. 'How is he? Did he say why he'd been away?'

Ted shrugged and gave a thoughtful pout. 'Seems all right. Tigi said Blue took occasional jobs of moving boats around the islands.' It appeared that was all she was going to get out of him. He was engrossed in lighting the barbecue. She felt a surprising amount of relief to hear that Blue was back and that no harm had come to him. Now she had to put her own feelings to one side and work out the best way to have a sensible conversation with him about the children.

Part way through the barbecue a familiar voice came from the driveway. 'Charlie!' Everyone paused. Millie was midway through a corn on the cob, her face covered in butter and yellow dots like she had a bad case of acne. Charlie tried to look casual as she left them but she could hear Fleur asking who it was. Charlie went through the villa and shut the door behind her, although it was likely their voices would carry to the back of the house on the warm evening air.

'Is that for me?' asked Blue, eyeing Charlie's hot dog.

'Er, no, but it's yours if you want it.'

'No, you're okay. They always strike me as a bit phallic.' Charlie stared at her innocent-looking hot dog. 'Large sausage nestled into a soft, doughy white bun?' Blue pointed at the hot dog as if it were a diagram. He shoved his hands into the pockets of his shorts as they both pulled their eyes away from the hot dog to survey each other.

'I'm sorry I had a go at you about the email. Where've you been?' said Charlie.

'I've been chilling out and doing some thinking. That's all really.'

'I see. So you've finished your meditating now, have you?'

Blue laughed at Charlie's words. 'Yeah, something like that. Look, I'm sorry I went off, but it was all a bit much.' He was smiling, but something of the sadness remained in his eyes.

'What made you come back?'

'I had a worse thought that you might leave now that you don't officially have a job.'

'And leave the kids behind?'

'I don't know. I was just worried you'd gone. That was all.' He straightened his creased t-shirt. It looked like he'd been sleeping in it.

Charlie relaxed her shoulders, only now realising how tense they had been. 'Do you want to join us?' She could see the resistance in his eyes and he stepped backwards slightly. 'Come on, perhaps we could talk about my job situation and a plan for the children when they've gone to bed?'

'Charlie, don't push me on this. I'm not trying to be awkward, but there's a lifetime of mess behind me that makes me a terrible candidate to be around these kids as anything other than 'the guy with the boat'…' he made inverted comma signs for emphasis.

'I'm not going to bully you into anything. Just come and have some food. The hot dogs are good, especially the phallic ones.' Her smile was disarming and Blue conceded silently and followed her round to the patio.

'Hello again, Felix,' said Fleur, looking rather surprised as Blue appeared behind Charlie. 'How long are you here on holiday for?'

'Fleur's got some catching up to do,' explained Charlie, as she popped her sausage out of the split roll and dropped it back onto the barbecue to reheat.

'Don't upset the system,' said Ted, giving Charlie a nudge and a broad smile. George was like Ted's shadow tonight and was eagerly hovering at his side with two sets of tongs, waiting for Ted's instruction to remove the cooked items and place on raw ones. Charlie waited around the barbecue with the boys drifting in and out of their conversation. She kept a watchful eye on Blue and Fleur, who were deep in discussion and she was unnerved when she saw Blue look over at her and then easily bring his eyes back to Fleur. Jealousy was an unpleasant feeling. After a couple of minutes, George retrieved Charlie's sausage and she shoved it back into the roll and bit into it savagely.

Charlie's plans were unravelling fast as Ted, Fleur and Blue were chatting amiably on the veranda whilst she was reading Millie yet another bedtime story. Millie was fighting hard to stay awake and wasn't going to admit defeat easily. She had been particularly clingy tonight and Charlie knew she wouldn't give in to sleep and lose the one-to-one time she was relishing with Charlie. She stroked Millie's cheek gently and whispered to her about the things they had done during the day and was thrilled to eventually see Millie's breathing set into a steady rhythm. She waited a few more minutes and tried to order her own thoughts and think through what her approach to Blue was going to be. At last she watched Millie sleeping peacefully and banished the thoughts of how many more times she would have the privilege of observing this idyllic scene.

When Charlie finally returned to the others, only Ted and Fleur remained.

Ted answered her thoughts, 'Blue had to go, something about an airport pick-up.'

'What are the odds of you bumping into him here? He looks very different...'

'With his clothes off,' butted in Charlie.

'I was going to say without so many layers. He's offered to show me round the island the day after tomorrow,' said Fleur, her demure smile at odds with her raised eyebrow and Charlie felt her emotional armour needed to be primed for battle.

Chapter Twenty-Eight

Blue came sprinting across the drive and leapt up the steps, making Charlie jump.

'Tropical rain storm coming!' said Blue, as he belted past her and into the villa. Charlie lifted up her sunglasses and looked at the sky. Granted it was a bit grey and swirly but it would most likely pass. The children were happily playing in the pool so, even if it did rain, they wouldn't be any wetter. She looked over to the doorway, where Blue stood beckoning her. She shrugged her shoulders at him; he was definitely over-reacting about this.

Blue pointed towards the sea and Charlie followed his gaze to the edge of the garden. She watched, utterly mesmerised, as a wall of rain streamed across the lawn like a floating curtain of water. There was a moment where half the garden was in torrential rain and the other dry; it was a sight to behold. Charlie was pulled from her trance by Blue shouting at her. She grabbed her paperback and wrapped it hastily in her towel before leaving her sun lounger. The rain reached the pool area and the pool occupants started shrieking. George and Eleanor were excited by it but Millie's was an anxious scream. The raindrops were hard and insistent, stinging Charlie's head as she ran to the poolside to scoop Millie out.

She ferried Millie into the doorway and Blue wrapped her in

a towel. The other two stuck it out like some sort of endurance test until Eleanor finally cracked and, without a word, marched inside, leaving a trail of water like an independent raincloud. George kept diving under the water for relief. Charlie knew there was no way he was going to admit defeat now.

'Need my 'brella,' wailed Millie, as Blue pulled a face at his lack of comprehension.

'Umbrella,' said Charlie.

'An umbrella wouldn't do you a lot of good against this storm,' said Blue, but Millie was still sobbing for it all the same.

They stood and watched the dollops of rain bounce high off the patio. Millie shivered although it still felt warm.

The storm was short and violent and the children were soon back in the water. After a few more minutes the clouds had departed and the only evidence of the storm were puddles and a renewed freshness in the air.

'We'll see you later,' said Blue, ushering Fleur to the jeep. Charlie pretended not to notice and mumbled a 'bye' but she had taken in that Fleur's outfit was very Audrey Hepburn and most definitely designed for maximum impact.

The day trundled by in an easy rhythm after the storm. Charlie heard Fleur's laughter before she was even in the drive and she knew what it meant. She knew the tone and the intent; Fleur was on a full-on seduction offensive. Fleur and Blue had been out all day together, just the two of them. Had Fleur fallen for Blue's thin charade of working lad made good? Perhaps it was the muscles that attracted Fleur time and again to such similar men. Charlie recalled that the suited variety, like Jonathan, were generally leaner on the muscle front.

The laughter grew closer and was now entwined with Blue's voice, until they appeared on the steps.

'You sound like you've had fun,' said Charlie, trying to sound breezy.

'It was totally amazing! I've eaten fresh pineapple, I've had a picnic on a deserted beach, fed a stingray and had the best time ever!' said Fleur, her excitement evident. 'I will update you on everything once I've had a shower.' She turned her attention to Blue. 'You're a doll, thank you so much. I will see you tomorrow.' She gave him a chaste kiss on the cheek and almost skipped inside.

Blue flopped down onto the sun lounger and stretched out, shielding his eyes from the waning sun with his forearm. Charlie looked at him, hoping for a bit more information.

'Good day? Itinerary sounded familiar,' said Charlie, unable to hide the hint of sarcasm.

Blue lifted his arm and opened one eye. 'I'm not local. It's the only route I know.' He gave her his cheeky grin and she resisted the urge to smile back at him. He was seriously getting under her skin.

'So, what are your credentials for running a boat tours company?'

'I don't have any, no qualifications as such, apart from the odd summer or two messing about with boats and jet skis when we were younger.' He slipped his yo-yo out of his pocket and idly started to throw it back and forth, whilst continuing to talk. 'I was running out of cash on Barbados; Sandy Lane uses it up quicker than pressing delete on your bank balance.' Charlie wasn't looking sympathetic but he continued anyway. 'I got a couple of jobs moving boats around the islands. By the time I met Tigi I had a bit of a reputation…' Charlie gave him an old-fashioned look. '…for my boat experience,' he emphasised, 'and the rest, as they say, is history.'

'All worked out perfectly,' said Charlie, trying not to be mesmerised by the yo-yo.

'I'm a bit of a fraud, really. I'm expecting to be found out any day now.'

'Someone once told me that the Ark was made by amateurs

and the Titanic by professionals. Which one would you rather have sailed in?'

Blue laughed, 'Fair point. I'll try to remember that, but I don't think I'll repeat it to my customers, if you don't mind.'

'Did you want a drink?'

'I'd love one,' he replied, swinging his legs off the sun lounger and Charlie felt something zing inside her. 'But I can't. I need to get back, eat, shower and do an airport pick-up. Jumby are having boat staff problems,' he explained as he gave the yo-yo a final flourish and returned it to his pocket.

'Who's Jumby?' asked Charlie, although the name was familiar.

'It's the island resort off the north-east side...'

'Where the big money people holiday,' remembered Charlie.

'You can come for the ride if you like. I could pick you up in about forty minutes?'

Charlie was wavering, although she knew Fleur would be fine to look after the children. She heard Fleur's footsteps behind her.

'Can I borrow your Victoria's Secret shower gel?' she asked, as she appeared briefly with a towel strategically wrapped around her.

'Of course, help yourself,' said Charlie and she watched as Fleur disappeared again. She turned back to Blue, who was looking at Fleur's sashaying behind, and her decision was made. 'Yes, I'll come.'

Fleur wasn't impressed with the thought of an evening on her own but if Blue needed a hand lugging cases for famous people that was definitely more up Charlie's street than hers. She curled up with a sparkling water with a squeeze of fresh lime and listened to her phone messages. Charlie had said something about the phone signal being a bit ropey but Fleur wasn't having a problem.

As she had predicted, there was a message from Rob offering to give up the flat and something about their drummer being offered a gig supporting a girl band that Rob was particularly disgruntled about. The boredom made her skip to the next message. There was no message left so she knew that would be her father. It beeped again and her mother's voice washed over her.

'Sweetie, please call me. I'm fretting. I know you can look after yourself but it doesn't stop me worrying about you. I'm sorry to have called but I need to know that you are safe and with Charlie. Not that you can't look after yourself… I love you.' And she was gone. There was a long pause at the start of the next message.

'Fleur, it's Jonathan. I… I'm so sorry about what happened. I am completely in the wrong. I just want you to know I am truly sorry. I won't bother you again… but you know where I am if you ever need anything. Anyway, I thought you might like this.' There was a slight pause before the opening chords of a very familiar song started.

'Her name was Lola, she was a showgirl.

With yellow feathers in her hair and dress cut down to there.

She would meringue and do the cha-cha.

And while she tried to be a star, Tony always tended bar.

Across the crowded floor, they worked from eight till four.

They were young and they had each other who could ask for more?'

But the sound of Barry Manilow's 'Copacabana' stopped abruptly and the electronic voice announced that that was the end of the messages.

Fleur pouted and pulled the fluffy white bathrobe a little tighter. All these people were worried about her. How much longer would that continue? Perhaps that was what bothered her the most, that one day they would stop worrying, that they would leave her to it and let her loose. Was that what she was really scared of? Not the thought of people interfering in her life but of them not. Who had really ever stopped her from taking control of things? Her father, perhaps. But he wasn't a bully, he was a man of action – if it needed doing he would get on and do it.

He wasn't like her mother who would neatly write the task on a list for the appropriate time.

She sipped her water. She envied Charlie, she always had. Charlie was permanently in control but then she never had the option of letting someone else take the lead for a change because there was nobody else in Charlie's life. There had never been anyone she trusted enough to steer her safely through life whilst she was a passenger. She was always so brave, taking a tight grip on life and telling it how it was going to be. Who else but Charlie would risk so much to bring the children to this beautiful place?

She wasn't the same as Charlie. In many ways they were opposites, but Fleur knew it was time to start making her own way. She felt a bit ashamed of herself for having run to Charlie in Antigua. It was another missed opportunity to stand on her own two feet and she sighed loudly. Fleur decided she would make a start by noting down each day what she had done for herself as well as what she had done for others because she was all too aware that that was another area in which she was lacking. Fleur zoned out of her thoughts and listened.

The tree frogs were humming their chorus, a mixture of chirrup and whistle. Paul McCartney and the frog chorus would have been proud. The noise was strangely melodic as if someone, somewhere, was dictating the tune. There must have been hundreds out tonight. However, they were nowhere to be seen but could be heard everywhere. Fleur had only ever seen one in her life when it had hopped up her leg in St Lucia and Poppy had insisted that it must have mistaken Fleur's leg for a tree trunk. She snorted at the memory. She started to realise that this was what Charlie was trying to do. She was building memories for the children. Moments that they could recall at any time in the future that would make them snort and make them feel the love. It was starting to make a little more sense and things were beginning to get clearer.

She finished her drink and went to throw the slice of lime in the bush, but as she got closer so did the sound of a distinct solo performer. There, in the bush, was a very tiny light-brown speckled frog, no bigger than her thumb. The bubble of air inflating under its mouth, enabling him to make his contribution to the chorus. Fleur watched him for a bit, recorded him on her phone and went inside, taking with her the lime slice and another memory to store.

The airport pick-up was obviously easy money for Blue. He had collected Charlie and they had parked right outside the terminal. She had waited in the minibus and, moments later, Blue had appeared with an American couple and a trolley full of matching luggage. The couple were quite chatty so Charlie just sat in the passenger seat and listened as Blue charmed them with stories of the island. The launch was only a couple of minutes from the airport so they were soon whipping across the Caribbean Sea in a catamaran. Two of Jumby Bay's usual crew were out of action so they had called on Blue as a reliable alternative to make the odd evening transfer.

Two members of uniformed staff were waiting at the Jumby Bay jetty as they moored up and greeted them all warmly. Charlie's eyes were on stalks as she took in as much of what she could see as possible. A palm-tree-lined beach was in front of her but they were ten a penny in Antigua or three hundred and sixty-five to be precise. It was dark now and there were only a few lights on the beach, so it was difficult to see. There was a restaurant behind the palm trees and she could hear the hum of talking and laughter. From what she could make out, it looked like it had a roof but no sides, so that the sea breeze could gently fan the guests as they ate.

The Americans tipped Blue and the staff shook his hand before he boarded the catamaran again. Charlie watched as a couple, hand in hand, slipped out from behind a palm tree and walked along the beach towards them. Blue started the catamaran and it purred into life. He manoeuvred it carefully away from the jetty. The couple were nearer to them now and Charlie was peering at them closely, the man was fair-haired and heavily tattooed, the woman was slender and dark-haired.

'They look a bit like the Beckhams,' laughed Charlie, as the man on the beach waved at them.

'Hiya, Blue, good to see you!' called the man, in a higher pitch than expected.

'You too, David!' replied Blue, and Charlie could have sworn that her jaw actually hit the deck.

The excitement of the Jumby Bay trip was a great distraction and had provided them with a good source of conversation back to St Johns. Charlie had at last calmed down after the excitement of her celebrity encounter, although infuriatingly, Blue would not confirm who the couple were, citing confidentiality clauses and complete discretion whenever she pushed him on it. Their chatter had been easy and the spark Charlie had felt as Blue lifted her off the vessel had shocked her.

Now, back in the minibus and retracing their path back across the island, there was silence. It was a comfortable silence, interspersed with the odd glance and smile from Blue. Charlie could get a good look at him when he was driving without it being too obvious. There was only the merest hint of a similarity to Toby, the only feature they shared were those freakishly blue eyes. Blue had a more lived-in face despite his younger years. There was a scar on his chin that stood out white against his tanned skin and he had a firm, manly jawline. He was strikingly good looking. Blue gave her another glance and she shot her eyes back to the darkness ahead.

'Penny for your thoughts?' asked Blue.

Charlie chuckled and paused, wondering whether or not to reveal the truth of what she was thinking, but she decided against it. 'I was thinking about tidying up the wardrobe, it's a bit of a mess with both mine and Fleur's clothes rammed in it.'

'That's a bit OCD.'

'If I had a penny for every time someone said I had OCD…' she paused as if thinking, 'I'd have eight hundred and seventeen pennies.'

'Oh, very clever,' laughed Blue, reaching out and squeezing her hand. The contact made her jolt, she hated not being able to control her reactions.

'Not my joke, I'm afraid, it was unashamedly stolen from someone I once knew.' More silence followed. 'I know it's a touchy subject, but can we talk?' asked Charlie.

'About us?' asked Blue, looking at Charlie and hitting a massive pothole, making the bus judder.

'Um, no, Blue, about what's likely to happen to the children when we have to go back to London?'

There was a long pause and it took a lot of patience for her to sit it out.

'I'm not sure what you mean, and I really don't want to sound harsh, but Ruth is going to be their guardian now and you need to find another job,' he said at last.

'Well,' she said, taking a big breath, 'she has to get through the assessment first and if she isn't successful they would go into care.' It took more effort than she had anticipated spelling it out. 'Even if she does pass muster as guardian I could still see them ending up with Social Services when it all gets too much for her, as I'm sure it will.'

'That's a bit dramatic!' he said, giving a brief chuckle before catching sight of Charlie's face.

'All I'm asking is that you rethink being their guardian. That way I can keep my job, me and the children can all go back to London, and you can stay here and carry on as before. You don't need to do anything else except visit every now and then. I'm just saying think about it.'

More silence suffocated the air and Charlie opened her window. As the stifling silence continued she decided to call time on the conversation and mentally rearrange her 'Kipper List' instead.

Chapter Twenty-Nine

There was something comforting about snuggling up in bed next to Fleur. It reminded Charlie of when she had been allowed to stay over at Fleur's house as a child and the secure feeling of being tucked in at night. Fleur had always wanted to talk into the small hours back then and that hadn't changed. Whilst the going to sleep was a calming feeling, the waking up next to her was an irritating one. It niggled Charlie that Fleur was still there. That she had got on a plane and appeared without any warning was typical Fleur. Whilst Fleur was doing her own thing she was still slap bang in the middle of the memories Charlie was trying so hard to create for the children. She slunk out of bed and went in search of breakfast.

As she shut the bedroom door behind her, she saw Eleanor sitting on the stairs. 'You okay?' she asked and Eleanor shrugged.

'Had some dreams, that's all.'

'Bad ones?' asked Charlie, combing her fingers through her bed-wrecked hair as she sat down next to Eleanor.

'Um, no. They were good ones about Mum. She was making clothes for Wriggly and he wouldn't wear the hat and it was funny,' a very brief smile broke her story.

'She'll always be a part of you. In your dreams and in your thoughts,' said Charlie.

'I know,' said Eleanor. 'Let's have pancakes for breakfast,' she added, taking Charlie's hand and clutching it all the way to the kitchen.

After breakfast Eleanor sat on the balcony with her legs dangling through the railings, her hands gripping them until her fingers turned white. Charlie was watching her from the gardens below and although she couldn't see the tears she knew they were there. Eleanor was staring out to sea, her legs swaying to an unheard rhythm. On the whole, Eleanor was brighter here and her sad days were fewer, but they were still there, and today was going to be one of them. Charlie knew she couldn't jolly Eleanor out of it and, to be honest, she didn't want to, Charlie knew too well the long-term damage of hiding your feelings. She had spent half her life catching her feelings like flailing butterflies and trapping them in imaginary glass jars; locking them away. It was far better to set them free.

Eleanor became aware of Charlie, her grip loosened and she turned her gaze. The tiniest flicker of a smile danced across her lips. Charlie smiled back and walked off, to leave Eleanor with her thoughts. What they had planned for later would hopefully cheer her up but, for now, it was best that she had some time to herself.

Inside, Charlie found George lying on the sofa in the TV room.

'Hiya, matey. You want a drink?'

'Noooo,' came the sighed response.

'You all right?'

'Bored,' he said, without diverting his eyes from the ceiling.

Charlie almost reeled out a speech about how lucky they were to be here and how could he possibly be bored, but instead opted for a more diplomatic approach. 'Why's that?' George shrugged. 'Is it because Ted's working?' George didn't answer her. It hadn't passed her by how close the two boys had become and, whilst the children strengthening their connections was exactly what she wanted to happen, she hadn't foreseen the obvious downside that the more connected the children were the harder it would be to tear them apart.

'Sure you won't have that drink? I was going to do banana milkshakes.'

'Oh-kay, then. A large one please.'

They had decided to have a change from their routine, on Berta's advice, as the excitement of the annual Antigua carnival was building and it was a good day to go to St Johns and see the floats being built and hear the bands. So, the morning was to be spent around the hotel pool and beach and then they were off to St Johns after lunch.

As they reached the beach she saw Blue was collecting a cool box of drinks from the pool bar and they exchanged the briefest of acknowledgements. Charlie really wished she knew where she stood with Blue. It all felt such a mess and their time on Antigua was running out. Just over a week left. She could practically feel the clock ticking.

Blue came over and plonked down the cool box. 'With Tigi and Ted on the boat I'm doing a bespoke island tour.'

'Won't you get lost if it's not the only tour you know?' teased Charlie.

'I'll make it a mystery tour. It's only a couple of hours, so I'll be back later.'

Charlie could hear the volume rising behind her and knew she had to intervene with the children before it reached the point of no return. 'Excuse me,' she said to Blue. 'Millie, stop pushing people in the swimming pool and come here please.' Millie blew a raspberry and, gripping her swim ring and favourite yellow bucket, she jumped into the pool.

Charlie called George and Eleanor over. 'Right, you two, these are the rules: no shouting, no sand in the pool, no running and no drowning each other.' She turned her attention back to Blue, who was staring at the pool and, despite his tan, looked a little pale. 'You okay?'

Blue came back to the present and blinked at her, 'Is Millie all right?'

Charlie turned to watch Millie proficiently doggy paddling about and gulping down pool water as she did so. 'If she'd let go of the bucket she'd be fine. George, help her, would you?'

Blue was still watching Millie, although he spoke to Charlie. 'Berta said you wanted to see the bands. If you like, I'll pick you up at about one to go to town.'

'Great, see you later,' and she watched Blue walk off across the sand. He looked sad, somehow, and didn't have his usual energy. It was nice to watch him when he wasn't aware of it, her eyes following him until he stepped off the beach and was gone and she exhaled slowly.

Charlie was sorting the towels out when Fleur appeared, and they pulled two sun loungers close to the pool and settled down to read. There was a period of tranquillity where the splashing ebbed into the distance, the sun warmed their skin and the pages turned.

There was a sudden bout of shouting from the pool and Charlie pulled her head out of her book to see a mass exodus of people from it. Lithe men were hauling themselves out, ladies were queuing at the steps and others were doing speed breaststroke. Children were crying and Millie was doing a frantic doggy paddle towards the deep end, despite being weighed down by the yellow bucket. Eleanor and George were nowhere to be seen. She scanned the pool for the source of the alarm and her eyes found something brown and turd-shaped floating in the middle of the pool.

'Poo!' spluttered Millie from the pool.

'Oh, dear God,' said Fleur, seeing the offending item at the same time, 'is it one of Millie's?'

'I can't really tell from this distance and, trust me, they all look the same.'

Charlie's acute hearing tuned into nearby giggling and she spun around to see a mop of fair hair bob down behind a bush.

'George!' she yelled and he came out clutching his sides for support. Eleanor appeared too and they erupted into hysterical laughter. A member of staff was hurrying towards the pool and Charlie could see how this was going to end.

'George, unless you want us banned from here, be the hero and scoop that up in Millie's bucket. Quick!'

Charlie hauled a choking Millie out of the pool and handed George the bucket. He threw it back in and dived in after it. Fleur was quick to intercept the member of staff and to highlight George's heroics.

'He's very brave, I wouldn't go near it. That water is contaminated now. Goodness knows what diseases you could catch from swimming in there.'

George looked suitably disgusted as he approached the floater and scooped it into the bucket. He got out of the pool and carried the bucket at arm's length and presented it to the member of staff. They all peered into the bucket, apart from George, who was excelling in his acting skills by pulling a face and looking over his left shoulder so as not to make eye contact with anyone or look at the bucket contents.

The member of staff spoke first, 'It looks like a… candy bar.'

Fleur's face showed recognition and she started to speak. 'It looks like a Mar…'

'Chocolate bar we call it, but I think you're right. Well done you!' interrupted Charlie, patting the man warmly on the back. 'That's good news, no need to clean the pool. Anyway I think we need to be packing up. Too much excitement for one day,' she said, folding towels rapidly.

George handed the man the bucket. 'Do you need this for evidence or something? 'cause my little sister will want her bucket back.' A shivering Millie stood next to him, looking anxious.

By the time they got back to the villa, they were all laughing. Charlie had got over her crossness quickly and, despite not being a fan of toilet humour, even Fleur could see the funny side.

'When you gave me the Mars Bar George knew straight away what we should do with it,' said Eleanor to Fleur.

'Oh, so it's my fault, is it? Thanks a bunch,' said Fleur as she started to chase them into the drive.

Despite the warnings from Blue nothing quite prepared them for the Antigua carnival. Different parts of it took place over different days, hundreds of people lined the streets and there were crowds everywhere. Everyone was dancing and, apart from the flamboyant coloured outfits of those in the parade, it would be difficult to tell who was in the carnival and who was there enjoying it. It was like one huge party that had spilled out onto the streets and everyone was invited.

The noise was astounding – huge trucks with bands performing live were trundled through the streets with speakers blaring at full tilt. Millie very quickly commandeered Ted's headphones in an attempt to block out some of the noise and she clung to Charlie. All the music had rhythm but some was more enticing than others and a few times Millie was persuaded to dance. The smaller floats had concentrated more on colour and design than volume and these appealed to Millie; the fact that their occupants waved back was the best thing ever. She particularly liked Miss Antigua, who she thought was a princess.

Blue found someone doing face-painting and Eleanor chose to have some flowers painted on her arm and hand as she felt she was getting a bit too old for face paints. Millie followed suit but alarmed the young lady when she was asked what she would like and she asked for 'Pooh on my hand, please.'

'These children have some sort of poo obsession today,' said Fleur, rolling her eyes.

Ted supervised a hot-dog run with George and they returned with giant sausages overhanging the rolls, which reduced Charlie and Blue to childish giggles but nobody else knew why. They nearly lost Millie and Eleanor to a troupe of cheerleaders. Especially when they spotted Esther at the back. Ted looked like he wanted to run when Esther waved her pom-poms at him. He gave her a shy wave and Blue, Charlie and Fleur all started whistling and acting like teenagers. Ted studiously ignored them.

Charlie heard the distinct sound of a steel band and grabbed Blue's arm in delight and then quickly let go.

'Sorry, I get so excited when I hear a steel band. It's so silly,' she said, taking her hair out of its ponytail before tying it back up again for no reason other than to occupy her hands and to stop them straying in Blue's direction.

'It's not silly,' shouted Blue over the noise, 'there's something evocative about them. I feel the same,' he said, but Charlie gave him a look that said she doubted him. 'Honest! Look,' he said, starting to dance to the rhythm.

As the steel band's sound took over from the last band, Charlie found herself dancing. But when she turned to Blue she found that Fleur was already there, instigating some sort of hip-bumping thing with him.

After a good hour, Fleur joined Millie's camp and announced she had a headache so they decided to leave the giant street party and head back to the villa. Millie insisted on sitting with Charlie on the way home, so Charlie was relegated to the back of the jeep and Fleur rode shotgun with Blue. The motion of the jeep sent Millie off to sleep and Charlie found herself dozing off too. Before long they were back at the villa, tired and happy.

Eleanor had decided during the trip that she needed more shells, so a reconnaissance party consisting of Eleanor, Millie, Charlie and Blue headed for the beach whilst Fleur and the boys chilled out at the villa. Millie clutched Charlie's hand on one side and her yellow bucket on the other.

The beach was a little breezier than it had been and that meant there were small waves breaking in long formation ripples on the sand, a white lace edge to each wave instead of the previous calm, which seemed to breathe new life into the beach. The girls got engrossed in shell-collecting as Blue and Charlie strolled ahead. Charlie carried her flip-flops and paddled in the warm water. It seemed even warmer than it had been and it lapped gently over her feet as they sank into the wet sand with each leisurely step.

'Thanks for taking us all to the carnival today. It was kind.'

'You're welcome. I enjoyed myself.' He paused. 'I know something is bothering you. Come on, out with it,' said Blue.

'Just the usual,' she said, breathing in deeply.

'Knowing my past, I'm a terrible choice as guardian.'

'Look, Blue, I know I don't know everything that happened, but you have to move on from all of that. It was a long time ago. Don't ruin the children's future because you're still hung up on the past.'

'You talk about me hanging on to the past but what about you and that tattoo?'

'What?' asked Charlie, feeling disheartened that he'd derailed the conversation.

'I think we're all agreed that it's hideous, so why do you keep it? Is it some sort of punishment for *your* past?'

'Spare me the amateur psychology!' Although his theory did come very close to the truth.

'Get it removed, they can laser them off these days, or a skilled tattooist could easily make it into something prettier.'

'Like what exactly?'

'I don't know. A butterfly?' He shrugged.

'Do I look like a butterfly kind of person to you?' said Charlie, a smirk escaping as she put her hands on her hips.

'Yeah, I think you could be.' Blue put his arm around her waist and they walked on.

'If I get the tattoo sorted would you consider being guardian?' Charlie bit her thumbnail. It was a very unlikely long shot, but that was all she was left with now.

'Charlie, don't you get it?' Charlie shrugged. 'If I agree to be their guardian then you will leave. You go back to London and I effectively commit you to looking after these kids for the rest of your life.'

'That's exactly what we want, don't you get that?'

'But then I don't get you?' he said, his voice soft as it trailed off.

'People rarely do get me. Someone called me obtuse once, I guess that's the same…'

'No. I mean I don't get to *be* with you.'

'What?' Charlie narrowed her eyes, deeply suspicious.

'Charlie…,' he sighed and rubbed his chin, 'I'm rubbish at this stuff.' He smiled at her but she was frowning deeply. 'You and me?'

'There is no 'You and me'. There was one night and then it all got complicated and you… well, I don't know exactly but I'm guessing you went looking for someone else to blow on your dice.'

Blue burst out laughing. 'There's nobody else 'blowing on my dice'. I promise you.'

Charlie didn't look convinced, 'You hardly know me.' Which, she thought, was probably why he might think he wants to be with me.

'There's something about you… Oh hell, I'm so useless at this. Charlie, I want us to be…' he seemed to struggle with finding a suitable word. 'I can't see how anything could happen between us with the children there too.'

Charlie felt as if a black hole had opened up at her feet. Trying to make sense of what Blue had put before her. 'You're giving me a choice: either the kids or you? Is that it?'

'That's not what I meant. It's just that I can see a chance for us here in Antigua. I've had an interview for a proper job and…'

Charlie's temper was rising. 'So, I dump the kids on a plane back to London and I stay here paddling my toes, playing holidays with you for the foreseeable future?'

'The children aren't your problem...'

'Yes, they are, and they should be yours!'

'Maybe with time...' but she didn't let him finish.

'That's exactly what we don't have!' said Charlie, her voice almost a growl.

The silence boiled between them as Blue looked as if he was desperately trying to think of a way out of the hole that had unexpectedly gobbled him up.

'Let's meet up later and talk more. Yeah?' he suggested.

'Talk gets us nowhere, Blue! It's a Cobley with a pulse and backbone that we need!' she said, striding off at speed-walking pace, but with less of the wiggle. She overtook the girls as she walked up the beach, staring at the waning sun and trying to control her breathing.

As they neared the beach bar she could see a crowd of people and it made her curious. Blue caught up with her but she didn't acknowledge him. As they got closer to the bar, they could see that everyone was glued to a news report on the small television behind the bar. The barman looked up and beckoned them over. 'You're from the UK, aren't you?' he asked. Charlie's feet stopped in mid-step and the bile rose in her throat. This was it, this was the moment she had been dreading. The barman was looking at Charlie and back at the television screen. He was starting to look puzzled, so he turned to Blue. 'She is British, isn't she?'

'Yeah, she's a Londoner through and through,' he said in a mockney accent and he put an arm around Charlie's waist but, realising that she wasn't moving, he stepped in front of her statue-like figure and waved a hand in front of her eyes. 'Have you been frozen by the White Witch?'

'Go and look what they're saying on the television and I'll... I don't know, I guess I hand myself in,' said Charlie, her voice soft, as if all power were draining from her.

Blue was already jumping up to sit on the bar for a good view of the screen, so her words were lost. The next few seconds seemed to creep by and the thundering of blood through her head was making Charlie feel dizzy. Eventually Blue turned and called her over, his face registering disbelief. 'You've got to see this.'

Charlie took a deep breath and prepared herself for the worst. As she reached the bar, Blue leant down and effortlessly lifted her onto the counter top. He held her tightly around the waist. She savoured the feeling of safety when all around her she felt the world was caving in. She closed her eyes, took a deep breath and forced herself to turn and look at the television screen. Charlie realised all the other eyes were now on her, awaiting her reaction. There was a news reporter and he was looking serious. She tried to focus on what he was saying. He was wearing a coat and the bottom of the screen said it was a report live from central London. She swallowed hard and tried to listen.

'The Thames has reached its highest level since records began and, with another thirty millimetres of rainfall expected in the next few hours, homes are being evacuated in preparation for the worst. Back to you, Fiona, in the studio.'

The eyes were still on her and she could feel a wave of cold sweat sweeping up her body. Had she missed it? The report about the kidnapped children? Her mug shot and CCTV pictures of them at the airport? She looked over her shoulder at Blue, the colour draining from her face.

'What did they say about the children?' she asked.

'Nothing, you loon. It was all about the weather. You are missing record rainfall and biblical floods in the UK and... Charlie!' Blue tightened his grip as Charlie's eyes rolled back into her head and her limp body slumped against him.

Chapter Thirty

'Really, I can't stand the fussing,' said Charlie, swatting people away like flies. It was a few hours since she'd passed out and, although everyone had been completely lovely and caring, they were now starting to drive her round the hat rack.

'But you should be resting,' said Fleur, leaning over and trying to feel Charlie's forehead for the umpteenth time.

Charlie waved both hands in front of her like a stilted conductor. 'Do you see what I mean?'

'Whoops, sorry,' said Fleur. 'Blue was awfully manly, though, carrying you all the way back here. I mean that's a long way to carry someone of your… well, it's a long way to carry anyone,' she corrected, as Charlie was tilting her head on one side and giving her one of her looks.

'Did you leave a light on for Millie?' asked Charlie.

'Yes, stop fretting. All the children are fine. I can cope, you know. Maybe you should let me cope more often. Give yourself a bit of a break. Not for a week or anything, I mean a weekend or an evening. Actually an evening would be best,' modified Fleur, as she left the room.

* * *

A few minutes later Fleur appeared with tall glasses of pineapple juice and they sipped them in silence for a bit.

'I'm thinking of booking my flight home soon,' said Fleur, eventually. 'This business idea is really buzzing in my head now and being here has let things settle. A little bit like sediment,' she said, swirling the bottom of her pineapple in the glass.

'I'm pleased,' said Charlie, 'about the business, not you going home... although it will be nice to have the last few days with the children to myself, if I'm honest.'

'It's okay, I get it.' Fleur gave her a hug.

It was all agreed, in spite of Charlie's protests, that the next day would be a day of rest for her. Fleur would be on Millie watch and Blue and Ted would take Eleanor and George out for the day. Blue had plans for fishing and playing cricket with some local children, so everyone seemed happy. Charlie reluctantly agreed. She only liked things organised when it was her doing the organising.

As it turned out, she had a restful day spent mainly on the beach. Esther had even called by to check on how she was and she couldn't fail to be touched by that. She had finished a great book that had kept her guessing about the killer until the last page and she had had at least two mini naps. She felt so relaxed that perhaps they had been right after all.

She collected up her things and sauntered up the windy hill road, smelling the air and taking in the flowers and even the cracks in the walls as she went by. She wanted to remember everything about Antigua. She couldn't see there being an opportunity to ever return, so she had to absorb it all while she was here. A deep breath took in a lungful of sweet, clean air. She felt peaceful and it was a good feeling. There was still the little niggle of what would be waiting for her in London, but she folded that up in her mind and locked it away.

Charlie saw Fleur come flying out of the house like an Olympic sprinter. Charlie quickened her pace and Fleur ran to meet her.

'Now, don't panic!' said Fleur. The words eliciting the opposite effect. 'I was playing hide and seek with Millie and she's hiding really well, that's all.'

'Fleur, hide and seek? You know I hate that game. When did you last see her?'

'She was playing in the bushes about twenty minutes ago.'

Millie was missing and Charlie could feel her insides dissolving in the acid of fear. 'Where have you looked?'

'House and garden, but she's hiding, Charlie. She'll pop up in a minute, I'm sure,' said Fleur, her face betraying the confidence of her words.

'Fleur, stop it! She could be anywhere after twenty minutes.' Charlie spun to look at the bushes, where she had last been seen. They were close to the road. 'What's she wearing?'

'Um, her pink swimsuit, I think.'

'Check the house again. Check under and in everything. I'll ask the neighbours.'

Fleur ran back up the steps to the house without arguing. Charlie followed to get her mobile before marching out of the drive. She started with the immediate neighbours, where no one was home, but a cursory look through their gardens showed no sign of Millie. Charlie checked her watch; that had taken four more minutes and panic was rising. She called Ted's mobile and left what she hoped was an urgent but coherent message.

She needed to do more – the door to door was too slow. Charlie ran onto the road and spun round frantically, trying desperately to catch sight of Millie. A glimpse of her dark hair or a flash of pink swimsuit was all she needed. In the distance and almost at the beach she saw a small child swinging a yellow bucket. Charlie burst into a run towards the child, her heart pounding. But a couple of strides forward made her spot the parents walking ahead of the child, who she could now see was a boy in red swim shorts.

These people were heading off for an afternoon of family fun on the beach. Their child was safe and all was perfect in their world. Charlie pulled her thoughts back to Millie and ran back to the house. She could hear Fleur inside calling Millie's name and she started to do the same but it kept catching in her throat and she couldn't call as loudly as she wanted to. She ran to the bottom of the garden and started pushing through the bushes and flowers, to be certain that she wasn't hiding there. A few more precious minutes passed and Charlie was sure that Millie wasn't in the garden and the realisation that she could have been kidnapped gripped her hard.

Ted came jogging into the garden, his face full of concern. 'We'd just docked at the jetty when I saw you'd called. Have you found her?'

'No.' Charlie didn't know what else to say and it was difficult to breathe and speak at the same time.

'Should we call the police?' he asked.

Charlie had considered the same thing but her automatic inclination to avoid the authorities had stopped her making the call.

'I don't know.' Her head was spinning and the tightness in her gut was making it hard to breathe properly.

'I'm going to call Blue. He'll know what to do,' said Ted, pulling out his phone. Charlie took a deep breath in an attempt to 'grip self' – another technique someone had once suggested.

'Ted, check the beach and the hotel. She loves the beach, that's where I'd go if I were her.' She hadn't seen Millie whilst she had been there but she was fast running out of places to check. Ted turned and sprinted off, speaking into his mobile as he went.

Fleur came out of the house, slumped onto the top step and started to cry. Charlie felt like doing the same but that wasn't going to solve anything. She went over and patted Fleur on the shoulder. 'I'm going to Berta's. She may be there. You stay here in case she comes back.'

Berta's was only a short stroll and when you were running full pelt it was actually very close. The small concrete block house was a yellow painted cube in a sea of frangipani flowers that were invading it from all directions. The ancient wooden door was open, revealing a dark interior and as she ran inside it took her eyes a moment to adjust. 'Millie!' Charlie's call was almost a screech as Berta appeared wiping her hands on a tea towel.

'Hello, Charlie.'

'Is Millie here, Berta? Have you seen her?'

'Not since lunch, what's wrong?'

'She's missing. I have to go. If you see her hold onto her and call the villa, please,' called Charlie, as she ran out of the small house and into the street.

A few desperate minutes later she was back in the villa gardens calling for Millie. Sweat trickled down her back and tears trickled down her face.

'Hiya!' called Blue, as he sauntered across the garden looking tanned and relaxed. 'Ted's with the terrible twosome. What's up?'

'Millie's gone missing,' said Charlie, glaring at Fleur as she joined them. 'Did you see anyone else before she went missing?' Charlie asked Fleur.

'Like who?' Fleur wiped the tears and snot roughly from her face.

'Anyone, someone who may have taken her.'

'I don't think so,' Fleur's forehead was creasing as she strained to think.

'Come on, Charlie,' Blue said, a small frown darting across his forehead, 'calm down. Don't you think you're overreacting? This is Antigua, not the East End.'

'Don't you think kidnapping could happen here? A quick boat trip and she could be on the coast of Venezuela and before bedtime she's being traded for coffee and cocaine in Columbia!'

Blue chuckled and stepped forward. 'Charlie, your imagination is amazing. She'll be playing somewhere. At worst, someone will have taken her in,' and, catching her look he quickly added, 'a kind person, who will make sure she's okay until we find her. That's what people are like here.'

'You don't know that for sure. We have to find her.' She checked her watch, 'She's been missing more than forty minutes. What do we do now?'

Charlie felt furious, helpless and totally overwhelmed by the situation and the horror in her mind that was fast becoming reality.

'Charlie, calm down,' said Blue, putting his hands on her forearms.

'Get off me! This is serious. Maybe if you had a heart,' she said, batting him across the chest, 'you might feel something. If you'd stayed around your family long enough to feel anything for anyone else, you might realise there's more to life than swanning around on fantasy bloody island playing with sodding boats!' she shouted. 'You're wasting time; she could be miles away by now. Why won't you help me?' and she lost the fight to keep the tears under control and started to sob.

Blue looked uncomfortable. 'All right. Let's divide and conquer. Fleur, you stay here in case she comes back. I'll call Tigi and we'll get the jeep and minibus out searching the streets for her. I'll call all the local hotels on English Harbour and ask them to look out for her. Okay?' he said, lowering his head so that he could look directly into her eyes.

Charlie took a deep breath and inelegantly sniffed back the tears. 'I'm coming with you.'

Blue nodded and strode off to call Tigi. Fleur and Charlie looked at each other and, although Charlie was crosser with her than she could ever remember being before, she couldn't help but feel for Fleur. She knew Fleur was sorry and was feeling the pain, but right now all she could focus on was finding Millie.

Blue finished his call and waved to Charlie. She gave Fleur the briefest of smiles jogged over to Blue and they headed out of the drive together. As they were about to step onto the road, Blue glanced over his shoulder and back at the villa. What he saw made him spin around.

Chapter Thirty-One

Millie was on Charlie's balcony, standing on the sun lounger, and was wobbling as she leaned precariously over the balcony railings.

Charlie realised Blue was running back to the villa, looked up and saw what was unfolding on the balcony. 'Millie!' shrieked Charlie, which made the toddler jerk upright and sway dangerously. Charlie gasped and ran towards the villa.

'Stay there, Millie,' said Blue calmly. Millie was throwing tampons off the balcony and lurching over the railings, each throw making her situation even more perilous. Charlie flew up the steps behind him as another tampon landed and Millie giggled. Running into the villa and up the stairs, her heart beating fast and her head swamped with the emotion of knowing Millie was here but still in danger, Charlie's sweaty hands fumbled with the bedroom door.

She flung it open and raced across the room to see Blue climbing onto the balcony. He picked up Millie, who waved a tampon around his head happily and stretched out her arms to Charlie. Charlie took Millie from Blue and hugged her tight, failing to smother the sobs that forced their way out.

'Where were you, Millie?' asked Blue.

'Sleep in the little room,' said Millie, pointing at the walk-in wardrobe. Blue smiled and shook his head.

Fleur leant against the doorframe, wiping away the tears. 'I'm so sorry,' she said.

Charlie clung to Millie. 'One day that won't be enough.'

Fleur looked as if the words had physically slapped her. She blinked hard, turned away and disappeared downstairs.

It took Charlie a while before she could let Millie go, which was long after Millie had wanted to be freed. She had finally conceded when Ted had returned with George and Eleanor, who were completely oblivious to the whole episode and were full of the great day out they'd had with Blue and Ted. Blue had clearly given them yet another fun day that had included a museum in St Johns, a tour of the Sir Vivian Richards Cricket Stadium, cricket on the beach and a visit to a friend of his who carved wooden creatures.

'I chose the turtle because it's an endangered species,' Eleanor explained to Millie, who was stroking its shell.

'What's dangered spee-spees?' she said, carefully mimicking the sounds of the unfamiliar words.

'It's when there aren't many of them left in the world. There is a danger that there will only be one or two and then they will die and we won't have that animal any more!'

Millie looked suitably shocked at the prospect. She stopped stroking the toy and clutched Pooh to her.

'Is Pooh a dangered see-spees?'

Eleanor was nodding, but Charlie intervened. 'No, sweetheart, he's unique because there is only one Winnie the Pooh and he's going to be here forever, so you don't need to worry.' She hugged Eleanor and gave her a wink and Eleanor revelled in the conspiratorial gesture.

The sun was thinking about setting as Charlie sat on the edge of the pool watching Millie push George, Ted, Eleanor and Blue in, time after time, giggling with each over-dramatic fall into the water.

'Bye, bye stupid man!' she said to Blue as she shoved him with both hands and he neatly dived in. It was all a far cry from the scenes earlier. Everything was back to normal, or so it would seem, but for Charlie something had changed. Charlie knew what she had experienced must be every parent's worst nightmare, but now she knew what it would feel like to not know where one of them was; she realised that simply knowing that they were safe wasn't going to be enough.

Blue looked up and Charlie smiled at him, noticing that his gaze was veering past her. Charlie turned to see Fleur lugging her designer case down the steps. Charlie hadn't spoken to Fleur since they had found Millie. She'd figured Fleur was mulling things over. Perhaps she had been too hard on her, although she knew she wouldn't be thinking that if Millie were still missing.

A taxi pulled into the drive and Blue acknowledged the driver, who got out and took the case from the struggling Fleur. Fleur stood for a moment, took a deep breath and strode over to Charlie. 'I love you and I would never do anything to hurt you. I am truly sorry and I take full responsibility for what happened. I'm going home because I think that's best. I'm not running away.' She looked at Charlie, her head held high.

'I will calm down eventually,' said Charlie, offering her arms out for a hug and Fleur gratefully stepped into it. They held each other tightly for a minute or so before Fleur released herself.

'Take care, Charlie. Bye Blue, bye kids,' and with that she got in the taxi and was gone.

Against all the odds, perhaps Fleur was actually growing up.

After the cacophony of Antigua airport, Fleur had been pleased to sleep in the peacefulness of first class on the way home. She wasn't pleased with the whole Millie mess, but she was satisfied with how she'd handled it. She had taken responsibility for her mistake and that was the way things were going to be from now on. She was also going to try her hardest to avoid making the mistakes in the first place.

It was early when they landed and as she trundled out of arrivals Fleur was wondering whether her father had picked up her text or whether she needed to get in a cab. She hadn't asked him to pick her up, she'd simply said she was coming home and that they needed to sort a few things out. The couple in front of her were walking slowly, creating a queue of tired travellers. Up ahead there were a few people hugging other passengers and babies being passed around. A few people with signs were looking very bored. Fleur was scanning the faces and suddenly she recognised two of them.

Rob was hanging over the barrier, looking pretty rough, with at least a week's stubble on his chin. Jonathan was standing upright about a metre further down, looking clean-shaven and holding aloft a neatly made sign that read 'Fleur Van Benton'. He saw her immediately and started waving. Fleur straightened her shoulders and walked to the barrier. Rob leapt over to intercept her and flung his arms around Fleur.

'Babe! I have missed you soooo much. We have loads to talk about. Let me take your case.'

Jonathan's face fell as he watched the happy reunion in front of him. Fleur was hugging the unkempt-looking bloke that had just arrived and pushed his way to the front. Jonathan had been there for over an hour. He lowered his sign and dragged his eyes away as they were now deep in conversation.

'Let go of my case before I scream thief and you end up being frogmarched off by security!' said Fleur, her voice almost a growl.

'Calm down, Babe. I wanted to see you. Now that's not a crime, is it?' He put his face close to hers and she could smell his un-brushed breath.

'How did you even know I was on this flight?'

'Your mum posted it on Facebook. You gotta love Mrs VB,' he said, trying to put his arm around Fleur's shoulders.

'Get off me, Rob,' said Fleur, trying to catch sight of Jonathan, who was no longer standing next to the barrier.

'Babe, you're tired. Let's get you home. Have you got cash for a cab?'

Fleur dropped the handle of her case and pushed Rob hard in the chest. He stumbled backwards and landed with a thump. He started laughing and held up his hands in surrender. Fleur was about to lunge at him when she felt a strong arm grab hold of her.

An offer of a day out with Blue was always going to be accepted. They were all on the boat and Blue was weaving his way around the smaller islands off Antigua's northeast tip. He slowed the motor and the boat bobbed past a large floating mass.

'Watch out for the seaweed,' called Blue.

'Is it deadly?' asked George, leaning over the side to grab some.

'No, this stuff's fine. We had a plague of sargassum seaweed a few years back and that was dangerous because we had tons of it floating about.'

'I'm dangered seaweed,' said Millie emphatically, which made Blue laugh.

'Really! Now, there's a thing,' he said.

'I think she means endangered species,' explained Eleanor, her face serious.

'There are millions of people on the planet, so how do you work that out, little one?'

'Only five left,' said Millie, holding up four fingers before quickly correcting her mistake.

Eleanor stepped in. 'She means that there's only five of us Cobleys left in the whole wide world,' she said, elaborately stretching her arms out in both directions. Blue stared at Millie and Eleanor. Charlie stared at Blue, waiting for a reaction. He shook his head and returned his attention to steering the boat.

'Welcome to Ibis Island,' said Blue, slowing the engine as the sea changed from deep velvet blue to a bright jewelled turquoise.

Ted jumped off the front of the boat and had judged it well as he could touch the bottom. He looked keen to help Esther off the boat but Millie was already in the front of the queue and launched herself into the water. Thankfully her life vest made her pop up quickly. Esther was laughing as Ted flicked the water splashes off his hair and, his annoyance quickly squashed, he laughed too as Millie's vigorous kicking sent yet more cascades of water over him. He reached out his hand to help Esther down the ladder, but as she was still laughing, he pulled her into the water instead. She was clearly not fazed by it and lots of splashing and laughter ensued.

'Ted, watch your sister!' called Charlie, who could see the doggy-paddling Millie nearing the shore.

'On it!' he called back.

George and Eleanor had jumped off the boat and were already swimming back for another go. Blue pulled off his shirt in one movement, slid into the water and reached up a hand to Charlie, the definition of his muscles side-tracking her thoughts momentarily as the sun shone on the blonde hairs on his arms.

'No chance! I saw what happened to Esther, I'll manage on my own, thanks.'

'Is that your philosophy for life?'

Charlie stopped as she was halfway down the ladder, the warm water lapping at her calves. 'Let's call a truce today. Let's make it a sniping-free zone. Okay?'

Blue looked hurt, 'I wasn't sniping. I admire that in you, Charlie – your strength and self-sufficiency. But obviously now I'll have to drown you,' and he grabbed her around the waist and dragged her screaming into the water.

The island had looked small when they had first seen it from the boat, but now they were on the shore the beach seemed to stretch out along the flank of the boomerang-shaped piece of land. Blue had a rucksack with drinks to keep them going until lunch but what he produced from the bag next captivated everyone.

'What is this?' said Blue, with eyes wide, his acting terrible as he unrolled a large brown-stained piece of paper.

Millie grabbed at it and pulled it down to her level, so that she could see it better. 'It's a map!' she squealed, making Esther wince at the high pitch.

'A treasure map,' added Eleanor, with obvious awe in her voice. Even George was clamouring for a look.

'It's the treasure map of the meanest, ugliest, scariest pirate that ever sailed the Caribbean Sea,' said Blue, his acting skills under yet more pressure.

'Is it you?' asked Millie, her eyes glued to Blue.

'Mills, Blue isn't a pirate,' said George.

'He got boat and treasure map,' pointed out Millie, with a pout.

'Fair point, Millie, but no, it's not me,' said Blue, before he slipped into an ill-rehearsed pirate accent. 'He lived a very long time ago and his name was Cap'n Bluebeard the Dreadful. He was as sly as a sea serpent and twice as slippery. A menace to all that had the misfortune of crossing his path. He was wanted by the Royal Navy, loathed by other pirates and feared by EVERYONE!' He shouted the last word, making everyone jump, and Millie squealed half in horror and half in delight.

Charlie was busy watching the faces of the others, who were all enthralled with the tale and, for a moment, allowed herself to dream a little. Was it too much to ask that Blue could have a place in the lives of these children? For someone who didn't have kids he was very good with them. And he was particularly good with these kids, so why wouldn't he do the simple act of securing their future? The answer Blue had already given her to this question flew to mind but she dismissed it quickly, there was no space for analysing what he may have meant about them being together. Charlie was brought back to the moment by Millie clapping her hands together as her excitement overflowed and the story reached its climax.

'And with his dying breath and the help of his parrot, he drew this map so that, one day, explorers like you could uncover the buried treasure of Cap'n Bluebeard the Dreadful.'

Ted started the applause and Millie jumped up and down as she clapped. Ted bent over and Blue spread the map on his back and everyone chipped in as they attempted to find a recognisable spot on the picture.

'Crescent beach!' shouted Eleanor, jabbing her finger into the map and consequently her brother's back.

'Haunted house? Is that the boarded-up bungalow on the hill?' said George, shielding his eyes from the sun with his hand as he looked up the nearby mound.

'Er, yeah. You may need to use your imagination,' said Blue.

'Okay,' said George, sticking his nose back into the map.

'Twees!' shouted Millie, and she started to point at the map and at the large wooded area in front of them.

'Good girl, Millie. You need to look for a special tree that has something carved into it,' said Blue, tapping the picture on the map and five heads all moved in for a closer look.

'Kiss!' said Millie.

'X marks the spot,' corrected Eleanor.

'Right, let's head off towards those trees and see what we can find,' said Blue. 'Do you and Esther want to relax on the beach for a bit, Charlie, while we do the treasure hunt?'

'Don't mind if I do,' said Charlie.

'Sure,' said Esther.

'Um, I was thinking Esther and I could go for a look round on our own,' said the map rest from his hunched position.

'Sorry, mate. I could do with a hand with all these land lubbers, ah-argh' said Blue, still in character as he relieved Ted of the map.

'Your acting really is shockingly bad,' said Ted, slapping Blue on the back, and they walked off companionably in the same direction as the children.

Esther looked across the small beach, 'looks like someone was here before us,' she said, indicating the rake marks in the sand. Charlie hadn't noticed them, but it made her smile to think that Blue had bothered to come out and set up the treasure hunt and rake the beach of seaweed. They found a shady spot under a clump of precarious-looking palm trees that were bowing down to the sand, laid out their towels and settled themselves without conversation, instead exchanging the odd half-smile.

Charlie glanced across at Esther's book and was surprised to see she was reading *The Catcher in the Rye*. Esther saw her looking and raised her eyebrows.

'Any good?' asked Charlie.

'It's an odd one,' said Esther, studying the cover, 'mainly in flashbacks covering key themes of rebellion, identity and independence. I'm not a fan of first-person narrative but it works well here.'

'Right,' said Charlie, surprised by the articulate response.

'How's yours?'

'Good,' said Charlie. Esther smiled and went back to reading.

Charlie must have nodded off as she was woken by squeals of delight. She quickly wiped her mouth in case she'd been dribbling, and sat up. Millie came running across the sand waving a pirate flag. 'We found the treasure, Charlie!' George was following her and was carrying what looked like a treasure chest but, as it got closer, Charlie could see that it was a large cardboard box that had been painted to look like one.

'Wow!' said Charlie, 'What's in the treasure chest?'

'Don't know yet,' said George. 'Blue said we had to open it together.' George looked so relaxed and happy since he'd been in Antigua; the anger was long gone, the boredom had subsided and it was good to see him having fun. He placed the box down on the sand between Charlie and Esther. Esther was looking hopefully at the trees from where they had appeared. Blue and Ted strode out together laughing and both Charlie and Esther instinctively leant forward.

Charlie watched the two men and it struck her for the first time that Ted had become a young man. His stance was different, he was walking upright, not the slouchy teenage lollop she was used to seeing in London. He had a purposeful stride that kept pace with Blue and he was looking more muscular than before, though his tan was perhaps emphasising that. Charlie looked at Esther and saw the adoration in her eyes, and it worried her.

Ted flicked his hair; it was sun-streaked and ridiculously long. She never had sorted out that hairdresser. 'You'll all need haircuts before...' Charlie realised she was saying her thoughts out loud and she stopped; she didn't want to spoil the moment by mentioning their departure, but it appeared no one had noticed until Esther chipped in, 'I could cut their hair. If you wanted me to.'

Charlie was expecting a lot of dissent from the troops but Ted led the chorus, 'Yeah, great idea. Thanks Est.' His easy acceptance was yet more evidence that he was growing up.

Millie was kneeling and jigging up and down on her heels as the anticipation powered her body.

'Go on, Mills, you can open it now,' said George, having a quick look over his shoulder to check that Blue was concurring with his instruction. Blue gave him a friendly slap on the back as he knelt down next to Charlie. Ted folded himself onto Esther's towel and she leaned into him.

Millie edged forward and slowly lifted the lid of the treasure box, her eyes widening as the inside was revealed. 'Wow!' she shouted, pushed the lid off and thrust her hands inside. She pulled out handfuls of toy gold coins and piled them onto the edge of Charlie's towel. More digging revealed some beaded necklaces and bracelets or 'jewels' as Millie declared them. Millie shared some jewels with Eleanor as George lost interest and sat back on the sand.

'Is that everything?' asked Blue.

'Yes,' said Millie, sticking her head inside the box.

'Are you sure?' asked Blue with a wink, which made Eleanor's face join Millie's in the box.

'There's a false bottom!' yelled Eleanor.

'Bottom!' giggled Millie, falling back against Charlie, who instinctively caught her in her arms.

Eleanor wrenched a large piece of cardboard out of the box and half threw it to Charlie. She took it from her and noted that someone had taken the trouble to paint it to look like wood planks. She felt that someone watching her and she looked up. She and Blue exchanged weak smiles. Eleanor still had her head in the box.

'There are bags for all of us,' said Eleanor, starting to hand out the brown paper bags. Each one had a neatly folded top, sealed with a skull and crossbones sticker and marked with their first names. 'Esther,' she said, handing her the first bag; as Esther leaned past Ted to reach it, the fact that she rubbed her cleavage against his arm was not missed by Charlie.

'Thanks,' said Esther to both Eleanor and Blue. All eyes were on her as she opened the bag and for the first time she looked quite shy. She reached in and took out a pen set, which she appeared genuinely pleased with and an Antigua bookmark, which made her smile. She crawled over the sand to kiss Blue a thank you, and Charlie noted the bird's-eye view that she and Blue had received of her abundant cleavage.

Eleanor handed out the other bags. Millie's revealed a pink flowery umbrella of the telescopic variety, which she was now waving in the air as she danced in the sand. George had a shark's tooth on a leather cord, as well as a musket ball from roughly the same time as when Nelson and his troops would have occupied the island.

Eleanor was thrilled with a photograph of Mr Wriggly in a shell-encrusted frame. 'I got the photo from Fleur,' said Blue, 'but you can put anything in it,' he added and he gave her a hug. Charlie was pleased by Eleanor's smiley face as, had he asked her, she would have advised against it for fear of Eleanor being upset. Ted opened his bag and pulled out a watch identical to Blue's; he forgot himself and bear-hugged Blue without any word of thanks, but it seemed the hug was more than enough for Blue. There was a lot of mutual manly slapping and Ted put the watch on.

Charlie was feeling a sense of tense anticipation of what was in her bag and she was tempted to say that she'd open it later, but the expectant faces forced her to unfasten it. She peered inside with caution, as if surveying a volatile substance. Inside was a small velvet box. Charlie stared at it as it sat in the unassuming paper bag.

'Come on, Charlie, what's in there?' asked Ted. Charlie looked up, terror etched on her face. She knew it was a ring box. What was Blue playing at? Had she been watching this in a film she would have thought what a marvellous setting for a proposal, but now, sitting here with a key role in a script she was not controlling, she was petrified. All the same, she reached in and pulled out the innocent box.

'Open it,' urged Esther. I bet you wish this were you, thought Charlie bitterly.

Chapter Thirty-Two

As if on autopilot, Charlie opened the small box, her eyes not immediately registering its contents. Millie appeared at her shoulder, 'Ooh, pretty ear things!' she cooed and skipped away. Charlie breathed again and blinked.

'If you don't like them, you can swap them,' said Blue, with caution in his voice.

'They're lovely,' she said, looking up at his hesitant face. She noticed the disappointment in Esther, who had shrunk back to Ted's side. She too must have made the same assumption as Charlie. 'Thank you,' Charlie added, somewhat belatedly. Now feeling embarrassed by her ridiculous assumption that he was giving her a ring.

'Right, who's up for a game of cricket before lunch?' said Blue, getting to his feet, and he was met by a mixture of cheers and groans.

George was victorious at cricket thanks to his brother's generosity of spirit at not catching the two balls he skied. Everyone was now flaked out on the sand, either reading or sunbathing, apart from Millie, who was merrily burying her own legs, something of a new favourite pastime. Charlie was keeping a watchful eye over the top of her book. She thought Blue was asleep next to her until he leant up on one elbow. 'Fancy a walk around the island?'

Charlie pulled a face. 'Not keen on leaving them.'

Esther put her book down. 'We'll watch them. Won't we Ted?' Ted was dozing, with his arm covering his eyes. He waved his hand slightly, which Charlie took to be his acceptance. Blue pulled Charlie to her feet and kept hold of her hand as they walked off along the beach. She liked the gesture; the closeness and she didn't want to let go.

They strolled slowly and in silence for a while. Blue with his feet in the filter-clear water and Charlie next to him, her feet sinking into the damp sand.

'I feel I owe you some answers,' said Blue, his voice soft.

'You don't owe me anything.'

'Well, I'm going to tell you some things anyway as they might help you to understand why I'm the way I am.'

Charlie kept quiet. She would never have asked, but if he was going to volunteer that was fine, as long as he wasn't expecting a mutual outpouring from her.

'Did Toby ever tell you about our brother, Seth, and what happened?'

'Seth died, didn't he?'

Blue looked down at his feet as they ambled along and let out a long, slow breath. 'I killed him.'

Charlie stopped walking and tried to look Blue in the eye, but he was staring, unblinking, at his own feet. 'Explain,' she said gently.

'The summer I was twelve, Seth and Tobes were meant to be looking after me. I was a lot younger than them, a bit of an afterthought on Mum and Dad's part, I think. Anyway, we used to spend days messing about down by the river near our house. We weren't meant to, but you know?' Charlie nodded her understanding and they started to walk again, perfectly in time with each other.

'We'd been flying my kite and I'd got it stuck in a tree. We couldn't reach it but I wouldn't give up. It was time to get back and I decided to have one last go, so I climbed up the tree. I thought if I kept going higher I would be able to grab it.'

'That sounds a lot like, George.'

'Yeah, I see a lot of me in him. He needs a close eye,' said Blue, before returning to the story. 'Seth was shouting at me to get down and I wouldn't. I thought I knew best. Eventually he lost his temper and started to climb up after me. Except he chose a slightly different route via the branches that overhung the river.' Blue took another deep breath and Charlie squeezed his hand. 'He was really cross and he wasn't concentrating on the climbing. He missed his footing and slipped. He banged his head as he went down and he landed in the river. He went under and that was it. Tobes dived in but he couldn't see anything. I was frozen to the tree like a fly to a web, unable to do anything. Toby shouted at me to get help, but I couldn't move. Toby lost his temper, got out of the river and pulled me down,' he said, rubbing the scar on his chin. 'So that's it. It was my fault Seth died.'

'Blue, that's an awful thing to have witnessed and I can see why you blame yourself, but it wasn't your fault. It was an accident.'

'Yeah, that's what the therapist said. I realise now, as I watch George, that I was only doing what kids do. I guess I'm starting to see that it was really bad luck, but it was an accident that I caused so it was my fault.'

'It says a lot about you that you didn't take the easy option. It's easy to blame other people. It's far harder to look to yourself for the answers.'

'That's a good quote, who said that?' asked Blue.

'Someone I used to know,' said Charlie, uneasy at the sudden change of attention in her direction.

'Charlie, this someone, was that your mother?'

Charlie half-snorted her reply, 'No! What made you think that?'

'It's the way you often have these pearls of advice that someone has given you. Who was it, then?'

It was Charlie's turn to stare at her feet and take in a deep breath. 'It wasn't one person, it was lots of people. Some I remember better than others; I was given a whole lot of advice when I was younger. Just about everyone had something to impart. I only remember the useful stuff.'

'Who were all these people? Friends? Family?'

'Foster parents mainly, social workers, advisers, some behavioural therapists. All sorts. I was in care from a young age, shuffled about by Social Services, so there were lots of different people. They all had a crack at 'sorting me out'.'

'That must have been tough?'

'Meh,' said Charlie with a sardonic shrug. 'Some people have it much worse. I'm still here to tell the tale.'

'Still, it can't have been easy. Do you have any family?'

'I thought we were talking about Seth?' she said, nudging his ribs with her elbow.

'Not a lot else to say, really.' He shrugged his shoulders but Charlie was gesturing for him to continue. 'We all muddled along as best we could. Tobes went to uni and I stayed home and got fussed over by our parents. Mum was diagnosed with cancer, most likely the stress of Seth's death, and she went to join him a few months after being diagnosed. Dad and I tried to carry on but it was all too much for him, really; he got old before his time. He had a variety of illnesses and then, when I was at uni, Tobes turned up unannounced to take me home and I knew Dad had gone, and that was it. That was the moment it all came crashing down around me. I realised that I had killed them all.' He stopped and took hold of Charlie's other hand. 'I make it sound all dramatic and I don't mean to. It's how I felt at the time. I needed to get away. I felt I needed to get away from Toby, so that I didn't jinx his life too.'

'Jinx? Now that would have been a better nickname than Blue.'

Blue laughed, the mood between them was one of calm under-standing. He leaned forward and kissed her ever so tenderly.

'That was presumptuous of me. I'm sorry.'

Charlie felt the sensation caress her body and she smiled. Surrounded by paradise this was a moment she would always remember. 'Forgiven.'

'Do you see now why I can't get close to the kids?'

'No,' said Charlie calmly, 'I'll never understand that. And, despite what you say, I think you are getting close to them.'

The beach ended and they climbed up some low rocks onto the narrowed middle of the elongated island. This part of the island was still green but rocky and Charlie was glad of her aqua shoes to protect her feet. Blue was like a mountain goat and bounded over the undulating surface with ease in his bare feet. They were soon on the higher side of the island. This side had no beach, the cliff edge dropping into the bright-blue sea beneath. There was a good view of the other islands from here and Blue went into tour-guide mode and rattled off their names and key birdlife. After sitting in silence for a while they eventually walked back through the trees and Blue showed Charlie the large sandy hole where the children had dug up the pirate treasure earlier.

'You went to a lot of trouble for the children today. Thanks.'

'You're welcome. They're lovely kids. They're coping well, with everything.'

'I think so, but that will all change when we get back to London.'

'Why should it? I'm sure they'll be fine.'

'Blue, you need to wake up and smell the Americano, my friend. They won't be fine unless we do something to sort out the guardianship.' Her voice was even and gentle.

'That again,' said Blue, the frustration evident in his voice. 'You have got yourself in too deep, you need to distance yourself. Look at it from another angle. Look at it from the point of view of the carefree single young woman you're meant to be.'

'I can't walk away. The children need me.'

'Do they? Or is it really that *you* need to be needed?'

'What do you mean by that?' Charlie felt the calm mood leave her instantly.

'Are you letting your hang up about Social Services cloud your judgement? You could be denying them the opportunity to find a new family. It does happen. You could be making them miss out on an opportunity of a better life.'

'If you honestly believe that the perfect family is sitting there waiting to take on four children, you are on another planet. First of all they will go into foster care while they wait to find this imaginary, perfect family. The chances of finding a foster family that can take all four together are ridiculously slim. If they're lucky, they might keep Ted and George together in one placement and Eleanor and Millie in another.'

'You're looking at this from the worst-case scenario…'

'No, I'm being realistic! Millie is the only one who stands a good chance of being adopted. Most adoptive parents want a baby or young child, which is always going to be their preference. I've heard of prospective adopters turning down three-year-olds because they wanted younger children.'

'Don't you think…?'

'I've not finished yet. Millie might be adopted and her new parents might let her see her siblings occasionally but they might not. As soon as George and Eleanor start playing up they will get moved on to the next foster family, Ted the same, but because he's older he'll probably end up in a children's home, where he'll learn how to lie, fight and run away. I know, because it happened to me! And that is why I can't walk away – it's got sod all to do with what I need!' and, with that, Charlie turned and stormed off. Blue sighed heavily as he watched her go.

Charlie could feel her fingernails digging into her palms and took a deep breath before releasing them. She wanted to lash out, to hit something and ideally that something would be Blue and with something a lot more substantial than a wet kipper. If she were a toddler, this is the point where she would be rolling on the floor screaming. She kicked a nearby tree and discovered how flimsy her aqua shoes were. She stood hopping on the spot and swearing.

'Um, you do know the others can hear you swearing,' said Ted, appearing, as if from nowhere. He pointed through the trees to the beach, where she could see the children mid-cricket match. Charlie realised that she and Blue must have walked a full circuit of the island.

'Sorry. Can I have a go in bat?' she asked, limping her way out of the trees.

The noise of the busy airport hummed in her ears as Fleur stood over Rob. The strong arm on her shoulder was urging her to turn around. She was about to fight against that, too, when she looked up to see a familiar face. Fleur threw herself into her father's arms and clung to him.

'Mr VB! Nice to see you, as always. Could you give us a hand here?' said Rob, from his supine position on the airport tiles.

'No. You can piss off, Rob,' he said, as he put one protective arm around his daughter, picked up the handle of her case and, without taking his malicious stare off Rob, he stepped over him.

'Ah, Mr VB, don't be like that. We're the same, you and me...' but nobody was listening.

The car journey home was uncomfortable for them both but it was Fleur who broke the prickly silence. 'I'm sorry, Pa. I shouldn't have been cross with you offering Rob the money and the flat and everything. I know you were trying to help. I should have directed my anger at Rob. I can see that now.'

Her father glanced away from the traffic for a moment, 'I didn't offer him anything. He came to me with the proposition,' he said firmly.

Fleur blinked slowly. 'Actually, that makes more sense,' she said, feeling even more of a fool. Why hadn't she seen through Rob's lies? 'How have things been at home?'

'Odd without you,' he said, with a quick glance at her. 'Your mother has fallen in love with Wriggly. I fear we might have to get a dog when he goes.'

'Well, let's see what happens with Charlie and the children first. Wriggly might yet need adopting.'

Mr Van Benton took his hand off the steering wheel to pat his daughter's hand affectionately, 'You're a good girl, Fleur.'

She smiled and returned his hand to the steering wheel. The motorway was hazardous enough without him driving one-handed – look at what happened to the Cobleys, she thought.

'So how was the holiday?'

'You'd like Antigua. Beautiful beaches, really pretty island. The Cobleys had picked a beautiful spot...' Fleur paused. 'That's why they were going there. God, I am thick.'

Her father laughed and looked puzzled.

'Toby's brother, Felix, runs a boat company near to where the villa was. Toby must have tracked him down. I can't believe I didn't work that out before,' she mused, as she chuckled to herself. 'Felix is actually a good person and he's great with the kids.'

'Does that mean the guardian problem is solved?'

'I wish it was that straightforward,' she said, shaking her head.

After a few patches of rainy bumper-to-bumper queues, they eventually pulled into the drive and Mrs Van Benton instantly appeared, almost running out of the front door, and Fleur felt a lurch of guilt at what she must have put her mother through.

After a few tears and mutual apologies they settled down in the kitchen as another rain shower battered the garden furniture outside. Everything looked the same, but Fleur somehow felt different. She felt that she was starting to take responsibility and make her own choices, and more importantly her own decisions. Wriggly had definitely settled in well and was sitting on Mrs Van Benton's lap, licking her fingers affectionately.

'I've been a total idiot,' said Fleur, and both her parents went to speak at the same time. She halted them by swiftly raising her palm. 'No, don't deny it. I have.'

'I wasn't going to,' said Mr Van Benton. 'I was going to completely agree with you,' he said, smiling broadly.

His wife shook her head. 'The thing is, you need to look forward to the future. So what are your plans?'

'I need to get this business off the ground. Pretty Saddles. I want to do it myself, but I also want your advice,' said Fleur, ticking things off on her fingers. 'I need to speak to Jonathan and sort things out there. I need to speak to Poppy because she's left, like, umpteen messages on my phone, each one getting louder and crosser. And, most importantly, I need to be the friend I always should have been for Charlie when she gets home to face whatever Social Services and Ruth are going to throw at her.' Her mother nodded her agreement, her pride almost palpable as she stroked the now-sleeping dog.

'Jonathan?' asked her father.

'He's that nice solicitor I used for the annulment. He was at the airport.' She noted the exchange of looks between her parents. 'He is just a friend.'

'Then he's a friend who cares a great deal about you. He's called here a few times while you've been away,' said Mrs Van Benton.

She was glad to be home and to have a plan. First on her list was to placate the irate Poppy and then she was going to sort things out with Jonathan.

Chapter Thirty-Three

Jonathan didn't recognise the entry in his diary. A Mrs Stakes had been put in for five-thirty by one of the legal secretaries and the only information was that she wanted advice regarding prochain ami, or Next Friend, as it was often called, which was a person who represents another who is under disability and who does not have a legal guardian. It wasn't his area of specialism, so he wasn't sure why it was booked in with him or why so late in the day. He dug out a couple of books that might be useful if he needed a reference and went to get a coffee – he had a few minutes to spare before the new client arrived.

Jonathan was sipping his coffee as he ambled back to his office, but he almost spat it out when he saw Fleur sitting in the waiting area.

'Steady on, Mr Steeple, don't go choking on me,' said Fleur, getting to her feet.

'Fleur, how lovely to see you. I'm really sorry but I've got a client arriving at any moment...' he said, looking around expectantly.

'Ah, yes, Miss Stakes,' said Fleur, with a giggle.

'Um, Mrs Stakes, actually, how did you...'

'It's me, silly. Miss Stakes. Mistakes,' she emphasised. 'I can't

301

believe they wrote it down wrong; that completely ruins the joke.'

'Are you here about prochain ami, Next Friend?' said Jonathan, his frown of confusion deepening.

'Sort of. It was me trying, and failing very badly, to say I've made mistakes and I'm sorry. Can we be friends?'

Jonathan looked less confused, but some of the light that had lit up his face earlier had been switched off. 'Right. Well, yes, of course. Friends it is,' he said, forcing a tortured smile that made him look as strange as the cartoon version of the Cheshire Cat. He held it for a moment, but it soon died. 'Did you want to come in?' he offered, as a way to avoid the crippling silence rather than anything else. He didn't really want to prolong the agony but didn't know what else to do and she was still standing there in a delicate pink shift dress, her hair cascading over her shoulders and generally looking totally stunning. He wondered why women always looked particularly gorgeous when they were breaking up with you or, in this case, reiterating that you never stood a chance in the first place. Did they do it on purpose?

Fleur went into Jonathan's office and settled herself into the nearest chair. Jonathan squeezed around to the other side of the oversized desk. He picked up his coffee cup and she watched him. 'Oh God, I'm so sorry. Did you want one?' he asked, getting to his feet and starting to squeeze past again.

'No, I'm fine. Relax.'

Yes, because being ordered to do it by a beautiful woman was always going to do the trick, he mused.

'Right,' he said, forcing his shoulders to slump so that at least he didn't look as tense as he felt.

'How are things with Ruth?' asked Fleur.

Jonathan rolled his eyes. 'Woman's a nightmare, but I have to say she is asking the right questions about what's best for the trust fund.' Fleur rolled her eyes. 'I don't think she's after the money, Fleur. She's not a people-person so she's focusing on the elements she thinks she can control. She doesn't trust Charlie at all; she thinks *she's* after the money!'

'That's outrageous!'

'I know, but it's what comes of families that don't discuss their wishes with each other before they die.' Which seemed to kill the conversation somewhat.

Fleur perked up, as if a thought had struck her. 'Thanks for the musical voicemail message. It made me smile,' she said, and she grinned, as if remembering.

'You can't beat a bit of 'Copacabana' to cheer you up.' He took another sip of coffee. 'How was the Caribbean?' he said, lifting his chin to show interest and now feeling thoroughly uncomfortable with his forced sloping shoulders and lifted chin.

'Good,' she nodded. 'Actually, not great. Antigua was stunning, weather was lovely, but Charlie and I fell out. Actually, I was an irresponsible fool and she called me on it – and rightly so.'

Jonathan wasn't sure how to respond and it was taking all his concentration to listen; there was something mesmerising about her moist lips in their perfect natural shade. He realised, a little too late, that Fleur was expecting a response, 'I see. And are you friends again now?'

'Oh we'll be fine. You know how it is?'

He nodded. 'You're all she's got.'

Fleur looked puzzled. 'How do you mean?'

'Well, with Charlie having no relatives, she's got you down as her next of kin.'

Fleur blinked hard. 'I assumed she had some relatives some-where...'

Jonathan was shaking his head. 'I've said too much.'

Fleur was frowning. 'We were in foster care together and we've always been very close. Two peas in a pod, Ma always says, but I didn't realise that she had nobody else.'

Jonathan breathed out slowly. 'You might want to talk to her about it. I really can't say anything else, I'm probably about to be struck off as it is. What with the forged letter and now this breach of confidence. I'm not cut out to be a solicitor.'

Fleur smiled at him. 'You could be right. You really are too much of a lovely person,' and she leaned over the desk to kiss him. Whether it was to be the air kiss of friends or a full-on tongue assault, Jonathan was destined never to find out as the massiveness of the desk between them made the distance insurmountable. Fleur smirked, shrugged her perfect shoulders and blew him a kiss as she left the room. Jonathan slumped back into his seat and rested his head on the desk; it was oddly comforting. The door opened again and he remained where he was.

'Good God, Jonathan! What on earth is going on?' boomed his grandfather's voice.

'I wish I knew,' said the small voice from the blotter, 'I really wish I knew.'

A day later, Charlie was watching from the patio area as Esther and Ted came up the villa steps hand in hand. Charlie tried very hard not to snigger, but it was quite entertaining watching Ted playing at grown ups. 'Hiya, you two, did you have a good time?' asked Charlie.

'Yes, thanks,' said Esther and she sat on the chair next to Charlie.

'I'll get the drinks,' said Ted and he disappeared inside.

'He's a different person here, you know,' said Charlie. 'He's changed a lot. All for the better.'

'I know you're a bit, well, suspicious of me,' said Esther, 'but I don't make a habit of going out with the tourists.'

'I won't deny it,' said Charlie. 'I've been a bit protective of him but that's good to know.'

Ted returned and placed the mugs of tea down on the table. It wasn't exactly what Charlie had expected and Esther also appeared a little bemused, but they thanked him anyway. He was looking particularly pleased with himself. He sat opposite the ladies, leant forward and rested his forearms on his thighs. 'Glad

I've got you two together. I want to talk to both of you.' He rubbed his hands together, as if warming them up. Charlie picked up her mug of tea and leaned back in the chair; whatever it was, she knew that not overreacting was the answer.

'I've been talking to Blue and he's agreed that I can stay here in Antigua. I can move schools and finish my exams here and I can help him run the business.' He relaxed into his chair, his arms hanging over the sides and his knees apart; he looked very confident and clearly pleased with himself.

Both women stared at him, neither speaking. Charlie was dusting off the 'Kipper List' and silently repeating her mantra to not overreact. She was really hoping that Esther would say something first, and thankfully she did.

'Why?' asked Esther. Charlie was very pleased at the question and especially her accusatory tone.

'So that we can be together.' He looked a tad incredulous.

'But I won't be here,' said Esther flatly and Charlie found she was warming to her by the second. 'I've got a place at university from January.'

Charlie realised she was grinning and stopped. This was great; at this rate the whole idea would be quashed without her having to say a word.

'You never said,' said Ted, his early confidence evaporating.

'I told you I was going to read psychology in Cuba!'

'I thought you meant for a holiday. But you do the hair-braiding with your mum.'

'Yeah, to help out. Not as a long-term career! Did you think that was all I was going to do for the rest of my life? All I'm worth?'

'No, I thought…' Ted was wrong-footed.

'No, that's exactly what you didn't do, think,' said Esther, getting to her feet. 'Night, Charlie. I swear I didn't know about any of this.'

'Esther, I have no doubt that he dreamed it all up on his own. You take care, now.' But Esther was already leaving.

Charlie sipped her tea. She glanced at Ted, who was scowling at the patio table. She kept quiet, the teenage male was a volatile creature, and she felt it would be best not to anger it further.

'She mentioned something about studying natural sciences, but I didn't know she was serious,' mumbled Ted. Charlie nodded and tried to hide her escaping smile behind her mug. She watched him and sipped her tea.

'I'm still staying in Antigua,' he said at last.

Charlie drank the last of her tea, 'How do you work that out?'

'Because I want to, whether Esther is here or not, and because Blue says I can.'

'I'm really sorry, Ted, but right now Blue is not signing up to be your guardian…'

'But he's our uncle,' protested Ted.

'Actually, he's not a blood relative of yours so, despite his promises, I'm afraid that's not an option.'

Charlie could see the flames of temper burning bright in his eyes. She knew that feeling all too well, but it was better to face the reality of this and be disappointed now than to build up his hopes and have them dashed. Well, at least she truly hoped this was the better option.

'Instead you're going to let me end up in some hell of a children's home full of delinquents?'

'Ted, I will do everything I can to keep this family together…'

'I'm not going back to London. Blue said I could stay with him. I'll work here and pay my way. I'm nearly sixteen!'

'I'm sorry, Ted, Blue had no right to promise you something like this.'

'At least he's trying to help me. What are you doing? Having a free holiday on Mum and Dad and and…' he ran out of steam and stood up. 'You're not in charge of me any more, Charlie,' and he went upstairs. Little did he know that she hadn't been employed for quite a few days now, so technically his statement was correct.

If she'd had the energy she would have been furious with Blue, but she felt weary and wanted to flop into bed and face it all tomorrow. Perhaps things would look a little brighter in the morning, although she very much doubted it.

The nightshift of tree frogs and crickets handed over to the more tuneful call of small birds, with the exception of the brown doves, which sounded as if they were learning the recorder, as they only knew three notes.

'Good morning, beautiful,' said an alluring voice. Charlie yawned, then stretched lazily and pushed away the covers as she did so. She blinked. The blackout curtains were parted a little and there was someone standing there. Charlie came round quickly, sat bolt upright and grabbed at the covers.

'Jesus Christ, Blue!' she hissed. 'What do you want?'

'Yes, I'd love to come in, thanks,' he said, opening the curtains wide, and letting the sun stream in. 'I want to talk to you properly.'

'We do have a door, you know, and I want to speak to you too,' she said, straightening the covers and checking that her cleavage was covered.

'Great. You first,' he said, dropping down onto the bed a little closer to her than was sensible.

'Ted.'

'Ted? Oh, staying on a bit longer. It's fine with me, if you're okay with it. He wanted to stay on so he could celebrate his sixteenth birthday with Esther,' he said, with a twitch of his eyebrow.

He was still smiling, so he obviously hadn't identified that the death stare that Charlie was emitting was meant to be terminal.

'Funnily enough, I'm not okay with him leaving a top UK private school halfway through his GCSEs to move to a school in Antigua with a different curriculum, and with his only ambitions in life to sleep with Esther and work on the boats with you until he retires.'

'Uh, it wasn't meant to be long-term. I didn't sign up for that.'

'There's a surprise,' said Charlie sarcastically, 'Anyway, if you could back me up that he can't stay here permanently, I'd be grateful.'

'I'll do my best. Now can I get a word in?'

'Be quick, they'll be waking up soon.' With that, there was the deafening sound of the front door being slammed shut with force. 'And I'm guessing Ted's not in the best place this morning.'

'Okay, leave it to me.' Blue kissed her on the forehead before jogging out to the balcony and disappearing over the side.

Charlie looked around the room. It was their last full day in Antigua. Tomorrow they needed to pack everything up and be at the airport for a half-eight evening flight back to London. She wouldn't let herself think beyond the flight. She feared she knew what was waiting for them all back in London and that was a heap full of crap to worry about, so for now she was going to put her energy into making sure everyone enjoyed their remaining time on an island they'd all grown to love.

The beach was busy and Charlie wasn't reading today. She was watching and listening and filling the photo album in her mind with endless gigabytes of data. Every laugh, every smile, she was taking a mental snap shot and a few on the camera too so that she could make each of the children a more tangible album of their own.

Blue came running across the sand like something out of a film; he was wet from having waded out of the sea, his muscles flexed in all the right places and he looked like he was modelling swimwear. Charlie watched him and took in every detail – she wanted to remember Blue when she was back home too. Despite everything, he was still one of her happy memories.

'Hiya, can't stop. We've got a quick turnaround today but the reason I came by earlier was to say that you, me and the kids need to get together tonight. Okay?'

Charlie wanted to ask questions. She wanted to manage her own expectations. 'Why?'

'It's important, Charlie,' his expression pained. 'That's all I can say right now.'

'Okay,' she shrugged. 'How's Ted?'

'Grumpy, but he'll get over it. Don't worry.' She watched him run back through the picture-postcard scene to the boat and she wasn't convinced that the back view of Blue running wasn't even better than the front.

There had been something in his voice that gave her the merest glimmer of hope. This was last-chance-saloon territory that they were entering. She had wanted Blue to get to the right answer on his own, but she had hoped it would have been a lot quicker than this.

Her attention was pulled back to the hotel pool and the game where Millie was Princess Seaweed and George was her pet dragon; it was an interesting twist on a classic legend, she thought. The children were all laughing and Millie was dishing out her orders, which were barely audible due to the giggling. It was certainly a sight to commit to her memory photo album.

The day went by as if someone had it on fast-forward, despite Charlie's best efforts to make it drag out. There had been lots of laughter and lots of silliness and it warmed her soul to have witnessed it. She felt calm, which was something new, and she guessed it might be close to the peaceful place that Blue had talked about.

When Blue arrived, dressed quite smartly for him, Charlie had all the children sitting waiting in the living room. Ted was on the floor with his ear buds in and a face that would frighten a troll.

'Hiya, folks. Let's go!' said Blue, waving everyone towards the door. Millie was already disappearing before Charlie could get her words out, 'I thought you wanted to talk to us all together?'

'Er, yeah. But not here. Down to the boat, everyone.' He gave Charlie what she expected was meant to be a reassuring wink, but she had no idea what he was trying to convey. She shook her head at him and he grinned back. 'Lovely dress, Elle. Green suits you.'

'Thanks,' smiled Eleanor as she skipped out of the room. Ted lumbered to his feet, his sloped shoulders had returned and made a great picture together with his miserable face. George was talking at him, but there wasn't even a flicker of recognition as they left the room.

Blue put his arm round Charlie's waist. 'Relax,' he said, giving her a gentle squeeze. 'You smell nice.'

'Hello Darling,' she replied.

'And hello to you too, darling,' he said, his eyebrows dancing.

'The smell is my Victoria's Secret body cream, it's called 'Hello Darling'.'

'Oh, right. Yeah, of course,' he said shaking his head slightly at his mistake.

The walk down to the beach seemed to take longer than it ever had before. Ted was walking as if his pumps were made of concrete but the others were marching on obliviously. Charlie sent Blue on ahead so that she could grab some time with Ted.

'Have you sorted things out with Esther?' asked Charlie. Ted didn't change his focus from the ground and didn't show any sign that he had heard her. He flicked his hair out of his eyes and straightened slightly.

'She won't speak to me,' he said, his voice a gruff monotone. When had that changed, she thought?

'She'll be pissed off with you for a bit, but she'll come round.'

'But what's the point? I won't be here when she does.' He quickened his pace and started to jog to catch the others, as if running away from the conversation.

Chapter Thirty-Four

The boat ride was short and, as the engines slowed, everyone recognised where they were going to moor up. Tiny Ibis Island was awash with white fairy lights and a party was already underway on the beach. The small group included Berta, Esther and some staff from the hotel who were all either clapping or waving at their arrival. Millie started to jump up and down on the boat, her excitement overflowing.

'Surprise!' said Blue, belatedly. Tigi waded in and helped Blue secure the boat in the shallows before carrying the children to the sand. Blue took Charlie into his arms and, for once, she didn't struggle or protest. The strength of him was reassuring, his body tantalisingly close to hers, and a moment later she was standing on the sand watching him pass things off the boat to Tigi.

The calypso was the happy pulse of the party beating out a steady tempo. A few people were dancing on the sand as the heat from two oil-drum barbecues blurred the picture. There was masses of food all lined up waiting to be cooked and Ted quickly took charge of one of the barbecues that was laden with the biggest prawns Charlie had ever seen. She was glad she'd brought the camera so she could take a picture of George eating one.

Blue had set up a coconut shy, with the aim being to see how many you could knock off with five cricket balls. Tigi quickly took the top score, despite George's best efforts to beat him. Millie nearly took out Berta when she strayed within five metres of the shy. Despite Millie not knocking off any, she was still insistent that she'd won and was now walking around hugging and talking to her coconut.

'Limbo!' announced Blue, driving two large poles into the sand. Anyone over ten groaned, but was soon jollied out of it by the sight of Millie and her coconut limbo-ing under an imaginary bar between the poles.

'Let me show you how it is done,' said Tigi, when the bar was in place. 'Now, none of this walking like a zombie that's pooed his pants,' he said, stretching his arms out in front of himself and bending his legs to fit his own description perfectly.

'He's right, you know, all the tourists look like that when they do the limbo,' said Blue. Tigi changed his stance, widened his gait and wiggled himself to nearly horizontal before he almost danced under the bar like a crab, to rapturous applause.

'This is precisely why you won't catch me doing it!' said Charlie.

'But it's compulsory. They won't let you leave the Caribbean unless you have made an enormous fool of yourself doing limbo,' and Tigi took her hand and dragged her to join the end of the line. The bar had been raised for the uninitiated. Blue took his turn. He had a good rhythm and his hips were flexing erotically. Charlie found it very hard to concentrate on anything else. The bar wasn't very low but Blue was almost on the sand as he went underneath.

Charlie wished she had stuck at the yoga classes – they might have been of help right now. As she waited for her turn, she noticed Ted and Esther were standing together talking and, from what she could make out, it looked amicable. Charlie hitched up her dress, put her hands out in front of her and tried very hard not to look like a zombie.

'Zombie!' shouted Millie repeatedly as she ran under the limbo pole without ducking.

Charlie made it underneath with a little space and with a small amount of her dignity intact. Blue wrapped his arms around her and pulled her into a hug. 'I've discovered that I fancy zombies.' He took her hand and, as the limbo continued, they disappeared into the trees and were soon on the rocky side of the island. There was no breeze tonight but there were a few clouds. They sat down and watched the sunset in silence, with the music and laughter a minor and distant interruption.

'This little island is amazing. I take it you have permission to use it?'

'Kind of,' said Blue. 'I've a friend who's a real-estate agent and she's selling the island for a client. They moved away years ago but hoped one day to come back but... I don't know what happened but they never did. She's very happy for me to show it off to prospective clients and what better way to show them what an amazing place it would be than to hold a lime?'

'You scammer! Who's supposed to be the prospective client?' asked Charlie.

'That'd be you.'

'If it's anything under a hundred dollars I'll take it!' They both chuckled but it wasn't easy laughter for either of them.

Blue had his arm around Charlie. 'You're tense,' he said, giving her an affectionate squeeze. Charlie didn't really know how to respond without sounding totally dramatic.

'I'm kind of still waiting for us to have the important talk you mentioned.' She kept her gaze on the dropping sun, the colours in the clouds changing from gold to pink before her eyes.

Blue hung his head, his eyes downcast. 'That was just the line I used to get you all to the party. Nothing has changed, Charlie. I still feel the same about you.'

'If you care as much as you say you do, why won't you do this for me?'

Blue leant back onto the hard stone and Charlie watched as the sun disappeared behind the last pillow of cloud and turned it a deep orange.

'I know you love the children, Charlie, but it's not just about them.'

'It's all that matters to me. I'm sorry, Blue, that's the way I feel. I don't understand how you can cut them out of your life.' She felt the emotion bubble inside and had to swallow hard and concentrate to keep it under control.

'I will keep in touch with them, I promise.'

'A letter once a year when they're sat round a stranger's Christmas tree will not make everything better.' She surprised herself at how calm she was.

'I know that you believe me being their guardian is their best option but I'm not convinced. There must be some other way. I can't help feeling that if I'm their only hope then they're doomed,' he said, before emitting a deep sigh. 'What is it that you want, Charlie? Children aside, what do you want from life?'

Charlie stopped herself from sounding like a parrot by taking a moment to think. To try to push the children to one side for a second and answer his question; he deserved that at least.

'I've always wanted to be part of a proper family.' She started to laugh when she saw the pity in Blue's eyes. 'I didn't mean to sound that pathetic. But it's the truth, it's what I've always wanted and it's why I can't bear to see this one torn apart.'

'I can't promise you a family, Charlie, and I don't have much, but I can offer you a new start here with me. And who knows where it might lead?'

Charlie was about to protest when they were both distracted by footsteps nearby. Blue put his finger to his lips and, without making a sound, carefully got to his feet. He crouched for a few moments, listening to the direction the footsteps were heading and, when they couldn't hear them any more, he crept away into the trees. Charlie threw her head back and quelled the desire to scream out her frustration. Why was it so hard to get through to him?

Blue returned after a few minutes looking flustered. He rubbed his chin and pointed into the trees. 'I think you might need to intervene.'

'Why? What's up?' said Charlie, instinctively getting to her feet.

'I think Ted and Esther have disappeared to... to make hot dogs,' said Blue, cringing at his own phrase.

'Christ, Blue, why didn't you stop them?'

Charlie ran into the trees and suddenly realised how dark it was. She stood still and listened. She could hear her heart beating, but nothing else. She closed her eyes to give her ears an advantage. She heard a noise to her left and started tentatively heading in that direction, pushing through the bushes. As she got closer she could hear muffled voices and a stifled giggle. Charlie started stomping on the spot and as soon as she heard the voices swearing, she stomped towards them, which was quite tricky in flip-flops. As she pushed vegetation out of the way she found them. They started to rearrange their clothes at high speed.

'Oh, um, hiya, Tigi. Berta. Sorry, I got lost... thanks for the party and everything,' and, with that, she almost ran back to Blue, who had followed her into the trees a little and was now trying to creep out.

'You idiot! It was Tigi and Berta!' she said, slapping him on the behind.

'Sorry, I assumed...'

'You didn't check who it was?' but Charlie was already laughing and her sides were starting to hurt. 'Come on, let's get back to the party,' she said, putting an arm around Blue's middle.

'I love you, Charlie.'

They both stopped walking and Charlie slowly turned to face Blue. She studied his face and looked into the Cobley blue eyes, but she had no words to reply with, so she kissed him instead.

It appeared they had only missed the toasting of the marshmallows and the best part of a game of French cricket, the excitement of which appeared to have been heightened by Millie's sugar intake. A short while later Millie flopped down onto Charlie's lap and Charlie knew it was time to go. Blue gazed at Charlie and watched Millie snuggling into her. Without a word, Blue stood up, went and said good night to people and started rounding up the other children.

The boat ride back to the bay was somewhat morose, like the last journey of the condemned. The smiles were gone; Millie's and Eleanor's had faded into sleep. Charlie watched Ibis Island disappear and immediately felt the loss; it was the perfect piece of paradise. Blue and Ted took the children back to the villa and let Charlie have a few minutes to herself on the beach.

Charlie held her flip-flops in her hand and swung them rhythmically as she meandered slowly across the deserted beach. The sea whispered to her, calming her senses as it methodically caressed the sand.

A few hours ago the sun had been up and the beach had been alive with bright, happy people. The sand had glowed flashbulb-white and the sea had been its usual felt-tip blue but now they were on the moon's shift and it was as if the whole scene had been painted over with a colourwash in office-block grey.

She sat down and hugged her knees to her and stared across the beach and out to sea. She wriggled her toes into the cool sand and gazed at the mass of glimmering silver that the surface of the sea had become.

Charlie thought about her time in Antigua. Four weeks ago, she had stepped into paradise and firmly closed the door on reality. Had it been the right thing to do? They had all made memories they would never forget, so that was one box ticked. They had found Felix, or rather Blue, which was something she never bargained for. She shut her eyes for a moment and let herself think about how she felt about him. If she could put aside her frustration over the children's situation, then her feelings towards Blue were very different. It was such an intense emotion and nothing before had ever come close, nothing had ever felt so right. It was as if all those clichéd lines in the books Fleur liked to read suddenly made sense.

If it had only been him and her, she knew she would be staying in Antigua, but it wasn't just the two of them; the children were relying on her and she wasn't about to let them down. She knew that this time tomorrow she would be on a plane to London and she was trying hard not to think about what the real world had in store for her.

Where was there in London that she could wander alone at night and let her thoughts drift off into the black hole of darkness? She could try Hyde Park, but that was a bit like displaying a flashing sign saying 'Victim seeks assailant. Apply now.'

As she strolled up the villa steps she could hear the argument drifting out on the warm evening air as it competed with the tree-frog chorus for her attention. At first she thought it was Ted and George, but as she quickened her pace up the steps she could hear that it was Ted and Blue.

'... you're the adult, you're meant to take responsibility, but it's all superficial isn't it? You want to play happy families to impress Charlie, but you couldn't give a stuff what happens to us!' yelled Ted.

'I do care, that's why I can't get involved. I'm a nightmare. I'm the nut job you said I was...'

'Er, volume, people! The others will hear you!' hissed Charlie when she found them on the veranda. They were standing dangerously close to each other and looked moments away from squaring up.

'They're asleep,' said Blue, taking a step back.

'I doubt it. I could hear you from the road.'

'Everything's okay,' said Blue, splaying out his hands as if about to join a séance, a gesture Charlie guessed was meant to make him appear in control of the situation, despite looking very out of his depth.

'No, it isn't! This family holiday isn't some massive coincidence,

317

you know. Dad must have booked this villa because he wanted us to get to know you and you want to bin us after four weeks. Then what? See you again in another six years!'

'Ted, I'm really sorry,' he said, before turning towards Charlie. 'I think I'd better go. I'll call round tomorrow to see you off. Tigi is going to take you to the airport. I'm no good at airport good-byes,' Blue said, with a ponderous smile.

'Oh, save us the sob story and don't bother coming round here tomorrow, we can say good-bye now. Bye Blue,' said Ted, holding out his hand to shake, his chest moving rapidly with the effort of containing his temper. Blue hesitated before shaking.

'Bye, mate, take care.'

'I'm going to bed,' said Ted, and for the first time he kissed Charlie's cheek before leaving the room, just as he used to do with Helen. Charlie blinked. Despite everything, the wave of joy she felt wrapped around her like a blanket and made her smile. Blue was giving her a very odd look.

'Sorry,' said Charlie.

'He's a bit hot-headed. I was like that once.'

'He's not like you,' snapped Charlie, feeling suddenly protective. 'He cares about his family.'

'Right,' said Blue, with a cursory nod, brushing past her as he left.

'Charlie!' yelled Eleanor. Charlie was already out of bed and across the landing before she was properly awake. She found Eleanor standing in the bathroom pointing at the toilet bowl. Charlie blinked and tried to focus. It was morning and she had managed very little sleep.

'What is it?' asked Charlie, peering at the small round object nestled at the bottom of the water.

'I think it's a coin,' said Eleanor as a sleepy-eyed Millie padded into the bathroom and they all studied the toilet like cats over a mouse hole.

'Someone made a wish,' said Millie, giving in to a large yawn.

'Or maybe it's fallen out of George or Ted's pocket,' said Charlie, reaching in and pulling out the small brown coin.

'Er, that means they were doing a poo!' said Eleanor, running from the bathroom, closely followed by a screaming Millie.

Charlie ignored the shrieking as it ebbed away and studied the coin; it appeared to be quite old. She rinsed it under the tap and washed her hands thoroughly.

The girls were fascinated by the coin over breakfast and it passed between the two of them at speed, like money on a Las Vegas gaming table. George flopped into a chair and put his head on his folded arms.

'George, look we found treasure!' said Millie, wrenching the coin away from Eleanor.

George sat up and looked a little more interested. 'Er, where did you find that?' he asked, his eyes following it as Millie waved it around. He saw Charlie watching him and dropped his head back onto his forearms.

'It was in the toilet,' said Eleanor, screwing up her nose.

'Someone made a wish!' added Millie.

'Do you know where it came from?' asked Charlie, her suspicion rising.

'No, not seen it before,' said George, without looking up.

Ted bounded into the room looking a lot brighter and successfully took the coin from Millie, who was now waving it above her head.

'Cool coin, Millie, is it pirate treasure?' he asked, returning it to her before she could protest.

'No... Yes! It's pirate treasure!' said Millie, hastily changing her mind and studying the coin more closely. 'There's a pirate on it!'

Eleanor leaned over for another look at the coin, 'No, that's a king, silly.'

Blue left the house early, grabbing the post from the side as he went and carefully closing the door; he didn't want to embarrass Berta by being there when she got up. He was really pleased for both of them. It was funny to think of Tigi settling down, but perhaps Berta was the ideal woman to do it with. She made a Jambalaya that could vaporise your tonsils, which he knew was a sure-fire way to capture Tigi's heart.

Blue loved the early morning in Antigua – before the tourists teemed out and before the party got started; it was tranquil and soothing. He opened his post as he went: the first was an insurance renewal for the boat, which made his eyes bulge, and he quickly folded it up and shoved it into his back pocket. The second was a job offer. The job he had attended an interview for weeks before and had almost forgotten about. This was what he wanted; his dream job in his dream location. So why wasn't he ecstatic?

Chapter Thirty-Five

George came downstairs, washed and dressed, and looking a lot perkier than he had done. 'I'm off to St Johns. Last-minute shopping,' he said, as he turned to leave.

'Not so fast,' said Charlie. 'Who are you going with?'

'Er, Tigi.'

'Does Tigi know?'

'Well, no, not exactly. But he did say last night that if there was anything he could do…'

'He'd been on the beer and, although I'm sure he meant it, I'm guessing he wasn't planning on you testing his word today.'

George's shoulders slumped and his expression became taut. 'Come on, Charlie, I can get the bus. The driver will make sure I get off at the right place. I'll be all right.'

'Nope, sorry.'

Ted flew past them into the kitchen. 'Ted'll come with me. Won't you?' said George frantically gesturing his pleas to Ted from behind Charlie's back.

Ted hesitated. 'Er, yeah, sure.'

Reluctantly, Charlie gave in and went to round up the girls for their final trip to the beach.

If Charlie was feeling low when she had completed the stroll up from the beach for the last time, she hit a new level as she saw the police car parked in the drive. She tightened her grip on each child's hand and walked up to the villa. She called out as she walked in and was quickly met by Berta.

'You've seen the car?' she asked. Charlie nodded and Berta joined her with a more exaggerated movement, 'The police brought George back from St Johns and he's telling some wild tales in there!' She pointed to the living room and headed off to the kitchen, taking Eleanor and Millie with her. Charlie blinked hard and waited for her pulse to steady. Thank God the police aren't here to arrest me, she thought, but what the hell has George been up to?

Charlie walked into the living room to find George in a chair, looking as if any colour he had had been scrubbed off. His lip wobbled as he saw her. She looked from George to the policeman. He was wearing a uniform of sorts; it looked very casual to Charlie and a little less authoritarian than at home, but the same old feelings of angst resurfaced.

Charlie smiled at the policeman, but turned to George. 'Tell me what happened.' George looked back at the policeman as if requesting permission.

'I'm Officer Rodell Gayle. The museum called me out because this one was kicking up a fuss,' he said.

'Thanks, officer, but I want to hear what George has to say.'

George looked surprised that he was going to get his say at all, let alone first. 'The truth please, George,' she added, and his expression changed.

George ran his hand through his hair and looked as though he was fighting back the tears.

'I had this idea that if we could miss our flight we'd have to stay a bit longer and you could sort out Uncle Felix,' he blurted. 'I thought if you got arrested we couldn't go home.'

Charlie looked alarmed, 'Arrested? What for?' The last thing she had expected was for the children to be the ones that would dob her in to the authorities.

'Nothing serious, only stealing the old coin.'

'The one from the toilet?' asked Charlie. The policeman looked as though he wasn't following the conversation.

'Yes. I took it from the museum when I was there with Blue.' He hung his head. 'Nobody saw and nobody had missed it and I had the idea that if I said you'd taken it...'

'Problem was,' piped up Officer Gayle, 'that the museum staff were very understanding and pleased to get it back.'

'Why did they call the police, then?' Charlie looked from the officer to George.

'I got cross and knocked over a postcard stand.'

'You have to control that temper and there's no excuse for stealing,' said Charlie.

Officer Gayle butted in again. He put his hand up to hide his mouth from George's sight, which was pointless as his voice was strident. 'They've got a lot of those coins, it's not worth much.'

'But stealing is stealing, George.'

'I'm sorry,' said George, looking sorrier than a house-trained pup that's had an accident. His big eyes scanned Charlie for a flicker of forgiveness.

'I'll leave you to deal with this,' said Officer Gayle, and Charlie warmed even more to the laid-back approach of the Caribbean.

'Thank you,' said Charlie, and she meant it. Charlie heard the officer say his goodbyes to Berta, who he clearly knew quite well. Like Blue said, it was a small island.

'George,' started Charlie, but she was winded by George catapulting himself from the chair and hugging her tightly. She felt his sobs but there was no sound. 'George, we'll sort something out. But I'm afraid staying here isn't the answer. Try not to worry.' She looked round. 'Did Ted go with you?'

'Yes, but he went off to meet Esther.'

Berta had kept the girls occupied with making themselves sandwiches, and smiled knowingly as Charlie and a red-eyed George joined them in the kitchen. George sat down at the table and looked at the girls, who were looking at him. He shrugged and Berta passed him some bread.

'Ted called. Esther will be here to do the haircuts in about twenty minutes,' said Berta, and Charlie wondered if Blue would drive her over.

He didn't. Charlie noticed a tear as Esther cut Ted's hair and she felt some sympathy for them both. Ted's first love and it wasn't ending as most of them did in a blazing row. Charlie left them to say their good-byes and gave herself a little moment to be sad in the privacy of the bathroom. That was until the door flung open and bounced off the towel rail.

'Found you!' announced Millie, as Charlie hastily wiped her eyes.

'Some privacy would be nice, Millie, please,' but Millie had already disappeared. Life was still one big game to Millie and it made Charlie smile, despite everything.

The journey to the airport had been subdued, the scenes out of the windows now familiar pictures to Charlie. It seemed impossible that they had been travelling in the opposite direction only four weeks before. The time had streaked past them; even though she'd made the effort to savour every day, it had still raced past like the proverbial hare. Ted and Tigi exchanged a few words in the front. Ted looked quite different from the boy that had left London. Esther's haircut had also made an impact, tidying him up around the edges. Tigi parked the van near a space and, as the others got out of the back, he bumped fists with Ted and a lot of manly slapping on backs followed before they straightened themselves and got out. Charlie and the others waited in a line like children in the school-dinner queue as Tigi and Ted passed them the cases.

Tigi hugged each of them in turn but lingered when he reached Charlie. 'I lied to you,' he said, his eyes full of remorse. Charlie looked uncertain and Tigi continued. 'You asked me if Blue had lots of women and I told you that he did. I don't know why I said that. It felt like the answer you expected, but it wasn't true. He's friendly with the ladies, all the ladies,' he said with a stifled laugh, 'but he never gets involved with any of them. He's always a true gentleman. Despite my advice, he's never made the most of the holiday trade. I'm sorry I misled you.'

'Thanks for telling me, Tigi. I'm afraid it changes nothing.' And she hugged him again.

Millie came back for another hug and looked very serious as he picked her up. She shook her head, 'changes nothing,' she said, mirroring Charlie, before taking her princess trolley and heading towards the airport building. Inside they were thrown into a melting pot of queues and noise. Somehow Charlie managed to herd everyone into the right queue. They checked in the cases with a very smiley young woman, who clearly loved her job. Charlie took the boarding passes and passports back and as she turned to leave the check in desk, there stood Blue.

Her heart flew up into the air but her expectations were on the ground.

'We'll be over there getting one last Wadadli,' said Ted, with a wink, but it barely registered with Charlie as he ushered the others away.

Blue stepped forward and they were inches apart. 'Charlie, I'm sorry.'

'What for?' asked Charlie, trying very hard not to cry.

'For not being who you want me to be.'

Charlie felt the tears starting to pool and blinked them away. 'Someone once told me, you have to be true to yourself. So I respect that,' she said, and she meant it.

'When things are sorted out with the children, would you come back?'

'It's not that simple, Blue,' said Charlie. She pushed thoughts of losing them to the back of her mind. 'I promise I'll let you know what happens.'

'Okay,' he said with a nod. 'I'll miss you, Charlie.'

He pulled her into a kiss but Charlie barely responded, the tears were dripping off her face and it was all she could do to not start bawling like a toddler. The sadness engulfed her. She was going to miss Blue and she was going to miss Antigua – and knowing she wouldn't see either again was too much to deal with.

'I need to go,' she whispered and pushed him away and, without a backward glance, headed for the toilets.

Blue turned around and could see the children sitting patiently. Ted stood protectively over them, his arms folded. Blue held up his hand in a half-wave but Ted didn't respond.

'Bye, bye, stupid pirate!' shouted Millie happily. Blue took a deep breath and left.

Charlie joined the others, having patched up her face, and slapped on the best she could muster in smiles. Post-holiday blues were going to be kicking in for all of them.

'You all right?' asked Ted.

'I'll live,' she said, pursing her lips. 'Be glad to get away from the flies.'

Ted looked pensive, 'What is it with you and flies?'

'Long story. Come on, let's get these through security and back to reality.'

Jonathan was pretty sure that it was the wrong thing to do, but he was going to do it anyway. He was going to speak to Fleur and get his message across like a man. Well, that was the plan, anyway. Mr Van Benton had provided his home details, so that was where Jonathan was heading. He was trying to think straight but all he had was a giant marshmallow of fog in his brain, so he was working on his instincts for the time being.

He pulled up in front of the house, had one last attempt at fog clearance and got out of the Audi. He wished he was a little taller and a fraction broader, but he would have to work with what he had. He wanted to run away but he simply wouldn't let himself, this was something he had to do. Jonathan knocked hard on the door and could instantly feel an apology trying to surface, but forced it back.

The door opened and a well-dressed woman greeted him warmly.

'Mrs Van Benton?'

'Yes,' she said, looking at him curiously.

'I'm Jonathan Steeple and I…'

'Oh, Jonathan, how lovely to meet you. Do come in,' and she almost dragged him inside. 'Thank you so much for all the support you've given Fleur. We are very grateful.'

'It was a pleasure. Is Fleur in?'

'She's down at the stables, I'll show you the way,' and she frogmarched him through the house and out the back, across a perfectly round lawn, then pointed him at the stables and, with a wave, left him to it.

He could hear classical music playing as he neared the stables and someone was talking.

'Now this is the last time. Do you understand? You have a serious attitude problem, Ralph, and you need to do something about it.'

Fleur came into view. Well, at least, her rear end did. This was not helping the brain spaghetti at all.

'Hi,' he said, completely forgetting about being more manly and forceful.

'Ooh, Jonathan, you made me jump,' she said, spinning around and self-consciously tucking her hair behind her ear. 'I was talking to Ralph here,' she said, indicating a very small, round horse that he would have sworn was glaring at him.

'Hi Ralph,' he said, with an almost jazz-hands wave before

shaking his head in an effort to stay on track. 'Look, I wanted to talk to you, Fleur.'

'Don't worry, I won't get you into any trouble about all this I promise. I've not said anything to anyone.'

'Oh, that's brilliant because I was a bit worried...' he stopped himself. 'That's not why I'm here. None of that matters,' he said, remembering that he was meant to be manly and irresistible. 'I want to talk about us. I don't want to be friends.' He was very pleased with his forceful delivery until he realised what he'd said.

'Oh, I see,' said Fleur, looking crestfallen.

'No! Sorry, that's not what I meant. I do want to be your friend. Obviously. Who wouldn't want to be your friend? What I meant to say was that I want to be more than that.'

'Oh,' said Fleur, which was a lot less than Jonathan was hoping for.

'I really like you, Fleur. I mean *really* like you. You came along and changed my world and, more than anything, I want to be the right person for you. But...erm... uh...' he ran out of things to say and was aware that he was mumbling now, so he stopped himself and threw up his hands. 'That was the end, the bit before the 'but'.'

Fleur looked demure in her riding jodhpurs and shirt with the cuffs turned back. Even her forearms were sexy, thought Jonathan.

'Jonathan, you are completely lovely and a very good friend.' Jonathan felt his shoulders start to sag and he forced them back up straight. Fleur stepped closer to him. 'You are so not my type. I never go for the nice boy with a good job and neat hair...'

'But I could change...' started Jonathan, self-consciously dragging his fingers through his hair. He was grateful that Fleur interrupted him as he had no idea where he was going with that.

'Let me finish,' she teased, 'but this time I'm going to make an exception.'

She leaned in and kissed him and he felt like every heroine in every love film he'd ever seen and almost melted. Sod being manly, he thought, this beats manly any day, and he kissed her back.

Chapter Thirty-Six

Charlie found it hard to keep still on the flight; she found she couldn't get comfortable and fidgeted constantly. A million different scenarios of what lay ahead had all been unleashed from their cell in her brain and were now running riot, creating all sorts of carnage.

She was relieved that the police didn't board the plane when they landed – this had been one of many possible scenarios – nor were they waiting at baggage collection or customs. They wandered out like lost souls caught in a gust of people and stood in line waiting for a taxi. It wasn't cold but the sky was grey and weighed heavy on them. The children had slept intermittently on the plane but all looked weary now.

The taxi deposited them outside their house and again, like the airport, there was nobody to meet them. It was all suspiciously quiet. Surely somebody had noticed that they had been missing for four weeks? There was some post and lots of free flyers on the doormat and the answer machine was flashing manically. Ted took the luggage upstairs and Charlie settled the others on the sofa with a Disney film and a blanket. It was mid-morning in the UK but it would have been super-early back in Antigua, so it would take them a while to adjust.

Charlie sorted out drinks and she and Ted stood next to the answerphone with a notepad. 'Ready?' Charlie asked.

'Go on…'

Charlie pressed play and tried to concentrate. The first message was from Fleur wishing them a nice holiday and Wriggly was barking in the background; she must have got their flight times wrong. There were a couple of marketing calls. It then moved on a few days and there was a series of calls from Mrs Van Benton and Poppy looking for Fleur. There were three messages where the caller put the phone down and left no message. Ted slumped against the wall and sipped his Coke.

It was now down to four remaining messages and Charlie found herself taking in lungfuls of air at the end of each one to steady herself. The next one was from Camille asking for an update and saying that people were getting worried, and then came a message from Ruth.

'You are no longer in the employ of the Cobley Trustees. Unless you contact me within the next twenty-four hours I will have to assume that you have taken unlawful action and I will be forced to notify the authorities.'

'She's still as charming as ever,' said Ted, letting his head fall back against the wall.

'Message was two days ago,' pointed out Charlie, 'and it's Sunday today, so we might be…' she fell quiet as the next message started to play.

'Hi Charlie, hi children,' came Camille's voice, 'please get in touch as soon as you get this message. An emergency meeting has been arranged for eleven o'clock, Monday, and it is key that everyone attends. You've got my numbers, but here they are again…' and she fired them off in quick succession.

'Meeting tomorrow, great,' sighed Charlie.

'Doesn't say where,' said Ted, who looked as if he was trying too hard to stay calm, but he kept twitching his hair out of his eyes, or he would have done had it still been long – it had become a nervous habit that needed breaking.

'Let's hope it's not at the police station.'

The last message started to play and there was silence until a hesitant voice kicked in, 'Er, hello Charlie, it's Roger here. I don't like these damned machines. Anyway, I wanted to talk to you about all this business with the children. Ruth is getting herself in a terrible state about it all. So that was all. Perhaps you'll call me. Bye.'

Ted and Charlie exchanged varying degrees of raised eyebrows. As Charlie pressed the delete button the phone sprang into life and they both jumped and smirked at each other. Charlie was tempted to let it go to voicemail, but after four rings she picked it up.

'You're home! Hurray!' said Fleur, and Charlie mouthed to Ted who it was but he had already worked it out and was walking away.

'Hello Fleur, how are you?'

'I'm brilliant. I couldn't remember when your flight was, but anyway you're home and you've not been arrested. Yay!'

'No, but there's some big meeting arranged for tomorrow, which I'm not looking forward to.'

'I'll be there to support you, Charlie. Just tell me where and when.'

'You don't need to…'

'No, I insist. I want to help and I won't take no for an answer.'

Fleur then babbled on about her business venture and Charlie had to wind up the call. They agreed that Fleur should come over that evening as she had lots she wanted to talk to Charlie about.

Charlie settled herself in the kitchen, ready to ring back Camille. Ted got another drink from the fridge and paused. 'I think I'm going to stay here for my A levels and go to uni in the Caribbean or America,' he said, as if it was the most normal piece of information to impart.

'Let's work out if you're all going to be flung into care first,' said Charlie, and she instantly regretted it. 'I'm really sorry, Ted. I shouldn't have said that. I can't think past tomorrow.' He looked at the floor, shrugged and went back upstairs. Charlie felt awful – he didn't need this regular slap of reality. He had grown up so much, but that still wasn't a good excuse to throw things like that at him. Her tongue was too quick for her brain sometimes.

She called Camille, who was overwhelmingly relieved to hear from her and must have been envisaging the worst. She explained about the meeting, which had the grand title of a 'family council' and involved everyone in the children's support network.

A number of times during the call Charlie nearly mentioned Blue. He kept popping into her head, but each time something stopped her. She wasn't sure what it was or why. Camille had had a lot of phone calls from Ruth and it sounded like she had worked hard to stop Ruth from going to the police. Camille promised to update Ruth after the call so that Charlie didn't have to speak to her, which was a small blessing.

In between calls a sleepy-looking Eleanor and Millie wandered into the kitchen and hugged Charlie in turn before sitting down.

'I miss Wriggly,' said Eleanor, 'and the beach,' she added with a yawn.

'Fleur's bringing him later,' said Charlie, and Eleanor instantly brightened up and her shoulders straightened.

'I miss the stupid pirate,' said Millie, with an even bigger yawn.

Not as much as I do, thought Charlie. 'How about some hot chocolate?' and she received two sleepy nods in response.

Charlie called Roger, who was thrilled to hear from her and they chatted for a while about the planned family council and Antigua. Charlie put each of the children on for him to speak to and, although listless, they did each manage a brief conversation with him. Eleanor handed the phone to Millie.

'...found pirate treasure with a pirate and fed a whale and there was poo in the pool. Bye-bye!' said Millie showing the most enthusiasm she had all day before she handed the phone back to Charlie and returned her attention to the television.

'You did the right thing, Charlie. They've all had a marvellous time. A holiday was exactly what they needed. Thank you.'

Charlie felt a lump in her throat and shook it away.

Charlie did the lazy thing and ordered pizza delivery for lunch – much to the delight of everyone. Excited barking at the front door interrupted more television.

'Wriggly!' yelled Eleanor, and she ran to get the door. The dog was so excited to see Eleanor he wee-weed on the front-door step. This was announced to the street and surrounding area by great shouts and broadcasts from the now-assembled children.

'Sorry,' said Fleur, when Charlie appeared with a mop.

'I'd assumed it was the dog,' said Charlie, as Fleur tip-toed around the puddle. Charlie had barely sorted out the clean-up when Fleur threw her arms around Charlie and squeezed her tightly.

'I've missed you, Charlie.'

'Hi, I've missed you too. Are you okay?'

'Me? Marvellous. Could not be better. Give me a hand with the things from the car, would you?'

'Christ, Fleur, you're only stopping two nights. How much did you bring?'

'Not luggage, silly! Shopping. I did a supermarket shop, as I knew you'd be tired, and I'm cooking tonight. No protests, please. You've looked after me often enough – now it's my turn.'

Charlie tilted her head to one side and studied the person in front of her, 'Who are you and what have you done with the real Fleur?' she asked, her face deadpan.

'You are funny,' said Fleur, giving her a playful shove.

The children beat an early and hasty retreat after dinner as they were all struggling with the combination of travelling and jetlag.

Fleur poured out wine for herself and Charlie and they relaxed back into the sofa.

'How did you leave things with Blue?' asked Fleur.

'Not great. His life is in Antigua. Mine is here. End of story. Let's not talk about him. So what did you want to talk to me about?'

Fleur smiled. 'I wanted to make sure that you knew how much I love you.'

Charlie took a sip of wine and raised an eyebrow. 'Don't tell me you're giving lesbianism a try?'

Fleur giggled. 'No, silly. I'm going out with Jonathan, but I'll tell you all about that in a minute. I know you had a rubbish childhood and you hate flies but other than that I don't know as much as I should about my best friend. You've been part of my life since... forever. I love you as much as I love Poppy and Ma and Pa. You're family to me, Charlie, and I want to get to know you as well as you know me. I'm starting with being there when you need me and listening more.'

Charlie was touched. 'Thanks, Fleur, that means a lot.'

'So what is it with the flies?'

Charlie sighed. 'My mother and I lived in a flat in Croydon. She was messed up with drink and used to go out, get wasted and then couldn't make it home. I got left on my own a lot.' Charlie paused. 'I've never shared this before.' Fleur took her hand and squeezed it reassuringly.

'There was often food left on dirty plates and it attracted flies. I loathed them,' Charlie shivered at the thought. 'She used to tell me to play hide and seek and then not come back for hours. Social Services tried loads of times to help my mother cope but she couldn't kick the drink. Eventually, when I was four, they took me into care. That's where I met you.'

Fleur hugged Charlie tightly and Charlie hugged her back. 'Whatever happens tomorrow, you'll always have me,' said Fleur. 'I promise.'

'Thanks, Fleur, and you know that if you wanted to trace your birth family I'd support you?'

Fleur nodded. 'I know, but I don't think I'm ready for that just yet. And, anyway, I've got all the family I need.' Fleur hugged Charlie tightly and Charlie hugged her back.

Chapter Thirty-Seven

Charlie woke and immediately a dark feeling crept over her and made her clutch at her covers. For a moment she looked around the room and took in the darkness created by the blackout blinds. No sun forcing its way through, she was back in London and something was wrong. Quite a few things were wrong. She knew she had a lot of explaining to do and there were most likely too many rucks to smooth things over this time. A look at the clock told her it was eight thirty-two – the jetlag had made her sleep in. But there was something else and she left her warm bed, dragged on her dressing gown and started checking the house.

The house was quiet. She stood on the landing and listened. She tried to feel what was unsettling her, wondering if she was losing her marbles; was her mind giving her off-beam messages? She opened George's bedroom door. George was in a star formation and out cold. She shut the door and went to check on Millie and Eleanor. Millie was on her knees with her bottom in the air, sound asleep, her hair covering her face and a glimpse of tatty Pooh poking out from the crook of her arm. Eleanor was reading a book with her book light shining on her, giving her an ethereal effect.

'Morning Charlie, did I wake you?' she whispered.

'No sweetie. The others are asleep. I'll start breakfast in a minute.' Back to the old routine, thought Charlie. There was no Berta here – she was on her own. She went to open Ted's door and it was already open. The dark feeling clawed at her gut. She pushed the door open and it slowly swung into the deserted room.

Charlie ran downstairs, tightening her dressing gown around her although she wasn't cold. She rushed into the kitchen, pulled open the pantry cupboard door and scanned the shelves as quickly as her tired eyes would allow. She went back to the top and started searching again, then she spotted it: the space where the honey jar used to sit. It was gone and she knew immediately that so was Ted.

Charlie got dressed at lightning speed and woke Fleur, who for once was ready to listen and do as she was told. Charlie grabbed the phone. She rang Ted's mobile and she heard it ring out in his room. It was no more than she expected.

She heard a noise in the bathroom and rushed inside in desperation to see a bleary-eyed Millie sitting on the toilet.

'Some piracy, please!' stated Millie firmly.

'Careful what you wish for, sweetheart,' said Charlie, shutting the door.

Charlie left the house in a daze. She needed to think like Ted, to think about the warnings she'd given him because now he was starting to heed them and use them to good effect. She needed to find him before the meeting at eleven and, far more importantly, before anything happened to him.

Charlie paced the nearby streets and checked the five nearest tube stations in case he had decided that Monday-morning commuters might be good for loose change. She was always going against the flow, always the one fish trying to swim against the tide of suits. She felt the panic rising in her and this time she let it out. She stood in the vast tunnel that led from South Kensington tube station, threw her face to the ceiling and yelled at the top of her voice. It wasn't a word, just a yell of emotion. She noted that she now had a good personal space around herself as people gave her a wider berth, although it didn't halt their journey in any way.

She gave herself a little shake. She definitely felt better for it and she carried on out of the station. As she was exiting up the many steps near the Natural History Museum her mobile rang; it was an unknown number.

'Ted?'

'Hi Charlie, it's Blue. How are you?' The sound of his voice made something switch back on inside of her, but that was an extra emotion that she wouldn't be able to manage right now.

Obviously timing wasn't Blue's strong point. 'Can I call you back?'

'Don't hang up. I've got a surprise for you.' And she heard the faint sound of a doorbell ringing in the background.

'Blue, really I've not got time for this.'

'Fleur? Hi, is Charlie in?'

'What the hell is going on?' asked Charlie, her small amount of patience ebbing away.

'I'm here in London. I called your home but it was engaged, so I called the mobile and I'm standing on your front doorstep!' She could hear the grin in his voice.

'Blue…' she started to talk but she could hear that Fleur had taken over at the other end and was calling the shots.

'…so Charlie has been looking for him for over an hour and if they are not back for this meeting, it won't look good. I need to stay here with the children and field any phone calls. What could you do to help?'

'I'm thinking. I've had a long flight, but I'm thinking.'

Charlie huffed impatiently on her end of the phone.

'Right, Charlie, you need to make sure that you are back for eleven whatever happens and you tell them that I've come to surprise you and I've taken Ted out. Okay?' said Blue.

'Okay,' agreed both Fleur and Charlie together.

'Ted asked me about survival techniques and I told him a few,' said Blue.

'Why would you do that?' snapped Charlie.

'Because he wanted to know and I'm an idiot. Now, where do you want me to look?' he asked, handing Fleur his case before he jogged down the steps.

'I don't know,' said Charlie, shaking her head. 'I've being looking for an hour and half but London is huge. I don't even know if he's still in London. He left his passport but that doesn't exactly leave us with a small search area.'

'We need to think like Ted. Where would Ted go?'

'I've been trying to do that all morning,' said Charlie, as defeat tried to wrestle her into submission, her anxiety starting to give way to despair.

Charlie talked Blue through all the places she had been and they agreed that she would check out the museum area. Blue headed towards the Thames.

Charlie's heart was beating a little faster to think that Blue was nearby, but she didn't dare to hope what his motivation for coming was. She saw a tall boy with short hair and slopey shoulders and all thoughts of Blue were lost as she broke into a run. She hurdled a park bench and nearly sent the slopey-shouldered youth to the ground.

'Watch it!' he shouted, his acne-ridden face twisting in alarm.

'I'm sorry. You looked like someone I'm looking for. Sorry. You've not seen someone who looks like you, have you?'

'Nutter,' he said and sidled off, shaking his head. Charlie stood and looked around. Where the hell was Ted?

A few minutes later Charlie's phone rang again – it was Blue. All he said was 'Do they still have boats on the Serpentine?'

'Er, yeah, they do.'

'Meet you there.' The phone went dead.

Charlie jogged back to the underground, glancing at her watch. It was nearly twenty past ten. If Blue was wrong about this hunch it was game over. There were so many people she had to queue to get back inside the tube station. The tube ride was hot, sweaty and, although there were seats, she chose to stand so that she could be first off the train. She looked around at the mixture of commuters, tourists and day trippers, some stony-faced, some animated but all trapped on a train for the duration.

It seemed to be taking forever, the train twisting and turning. Eventually, they came out of the tunnel and into the artificial light of Knightsbridge tube station. Charlie ran off the platform, swore at the ticket barrier, which took two attempts to recognise her Oyster card and sprinted out of the station. She knew there was a way through to the park down the side of the Mandarin Oriental Hotel. She ran until she had to stop for breath. She bent double and stood for a moment, filling her burning lungs. Charlie looked up and was pleased to see the massive hotel ahead of her as she rubbed at the stitch in her side.

It was an impressive building of ornate red brick and had been the tallest building in London when it had been built over a hundred years earlier; more useless information someone had imparted to her. She stopped for a second – it had been Helen. Helen had told her all about the Mandarin Oriental and she swallowed hard at her memory. She needed to concentrate and find Helen's son.

Charlie took a deep breath and tried to run again, but the pain in her side was a hindrance. She jogged as best she could down the side of the hotel and round to the original entrance at the back of the hotel, which was now reserved for the Royal Family and special occasions, past it and into the park. She found herself near to the Serpentine and scanned the area for anyone looking like Ted. Blue rang again.

'Where are you?'

'The moon,' said Charlie. 'Sodding Hyde Park, where are you?'

'Hyde Park Corner tube.'

'What makes you think he's there anyway – we could be wasting time.'

There was a pause. 'It's where I would go. I'd want to escape to water, to feel the rhythm of its movement.' He stopped talking. Charlie was breathing heavily on the other end. 'It's the boathouse we need to aim for.'

'Get a bloody move-on then, I'm near the Serpentine.'

'Wait there, I'm on my way.'

Charlie had no intention of waiting. Her stitch was easing, so she speed-walked nearer to the lake. It was vast and the boathouse was on the opposite side. Charlie turned right and followed the line of the water past the Queen Caroline memorial. She heard a familiar voice calling her name, but she was on a mission. The boathouse was in sight.

Blue appeared at her side, 'I know you heard me,' he said falling into step, 'can we talk as we walk?'

'If he's not here, we are totally kippered.'

'I know. Hello, by the way,' he said, leaning in for a fleeting kiss as they continued to speed-walk.

'Hello,' said Charlie and a brief smile escaped as she took in the shirt with rolled-back cuffs and the trousers he was wearing rather than his usual t-shirt and shorts. 'Why are you here?'

'Because I need to tell you something, but now might not be the time.'

'I'm listening,' she said, a tad impatiently.

Blue took a deep breath, 'When I met you something happened, something I never expected to happen and, to be honest, it was a hell of a shock.' He paused, but there was no response, so he twitched his head and carried on. 'You drive me totally crackers, Charlie French, but I need you. My sad heart needs you. I thought it hurt when I left London but when you left Antigua it was like…'

'Is this going to take long? Because I'm having a bit of a crisis,' said Charlie, her tone matter-of-fact.

'I know. I said it might not be the right time, but I've started now and I've travelled…' Blue squinted, as if trying to work out the distance, 'a bloody long way to tell you this.'

'And that's lovely but it's not going to change anything if it's the same conversation we kept having in Antigua. Is that him over there?' said Charlie, stopping to focus her tired eyes properly.

'No, it's a tree stump. You need glasses. Charlie, please listen. I know you and the kids come as a package and I still think they have better options than me…' Charlie opened her mouth to butt in but Blue kept going, 'and I know you disagree. So let's give it a go.'

Blue studied her face, the seconds ticking by until Charlie turned away and marched off. Blue took a deep breath and followed her. They carried on for a couple more paces until Charlie stopped dead. 'What do you mean 'Give it a go'? You're not changing your sodding washing powder! It's not a new syrup in your coffee!'

'I mean, I have never been so bloody scared in my whole life as I am right now, but I'm here doing it anyway because I need my family around me and that's you and the kids.'

'Have you really thought this through?'

'No, not in the slightest. If I were going to think it through I would be lying in a hammock sipping a Wadadli right now. But I know all I need to know.' He paused and took a breath. 'I know I love you.'

Charlie narrowed her eyes, 'How do you know that?'

Blue laughed, his eyes looking brighter and bluer than ever. 'Because you drive me insane, you are all I think about all the time. When you left it was like… you'd died. It felt like all the pain had returned.' Charlie continued to eye him suspiciously. 'How about you? How do you feel?' asked Blue.

'We need to find Ted. This can wait,' she said and carried on round to the boathouse at a pace. Blue stood for a moment, looking panicked, and laced his fingers together on top of his head as he watched her march off. He let out a long, slow breath, shook his head and followed her.

Charlie carried on walking, staring straight ahead but not really seeing anything. Why did she feel so despondent if Blue was here, telling her he loved her? She already knew she loved him too. Because none of it matters if I can't find Ted, she thought miserably. She reached the boathouse and stood on the decking. The boathouse was closed but there was movement inside.

She peered in the window and got shooed away by a grey-haired man. Charlie turned around to face the lake. She scanned the still water. There was nobody there apart from a couple of ducks.

'Ted!' she yelled and she heard an echo as Blue got nearer and started to call out too.

'Ted!' they shouted together and as he neared they locked eyes and a look of shared pain shot between them. For a moment there was nothing but the noise of an irritated duck further along the lake.

Blue got out his yo-yo and started to play. Charlie glowered at him. 'Seriously, you're playing with that now?'

'It helps with stress,' he said, reluctantly putting it away.

'I have something similar,' she said, rearranging the 'Kipper List' and Blue's name dropped off the bottom. There were lots of things she wanted to do to him but slap him with a kipper wasn't one of them. They both started to pace the decking and call Ted's name in turn.

'We've got it wrong,' said Charlie after a few seconds. 'Actually, you got it wrong.'

'He might still turn up. He loved the boat, he was a natural. It's where I'd go.'

'You keep saying that, but he's not you. He's Ted and he has a mind of his own.'

'Look, let's wait here and…'

'Teeeeeeeeeeeed!' howled Charlie, her pain cutting through her voice.

One of the rowing boats started to rock in the water and Ted hitched himself up onto one elbow. 'Trying to get some sleep here,' he said, before doing a double take at Blue, who threw up his arms theatrically in relief. 'What are you doing here?' asked Ted.

'Looking for you, you goon,' said Blue.

'I'm not coming back,' said Ted, his voice calm and reasoned. 'I'm sorry, Charlie. I've changed and I can't let this happen to me. I have to do something.' He shot Blue an accusatory glance.

'Ted, I think it's going to be okay.' Charlie's voice was hesitant and she looked at Blue for reassurance.

'It is. I've sold my share of the business to Tigi, Berta has promised to keep him in check and I'm here on a one-way ticket,' said Blue and Charlie turned to stare at him, her eyebrows high.

After a moment, she turned back to Ted. 'It'll be okay,' said Charlie and this time she was starting to believe it herself.

'Are you saying all that just to get me out of the boat?' asked Ted.

'No, don't be an arse. There's a meeting at eleven, isn't there?' said Charlie, wiping away a stray tear of relief.

Ted grinned and started to climb out of his boat and across three others, which all rocked precariously until he made it onto the decking. Charlie forgot herself and hugged him tight and he let her. She had suddenly gone from despair to the happiest person on the planet and it was exhausting.

'You know I hate hide and seek,' said Charlie, and Ted put his arm around her and gave her a squeeze.

'Sorry.'

'Wah gwan,' said Blue as he fist-bumped Ted and they embraced each other, which was followed by the now-traditional backslapping.

Ted looked quizzical as he eyed Blue. 'When you got on a flight I would have still been at home. So what made you leave Antigua?' he asked. Both he and Charlie had their eyes fixed on Blue.

'Because I want to be your guardian,' he said, pointing at Ted.

'Just like that?'

'Yep… well, with the proviso that all family holidays are spent in Antigua,' said Blue, giving Ted another friendly slap on the back. 'Come on, let's get back for this meeting. I can't wait to see Ruth again!'

Charlie telephoned ahead to update Fleur, who sounded thrilled to be able to relay the information to the others, who had already arrived – especially Ruth.

They turned the corner into their road with moments to spare.

'You go ahead,' said Charlie to Ted, 'we'll be there in a minute.' He smiled back his reply and strode off with his head held high.

'I want to be sure I've got this right,' said Charlie, the breeziness in her voice disappearing in an instant, 'you are giving up everything to be their guardian?'

'No, I'm being totally selfish – so I can be with the people I love.'

'Love,' repeated Charlie, looking stunned.

'Turns out I had a vacancy here,' he thumped his chest, 'and now you, all of you, have barrelled into my life and occupied it and you are bloody impossible to evict.' He gave her his best cheeky grin.

Charlie's forehead was creased and she was looking stern. 'Let's say you go ahead with this. You can't run away at the first sign of trouble. I don't give a stuff about me, but you can't screw up the children; they deserve better!' Charlie's breathing was coming in gasps and she was fighting hard to keep calm.

'Charlie, you're talking as if it's going to happen and it's not. Trust me.'

There was an excruciatingly long pause, in which Charlie's eyes darted about Blue's face. 'I'll try. But if you do anything to hurt those children I swear I will hunt you down and beat you to a pulp. And you know I mean it.'

He held her shoulders and looked her square in the eyes. 'Charlie, calm down. I promise you, I'm going nowhere.'

'So, are you moving to London?'

'Yes, I'm moving in here,' he said, pointing at the house.

'Oh, you think so?' said Charlie, her breathing starting to return to normal.

'Yes, because I am never letting you out of my sight again. Assuming that you still fancy me, that is.'

The first real smile appeared on Charlie's face.

'As it turns out I quite fancy you fully clothed. Obviously I'm a woman of integrity and it's what's inside that's most important… but that shirt definitely helps.'

He lifted her up and spun her around before letting her slide back into his arms and they connected with a soft kiss. Their lips moulded together and they kissed a slow, passionate kiss, lost for a moment.

They were disturbed by a large round of applause and unseemly whistling, which came from the now-assembled family on the steps of the house, accompanied by barking from Wriggly.

'Charlie kissed the pirate!' yelled Millie, as her hands covered her face in glee.

Epilogue

Eighteen months later

Charlie shivered. The windowless room made her more than uneasy and she took in a deep breath to try to steady herself. Another shiver made her jolt nervously. The courtroom was a little cool due to the air conditioning, but that wasn't what was making her tremble. Charlie closed her eyes for a moment and tried to gather her thoughts, but there was nothing but blankness edged with blind panic. She rested her hands in her lap and studied her new black skirt. It wasn't the sort of thing she usually bought, but it seemed appropriate.

The far end of the courtroom was all wood-panelled with an oversized version of the Queen's coat of arms in the centre. Charlie stared at it and tried hard to focus. This was serious and she needed to stay calm. The door to the right of the coat of arms opened and the judge emerged. He was in full robes and wig and Charlie felt herself break out in a sweat despite the air conditioning, which was humming loudly above her. A court assistant, wearing a black suit, followed him out. She nodded at Charlie and started to talk to the judge and shuffle papers in front of him.

Charlie felt sick and her palms were ridiculously sweaty. She wiped them down her black skirt and rested them on her thighs, both of which were jiggling nervously up and down. At almost the same time a large hand engulfed hers on her left side and a small, equally sweaty, hand entwined itself with her right. Charlie breathed out slowly and looked to her right.

'You okay, sweetie?' asked Charlie.

'I'm not laughing at the silly wig,' stated Millie loudly, her face deadly serious. Charlie glanced at the judge, who was smiling but pretending not to notice. Charlie looked to her left. Blue squeezed her hand.

'You're doing really well, you haven't run out yet,' he said, his eyes full of love.

'Doesn't mean I don't want to.' The thought of having to go to court had had Charlie in a panic for the last few weeks.

'Is this going to take long? I don't want to be late picking up Esther,' came Ted's voice.

'Ted, mate, we have loads of time. She doesn't land for another three hours,' said Blue to the disembodied head that had appeared from the other side of Millie.

The judge cleared his throat.

'SHHHH!' said Millie loudly.

'Thank you, young lady,' said the judge.

'You're welcome,' said Millie, with a confident nod.

'My name is Judge Lombardi...'

'That's a mafia name,' whispered George to Eleanor and she giggled.

'... and I am here today to conduct the adoption hearing for,' he consulted his papers, 'Edward, George, Eleanor and Amelia Cobley. Is that correct?'

'Yes, it is,' said Millie, before anyone else had a chance.

'Well, young lady, would you like to introduce everyone?'

Millie nodded. She let go of Charlie's hand and went to the end of the row.

'This is Granddad Roger,' she said, pointing to the old man in a wheelchair with a tartan rug neatly wrapped around his legs and then looked at the judge, who nodded, and she moved on to the next seat. 'Auntie Ruth,' who smiled briefly and glanced at her watch. 'Camille,' who exchanged smiles with the courtroom assistant, 'Jonathan, Fleur and her mummy and daddy,' said Millie. Mrs Van Benton gave a little wave and her husband rolled his eyes.

'...and George, Eleanor and Ted.' She reached her own seat and picked up two photographs, 'This is our first mummy and daddy, they couldn't come because they died,' said Millie, holding the photo at arms-length towards the judge, who very helpfully nodded, although it was doubtful that he could see from that distance. Millie showed him the other photograph. 'This is Wriggly, he wanted to come but he wasn't allowed because he does wee-wees when he gets too excited.' She put down the photos and continued to the last two people. 'And this is Mummy Charlie and Daddy Blue.'

THE END

Acknowledgements

Let's start the Thank yous off with my terrific technical experts: thank you to Louise and Diana for checking my Social Services interactions. Thank you to Christine Thorley for airline procedures and to Carol Lewington for Private Schools policies.

Special Antigua thank yous: Thank you to Henson Martin, our fabulous tour guide, for his extensive knowledge of Antigua and taking us on an unforgettable island tour and putting up with all my questions and constant scribbling in the back! Thanks too to the wonderfully friendly people of Antigua for their hospitality.

Thank you to my early beta readers: Beryl Taylor, Pat Mahon, Louise Reid, Zoe Baldwin, Karen Key, Charlotte Bennett, Bev Ball, Polly Fishwick, Lesley Elder (excellent life coach type person – look her up), Mick Arnold and Julie Smith. Special thanks to my amazing grammar guru Chris Goodwin.

Special thanks to Laura Parish and all at Novel Kicks for giving me the opportunity to write a regular column and share my writing journey and other witterings!

Thank you to those that unwittingly supplied a couple of comedy moments that spawned scenes in this novel in particular Cherie Niles, Caroline East and Caroline Russell – it's all right they'll never know which ones were yours!

Thank you to my wonderful crew of generally supportive folk that supply cake, wine and laughter in varying quantities depending on my needs: my writing friends from the Romantic Novelists' Association (RNA) and in particular the Birmingham Chapter, Gill Vickery and the folks that attend her Writing Fiction class (special mention to the naughty table) and my most excellent friends the members of the boozy book club.

My wonderful editor, and most possibly the nicest person on the planet, Charlotte Ledger has worked her socks off along with the fabulous team at HarperCollins to get this looking like an actual proper book – I am forever in your debt.

Thanks to my agent, Kate Nash, who is always on hand to provide guidance and steer me through the wonderful world of publishing. I'm so lucky to have you in my corner.

A massive thank you to my writing fairy godmother, Katie Fforde, for the in-depth discussions, valuable advice and giggles. I am so very grateful.

Thank yous and hugs all round to the amazingly supportive blogging community, the unsung heroes of the book world – you are all amazing!

Much love to my husband, daughter, family and friends who have supplied tea, love and support when the going got tough.

Anyone who is reading this and thinking she's not mentioned me yet, I'm mentioning you now – thank you!

Lastly thank YOU for buying and reading my book.